小婦人
Little Women

中英雙語典藏版

露意莎·梅·艾考特——著

那培玄、法蘭克·T·麥瑞爾、鐘文君——繪

張琰——譯

晨星出版

化身喬的露意莎
（1832 ～ 1888）

　　露意莎・梅・艾考特生於距今一百六十年前的美國賓州，是位思想相當先進的女文學家。

　　露易莎是家中的次女，她的個性活潑開朗，對人生充滿積極觀念，極似母親。露意莎甚至自嘲：「我生下來時皮膚黝黑，哭個不停，那聲音還很宏亮，我生於一年之中最昏沉的十一月，所以我相信也許我的一生是悲苦的，但我不放棄，我一定會克服。」

　　她的一生有多次遷徙，也因此愛上了變化多端的世界，其中某次在波士頓走失，雖獨自身處異地卻沒有恐懼，有的只是感受周遭與眾不同的環境，而這反而成了她自己到老最珍藏的美麗回憶。之後多次遠赴歐陸旅行，有次因自願照顧生病的姪女，她有機會造訪各國，一年中，其芳蹤遍及德、義、瑞、法等國。

　　露意莎的一生是孤獨的，甚至因為大姐要嫁為人婦而心有氣憤，最終仍是祝福她並跟自己說：「我們倆姊妹的人生也許是不同的，我知道梅格會幸福，但我相信我也可以自己走完我的人生，靠我自己。」

　　一生著作膾炙人口，包括：《小婦人》、《好妻子》、《小紳士》……等，我們在她的作品當中沒有看到一絲的憂鬱色彩，只有奮力不懈的人生，露意莎在作品中充分發揮她對人生光明的一面，這也是她的作品能譯成多國語言、風靡全球的原因；一本讀起來永遠樂觀正向的書，誰都會樂此不疲的。

目録

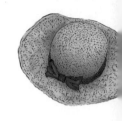

CONTENTS

第 1 章
演出天路歷程

「沒有禮物，聖誕節就不是聖誕節了。」躺在地毯上的喬嘟嚷著說。「當個窮人好慘喔！」梅格嘆著氣，低頭看著自己一身舊衣。

「有些女孩有好多漂亮東西，有些女孩什麼也沒有，我覺得很不公平。」艾美加上一句，一邊傷心地吸吸鼻子。

「我們有爸爸媽媽和彼此呀。」待在角落的貝絲心滿意足地說。

爐火照亮的四張年輕臉孔隨著這句使人振奮的話而開朗了。

「可是爸爸現在不在，我們也會有很長的時間看不到他。」喬哀傷地說。大家聽了這句話，臉色又黯淡了下來。每個人都想起遠在戰場作戰的父親。

一時間沒有人開口，梅格語氣一改：「你們知道，媽媽提議今年聖誕節不要發禮物，因為寒冬就要來了，而我們的男人在軍中受苦受難，我們不應該花錢尋樂。我們能做的不多，不過我們可以做一點小小的犧牲，並且應該開開心心的。只是我可不開心。」梅格想到她夢寐以求的那些漂亮東西，難過地搖了搖頭。

「可是我想我們就算少花一點錢也不會有什麼用處。我們每個人只有一塊錢，把錢捐出去，對軍隊也沒什麼幫助。我不期待

媽媽和你們送禮物給我，可是我真的很想買一本《渦堤孩》，我想好久了。」愛看書的喬說。

「我打算用我的錢去買些新樂譜。」貝絲輕輕嘆了口氣。

「我要買一盒法珀牌的畫筆，我真的很需要。」艾美語氣堅決地說。

「媽媽沒有提到我們的錢，她也不會希望我們把所有事情都放棄。我們各買各的，快活一下嘛。我相信我們都是辛辛苦苦賺來這些錢的。」喬一邊大聲說一邊用男人般的姿態檢查她的鞋跟。

「可不是嘛——比起整天教那些煩死人的小孩，我是多麼想一個人待在家裡快活呢。」梅格又開始抱怨了。

「你的辛苦還比不上我的一半呢。」喬說。「你喜歡跟一個神經兮兮、愛挑毛病的老太婆關在一起好幾個鐘頭嗎？這個老太婆老煩得你恨不得從窗子逃出去或是放聲大喊！」

「雖然怨天尤人並不好，不過洗碗和打掃房子真是世界上最糟的工作，讓我脾氣暴躁，雙手也變得好僵硬，根本練不好琴。」貝絲嘆了一口氣。

「我相信你們誰都沒有我受的苦多，」艾美大叫，「因為你們用不著和那些沒有禮貌的女生同班上課，如果你功課不會寫，她們就會一直煩你，還會笑你的衣服。爸爸沒有錢要被她們標價，鼻子長得不好看也要被她們侮辱。」

「你是說『誹謗』吧？別說成『標價』，好像爸爸是一瓶醃黃瓜。」喬邊笑邊糾正。

「我知道我在說什麼，你不必這樣『冷嘲日諷』，用好的字眼沒什麼不對，這有助於增加『次彙』。」艾美義正辭嚴地反擊。

「別鬥嘴了，姑娘們。喬，你不希望我們像小時候那樣有錢嗎？唉，如果沒有煩惱，我們會多麼快活呀！」還能記得往日好時光的梅格說。

「你前幾天才說你認為我們要比金家的孩子快樂得多，因為他們雖然有錢，卻總是吵鬧不停。」

「我是說過，貝絲。我認為我們是快樂得多，雖然我們必須工作，我們也能自尋快活，就像喬說的，我們是快活幫呢。」

「喬就是會說這種話。」艾美說，並用責備的目光望著躺在地毯上的修長身軀一眼。喬立刻笑了起來，雙手插在口袋裡，開始吹起口哨。

「喬，別吹了，太男孩子氣了。」

「就是因為這樣我才要吹。」

「我討厭粗線條、一點女孩子樣都沒有的女生！」

「我討厭裝模作樣、故作優雅的小孩子。」

「『小小窩裡的鳥兒也同意』。」貝絲這個和事佬扮鬼臉唱了起來，兩個尖銳的聲音軟化成笑聲，於是這個「互挑毛病」的風波暫時止息。

「真是的，兩位，你們兩個都有錯，」梅格擺出大姐的派頭，開始教訓她們。「喬，你已經長大了，不該再像個男孩子一樣，應該優雅一點。如果你還小也就算了，但是你現在長那麼

第 1 章

高，而且也網起頭髮，你就應該記住你是個年輕淑女了。」

「我才不是呢！如果網起頭髮就會讓人變成年輕淑女，那我要梳兩個馬尾梳到二十歲！」喬大叫，「我討厭長大變成瑪區小姐，穿長裙、一本正經的模樣。我喜歡男孩子的遊戲，男孩子的工作以及男孩子的氣度，卻偏偏是個女孩子，真是倒霉透了。做不成男孩真讓我止不住失望，可現在比以往任何時候都要糟，因為我好想跟爸爸一起去打仗，但卻只能待在家裡打毛線，像個要死不活的老太婆！」

喬甩動藍色的軍襪，把裡面的毛線針抖得像響板一樣嘎啦嘎啦響，線團也滾到房間地上。

「可憐的喬！真是太慘了，但是也沒辦法，所以你只好把名字改得像男生，假裝是我們這些女生的兄弟。」貝絲說，她用一隻再怎麼洗碗、打掃也不會變粗的手揉著膝頭。

「而你呢，艾美，」梅格接著說，「你太講究又太正經了。你那種做作的模樣很可笑，如果你不留意，你長大以後就會是個裝腔作勢的小傻瓜。我喜歡你自然有禮貌和文雅的說話方式，只是你那些荒謬的用詞和喬的俚語一樣糟。」

「如果喬是個男人婆，艾美是個小傻瓜，那我是什麼呢？」準備一起聽訓的貝絲問道。

「你是個道道地地的小可愛呢。」梅格柔聲地說。沒有人有異議，因為「小老鼠」是全家人都喜愛的。

年輕讀者都希望知道「她們長得怎麼樣」，我們趁此機會把坐在黃昏餘暉下做針線活兒的四姐妹概略描述一下。此時屋外的

多雪正輕輕飄落，屋內爐火劈啪歡響。雖然這間舊房子鋪著褪了色的地毯，擺設也相當簡單，但卻顯得十分舒適：牆上掛著一兩幅雅致的圖畫，壁凹內堆滿了書本，窗台上是綻放的菊花和聖誕花，屋裡洋溢著一片寧靜、溫馨的氣氛。

四姐妹的老大是瑪格麗特，十六歲，體態豐腴，相貌秀麗，大大的眼睛，一頭濃密而柔軟的棕髮，嘴型甜美，還有一雙她頗為得意的白皙的手。十五歲的喬個兒高，很瘦，棕色的皮膚，讓人想到一匹小馬，因為她似乎永遠也不知道該怎麼擺放那礙著她的長手長腳。她有一張堅毅的嘴、一個俏皮的鼻子，以及一雙銳利的灰色眼睛，似乎能看穿一切，有時候嚴厲、有時候滑稽、有時候若有所思。濃密的長髮使她顯得特別美麗，但為了方便，長髮通常被她束入髮網。喬雙肩圓潤，大手大腳，衣著有種輕浮不定的感覺。她正迅速長成一個成熟的女性，心裡卻極不願，因此常常流露出這個階段的女孩所特有的尷尬神情。伊莉莎白——每個人都叫她貝絲——是個膚色紅潤、頭髮光滑、雙眸明亮的十三歲女孩，舉止害羞、聲音膽怯，神情總是安詳平靜，很少受到干擾。她父親叫她作「小安」，這個小名再適合不過了，因為她似乎生活在自己的快樂世界中，只有在和她信任而且摯愛的人相見時才肯走出來。艾美雖然是老么，卻是最重要的人物——至少她自我感覺如此。她的皮膚白皙，有一雙藍色的眼睛，一頭黃色鬈髮垂在肩頭，細細瘦瘦，總是像個注意禮儀的年輕女士一樣舉止自若。至於四位姐妹的性格如何，請待後續揭曉。

鐘敲了六下，貝絲已經清掃過壁爐，把一雙拖鞋放到上面烘

乾。看到這雙舊鞋，對女孩子們倒有些正面影響，因為媽媽就要回來了，每個人都開心地準備迎接她。

「這雙鞋都穿破了，媽媽應該要有雙新鞋才行。」

「我想用我那一塊錢給她買一雙。」貝絲說。

「不行，我要買！」艾美叫道。

「我是老大──」梅格才開口，喬就用堅決的語氣說了：

「爸爸不在家，如今我是家裡的男人了，我來買鞋，爸爸要我在他出門的時候好好照顧媽媽。」

「我告訴你們該怎麼辦，」貝絲說，「我們不要幫自己買什麼禮物了，我們每個人送媽媽一份聖誕禮物。」

「真不愧是你！我們要送什麼呢？」喬驚嘆道。

於是每個人都冷靜地想了一會兒。梅格或許是從她自己那雙漂亮的手得到啟發，她宣布：「我要送她一副好手套。」

「最好送她雙軍鞋。」喬大叫。

「有縫邊的手帕。」貝絲說。

「我要買一小瓶古龍水，因為媽媽喜歡，又不用花很多錢，這樣我就可以留下一些錢拿來買鉛筆了。」艾美說。

「我們要怎麼送出這些東西呢？」梅格問。

「把它們放在桌上，請她進來，要她拆禮物。你忘記以前我們過生日的時候是怎麼做的了嗎？讓媽媽以為我們是在互送禮物，然後給她一個驚喜。我們明天下午必須去買東西，梅格。」喬說。

門口傳來一個快活的聲音，於是她們全都轉過身去迎接一位

高尚的慈祥女士。她的衣著並不是很考究，但是看起來十分高貴。四姐妹都認爲在一身灰斗篷和過時的軟帽下的母親，是世界上最棒的母親。

「乖女兒們，今天你們過得怎樣？今天事情太多了，要把那些箱子準備好明天運走，所以我沒有回家吃午餐。有沒有人來家裡呀，貝絲？你的感冒怎麼樣了，梅格？喬呀，你看起來累得要死呢。過來親親我，小寶貝。」

瑪區太太一邊發出這些做母親的探問，一邊把濕衣服脫下，穿上暖和的便鞋，在安樂椅上坐下，把艾美抱到大腿上，準備享受她忙碌的一天中最快樂的時刻。四姐妹來回奔忙，每個人都以自己的方式想使母親舒服自在。

她們圍在茶几旁後，瑪區太太特別開懷地說：「晚飯後我有個好消息要告訴你們喔。」

一抹燦爛的笑容像一道陽光般綻開在每個人臉上。貝絲不顧手上拿著的餅乾就拍起手來，喬把餐巾往上一拋，大叫：「信！信！我們替爸爸歡呼三聲！」

「是的，是一封很棒的長信。爸爸很好，他認爲他可以熬過寒冷的季節，不需要我們擔憂。他給我們各種聖誕節的祝福，還特別寫了些話給你們。」瑪區太太說，她拍拍口袋，彷彿那裡有份寶藏。

她們全都靠近爐火，媽媽坐在大椅子上，貝絲坐在她腳邊，梅格和艾美坐在椅子的兩個扶手上，喬靠在椅背後。喬靠在椅背後，這樣的話，如果這封信很感人，誰都不會看到有人流露出情

小婦人

感。

在這段艱困的日子裡，幾乎沒有一封信不感人，尤其是父親寫回家的信。在這一封信裡面，做父親的很少提到受的苦、面對的危險，或是克服了的思鄉愁緒，這是一封快活而且充滿希望的信，字裡行間全是對於軍營生活、行軍、軍聞的活潑生動的描述，只在信末才流露出對家中小女孩們的父愛和渴望。

「代我給她們我全部的愛和親吻。告訴她們我白天思念她們、夜晚為她們祈禱，而無時無刻不在她們的深情中找到最大的安慰。再見到她們還要一年的時間，似乎太久了，但是提醒她們：我們要一邊等待一邊工作，不要讓這些艱困的日子虛擲。我知道她們會記得我對她們說過的所有話，她們會是你的貼心孩子，也會盡責地做分內的事，勇敢地對抗自己的大敵、打場漂亮的勝仗，使我回到她們身邊的時候，會對我這些小婦人們更為疼愛、更為驕傲。」

聽到這裡，每個人都吸著鼻子。喬對於從她鼻尖落下的大粒淚珠並不感覺羞恥，艾美把臉埋在母親肩頭，放聲哭了出來，也不在乎自己的鬢髮弄亂。「我是個自私的人！但是我會努力改善，不要讓爸爸對我失望。」

「我們都要努力！」梅格哭了。「我只顧著外表，不喜歡做事，但是我以後不會再這樣了。」

「我會努力去做個爸爸叫我的『小婦人』，不要有粗野的動作，專心做好我在家裡的工作，而不是一心想到別的地方。」喬也說了，但是她心裡想，要她在家裡收斂自己的脾氣，那可是比

在南方面對一、兩個南軍還要困難的工作呢。

　　貝絲什麼話也沒有說，只是用編織的藍色軍襪拭去眼淚，努力打起毛線來，不浪費一點時間，同時在她安靜的小小心靈中也下了決心，要讓自己在一年後父親返家時做到父親希望她做到的地步。

　　喬說完話後是一陣沉默。這時瑪區太太用快活的語氣說：「你們還記得你們小的時候都會演『天路歷程』嗎？」

　　「那是多麼有趣的事呀！尤其是經過那些獅子群和惡魔作戰，還有通過有妖魔的山岩！」喬說道。

　　「我喜歡包袱掉下來，滾到樓下去的那段。」梅格說。

　　「我最喜歡的部分是我們走到屋子的天台上，也就是放著我們的花和矮樹和好東西的地方，然後全體站在那兒，為著陽光中的喜樂唱歌的那段。」貝絲露出微笑說著，彷彿那段快樂時光再次來到一般。

　　「我記不得很多了，只除了我很害怕地窖和那個陰暗的門口，還有我總是喜歡在屋頂上吃蛋糕喝牛奶。要不是我年紀太大，不適合這種事，我倒真想再演一次呢。」艾美說，她已經口口聲聲說要在「成熟」的十二歲時拋開幼稚的玩意了。

　　「做這件事我們永遠也不嫌年齡大的，我親愛的，因為這是一齣我們始終在用不同方式演出的戲。我們的包袱在這裡，我們的路在前面，而那善良和快樂的渴望，就是帶領我們走過許多困難和錯誤，走向平靜的嚮導，而平靜是真正的『天國』。好啦，我的小小朝聖者們，你們不妨開始吧，不是玩笑式的，而是真心

真意的，我們看看在爸爸回家以前你們能走多遠。」

「真的嗎，媽媽？那我們的包袱在哪裡？」艾美問，她是個一板一眼的小女生。

「你們每個人都說說看此時此刻你們的包袱是什麼，貝絲除外，我猜她沒有什麼負擔。」母親說。

「我有的。我的包袱是碗盤和撢子，以及嫉妒家裡有好鋼琴的女孩子，還有怕生。」

貝絲的包袱太可笑了，每個人都想笑，但是沒有人笑出來，因為那會大大傷了她的心。

「我們就照做吧！」梅格沉思著說。「這不過是行善換個名字做罷了，而且這個故事還能夠幫助我們呢，因為雖然我們有心行善，但是卻不容易，我們又常會忘記，而沒有盡力去做。」

「我們今天晚上是在『沮喪的深淵』裡，媽媽過來把我們救出去，就像書裡面那個『救援』。我們應該有路線圖的，就像基督徒一樣。這一點我們要怎麼辦？」喬發問了，盡本分這種枯燥工作，如果可以因為想像而增加一些浪漫，她可是很開心的。

「聖誕節早晨到你們枕頭底下找，你們就會找到你們的路線指南了。」瑪區太太回答道。

於是在漢娜清理桌子的時候，她們就討論著這個新計畫，而後她們拿出四個女紅籃，為瑪區嬸婆縫被單，縫衣針飛快地上上下下，這縫紉的工作十分無趣，但是今天晚上沒有人抱怨。

九點鐘，她們停下活兒，像平常一樣在睡前先唱唱歌。只有貝絲能從這架很舊的鋼琴上彈出很多音樂，而她自有一種方法去

輕觸黃色琴鍵，為她們唱出的簡單歌曲彈出動人的伴奏。梅格的歌喉像笛音般清亮，這個小小合唱團就由她和母親擔任主唱。艾美吱吱喳喳地唱，像隻蟋蟀，喬是隨著自己的意思讓歌聲在空氣中飄蕩，而總是在不該停頓的地方停頓，發出咕嚕聲或是顫音，把最最憂傷的曲子都破壞掉了。她們從小時候還口齒不清地唱著「一閃一閃亮晶晶！」的時候就這麼做了，從此這也成為家裡的傳統，因為媽媽是個天生的歌唱好手。每天清晨的第一個聲音就是她的聲音，她會唱出雲雀般的歌聲，在房裡四處走動；夜晚最後的聲音也是同樣的快活歌聲，因為那熟悉的搖籃曲是女孩子們不論到幾歲都聽不膩的。

第 2 章
快樂聖誕

　　喬是聖誕節當天第一個在灰濛濛的清晨起來的人。壁爐上沒有掛著襪子，一時間她覺得和好久以前她的小襪子因為塞滿了糖果而掉到地上時同樣失望。然後她想起母親的承諾，就把手往枕頭下面摸，摸出一本深紅色封皮的小書。這本書她很熟悉，因為這是描述最美好生命的美麗古老故事，喬認為這是任何一個要長途跋涉的朝聖者真正的指南。她用一句「聖誕快樂」把梅格叫醒，要她去看看她的枕頭底下有什麼。那是一本綠皮的書，裡面也有相同的圖，還有母親寫的幾句話，這使得她們的禮物在各自眼中都變得更為珍貴了。沒多久，貝絲和艾美也都醒來，並且在枕頭下翻出她們的小書——一本是灰色的皮，另一本是藍皮。於是四個人就在東方天空漸漸變為粉紅色之時，坐在那裡談著這些書。

　　「媽媽在哪？」半小時之後，梅格和喬跑下樓要謝謝母親的禮物，梅格問道。

　　「天知道去了哪裡。有個可憐人過來討飯，你媽媽就立刻去看看還需要什麼了。從沒看過這麼會把吃的、喝的、穿的、柴火送給人的女人。」漢娜說。漢娜從梅格出生以後就和這家人一起生活了，全家人都不把她看成僕人，而當成了朋友。

「她很快就會回來了，我想。你先煎餅吧，把一切都準備妥當。」梅格說，一邊檢視放在一個籃子裡的禮物，籃子放在沙發底下，準備要在適當時間拿出來。「咦？艾美那瓶古龍水呢？」她發現沒有看到那個小瓶子，又問了一句。

「她一分鐘前才把它拿出來，後來又拿走了，要在上頭綁緞帶或是那一類的東西。」喬回答道。她在房裡四處舞著，好讓新的軍鞋穿起來沒那麼僵硬。

「我的手帕看起來多好呀，不是嗎？漢娜替我洗好、燙過。上頭的字全是我繡的呢。」貝絲說道，得意地看著她費好大氣力繡出來但有些不平的字母。

「天啊！她在上頭繡『媽媽』！」喬拿起一條手帕說著。

「這不對嗎？我還以為這樣比較好，我不希望媽媽以外的人用這些手帕。」貝絲看起來很困擾地說。

「親愛的，這是個很好的想法。媽媽一定會很開心的。」梅格說，她對喬皺起眉頭，又給貝絲一個微笑。

「媽媽來了。快把籃子藏起來！」門砰的一聲關上，門廳裡傳來腳步聲，喬立刻大叫。

「聖誕快樂，媽媽！謝謝你送我們的書，我們已經看了一些，而且以後每天都要看呢。」她們齊聲喊道。

「聖誕快樂，女兒們！我很高興你們立刻就開始了，希望你們能繼續保持下去。但是在我們坐下來之前，我想要說一件事。離這裡不遠有個可憐女人和新生的小嬰兒躺在那裡。六個孩子擠在一張床上取暖，因為他們家沒有生火，也沒有食物。他們家的

大男孩告訴我說他們又餓又冷。孩子們，你們願不願意把你們的早餐給他們，當成是聖誕禮物？」

　　她們已經等了將近一個鐘頭，早就餓得很了，一時間沒有人開口，但也只有一下子，因為喬激動地喊道——

　　「我真高興你在我們開始吃以前回來！」

　　「我可不可以幫忙把東西拿去給那些可憐的小孩？」貝絲急切地問。

　　「我來拿奶油和鬆餅。」艾美加上一句，她很英勇地放棄了自己最喜歡的東西。

　　梅格已經把蕎麥煎餅用東西蓋住，並且把麵包堆到一個大盤子裡。

　　「我就猜你們一定願意。」瑪區太太彷彿很滿意地笑著。「你們全都一起去幫我，回來以後我們就吃麵包喝牛奶當作早餐，晚餐再補回來。」

　　她們很快就準備妥當，於是一行人便出發了。

　　那是一間四壁蕭條的陋室，窗子殘破，沒有爐火，床單也是破破爛爛。一個生病的母親、一個啼哭的嬰兒，還有一群面容蒼白的饑餓小孩，全都擠在一條舊被子下面取暖。

　　「啊，我的天啊！善心的天使來救我們了！」這個可憐的婦人說著，喜極而泣。

　　「戴著帽兜、戴著手套的怪天使呢！」喬說的話讓他們全都笑了起來。

　　「真係好！仄些天使襖心人！」這些可憐的小朋友一邊吃東

西，一邊把凍得青紫的手放在舒適的溫暖火光前烤暖，嘴裡這樣喊著。

　　女孩子們從沒有被人稱作天使小孩過，這個稱呼聽起來很令她們開心，尤其是喬，她從生下來就被人認為是個粗枝大葉的人。這頓早餐很快樂，雖然她們一點也沒有吃到。當她們離開這家人且留下安慰給他們之後，我相信這座城市裡絕對不會有人比這些饑腸轆轆的女孩子更快樂的了。她們奉獻出自己的早餐，在聖誕節早晨只吃麵包，喝牛奶，就心滿意足了。

　　「這就是愛鄰人勝過愛自己了，我喜歡這樣。」梅格說。她們正拿出各自的禮物，母親則在樓上收集送給可憐的胡梅爾家的衣服。

　　禮物看起來不是很豪華，不過這稀少的包裹裡卻飽含了濃濃的愛心，而放在桌子中間那插著紅玫瑰、白菊花和垂掛著蔓藤的高高花瓶，為桌子增添十分優雅的氣氛。

　　「她來了！開始啦，貝絲！開門，艾美！為媽媽歡呼三聲！」喬得意洋洋地來回走著，梅格走過去，將母親領到貴賓席。

　　貝絲彈起最輕快的進行曲，艾美把門一推而開，梅格以莊嚴肅穆的神態護送著母親。瑪區太太既驚喜又感動，一一詳視了禮物，還看了附在禮物上的紙條，睜大著眼睛露出笑容。她立刻穿上新的室內鞋，把新手帕塞進口袋裡，手帕上已經灑了艾美的古龍水，所以聞起來香噴噴的，玫瑰花也別在她胸前，她還說那雙美麗的手套是「絕佳搭配」呢。

接著是她們的歡笑、親吻和解釋，這幕景象是那麼地單純而且充滿關愛，眾人和樂融融，日後更是甜蜜的回憶。之後所有人就開始工作了。

由於早晨的善行和送禮儀式用去太多時間，這一天其餘的時間就全部用來準備晚上的慶祝活動。四姐妹年齡還太小，不能經常去戲院，也沒有錢花大筆費用做私人的表演，因此就盡量發揮聰明心思；再加上「需要為發明之母」，所以她們缺什麼就自己做什麼。劇團規模小，兩個主要演員就必須一人分飾數角，而她們辛苦地扮演三、四個角色，飛快穿脫不同戲服，還要管理舞台，確實值得人稱讚。這對於她們的記憶力是一種絕佳的練習，也是一項無傷大雅的娛樂，反正這些時間也無聊，再不就是耗在無益的交際上。

聖誕節的晚上，充作包廂的大床上擠了十幾個女孩子，面前是藍黃兩色的印花布幕，她們都以一種令人歡喜的神態滿心期待著。布幕後面傳來衣物的窸窣和低聲細語，些微油燈的煙味，偶爾還會有艾美的嘻嘻笑聲；在當前的刺激狀況下，她很容易就變得歇斯底里。不久後響起鈴聲，幕開了，這齣「悲歌劇」便開始了。

演出一結束，漢娜就出現了，對她們說：「瑪區太太要招待各位，各位小姐請下樓用餐好嗎？」

這真是個驚喜，就連這些演員也這麼覺得呢。而當她們看到桌上情形，她們又驚又喜地彼此望著。媽媽一向會為她們準備一些點心，但是像這樣精緻的東西，從已經遠去的富裕日子之後就

再也沒見過了。桌上有冰淇淋——共有兩盤，一盤是粉紅色、一盤是白色——和蛋糕、水果，以及教人愉快的法國糖果。在桌子中央還有四大束溫室栽培的花束呢！

這場面使她們屏氣凝神，她們先盯著桌子，然後望著母親，母親的表情似乎非常開心。

「是仙女送的嗎？」艾美問。

「是聖誕老人送的。」貝絲說。

「是媽媽做的。」梅格露出最甜美的笑容，雖然她還留著灰鬍子、白眉毛。

「瑪區嬤婆心情特別好，送我們一頓好東西。」喬靈機一動，大喊道。

「全都猜錯了。是老羅倫斯先生送的。」瑪區太太回答。

「羅倫斯男孩的爺爺！他怎麼會想到這種事？我們又不認識他！」梅格嘆道。

「漢娜把你們早上的事告訴他一個僕人。他是個古怪的老先生，但是這件事讓他很歡喜。他認識你們外祖父，那是好多年以前的事了。今天下午他派人送給我一張很客氣的紙條，說希望我讓他表達對我孩子們的心意，他要送些小東西給她們，來慶祝這個節日。我不能拒絕，所以你們晚上就有頓小小的饗宴，可以彌補那頓麵包和牛奶的早餐了。」

「那男孩告訴他的，我知道！他是個好人呢，我希望我們能認識。他看樣子很想認識我們，可是他很害羞，而梅格又太一本正經了，我們走過他身邊的時候她又不讓我同他說話。」喬說。

「你說的是住在隔壁那幢大房子裡的人吧？」一個女孩子問。「我媽媽認得老羅倫斯先生，可是她說他很自傲，不喜歡跟鄰居來往。他的孫子沒有在騎馬或是和家庭教師一起散步的時候，他都把他關在家裡，要他認真唸書呢。我們邀請他來參加我們家的聚會，他都不來。我媽媽說他人很好，只是從來沒有跟我們女生說過話。」

「我們家的貓有一次跑掉了，他把牠送回來，我們就隔著圍籬說話。我們聊得很愉快——聊些板球的事，等等——一直到他看到梅格走來，才走掉。我希望哪一天能認識他，因為他需要有些娛樂，我確信。」喬堅決地說。

「我喜歡他的態度，他看起來像是個小紳士。」

「幸好你沒有邀他來呢，媽媽！」喬笑著說，望著她的靴子。「不過我們可以另外演一齣戲，他可以來看。也許他還可以幫忙演個角色呢，那不是挺快活的事嗎？」

「我從來沒有收過這麼美麗的花束呢！多漂亮呀！」梅格滿懷興趣地檢查她的花。

「真是好可愛呀！不過貝絲的玫瑰對我來說還更香呢。」瑪區太太聞著緞帶上已經半枯萎的花朵說道。

貝絲挨擠到她身邊，輕聲說：「我希望能把我的花送給爸爸。我想他的聖誕節恐怕沒有我們的快樂呢。」

第 3 章
羅倫斯家的男孩

「喬！喬！你在哪裡？」梅格站在閣樓樓梯底喊著。

「這裡！」上頭傳來一聲粗粗的回答。梅格跑上樓，發現妹妹裹著一條被單，坐在陽光下的窗邊一把三條腿的舊沙發上，正一邊啃著蘋果，一邊為《雷克利夫的繼承人》流眼淚呢。這裡是喬最喜歡待的地方，她喜歡帶六、七個蘋果和一本好書躲到這裡，享受這裡的寧靜和一隻老鼠的陪伴，老鼠就住在附近，對她毫無戒心。梅格一出現，「史瓜寶」就一溜煙竄進牠的洞裡了。喬搖搖頭，甩開眼淚，等著聽消息。

「多有趣呀！你瞧瞧！葛帝納太太給我們一份正式請束呢，邀我們明天晚上過去！」梅格叫道，揮動手裡這份珍貴的紙張。

「『葛帝納太太敬邀瑪區小姐與喬瑟芬小姐參加除夕夜舞會。』媽媽同意我們去了，那我們該穿什麼好呢？」

「你明明知道我們除了厚厚的黑呢裙以外也沒有別的衣服好穿，問這做什麼？」喬回答她，嘴裡塞滿東西。

「要是我有絲綢禮服就好了！」梅格嘆口氣，「媽媽說我十八歲的時候可以穿。可是兩年的時間像是一輩子呢。」

「我相信我們的黑呢裙子看起來像是絲綢，穿起來也夠好看了。你的衣服還像新的，不過我忘了，我衣服上還有燒焦和撕破

的地方。我該怎麼辦？燒焦的地方很明顯，我又不能把它弄掉。」

「你就盡量坐著別動，不要讓人看到你的背後，前面還好。我會用一條新的緞帶綁住頭髮，媽媽要借我她的珍珠胸針，我的新鞋很漂亮，手套也可以，只是沒有我想要的那麼好。」

「我的手套被檸檬汁弄髒了，又找不到新手套，那我就只好不戴手套了。」喬說，她從來不會為衣著操太多心。

「你非戴手套不可，不然我不去。」梅格堅決地說。「手套比任何東西都重要，沒有手套你根本不能跳舞，如果你不戴手套，我會丟臉死的。」

「我可以把手套抓在手裡，就不會有人知道手套有多髒了，我只能做到這個地步。不對！我告訴你我們用什麼方法，我們各戴一隻好的手套，不好的那隻就拿在手裡，你明白了嗎？」

「你的手比我手大，你會把我的手套撐壞。」梅格說。她把手套視為心肝寶貝。

「那我就不戴手套。我才不在乎別人怎麼說呢！」喬說著把書拿起來。

「好吧，好吧，你拿去嘛！可是你別弄髒了，而且拜託你文靜一點。不要把兩隻手放在身後或是瞪著別人，或者說『哎喲喂呀』，好嗎？」

「不用擔心，我會盡量一本正經不跟人吵架的。你去回你的信吧，讓我把這個精采的故事看完。」

於是梅格就去寫「謝函」信、檢視她的衣裙，並且一邊開懷

唱著歌，一邊縫上她唯一的蕾絲裙邊。而喬這時候也看完了故事，吃了四個蘋果，還和「史瓜寶」玩了一下。

除夕夜，客廳空盪盪的，因為兩個小妹妹擔任起侍候更衣的女僕，而兩個大姐姐則沉浸在「為舞會準備」這件最重要的事情中。

梅格終於打扮妥當，而在全家人的共同努力下，喬也把頭髮梳上去，衣服穿好了。她們穿著樣式簡單的衣服，非常出色。梅格穿著蕾絲荷葉邊的銀棕色衣裙，戴著一頂藍色天鵝絨兜帽，還別著一枚珍珠胸針；喬穿著茶色衣裙，上衣有一個亞麻布做的帥氣硬領，身上唯一的裝飾是一、兩朵菊花。她倆全都戴著一隻淺色的漂亮手套，把一隻髒手套拿在手上，而營造出十分「優雅和安逸」的效果。梅格的高跟鞋很緊，讓她腳痛，不過她是絕不會承認的；喬頭上的十九根髮夾全都像是直直刺進她腦袋裡，實在是不怎麼舒服，不過，不讓我們優雅動人，不如讓我們死掉算了！

「好好地去玩吧，親愛的，」兩姐妹優雅地走在路上時，瑪區太太說。「晚餐不要吃太多。十一點要回來，我會讓漢娜去接你們。」大門在她們身後關上時，一扇窗子裡傳出叫喊的聲音──

「你們兩個！你們兩個！你們有沒有帶乾淨手帕？」

「帶了，帶了，乾淨得很呢，梅格的上面還灑了古龍水呢。」喬也叫著，還笑著加了一句，兩人繼續走著。「我相信就算我們在躲地震，媽媽也會問我們這句話。」

「那是她高貴的品味之一，也很對，因為一個真正的淑女，是可以從她整潔的鞋子、手套和手帕看出來的。」梅格答道，她自己也有不少小小的「高貴品味」。

「好，記住，不要讓人看到衣服燒到的地方，喬。我的披肩位置對嗎？我的頭髮看起來很糟嗎？」梅格對鏡梳整好長一段時間之後，從葛帝納太太的更衣室鏡前轉過身說。

「我知道我會忘記。如果你看到我做不對，你就眨眨眼提醒我，好嗎？」喬回答。她扯了扯領子，又匆匆把頭髮梳了梳。

「不行，眨眼睛太不淑女了，如果有什麼不對勁的地方，我就會抬眉毛，如果你做得沒錯，我就點點頭。你要抬頭挺胸，走碎步，如果人家把你介紹給別人，你可別去跟人握手，那是不對的。」

「你怎麼會知道這些禮節啊？我從來都不知道呢。你聽，這音樂真輕快呢！」

她們走下樓，心裡有些膽怯，因為她們很少參加舞會，這個小小的聚會雖然不是正式的場合，但對她們來說卻也是件大事。莊嚴的葛帝納老太太親切地和她們打招呼，並且把她們交給她六個女兒中的老大去招呼。梅格認識莎麗，很快就非常自在，但是喬不太喜歡女孩子，也不喜歡女孩子間的閒談，所以小心翼翼地背對牆站著，覺得自己像小馬進到花園裡般格格不入。由於衣服上的一塊焦痕，她不能四處走動找些樂事，只好可憐兮兮地看著別人，直到舞會開始。梅格立刻就有人邀舞了，而那雙很緊的鞋輕快地來回舞著，沒有人猜得到穿這雙鞋的人面帶微笑所承受的

疼痛。喬看到一個紅頭髮的大塊頭青年朝她這個角落走來，她怕他會請她跳舞，便溜進一個掛著布幔的牆凹裡，打算從布幔裡面往外偷窺，安安靜靜獨享快活。不幸的是，還有一個害羞的人也選了同一個避難所；當布幔在她身後垂下時，她發現自己正和「羅倫斯家男孩」面對面。

「天啊，我不知道這裡還有人！」喬結結巴巴地說，打算用闖進來時同樣的速度退出去。

不料男孩子卻笑了，表情略顯驚訝，他愉快地說：「不用管我，你願意就留在這裡吧。」

「我不會打擾你嗎？」

「才不會呢。我進到這裡是因為我認識的人不多，起初會覺得很不自在，你知道。」

「我也是。請你不要走開，除非你想要走開。」

男孩又坐下了，一直盯著自己的輕便跳舞鞋，等到想表現出禮貌和自在的喬開了口：

「我想我見過你，你住在我們家附近，是不是？」

「隔壁。」他抬頭往上看，直接就笑出來了，因為他記得他把貓送回家時他們還討論過板球，而此刻喬的正經態度就顯得相當可笑。

這麼一來，喬倒是自在了，她也開懷大笑著說：「你們那份很棒的聖誕禮物讓我們開心了好一段時間喔。」

「是我爺爺送的。」

「但是，是你告訴他的吧，對不對？」

「你的貓怎麼樣了，瑪區小姐？」男孩問，他力圖鎮靜，但是黑眼睛裡卻顯現著興味十足的樣子。

「很好啊，謝謝你，羅倫斯先生，不過我不是瑪區小姐，我只是喬。」少女回答。

「我不是羅倫斯先生，我只是羅瑞。」

「羅瑞·羅倫斯——多怪的名字。」

「你不喜歡跳舞嗎，喬小姐？」羅瑞問，他似乎認為這個名字很適合她。

「如果地方夠大，每個人都很活潑，我是很喜歡的。但是在這種地方我是一定會弄壞什麼東西、踩到別人的腳，或是闖出大禍的，所以我就避開，讓梅格去跳舞。你跳不跳舞？」

「有時候。我在國外待了很多年，跟這裡的人交往不多，不知道你們這裡的情形。」

「國外！」喬喊道，「噢，告訴我國外的事情吧！我好喜歡聽人家說起他們旅遊的事情呢！」

羅瑞似乎不知道該從何說起，不過喬那些急切的問題很快就使他侃侃而談了起來。

喬像男生一樣的態度使羅瑞覺得很有意思，也就變得自在了，因此他的羞怯很快就消失；而喬也回復了快活的本性，因為她已經忘了自己衣裙的事，而且也沒有人對她抬眉毛了。她比以前更喜歡「羅倫斯家的男孩」，於是好生打量了他幾眼，好讓她能夠跟姐妹們描述他。她們沒有兄弟，堂表兄弟又少，男孩子對她們來說幾乎是陌生的生物。

「鬈鬈的黑髮、棕色皮膚、大大的黑眼睛、漂亮的鼻子、整齊的牙齒、手腳都很小，比我高。以男孩子來說，很有禮貌，整個人是很不錯。不知道他多大？」

這句問話已經在她舌尖，不過她及時忍住了，並且用少見的技巧試圖以迂迴的方式找出答案。

「我猜你很快就要進大學了吧？我看到你辛辛苦苦在啃書──不，我是說你很用功唸書。」喬對自己不小心說出「辛苦啃書」感到很不好意思。

羅瑞笑了笑，看起來並不驚訝的樣子。他聳聳肩回答道：

「一、兩年內是不會的。反正我十七歲以前也不能進去。」

「你才十五歲嗎？」喬問他，她注視這個她已經想成十七歲的高個子男孩。

「下個月十六歲。」

「我多希望是我要去上大學！你看起來好像不太喜歡。」

「我討厭上學！」

「那你喜歡什麼？」

「住在義大利，自尋快樂。」

喬很想問他的快樂是什麼，不過他皺起眉頭時那兩道黑眉看起來教人擔心，於是她就改變話題，在她的腳打拍子的時候說：「這是一首很棒的波卡舞曲呢！你怎麼不去試試？」

「除非你跟我一起去。」他殷切地鞠了個躬說道。

「不行，我告訴梅格說我不會跳的，因為 ──」話說到這裡，喬停住了。

「因為什麼？」羅瑞好奇地問。

「你不會說出去嗎？」

「絕對不會說！」

「是這樣的，我身上這件衣服被我燒壞了，雖然補得很好，還是看得出來，所以梅格要我不能亂動，這樣就不會有人看到了。你想笑就笑吧，這的確很好笑，我知道。」

但是羅瑞並沒有笑，他只低頭看了一下，臉上的表情讓喬很困惑，他輕柔地說：

「別管這個啦。我告訴你我們怎麼辦：外面有個很狹長的大廳，我們可以跳個痛快，也不會有人看到。我們去吧，好嗎？」

喬謝了他，就高高興興去了，而看到她的舞伴戴著那隻漂亮的珍珠色手套時，她就希望自己能有兩隻好手套了。大廳空無一人，於是他們跳了一首波卡舞曲，羅瑞舞跳得很好，還教喬德國式舞步，讓喬很開心。音樂停下來之後，他倆就坐在台階上喘口氣，羅瑞說起海德堡一種學生慶典的故事，說到一半，來找妹妹的梅格就出現了。她招了招手，喬不怎麼情願地跟她走進一間側屋，看到她面色慘白地坐在一張沙發上，手握住一隻腳。

「我扭到腳踝了。那雙笨高跟鞋歪了一下，我就扭到了。好痛喔，我幾乎站不住，我也不知道要怎麼回家。」她說，身體痛苦地前後搖晃著。

「我就知道那雙愚蠢的鞋子會弄痛你的腳。我很難過，不過我看不出你能怎麼辦，除非去叫輛馬車來，不然就是在這裡待上一整晚。」喬說，一邊輕柔地揉著那可憐的腳踝。

「叫輛馬車一定得花很多錢。我敢說我連一輛也叫不到，因為大部分的人都是坐自己的馬車來的，而到馬廄又是好遠的路，又沒有人可以去。」

「我去。」

「絕對不行！已經過了九點鐘，外頭黑得跟什麼一樣。我就休息到漢娜來吧，然後就盡量看著辦了。」

「我去找羅瑞，他會去。」喬說，這個念頭使她看起來鬆了一口氣。

「老天爺，不行！不要找人，也不要告訴任何人。把我的橡膠鞋拿來，把這雙高跟鞋和我們的東西放在一起。我不能再跳舞了，不過等到晚餐過後就要注意漢娜來了沒有，她一到就告訴我。」

當漢娜出現時，他們正和兩、三個無意間走過來的年輕人玩「比手畫腳」遊戲玩到一半。梅格忘了腳痛，猛地站起來，使她痛得大叫一聲，緊緊抓住了喬。

「噓！什麼都不要說！」她低聲說，然後大聲加上一句：「沒事的！我稍微扭了一下腳──如此而已！」說完就一跛一跛地上樓去穿戴整齊。

漢娜責罵起來，梅格就哭了，喬無計可施，最後她決定插手管這件事。她溜出去並跑下樓，找到一個僕人，問他可不可以幫她叫輛馬車。不巧這人是雇來的服務生，對這一帶毫無所知。於是喬四下張望想找救兵，這時候羅瑞來了並聽到她說的話，主動要讓她們用他爺爺的馬車，馬車才剛來接他，他說。

「現在還早呢！你不會真的要走吧？」喬說，她看起來如釋重負，但是仍遲疑著，不知道該不該接受這個提議。

「我一向都早走，真的。請讓我送你們回家好嗎？這完全順路的，你知道。而且他們說現在下雨了。」

於是就這麼解決了。喬一邊告訴他梅格的不幸，一邊感激地接受了他的好意，而後衝上樓去把其他人帶下來。漢娜不喜歡下雨，所以一點也不囉唆。她們坐上這輛廂型豪華馬車，感覺既開心又優雅。羅瑞坐在車廂外的座位上，這讓梅格不僅可以把腳抬高，女孩子又可以自由自在談起舞會。

「我玩得好開心呀，你呢？」喬問，同時把她的頭髮撥得亂蓬蓬，讓自己舒適自在。

「我也是，一直到我扭傷為止。莎麗的朋友安妮‧莫法特很喜歡我，邀我跟莎麗去她家住一個星期。莎麗要在春天去她家，那時候歌劇也開始演出了，如果媽媽准我去，那就太好了。」梅格回答，這個念頭使她很開心。

喬把自己的冒險經過告訴她，等到她說完，她們也到家了。連連道謝之後，她們互道「晚安」，就悄悄進入屋裡，希望不要打擾到任何人。沒想到她們的房間門才剛發出嘎吱的聲音，兩頂小小的睡帽就突然冒出來，兩個睡意很濃但急切的聲音喊了出來——

「說說看舞會的事！說說看舞會的事！」

喬以梅格說是「萬分失態」的方式藏了一些糖果給妹妹們，她們在聽完當晚最刺激的事情後也很快就去睡了。

第 4 章
包袱

「天啊，現在要扛起我們的包袱，繼續往前走，看起來的確好困難呢！」舞會後第二天早晨，梅格嘆口氣說了。假期結束，這一整個星期的歡樂使她更難面對她從來就不喜歡的工作。

「我希望天天都是聖誕節或是新年，那不是很有趣嗎？」喬回答，愁苦地打著呵欠。

「我們連像現在這樣的享受都不應該有。不過能夠有頓餐宴、有人送花，參加舞會，坐著馬車回家，看看書，休息休息，不用工作，倒真是不錯。就像別人一樣，你知道我一向羨慕能這麼做的女孩。我太喜歡舒適安逸了。」梅格說，一邊思考著手裡的兩件破舊衣裙中哪一件比較不那麼破舊。

「反正我們是沒辦法過這種生活的，就別抱怨了吧，扛起我們的包袱，學媽媽一樣快快樂樂地往前走吧。」

但是梅格卻沒有開朗起來，因為她的包袱是四個被寵壞的孩子，而這個包袱似乎比以前更重了。她甚至沒有心思把自己像往常一樣打扮漂亮、在脖子上繫條緞帶、梳個最好看的髮式。

「看起來好看有什麼用？除了四個壞脾氣的小鬼看得到我以外沒有人會看到，也沒有人在乎我好不好看！」她喃喃說著，用力關上抽屜。「我只能成日辛苦，偶爾有些小小樂事，慢慢變老

變得壞脾氣：就因為我沒有錢，不能像別的女孩子那樣享受我的生活。真可悲！」

於是梅格滿臉悲憤地下了樓，早餐時候一點也不客氣。每個人似乎心情都不好，說起話都哭喪著臉。

「從沒有看過這麼愛生氣的一家人！」喬叫道。

「女兒們，女兒們，請安靜一分鐘好嗎？我必須趁早班郵件時把這封信寄出去，你們那些煩惱都讓我沒法專心了！」瑪區太太刪去信上第三段寫錯的句子，一邊叫道。

之後有片刻的平靜，卻被漢娜打斷了。她悄悄走進來，在飯桌上放了兩塊熱騰騰的捲酥餅，又悄悄走了出去。漢娜從來不會忘記給她們做捲酥餅，因為那段路走起來又長又荒涼，這兩個可憐的孩子也沒有別的午餐，而且很少會在兩點鐘以前回得了家。

「再見了，媽媽，今天早晨我們像是壞蛋一樣，但是我們回來時就會像個十足的天使了。走吧，梅格！」喬邁步走了，她覺得這些朝聖者並沒有做出該做的事。

她們轉過路口前總會回頭看，因為母親總是會站在窗前點頭微笑，朝她們揮著手。不知怎麼的，她們好像不這樣就很難度過一天，因為不論她們的心情如何，只要能再看母親一眼，那張臉就會像是溫暖的陽光一樣帶給她們暖意。

當她倆準備就此分開各過這一天的時候，喬在姐姐肩上鼓勵式地拍了拍，她們從這裡要走不同的路，各自握著手中溫暖的捲酥餅，試圖不受寒多天氣、辛勤工作，以及年輕人玩心無法滿足的影響，依然保有開懷的心情。

　　瑪區先生因為幫助一個不幸的朋友而失去所有財產時，兩個大的女兒央求父母讓她們做點事，至少可以養活自己一些。做父母的相信，培養力量、勤奮和獨立，任何年齡都不算早，便同意了，於是兩人便帶著一股熱切的好意開始工作。

　　梅格找到一個保母的職位，微薄的薪資也使她感覺十分富足。她發現自己比其他人更難忍受，因為她還能夠記得家裡很漂亮、生活充滿安逸與享樂、從不知匱乏為何物的時候。她試著不去嫉妒或是不滿，但是少女渴望美麗的事物、快活的朋友、社交上的才藝和快樂的生活，是非常自然的事。在金家，她每天都會看到自己欠缺的一切，也看到大筆的錢用在一些瑣事上，而這些瑣事卻可能對她而言非常珍貴。可憐的梅格不常抱怨，但是一種忿忿不平的感覺卻使她有時候會對每個人都很偏激。她還不知道自己在享有的恩賜中是多麼富有，單單這種恩賜就足以使得生活幸福了。

　　喬剛好很適合瑪區嬸婆，瑪區嬸婆腳不方便，需要一個活潑的人侍候。這位老太太沒有小孩，她們家出問題的時候曾經想要收養四姐妹中的一個，但是遭到拒絕，她非常生氣。其他朋友告訴瑪區家人說他們已經沒機會被列在這位富有老太太的遺囑裡了，然而瑪區這家對名利無動於衷的人卻只說：

　　「給我們再多的錢，我們也不會把孩子送人。不管是富是貧，我們都要在一起，快快樂樂做伴。」

　　老太太有一段時間不肯跟他們說話，後來有一次在朋友家剛好遇到了喬，喬那張有喜感的臉和直率的態度十分討老太太的歡

心，她想要喬陪她做伴。這工作一點也不合喬的興趣，但是她還是接受了，因為眼前也沒有更好的工作。結果她倒是和這個暴躁的親戚處得相當好，讓每個人都嚇了一跳。偶爾兩人會有番大吵，有一次喬甚至還走回家說她再也不能忍受了，不過瑪區嬸婆總是一下子就雨過天青，然後又急急忙忙找她回去，使她不能拒絕。其實在她心裡，她倒是挺喜歡這個火爆的老太太。

我猜，真正吸引她的是那擺滿好書的大圖書室。自從瑪區叔公過世之後，這間房就任由塵灰滿布，甚至還有蜘蛛進駐。陰暗而滿布灰塵的房間裡，那些胸像從高高的書櫃上方往下凝視，而舒適的椅子、地球儀，以及其中最好的——大片的書海，她可以隨自己的喜愛漫步其中——這一切都使得圖書室對她像是一個幸福的所在。

瑪區嬸婆才打上盹或是忙著招呼客人，喬就急忙來到這個安靜的地方，把自己縮在安樂椅中貪婪地吞噬詩篇、浪漫小說、歷史、遊記和圖畫，像是一隻十足的書蟲。不過這也和所有的快樂一樣，維持不了很久。因為只要她剛剛看到故事的精采處、詩歌最甜美的句子，或是旅人最危險的冒險經歷時，就會有個尖銳的聲音叫著：「喬瑟——芬！」她就只能告別她的樂園去纏毛線、給那隻獅子狗洗澡，或是唸上一小時貝爾沙的文章。

喬的志向是做了不起的大事，至於是什麼，她還不清楚，要讓時間告訴她。而在同時，她也發現自己最大的悲哀是她不能隨自己所願地看書、跑步、騎馬。一個脾氣壞、嘴巴毒、喜怒無常的人老要找她吵架，使她的生活充斥一連串的起伏情緒，既滑稽

又可悲。不過她在瑪區嬸婆家所受的訓練正是她需要的,而且想到她也在謀自己的生計,這一點也令她很快活,雖然那「喬瑟──芬!」的呼喚永遠也叫不完。

貝絲害羞不敢去上學,家人曾經試過讓她去,但是她卻非常痛苦,於是就放棄這個想法並讓她在家接受父親的教育。即使父親遠行,母親被找去為「軍人之友社」奉獻技術和氣力的時候,貝絲仍然規矩地自己唸書,也盡量用功。她是個賢妻良母型的小傢伙,會幫助漢娜把家整理得整潔而且舒適,從不要求任何報酬,只要大家愛她。她安安靜靜過著漫漫長日,但是她可不是孤單而且無聊的,因為她的小小世界裡充滿了想像的朋友,每天早晨她都要拿起六個玩偶,給它們穿衣打扮。貝絲還是個孩子,對她的玩具可是愛得很呢。這些娃娃沒有一個是完整的,也沒有一個稱得上漂亮。它們都是別人玩過丟棄了,被貝絲撿回來的。她的姐妹們玩膩了這些娃娃,而艾美不肯要舊的或是醜的,就會把它們給她。就因為這樣,貝絲更是溫柔地對待它們,還為受了傷的娃娃建了一間醫院。

貝絲也和其他人一樣,有她的困擾,她經常會因為不能學琴和有架好琴而──套句喬的話──「小哭一場」。她深愛音樂,辛苦地練琴,在叮叮咚咚的舊鋼琴上非常有耐心地練著。你也許認為應該有人會伸出援手幫助她,但事實上沒有人伸出援手,也沒有人看到貝絲獨處時把淚水從那走音的泛黃琴鍵上抹去。她的歌聲有如雲雀一般,為媽媽和姐妹們彈琴永不嫌累,而日復一日她都滿懷希望地對自己說:「我知道如果我表現得很乖的話,總

有一天可以學琴的。」

如果有人問艾美她生命中最大的磨難是什麼，她一定會立刻回答：「我的鼻子。」她還是嬰兒的時候，喬曾經不小心把她摔到煤斗裡，艾美一口咬定那次摔落永遠毀了她的鼻子。她的鼻子不大也不紅，只是比較扁，再怎麼捏也捏不出有貴族味道的鼻尖來。除了她自己以外誰也不在意，而這個鼻子也很努力地在長，但是艾美仍然深深感到自己欠缺了一個希臘式鼻子，於是畫了一張又一張漂亮的鼻子好安慰自己。

這個姐妹口中的「小拉斐爾」有明顯的繪畫天分，而她在臨摹花朵、設計仙女模樣，或是畫著古怪的故事插畫時候是最開心的。她的脾氣溫和，又有輕易就能使人快樂的本領，所以在同學間人緣很好。

艾美很可能會被寵壞，因為每個人都疼她，而她那小小的虛榮心和自私心態也漸漸滋長。不過有一件事倒是挫了她的虛榮心，那就是她必須穿她表姐的衣服。佛羅倫絲的媽媽一點品味也沒有，所以艾美深感痛苦。每件衣服質料都很好、手工精細，穿過的次數也不多，但是艾美富有藝術眼光的雙眼卻很痛苦。尤其是今年冬天，她的上學衣裙是一種暗紫色帶黃點的衣服，沒有任何裝飾。

梅格是艾美傾訴的對象，也是她的監督者，而因為某種奇異的相反性格會互相吸引的道理，喬成為溫柔的貝絲傾訴心事的對象和監督者。這個靦腆的孩子只把心事告訴喬一個人，而貝絲對於這個粗線條作風的姐姐具有不自覺的影響力，比起家中任何人

都大。兩個姐姐彼此很親,但是她們卻也各自負責一個妹妹,照顧她、管教她,她們形容這是「扮媽媽」,把妹妹們當成被丟棄的玩偶一般,用小女人的母性本能照顧她們。

「有沒有誰有事情可以說?今天過得很無趣,我可真想要有些娛樂。」這天晚上她們坐在房裡做著縫紉活兒時梅格說。

貝絲說了一個故事讓大家哈哈大笑,然後她們要母親也說個故事,母親思索了一會兒,正色說道:

「從前有四個女孩子,她們吃得飽,喝得足,穿得暖,有許多值得安慰和歡樂的事,有深愛她們的和善朋友和雙親,但是她們卻不滿足。」話說到這裡,聽者偷偷瞄著彼此,並且開始勤奮地縫著。「這些女孩子一心想求好,也經常說『要是我們有這個就好了』,或是『要是我們能做那件事就好了』,她們忘了她們已經擁有許多,也忘了她們其實可以做很多快樂的事情。於是她們問一個老婦人說,她們要用什麼符咒使她們快樂呢?老婦人就說:『當你們覺得不滿足的時候,想想你們的福分,並且心存感激。』」這時候喬很快抬眼看,彷彿要說話,但是發現這個故事還沒有說完,就改變主意了。

「因為她們都是明理的女孩,所以決定試著照老婦人的建議去做,她們很快就發現她們自己是多麼幸福。一個人發現金錢也不能使富有人家遠離羞恥和悲愁;另一個人發現自己雖然窮,但有青春、健康和愉快的心境,她要比某個脾氣暴躁、身體孱弱、無法享受舒適生活的老太太快樂許多。第三個女孩發現,雖然幫人準備午餐不是件開心的事,但是向人乞討午餐卻更困難;第四

個女孩發現的是，即使紅玉戒指也沒有良好的行爲珍貴。所以她們一致同意不要再抱怨，而要享受她們已經擁有的福分，並且努力讓自己不負這些福分，以免福分不增反減。我相信她們聽那個老婦人的勸告是絕對不會失望或是後悔的。」

「媽，您太厲害了，竟然用我們自己的故事來教訓我們，不告訴我們一個浪漫故事，反倒訓了我們一頓。」梅格叫道。

「我喜歡這樣的訓話，爸爸從前告訴我們的就是這種。」貝絲把毛線針直接放在喬的靠墊上，若有所思地說。

「我不像其他人那樣愛抱怨，從今以後我也會更加小心。」艾美道貌岸然地說。

「我們需要那個教訓，我們不會忘記的。如果我們忘了，您只管對我們說，就像老克羅在《黑奴籲天錄》裡面說的：『想想你的天賜恩惠，孩子們！想想你的天賜恩惠，孩子們！』」喬加上一句，她是怎麼也忍不住要從這小小的講道中找點樂趣的，雖然她也和其他人一樣，已經牢牢記住這個教訓了。

第 5 章
睦鄰

「你究竟要幹什麼呀，喬？」一個下雪的午後，梅格問道，這時候她妹妹穿著橡膠鞋、舊大衣，戴著兜帽，一手拿著掃帚一手拿著鏟子，大步跨過門廳。

「出去運動。」喬說，眼睛閃著促狹的亮光。

梅格回去烘她的腳，一邊看《撒克遜英雄傳》，喬開始拚命在雪地裡挖出道路來。雪下得很少，她用掃帚很快就在花園四周挖出一條路，要讓貝絲帶著那些需要空氣的傷病娃娃在太陽出來後散步用。這座花園隔開了瑪區家和羅倫斯家。兩家的房子都在城郊，這裡仍然很像鄉下，有矮叢和草坪、偌大的花園和寧靜的街道。一道低矮的樹籬將兩座莊園分開。一邊是一幢棕色的舊房屋，看起來老舊而且光禿，沒有在夏天裡可以遮住四牆的蔓藤，也沒有長在四周的花朵。樹籬另一邊是一幢堂皇的石造大宅，從寬敞的馬車車房和保養得宜的草地，到溫室花房，到偶爾可以從那富麗的窗簾之間瞥見的美好物品，清清楚楚地說明了這戶人家有各種生活上的舒適和豪華。然而它似乎是個寂寞而死氣沉沉的房子，因為它的草坪上沒有孩童嬉戲，窗前沒有做母親的笑臉，除了那位老先生和他的孫子以外，幾乎沒有什麼人進出。

在喬生動的想像中，這幢華宅似乎是一座魔宮，充滿了奇妙

而且歡樂的事物，卻沒有人享受。她早就想要一睹其中那些隱藏著的光華，並且認識那個「羅倫斯男孩」，他看起來很想認識人，卻不知道該如何開始。自從那次舞會後，她比以前更渴望，並且還計畫了很多種方法要和他做朋友，只是最近她都沒有看到他。她原本猜想他已經離開了，後來有一天她看到樓上一扇窗戶後頭有一張棕色的臉，正羨慕地望著下方她們家的花園，貝絲和艾美正在互相丟雪球。

「那個男生好想要有社交和歡樂，」她自言自語。「他爺爺不知道什麼事對他有益，把他一個人關起來。他需要有一群男生陪他一起玩，或是一個年輕活潑的人。我很願意過去告訴那位老先生。」

這想法讓喬很快活，她喜歡做些大膽的事，總是用她那些奇怪的言行讓梅格憤慨不已。她沒有忘記這個「過去」的計畫，而當這個飄著雪的下午時分到來時，喬決定試試看。她看到羅倫斯先生駕車出去後，就衝出家門用掃帚一路掃到樹籬邊，再停下來探查一番。這裡是靜悄悄的——樓下窗戶的窗簾全都拉上，一個僕人也看不到；除了樓上窗裡一個黑鬈髮腦袋支在一隻細瘦的手上之外，看不到一個人影。

「他在那裡，」喬心想。「可憐的人！在這種陰沉日子裡孤單一人又生著病。真可憐！我丟個雪球上去，要他往外看，然後跟他說些安慰的話。」

於是一顆柔軟的雪球丟了上去，那顆腦袋立刻轉過來現出一張臉。只見那原本無精打采的表情立即消失，一雙大眼睛亮了起

來，嘴角也開始漾出笑意。喬點點頭，笑了起來，一邊喊一邊揮舞她的掃帚。

「你好嗎？你是不是生病啦？」

羅瑞打開窗戶，用烏鴉一般的粗啞聲喊著：

「已經好多了，謝謝你。我得了重感冒，已經關了一個星期了。」

「我很遺憾。那你都做什麼消遣呢？」

「什麼也沒有。這裡跟墳墓一樣無聊。」

「你不看書嗎？」

「不太看。他們不准我看。」

「別人不能唸給你聽嗎？」

「爺爺有唸，有時候，可是我的書他沒有興趣，我也不喜歡老是要布魯克唸給我聽。」

「那你可以找人去看你呀。」

「我沒有什麼想要看到的人。男孩子會很喧鬧，而我的頭又受不了。」

「難道沒有什麼願意唸書給你聽的好女孩嗎？女孩子都文靜，也喜歡當護士照顧別人。」

「我不認識任何女生。」

「你認識我們呀。」喬說，然後笑了起來，但又停住了。

「對呀！那你過來好嗎，拜託？」羅瑞叫道。

「我可不文靜也不乖巧，不過我願意去，只要我媽允許。我去問她。你關上窗子等我。」

小婦人

　　說完，喬扛起掃帚就大步進了屋裡，一邊想她們會對她說什麼。羅瑞想到有人要來簡直興奮得不得了，來來回回忙著準備，因爲他正如同瑪區太太所言，是「一位小紳士」。爲了向即將光臨的客人表達敬意，特地梳了梳他的鬈髮，換了新的衣領，還試著把他的房間清理了一下。他家雖有五、六個僕人，但是這個房間卻一點也不整齊。很快地傳來一陣很大聲的鈴聲，接著是一個口氣明確的人聲，要見「羅瑞先生」，然後是一個滿臉驚訝的僕人跑上樓，說有位年輕女士來訪。

　　「好，請她上來，那是喬小姐。」羅瑞說，他走到他那間小客廳門口迎接喬。喬出現了，神情愉快，十分親切也很自在，一手拎著一個蓋起來的碟子，另一隻手抱著貝絲的三隻小貓咪。

　　「我來啦，帶著全部家當呢。」她簡短地說著。「我媽要我替她問候你，她很高興我能爲你做點事。梅格要我帶一些她的奶凍，她做得很好；貝絲認爲她的貓可以給你安慰。我知道你會笑的，可是我不能拒絕，她那麼急著想要做點事。」

　　結果貝絲借出來的小貓咪卻是再恰當不過的，因爲羅瑞看到這些小貓咪就笑了，忘掉了自己的靦腆，立刻就可以自在說笑了。

　　「這些看起來太漂亮了，教人捨不得吃。」喬把碟子拿出來，奶凍周圍是由綠葉和艾美最喜歡的天竺葵的深紅花朵形成的花圈，他高興地笑著說。

　　「這沒有什麼，她們都想對你表達自己的善意。你叫女僕把它拿去放，配你的茶吃。這很簡單，你可以吃，而且它很軟，一

吞就滑進你肚子裡，不會傷到你疼痛的喉嚨。這間屋子好舒服呢！」

「如果有好好整理的話或許是吧，不過女僕們都好懶惰，我也不知道要怎麼讓她們用心一些。我挺煩惱的。」

「我可以在兩分鐘之內整理好，你只需要把爐子這裡掃一下——像這樣——壁爐台上的東西放整齊，像這樣；書放在這裡，瓶子放在那裡，你的沙發椅轉過來，背著光；再把枕頭拍鬆一點。好啦，這樣就弄好啦。」

果真如此。因為喬在說說笑笑之際也很快就把東西擺放到適當位置上，使房裡的氣氛大為不同。羅瑞充滿敬意地默默看著她，當她招手要他坐到沙發上時，他滿意地嘆口氣坐下來，感激地說：

「你真好心呢！沒錯，這房間就是需要這樣子。現在請你坐那張大椅子，讓我做些事娛樂我的客人吧。」

「不，我是來娛樂你的。要不要我唸書給你聽？」喬以愛慕的眼光望著附近一些很吸引人的書。

「謝謝你，這些書我全都看過了。如果你不介意的話，我倒願意聊聊天。」羅瑞回答道。

「我一點也不介意。只要你讓我開始說話，我可以說上一整天。貝絲說我永遠也不知道什麼時候該住嘴。」

「貝絲是那個粉嫩皮膚、常常待在家裡，有時候會拎著小籃子出門的那個嗎？」羅瑞很有興趣地問。

「是的，那是貝絲，她是歸我管的，她的確非常乖。」

「很漂亮的那個是梅格，頭髮鬈鬈的是艾美吧？」

「你怎麼知道？」

羅瑞臉紅了起來，但是回答得倒坦白：「是這樣子的，我時常聽到你們彼此叫喚，當我獨自一人在這個樓上，我總忍不住會往你們家看去，你們好像總是很快樂。請原諒我這麼沒禮貌，但是有時候你們忘了拉下種著花的那扇窗戶的窗簾，等到點亮燈的時候，就很像是看著一幅圖畫；看到燈火，看到你們和母親圍坐在桌旁，你母親的臉正對著我，她的臉從花的後面看過去十分祥和呢，我忍不住會一直看。我沒有母親，你知道。」羅瑞撥著壁爐火，掩藏他忍不住抽動的嘴唇。

羅瑞生病了，又很寂寞，喬感到自己在家庭親情和幸福當中是多麼富有，所以樂於和他分享。她的神情非常友善，她那尖銳的聲音也在說話時變得少見的溫柔：

「我們永遠也不會把窗簾拉上了，而且我准你愛看多久就看多久。不過我希望你不要偷看，而是到我們家來看我們。我媽媽手藝好了不起，會給你做好多好多好吃東西；貝絲會唱歌給你聽，如果我求她的話；艾美還會跳舞。我和梅格滑稽的舞台道具會讓你大笑，我們會很開心的。你爺爺會不會讓你來？」

「如果你母親問他的話，我想他會的。他人很好心，只是看起來不像；他通常都准我做我要做的事，只是他害怕我會給陌生人帶來麻煩。」羅瑞說，他越來越開朗了。

「我們不是陌生人，我們是鄰居呢，而且你不用認為會給我們帶來麻煩。我們想要認識你，而且我早就想要這麼做了。我們

住在這裡並不久,你知道,可是我們已經認識所有的鄰居了,除了你們。」

「你知道,我爺爺活在他的書當中,不太理會外界發生的事。布魯克先生是我的家庭老師,他又不住在這裡,我旁邊沒有什麼人,所以只好待在家裡。」

「那樣不好。你應該試試看,人家請你去你就去,這樣你就會有許多朋友,還有愉快的地方可以去了。不要在意你多麼害羞,只要你經常出去,這種情形也不會長久的。」

羅瑞臉又紅了,但是被人說很害羞他倒不生氣,因為喬的話是好意,她那些直率的話只能被當成出自好意。

「你喜歡你的學校嗎?」兩人間有一段短短的停頓,這時候他盯著爐火瞧,而喬滿意地打量著四周,之後男孩子換個話題問道。

「我沒有上學,我在做事——是個職業婦女呢。我的工作是侍候我嬸婆,她還真是個壞脾氣的老太太呢。」喬回答。

羅瑞張口正要問另一個問題,及時想到打探別人太多私事是沒有禮貌的,因此閉上嘴,看起來很不自在。喬很喜歡他的好教養,也不在意說瑪區嬸婆的笑話,於是她對他生動描述了這位壞脾氣的老太太、她那隻肥獅子狗、那隻會說西班牙語的鸚鵡,還有她愛沉迷其中的圖書室。他們接著又談到了書,而讓喬開心的是,她發現羅瑞和她一樣愛書,看過的書甚至比她還多。

「如果你那麼喜歡書,我們下樓去,你可以看看我們的書。爺爺出去了,所以你不用害怕。」羅瑞說著站了起來。

「我什麼都不怕。」喬把頭一揚，回答他。「我相信！」男孩嘆道，以無比的羨慕眼神看著她，不過私底下他猜想，如果她碰巧遇上爺爺情緒差的時候，她對這位老先生就會有幾分畏懼了。

這整幢房屋的空氣像夏天一樣暖和，羅瑞領著她從一個房間走到另一個房間。終於，他們來到了圖書室，她拍著雙手，歡喜地跳了起來，她特別開心的時候都會這麼做。圖書室裡擺滿了書籍、畫、雕像、滿是錢幣和珍奇物品的小櫃子、躺椅和古怪的桌子，以及銅器。最棒的是，還有一座大型的開放式壁爐，壁爐周圍鋪著奇特的磁磚。

「多麼富有呀！」喬嘆道，跌坐在一張天鵝絨椅的深處，用大為滿足的神色打量四周。「狄奧多‧羅倫斯，你應該是全世界最幸福的男孩子了。」她強調地加上一句。

「人不能只靠書本生活。」羅瑞說，他坐在對面一張桌子上，搖搖頭。

他還來不及再說些話，鈴聲響起，喬立刻跳起來並驚恐地叫道：「天啊！是你爺爺！」

「如果是的話，又怎麼樣呢？你什麼也不怕呀，你知道。」男孩回道，看起來一臉戲謔。

「我想我是有一點怕他的，只是我不知道為什麼會怕他。我媽媽說我可以來，我想你身體也沒有因此變差。」喬強作鎮定，不過眼睛仍然直盯著門。

「我已經好太多了，而且感激不盡。我只怕你跟我說話會感

到厭煩，這真是太愉快了，我不想停止。」羅瑞很感激地說。

「大夫來看您了，先生。」女僕邊說邊招手。

「你不介意我離開你片刻吧？我想我必須見他。」羅瑞說。

「別管我。我在這裡快活得很呢。」喬回答道。

羅瑞走開了，於是他的客人也自得其樂起來。她站在那位老先生的精細畫像前，這時門又開了，她頭也不回地用堅定的語氣說：「我現在很確定，我應該不會害怕他了，雖然他的嘴好像很嚴厲，他的人看起來非常有主見，但是他卻有一雙慈祥的眼睛。他沒有我外公好看，可是我喜歡他。」

「謝謝你，女士。」她身後響起一個沙啞的聲音，她驚惶失措起來，原來老羅倫斯先生就站在身後。

可憐的喬，臉紅得不得了，她想到自己說過什麼話，心跳就不自在地加快了起來。一時間她只想快快逃走，但是那樣太懦弱了，姐妹們也會笑她，所以她決定待在那裡，並且盡量想辦法脫困。再看第二眼，她發現這對濃濃的灰色眉毛下活生生的雙眼，甚至要比畫裡頭的還要慈祥，而這雙眼睛中閃著一抹狡黠的光亮，使她的恐懼大為減輕。經過一段令人恐懼的靜止時刻後，老先生突然開了口，他那沙啞的聲音變得更沙啞了：「這麼說來，你不怕我囉？」

「不太怕了，先生。」

「而你認為我沒有你外公好看？」

「不太比得上，先生。」

「而我非常有主見，是嗎？」

「我只說我覺得如此。」

「不過你還是喜歡我就是了？」

「是的，先生。」

這個回答使老先生很滿意，他笑了兩聲並和她握了手，然後把手指放在她下巴下方抬起她的臉，神色嚴肅地端詳著再放開手，點點頭說：「就算你沒有你外公的長相，你也有他的精神。他是個好人，孩子；但更好的是，他也是個勇敢而且誠實的人，我很榮幸能做他的朋友。」

「謝謝您，先生。」這番話之後喬就相當自在了，因為她對這話深有同感。

下一個問題是：「你對我這個孫子做了什麼事呀？」問得很尖銳。

「只是想要敦親睦鄰而已，先生。」於是喬就把自己怎麼會來的情形告訴了他。

「你認為他應該快活點，是不是？」

「是的，先生。他看起來有點寂寞，年輕人對他也許會有幫助。我們只是女孩子，不過我們很樂意幫助他，因為我們沒有忘記您送給我們那美好的聖誕禮物。」喬熱切地說。

「嘖，嘖！那是我孫子的事呀。那個可憐婦人怎麼樣了？」

「很不錯呢，先生。」於是喬很快地說起胡梅爾家情況。她母親已經要一些富裕的朋友開始關心這家人了。

「跟她父親行善是一個樣。哪一天我會去探望你母親。你告訴她一聲。喝茶鈴聲響了，我們喝茶時間比較早，是因為我孫子

的關係。我們下去吧，你繼續做你的睦鄰工作吧。」

「如果您願意讓我加入的話，先生。」

「如果我不願意，我就不會問了。」羅倫斯先生行老派的禮節，把手臂伸向她，讓她搭著。

「不曉得梅格對這些事情會怎麼說呢？」喬被羅倫斯先生帶開時心裡想道，她想像自己在家裡說起這件事的情形，眼光也流露出興味。

這時候羅瑞正跑下樓梯，看到喬和他那令人敬畏的爺爺手挽著手這幅驚人的景象，嚇了一大跳，突然停下腳步。

「我不知道您回來了，爺爺。」他說，喬用勝利的眼光望了他一眼。

「從你乒乒乓乓衝下樓的情形看來，顯然如此。來喝茶吧，先生，舉止要像個紳士一樣。」羅倫斯先生疼愛地抓了抓孫子的頭髮後便繼續走著，而羅瑞在他們背後做出一連串滑稽的動作，幾乎讓喬笑出聲來。

老先生連喝了四杯茶，沒說什麼話，不過卻觀察這對年輕人，只見他們很快就像老友般聊起天來，而孫子的改變可沒有逃過他的眼睛。如今他的臉上有了神彩、有了光亮，也有了生命；他的態度活潑；他的笑聲中也有真正的快活。

「她的話沒錯，這孩子是很寂寞。我倒要看看這些小女生能幫他什麼忙。」羅倫斯先生一邊看他們，聽他們說，一邊思忖著。他喜歡喬，因為她那種古怪而且率直的作風很合他意，而且她了解這個男孩，幾乎像她自己就是個男孩一樣。

第 5 章

　　如果羅倫斯祖孫是喬所說的「古板又遲鈍」的人，她根本就不會和他們相處，因為這種人總會教她害羞而且尷尬。發現他們其實很隨和之後，她就更為自在，也給他們留下很好的印象。當他們站起來後她提議要走了，但是羅瑞說他還有東西要給她看，就把她帶到溫室花房去，花房的燈已經先為她點了起來。對喬來說這裡真像是童話仙境。她在走道上來回走動，享受兩旁盛開的花朵、柔和的燈光、香甜的潮濕空氣，和她上方垂吊下來的美麗蔓藤和樹木。她的新朋友剪下最嬌美的花朵，直到他雙手捧滿了花。而後他把花綁成一束，帶著喬喜歡的快活神情說：「請把這些花送給你母親，告訴她我非常喜歡她給我的藥。」他們發現羅倫斯先生正站在大客廳的壁爐前面，但是喬的注意力卻完全被一架打開著的平台鋼琴所吸引。

　　「你會彈琴嗎？」她轉身面對羅瑞，用一種尊敬的神情問。

　　「有時候。」他謙虛地說。

　　「請你現在彈一下，我想聽聽，好告訴貝絲。」

　　「你先彈吧！」

　　「我不會彈。太笨了學不會，不過我非常喜歡音樂。」

　　於是羅瑞就彈起琴來。喬把鼻子深深埋進向日葵花和薔薇中，對於「羅倫斯家男孩」的敬意增添了許多，因為他琴彈得真好，又不擺架子。她真希望貝絲也能聽到，不過她沒有說，只是一個勁地稱讚他，使他脹紅了臉，還是他爺爺過來解了圍。

　　「這樣就行了，這樣就行了，小姑娘。太多的讚美對他可不好呢。他的琴彈得不錯，不過我希望他在重要的事情上做得也同

樣好。要走了嗎？噢，真謝謝你了，我希望你能再來玩。替我向你母親問好。晚安，喬大夫。」

他和氣地握了手，但是看起來好像有什麼事而不悅的樣子。他們走到大廳以後，喬問羅瑞說她是不是有什麼地方失言了，他搖搖頭。

「不是，是因為我的關係。他不喜歡聽到我彈琴。」

「為什麼呢？」

「改天再告訴你。約翰要送你回家，我不能去。」

「用不著，我又不是小女生，而且也只有兩步路。好好保重，好嗎？」

「好。但是你會再來吧，我希望？」

「只要你答應病好了就到我們家來玩。」

「我會的。」

「晚安，羅瑞！」

「晚安，喬，晚安！」

這場下午的冒險故事說完之後，全家人都想一起去拜訪一下，因為每個人都發現樹籬另一邊的那個大房子裡有吸引人的東西。瑪區太太想和那位仍未忘記她父親的老先生談談父親；梅格很想到溫室花房走走；貝絲為那架平台鋼琴嘆著氣；艾美好想欣賞那些精美的圖畫和雕像。

「媽媽，為什麼羅倫斯先生不喜歡羅瑞彈琴？」天生就好問的喬問道。

「我不清楚，不過我猜那是因為他兒子——也就是羅瑞的父

親——娶了一個義大利女孩,那女孩是個音樂家,老先生對這件事很不高興,因為他是個很自負的人。那個女孩子人很好,可愛又有才華,但是他不喜歡她,在兒子結婚以後就再也不肯見兒子了。羅瑞小時候父母親就去世了,於是爺爺就把他帶回家。我猜這個在義大利出生的男孩身體不是很強壯,老先生很怕失去他,所以他才那麼小心翼翼。羅瑞天生就喜歡音樂,因為他像他母親,我敢說他爺爺一定是害怕他當音樂家,不管怎麼說,總之他的琴藝使老先生想起那個他不喜歡的女人了,所以他才會『大皺眉頭』——像喬說的那樣吧!」

「天啊!好浪漫呀!」梅格嘆道。

「好可笑呀!」喬說。「如果他願意,就讓他去做音樂家嘛,明明他不喜歡進大學何必非要他去,讓他痛苦得要命!」

「所以他才會有那麼漂亮的黑眼睛和優雅的風度,我猜。義大利人一向都很溫文有禮。」梅格說,她是有點感情豐富的人。

「你知道什麼眼睛和風度呀?你幾乎從沒有跟他說過話呢!」喬大叫,她可不是多愁善感的人。

「我在舞會上看過他呀,而且從你說的話裡可以看出他很懂得分寸。他說起媽媽送給他的藥那番話,就說得很好。」

「我猜他指的是奶凍吧。」

「你怎麼那麼笨呀,孩子!他說的是你呀,當然囉!」

「是嗎?」喬睜大了眼睛,好像她從來都沒想到一樣。

「我從來沒見過這種女孩子!人家稱讚你,你都還不知道!」梅格說,她流露出對這件事無所不知的神情。

「我認爲讚美全都是胡說八道，而我還要謝謝你沒有做傻事，破壞我的玩興呢。羅瑞是個好孩子，我很喜歡他，我對那些讚美之類的廢話是不會感情用事的。我們都要對他好喔，因爲他沒有媽媽，而且他也可能會過來看我們，媽媽，他可不可以來我們家？」

「當然可以呀，喬，我很歡迎你的小朋友呢，而我希望梅格能記住一件事，就是小孩子應該盡量天眞無邪。」

「我不認爲我是小孩子，我也還沒有到青少年的年紀呀，」艾美說。「你的看法呢，貝絲？」

「我在想我們的《天路歷程》呢。」貝絲答道，她根本沒有聽到半句話。「我們要怎麼走出『絕望的泥沼』，透過試煉，爬上陡坡，並走出『邊門』？也許隔壁那幢房子，那幢滿是美好東西的房子，就是我們的『美麗宮殿』呢。」

「那我們還得先通過書裡面『獅子』那一關呢。」喬說，她倒像是挺喜歡那幕景象的呢。

第 6 章
美麗宮殿

那幢大宅果然是座「美麗宮殿」，在這段期間發生了各種各樣快活的事情，因為這新的友誼像春天的青草一般欣欣向榮。每個人都喜歡羅瑞，而羅瑞私底下也告訴他的家庭老師說：「瑪區家的女孩子都是非常好的女孩子。」從小沒有母親也沒有姐妹的他，很快就感受到她們帶給他的影響；而她們忙碌又活潑的態度也使他對於自己過的懶散生活感到羞恥。如今他對書本已經厭倦了，反而覺得人才是有趣的東西，這使得布魯克先生不得不告狀，因為羅瑞老是逃課跑到隔壁瑪區家。

「沒關係的，讓他放個假吧，過後再補上好了，」老先生說。「隔壁的好心女士說他唸書唸得太辛苦了，需要結交年輕朋友、要有娛樂和運動。我想她的話沒錯，而我也一直太呵護他，好像我是他奶奶一樣。就讓他愛做什麼就做什麼吧，只要他開心就好。」

他們過了多少快樂時光啊！演戲劇、乘雪橇、溜冰玩耍、在老客廳度過快活夜晚，偶爾在大宅子裡舉行歡樂的小小派對。梅格可以隨時到溫室花房裡散步，沉迷在花束之中；喬貪婪地在新的圖書室中瀏覽，她的高談闊論總會讓老先生捧腹大笑；艾美臨摹那些圖畫，開懷地欣賞美麗事物；羅瑞則以最教人快活的方式

扮演「莊園主人」的角色。

　　但是，對平台鋼琴無限渴望的貝絲，卻鼓不起勇氣前去「幸福宅邸」——梅格這麼稱呼那裡。貝絲和喬去過一次，但是老先生不知道她性情柔弱，而從他粗粗的眉毛下嚴厲地瞪著她，用好大的聲音說了「嗨！」一個字，把她嚇得「兩隻腳在地板上打顫」——她這麼告訴母親——她就跑走了，並且宣布再也不去了，就算去看那架好棒的鋼琴也不去了。不論人家怎麼勸說、怎麼利誘都克服不了她的恐懼，後來這件事以一種神祕的方式傳到羅倫斯先生的耳中，他便決定要做點補償。在一次短暫的拜訪中他很有技巧地把話題轉向音樂，談起他見過的偉大聲樂家，他聽過的好管風琴，還說起許多有趣的軼事；實在太有趣了，使得貝絲覺得不該繼續待在遠遠的角落裡，只能越靠越近，像是被迷住了一樣。走到他的椅子後面時，她停住並睜著大眼聽，因為他絕佳的表演興奮得兩頰通紅。羅倫斯先生對她毫不在意，彷彿她是隻蒼蠅，逕自說起羅瑞的課和老師們。然後，像是突然想到了一樣，羅倫斯對瑪區太太說：

　　「這孩子現在疏忽音樂，我倒很高興，因為他太喜歡它了。可是鋼琴不用也不好，你們家女孩子可不可以偶爾過來練練琴，免得琴走音了？」

　　瑪區太太還來不及回答，羅倫斯先生就很奇怪地微微點點頭，笑道：

　　「她們用不著去看到誰或是跟誰說話，儘管隨時進來；因為我都關在房子另一頭的書房裡，羅瑞又常常跑到外頭，而僕人們

過了九點以後是絕對不會走近起居室的。」

　　說到這裡他站了起來，像是準備走了一樣，而貝絲也下定決心要說話了，因為這最後的一項安排已經使她別無所求。「請把我的話告訴那些姑娘，如果她們不想來，唉，那也沒關係。」這時候一隻小手伸進他手裡；貝絲仰起頭，一臉感激地看著他，熱切而又膽怯地說：

　　「噢，先生，她們很想很想去的！」

　　「你就是那個喜歡音樂的小姑娘嗎？」他低下頭，慈祥地看著她問，沒有說出什麼嚇人一跳的「嗨！」

　　「我是貝絲。我很喜歡呢，如果您確定不會有人聽到，而且不會被我打擾的話，我會去的。」她害怕自己太魯莽，還加了一句，並且為了自己的大膽渾身顫抖呢。

　　「絕對不會有一個人聽到呢，小姑娘。我的房子半天都是空的，所以請過來，隨你愛彈多久就彈多久，我會很感激你的。」

　　「您好好喲，先生！」

　　在他友善的神情注視下，貝絲臉紅得像朵玫瑰一樣，不過現在她不怕了，所以她感激地握了這隻大手，因為她無法用言語表達她對這份珍貴禮物的謝意。老先生輕輕摸了摸她額頭上的頭髮，彎腰親了親她，並且用一種幾乎沒有人聽過的語氣說：

　　「我也曾經有一個小女孩，眼睛也像你一樣。上天保佑你，我親愛的！再會了，夫人。」於是他急匆匆走了。

　　貝絲和母親欣喜若狂了好一會兒，當天晚上她唱歌唱得多快活呀！又因為她在夜裡把艾美的睡臉當鋼琴練，結果吵醒了艾

美，全家都笑她。第二天，貝絲眼看著隔壁一老一小兩個男生都離開家了，又退卻了兩、三次之後終於走進邊門，像老鼠一般無聲無息地走到起居室。她心中的偶像就立在那裡。當然啦，正巧鋼琴上放著一些漂亮又容易彈的樂譜，於是貝絲終於伸出顫抖的手指，在停頓多次、四下張望以後，碰觸了這架偉大的樂器。她立刻就忘了恐懼、忘了她自己，以及其他的一切，心中只剩音樂給予她的那種無法言喻的快活，因為音樂像是一個親愛的朋友正說著話。

她一直待到漢娜來接她回去吃晚飯，但是她毫無食欲，只能坐在那裡，用一種處於幸福中的神情對著每個人微笑。

從此以後，那個小小棕色兜帽就幾乎每天都會穿過矮樹籬，而那間偌大的起居室像是有個音樂精靈住在裡頭似的，沒有人看到精靈的來去。但是她從不知道羅倫斯先生常常打開書房門，聆聽他喜愛的古老旋律；從沒有看過羅瑞站在大廳當守衛，警告僕人不得靠近；從沒有猜到她在架子上發現的練習本和新樂譜都是別人特別為了她放的，而當他在家中跟她談起音樂的時候，她只想到他真好心，還會告訴她能給她很大幫助的事情。於是她開心極了，也發現自己唯一的願望成真 —— 雖然世事並不是永遠如此。

「媽媽，我要做雙鞋子送給羅倫斯先生。他對我真好，我必須要謝謝他，這是我唯一能做的事情，可以嗎？」在老先生那次重大的拜訪之後的幾個星期，貝絲問道。

「可以呀，親愛的。那會使他很開心呢，而且也是很好的道

謝方式。」瑪區太太說，她對於能答應貝絲的要求特別快樂，因為貝絲很少為自己要求過任何東西。

她是個靈敏的小小裁縫師，所以在誰都還沒有感到厭煩的時候，這雙鞋就做好啦。於是她寫了一封短箋，在羅瑞的幫助下，在一早上老先生還沒起床的時候把鞋子偷偷放到書房的書桌上。

等這陣興奮過後，貝絲就等著看會有什麼事情發生。當天過去了，第二天也過了一半，卻沒有任何回卡送到，她開始害怕她惹這個脾氣不好的朋友生氣了。第二天下午她出去跑腿，順便也帶可憐的瓊安娜──那個身障娃娃──做每天必做的運動。等她走在回家的街上時，她看到三個──噢，是四個人的腦袋在起居室的窗子裡探進探出，且一看到她，好幾隻手就揮了起來，還有好幾個快活的聲音尖叫著──

「隔壁老先生來信了！快回來，快來看呀！」

「噢，貝絲！他送你──」艾美開始用並不適當的氣力比手畫腳起來，但是沒比劃多久，喬就把窗子用力拉下並阻止了她。

貝絲惶惑不安地趕忙回家，走到門口時，她的姐妹們就抓住她，以一個勝利的遊行隊伍之勢把她推到起居室，所有人同時手指著說：「你看那裡！你看那裡！」貝絲看了，立刻因為歡喜和驚訝臉色發白，因為房裡立著一架小型的直立式鋼琴。光滑明亮的鋼琴蓋上擺著一封信，像塊招牌一樣，寫著「伊莉莎白·瑪區小姐」收。

「給我的嗎？」貝絲倒抽一口氣，緊抓著喬，覺得自己快要昏倒，畢竟這件事太教人吃驚了。

「是呀，全是你的呢，乖孩子！他可真是個好人呢，不是嗎？你不覺得他是全世界最最可愛的老人家嗎？這是信裡面附的鑰匙。我們沒有把信打開，可是我們好想知道他說些什麼呢！」喬喊道，她摟住妹妹，並且把信交給她。

「你唸信吧！我不能唸，我感覺好怪喔。噢，這實在是太好了！」說著貝絲把臉埋進喬的圍裙裡，被這份禮物攪得心緒不寧。

喬一打開信就笑了起來，因為她看到的第一句就是：

「瑪區小姐：親愛的女士──」

「聽起來多好聽呀！我真希望也有人能這樣子寫信給我呢！」艾美說道，她認為這種老式的稱謂非常典雅。

「我一生中有過許多雙便鞋，但是從沒有穿過像你送我的那麼合腳的鞋，」喬繼續唸下去：「野生三色堇是我最喜歡的花，這些花無時無刻不使我想到那位溫柔的送禮者。我希望能表示我的謝意，並且我知道你會准許『這個老先生』送給你一件，曾經屬於他已逝小孫女的東西。懷著衷心的感謝以及誠摯的祝福，我仍然會是『感激不盡的朋友及謙卑的僕人』詹姆斯·羅倫斯 敬上。」

「你看看，貝絲，這真是值得驕傲的榮幸呢！羅瑞告訴過我，羅倫斯先生很疼他那個死去的孩子，還說他都小心保存她的小東西。想想看，他把她的鋼琴都送你了。這是因為你有雙大大的藍眼睛，又喜歡音樂呢。」一心想安慰貝絲的喬說。貝絲全身顫抖，從沒有這麼興奮過。

「試試這架琴吧，親愛的。讓我們聽聽這架鋼琴寶寶的聲音。」漢娜說，家人的喜怒哀樂，她總願意一起分享。

於是貝絲試彈了一下，每個人都說這真是她們聽過最好的鋼琴了。「你必須去當面謝謝他。」喬開玩笑說道，其實她腦中從來沒有想到要讓這孩子真的去謝謝人家。

「是呀，我想要去。我想我現在就去吧，趁我還沒有一想到就害怕。」於是在全家人的驚異當中，貝絲竟然當真走到花園，穿過矮樹籬，來到了羅倫斯家門口。

要是她們看見貝絲後來做了什麼事，她們會更驚異。各位且聽我說，她還沒讓自己有時間思考就去敲書房門，等到一個沙啞的聲音往外喊「進來！」，她也就真的進去，並且直直走到看起來嚇了一跳的羅倫斯先生面前。她用微微顫抖的聲音說：「我是來謝謝您 —— 」但是她沒有繼續說下去，因為他看起來那麼地友善，她忘了該說什麼，再加上她只記得他失去了疼愛的小女孩，就用兩手抱住他的脖子親親他。

就算這幢房子突然被風吹得掀了頂，老先生也不會更驚訝，不過他很喜歡這個舉動 —— 噢，是的，他可喜歡呢！ —— 這親暱的小小親吻使他大為感動又歡喜，他所有的暴躁脾氣都不見了。他讓她坐在他膝頭，用他皺紋滿布的臉貼著她紅潤的臉蛋，感覺他自己的小孫女又回來了。從這一刻起貝絲就不再怕他，且坐在那兒自在地同他說著話，就像她已經認識他一輩子了呢。這全是因為愛會逐走恐懼，而感激可以征服驕傲。她回家的時候，他陪她走到家門口，誠誠懇懇地和她握了手並碰了碰帽子，再大步走

回家。羅倫斯先生身體挺直又莊嚴，像個英俊又英勇的老紳士，而他本來就是這樣的人。

　　女孩子們看到這一幕，喬跳了一段捷格舞，表示她的滿意；艾美驚訝得幾乎摔出窗子；梅格舉起雙手嘆道：「呵，我真的相信世界末日來臨了！」

第 7 章
飽嘗羞辱

「我很需要錢，我欠了好多的債；又還要一個月才能有零用錢。」艾美說。

「欠債，艾美？這是什麼意思？」梅格神情凝重。

「噢，我欠人家至少十幾個醃萊姆，可是我又要等到有錢了才能還人家，你知道的，因為媽媽不准我到店裡賒帳。」

「還用得著你說嗎？現在流行用萊姆了嗎？以前我們都是把橡皮擦削成小球。」梅格努力不讓她難堪，艾美看起來一本正經，神氣活現的樣子。

「你知道嗎，那些女生老是在買萊姆，除非你想要被人家認為很小氣，不然也非得照做。現在大家都在迷萊姆，因為上課時候每個人都在座位上吸萊姆汁，下課以後又用萊姆去換鉛筆呀、珠珠戒指呀，或是紙娃娃之類的東西。如果一個女生喜歡另一個女生，她就會送她一個萊姆；如果她生她的氣，她就在她面前吃萊姆，連一口也不給她吸。她們會輪流請客，我拿了人家太多了，可是都沒有回請她們，而我是應該回請的，因為這些是光榮的債，你知道。」

「要多少錢才能還清欠人的萊姆，恢復你的信用呢？」梅格拿出錢包問道。

「兩毛五分就很夠了，還可以剩下幾分錢，請你吃一些。」

「錢在這裡，盡量不要用完，因為其實這也不多，你知道。」

「噢，謝謝你！有零用錢真好！」

第二天，艾美到學校挺晚，但是她卻抵不過誘惑，用一種可以原諒的得意展示一個濕牛皮紙袋，讓同學看過才把它放進書桌最裡面。接下來幾分鐘，話就在她那夥人當中傳了開來；說艾美・瑪區帶了二十四個好吃的萊姆（她在路上吃了一個），等會兒要請大家吃呢，而她朋友們的關注也如排山倒海般湧來。凱蒂・布朗當場就請她參加她下一次的派對；瑪麗・金斯利堅持要把錶借她戴到下課；珍妮・史諾那個愛諷刺別人的女生，之前曾經卑劣地挖苦過艾美沒有萊姆，這會兒卻立刻要求和好了，還要告訴她一些算術題的答案呢。不過艾美可沒忘記史諾那些刻薄的話。

剛好這天早上來了個有名的大人物到學校參觀，而艾美畫得很漂亮的地圖受到了稱讚，這項榮譽在她的敵人史諾看來更是痛恨，也使得這位瑪區小姐有股洋洋自得的小孔雀的神態。可是，哎呀呀！驕者必敗，那個一心想復仇的史諾扭轉了形勢，而且大獲成功。客人才說完老套的讚美之詞、鞠躬離去，珍妮就假裝要問一個重要問題，向老師戴維斯先生告了一狀，說艾美・瑪區書桌抽屜裡有醃萊姆。

要知道，戴維斯先生曾經宣布說萊姆是違禁品，並且誓言第一個被發現違反這條規定的人，他一定會公然懲處。

「瑪區小姐，到講桌這裡來。」

艾美外表鎮定地乖乖站起來，但是私底下卻有種恐懼壓迫著她，因為那些萊姆已經成為她良心的重擔了。

「把你書桌裡的萊姆拿過來。」這句沒有料到的命令使她還沒走出座位就停住了。

她用絕望的目光瞥了她那些醜萊姆一眼，乖乖照做了。

「現在你把這些討人厭的東西兩個兩個拿著，丟到窗外。」

艾美又羞又怒，臉脹得通紅，來回走了六趟。艾美走完最後一趟，正往回走的時候，戴維斯先生發出一聲很不祥的清喉嚨聲，然後用他最最讓人不敢輕忽的態度說了：

「各位同學，你們都記得我在一個禮拜前對你們說過的話。我很遺憾發生了這件事情，但是我絕對不許有人破壞我的規矩，我也從來不食言。瑪區小姐，伸出手來。」

艾美嚇了一跳，把兩手放到身後，轉向老師，露出懇求的眼神，這種眼神要比她說不出口的言語更能替她求情。

「伸手，瑪區小姐！」是她沉默的懇求得到的唯一答覆，於是艾美——她自尊心很強，不肯哭出來也不肯開口求情——把牙咬緊，將頭往後不屑地揚起，就毫不畏縮地讓小小的手心上挨了幾次刺痛的抽打。她這輩子第一次被打，而這種羞辱在她心中就像把她打到地上去一樣地深。

「你現在就站到講台上，站到下課。」戴維斯先生說，既然事情已經開始，他就下決心要貫徹到底。

在後來的十五分鐘裡，這個自負而又敏感的小女孩飽受她永

遠也忘不掉的屈辱和痛苦。別人看起來或許覺得這是件滑稽抑或是微不足道的事，但是在她看來卻是個不好受的經驗；因爲在她十二年的生命中，管教她的只是愛，從沒有碰過這樣的打擊。而手心的疼和心中的痛在「我回家以後必須說這件事，而她們會對我好失望！」的想法刺痛之下，全忘光了。

十五分鐘像是有一個小時那麼久，不過也終於熬完了，而「下課！」這句話從來沒有現在這麼受她歡迎過。

「你可以走了，瑪區小姐。」戴維斯先生說，他的樣子不怎麼自在。

艾美臨走前投給他的責備眼光，他久久難忘。她一句話也不跟人說，逕自走到前室，一把抓過自己的東西，就因此「永遠」——她熱切地向自己宣稱——離開了學校。回到家時，她人還處在一個哀傷的狀態中，而等到姐姐們過後也回到家，她們立刻開了一場憤怒的會議。瑪區太太沒說什麼，但是面露愁煩，而用最最溫柔的態度安慰她痛苦的小女兒。梅格用甘油和淚水塗在她那隻受到侮辱的手上；貝絲覺得要撫平像這樣的哀痛，就連她最喜愛的小貓咪都不夠呢；而喬氣憤地提議說，戴維斯先生應該立刻被捕；漢娜對這個「惡棍」揮著拳頭，她搗著晚餐要用的馬鈴薯，就像她那杵下搗的是他一樣。

「好，你可以暫時放個假，不去上學，但是我要你每天讀一點書，跟貝絲一起。」這天晚上瑪區太太說。「我不贊成體罰，尤其是對女孩子體罰。我也不喜歡戴維斯先生教書的方法，我更不認爲你交的朋友對你有任何益處，所以我得先問問你爸爸的意

見，再看看把你送到什麼地方。」

「我希望所有同學都離開，讓這間老學校完蛋！想到那些好好吃的萊姆，我簡直要氣死了。」艾美用壯烈的神情嘆了口氣。

「你丟掉那些萊姆我並不可惜，因為你違背規矩，本來就應該受到不聽話的懲罰。」這句嚴厲的回答讓這位少女頗失望，她原以為別人對她只有同情，沒有其他想法。

「你是說你很高興我在全班面前丟臉嗎？」艾美喊道。

「我不會用這種方法去糾正一個錯誤，」她母親回答。「不過我不確定這種方法比起溫和的方法，是不是對你更有好處。你變得自負了，我親愛的，而現在你也該改一改了。你有很多小小天賦和好德行，但是你用不著一一炫耀，因為自負會破壞最好的天才。真正的才能或是善良是不太可能被長久忽視的，就算是被忽視了，你知道自己擁有這種才能或是善良，並且可以發揮出來，就應該可以讓你滿足了。況且所有力量最大的魅力就是謙虛。」

「的確沒錯！」正在角落裡和喬下棋的羅瑞喊道。「我從前認識一個女孩子，她對音樂真的是有了不起的天分，但是她不知道。她從來沒想過自己的自創曲有多麼好聽，就算是有人告訴她，她也不相信呢。」

貝絲突然臉色脹得通紅，把臉埋進沙發靠墊中，突然的發現讓她很不好意思。於是這番訓話在一陣笑聲中結束。

第 8 章

報復

「嘿，你們要去哪裡呀？」艾美問。一個星期六下午，艾美正走進她們房間，卻發現她們神祕兮兮地準備要出門，這激起了她的好奇心。

「你別管。小女生不可以問問題。」喬厲聲回她。

「你們要跟羅瑞去什麼地方，我知道。你們昨天晚上在沙發上說悄悄話，還一起笑，我一走進屋裡你們就停住了。你們不是要跟他一起去嗎？」

「對啦，我們是要一起去。好啦，安靜，別再煩人了。」

艾美住嘴了，但是她用眼睛看，看到梅格把一把扇子塞進她口袋。

「我知道了！我知道了！你們要去戲院看《七城堡》！」她大叫，並且堅決地又加上一句：「那我要去，媽媽說我可以看，我也有零用錢，你們不早點告訴我，真的很壞心呢。」

「你不能跟我們坐在一起，因為我們的座位是預訂了的；可是你又不能自己一個人坐，所以羅瑞就會把他的座位讓給你，那樣就破壞我們的樂趣了。再不然他會再弄個座位給你，那又不妥當，因為人家並沒有邀你。所以你最好待在這裡吧。」喬罵她。喬在急急忙忙中把一根手指扎到，火氣更大了。

第 8 章

　　艾美一隻腳穿著鞋，坐在地上就開始哭了，梅格才要跟她講道理，羅瑞已經在樓下喊，於是兩個女孩子急忙下樓，丟下妹妹在那裡大哭。就在一夥人要出門的時候，艾美靠在樓梯欄杆上用威脅的口氣大叫：「你會後悔的，喬·瑪區，你等著看好了！」

　　「胡說八道！」喬也回敬一句，並且把門用力摔上。

　　他們看得好快活，因為《鑽石湖七城堡》就像你預期的那麼精采。不過，雖然有那些滑稽的紅小鬼、閃閃發亮的小精靈，以及俊美的王子和嬌豔的公主，喬的快活當中卻有一絲絲感傷：仙后的黃色鬈髮讓她想起艾美，而在兩幕戲之間，她就猜想妹妹會做什麼事讓她「後悔」。

　　回到家裡，他們發現艾美在起居室看書。她們走進來的時候，她是帶著一種受了傷的神色，目光壓根兒沒有從書上抬起，也沒有問一個問題。喬上樓收好自己最好的帽子，她第一眼就朝五斗櫃看了看，因為上次吵架的時候，艾美平息怒氣的方法是把喬的衣櫃最上層抽屜倒在地板上。不過此刻每樣東西都在原位，而喬在匆匆檢查了各櫥櫃、皮包和箱盒以後，認定艾美已經忘了她的不是，也原諒了她。

　　殊不知，喬錯了，因為第二天她發現了一件事，就此釀成了一場風暴。下午稍晚時，梅格、貝絲和艾美一起坐著，這時候喬神情激動地衝進房裡，氣喘吁吁地問：「有沒有人拿了我的書？」

　　梅格和貝絲立刻說「沒有」，並且露出驚訝的表情：艾美撥著壁爐爐火，一句話也沒說。喬看到她臉轉成紅色，立刻衝到她

面前。

「艾美，是你拿了嗎？」

「我燒了。」

「什麼？我那麼喜歡的那本小書，我那麼辛辛苦苦寫的，想要在爸爸回家以前寫好的書嗎？你是真的把它燒了嗎？」喬說著，她的臉色發白，眼神發亮，雙手激動地緊抓著艾美。

「對啦，我就是燒了！我告訴過你，我要你為了昨天發那麼大的脾氣付出代價，所以──」

艾美不敢往下再說，因為喬早已怒髮衝冠，她狠勁猛搖艾美，把她弄得牙齒格格作響，一面悲憤交加地大叫道──

「你這個壞透、壞透了的女孩子！我再也寫不出來了啦，我一輩子也不會原諒你的！」

梅格飛快跑過去救艾美，而貝絲也很快過去安撫喬，但是喬已經接近瘋狂了。她衝出房門──臨走前賞了妹妹一記耳光──跑到閣樓的舊沙發上，獨自發脾氣。

樓下這陣風暴倒平靜了，因為瑪區太太回來了，並且在聽說這件事了以後立刻讓艾美了解對姐姐做的事是不對的。喬的書是她相當自豪的事，家人也都把它看成是前景可期的文學新作。這書只是六、七篇小小的童話故事，但是卻是喬全心投入、耐心寫出的東西，希望能寫成一本好書付印。她才剛仔仔細細謄寫好，把舊的草稿撕了，所以艾美那把火毀掉的是好幾年的心血。也許這在別人看來只是小損失，但是對喬而言卻是可怕的災禍，她覺得永遠也無法補償了。貝絲難過得像是死了一隻小貓咪，梅格也

第 8 章

不願意爲她寵愛的妹妹辯護；瑪區太太神情凝重而且難過，艾美覺得除非要爲這個行爲請求寬恕，否則沒有人會再愛她了，如今她比誰都後悔自己的行爲。

喝茶鈴聲響起，喬出現了，但是她看起來冷冷的，教人不敢接近，艾美鼓足了勇氣才柔聲問：

「請你原諒我嘛，喬。我非常非常對不起。」

「我永遠也不會原諒你的。」這是喬嚴厲的回答，從這時候起，她對艾美完全不加理睬。

瑪區太太親吻喬道晚安時，輕柔地對她說：

「我親愛的，不要在太陽下山時還留著怒氣；要互相原諒，互相幫助，明天重新開始。」

喬很想把頭靠在母親胸前，哭出她的哀傷和憤怒，可是眼淚是軟弱的象徵；況且她覺得自己受到重重的傷害，現在還不能眞正地原諒對方，於是她拚命眨眼不讓自己哭出來，並且搖了搖頭，用粗啞的聲音說——因爲艾美也在一旁聽——

「這件事太可惡了，她不配我原諒。」

說完這句話，她大步走向床前，當天晚上沒有人說悄悄話。

求和還被拒絕，艾美很生氣，恨不得自己沒有那麼卑下地求原諒過；她覺得自尊比之前更受到損傷，卻也爲自己高貴的品行頗爲得意，得意到令人生氣的地步。喬仍然看起來像陰晴不定的烏雲，一整天沒有一件事對勁：早晨天氣奇冷、她把她那珍貴的捲酥餅掉到水溝裡了、瑪區嬤婆突然心情煩躁了一陣、梅格憂心忡忡、貝絲回到家就會露出那憂愁又若有所思的神情，而艾美又

不停地說有些人老是說要行善，可是當別人給她們立了個好榜樣的時候，自己又不肯照做。

「每個人都好討厭，我去找羅瑞溜冰去。他一向和氣又快活，他會讓我恢復正常，我知道。」喬自言自語，說罷就出門了。

艾美聽到溜冰鞋的嘎啦嘎啦聲，便往外瞧，一邊還不耐煩地說：

「你看！她答應過我下次可以去的，這是湖水結冰的最後一段時間了。可是要這麼個壞脾氣的人帶我去是沒有用的啦。」

「別這樣說話。你的確是調皮的呀，而且要她原諒你毀掉她那本珍貴小書的錯也真的很難，不過我想她現在也許可以原諒你了。」梅格說。「你跟他們去，先什麼話都不要說，等到喬和羅瑞在一起心情好了以後，再趁個安靜時刻去親她，或者做件貼心的事。我相信她又會真心地跟你和好的。」

「我要試試看。」艾美說，因為這個建議很適合她。一陣混亂後她準備妥當了，於是就去追趕那兩個朋友，而他倆才剛剛翻過山丘。

喬聽到艾美在她身後喘氣、跺腳、對著指頭吐氣，想要把溜冰鞋穿上；但是喬就偏不轉過身，反而不慌不忙地用「之」字形的路線在河面上溜著，對妹妹的問題產生一種狠心的報復快感。羅瑞滑過河灣時回頭高喊：

「盡量靠岸邊溜，河中間不安全。」

喬是聽到了，但是艾美正掙扎著想要站起來，所以一個字也

沒聽到。喬往身後一瞥，而她心中藏著的小惡魔卻在她身邊說：

「不管她有沒有聽到，就讓她自己小心點吧。」

羅瑞繞過河灣，看不見了，喬正要轉過去，而遙遙在後的艾美則是剛往河中央比較平滑的冰面出發。喬定定站在原地一分鐘，心裡有種很奇怪的感覺，然後她下決心繼續往前溜，但是有什麼東西攔住她，並且讓她轉過身。於此同時，她正好看到薄脆的冰面突然嘎啦一聲破開，艾美兩手往上一揮，在嘩啦啦的濺水聲和一聲教喬心驚膽戰的叫聲中，人就落到水裡了。

她想要叫羅瑞，但是她發不出聲音；她想要衝過去，但是兩條腿似乎完全沒有力量，一時間她只能動也不動地站著，帶著驚恐的表情盯著黑呼呼的河水上方那頂小小的藍色兜帽。有樣東西飛快衝過她身邊，羅瑞的聲音大喊：

「去拿根欄杆木頭，快，快！」

她是怎麼做到的她根本不知道，但是接下來幾分鐘裡她卻像是著了魔似地盲目聽從羅瑞指揮做事。羅瑞倒是非常地鎮定，他平躺在河面，用手臂和曲棍球棒抓住艾美，等到喬從籬笆裡抽出一根木頭，兩個人才合力把艾美救出。要說艾美是受傷，還不如說是嚇到了。

他們把全身發抖滴著水、哭哭啼啼的艾美送回家，在一陣慌亂之後，她裹著毛毯在溫暖的爐火前睡著了。「你確定她現在安全了嗎？」喬低聲問，悔恨交加地望著那個險些在驚險的冰層下，永遠從她視線中消失的金髮腦袋。

「很安全，親愛的。她沒有受傷，甚至也沒有著涼，我猜。

你們很快把她包暖和，送回家，這作法很對。」她母親開心地回答。

「那都是羅瑞做的，我只是任由她自己去。媽，如果她死了，那全是我的錯。」喬跌坐在床邊，在一陣悔罪的淚水中，把事情一五一十地全說了；一邊痛罵自己的鐵石心腸，一邊哭哭啼啼地說自己差點受到嚴重的懲罰，實在是謝天謝地。

「我發起脾氣來好像什麼事都做得出來，我會變得好殘暴、我會傷害任何人，而且還很開心。我好怕有一天我會做出什麼可怕的事毀了我的一生，使每個人都討厭我。噢，媽，你幫幫我，你要幫幫我！」

「我會的，孩子，我會的。別哭得這麼傷心，但是要記住今天並且痛下決心，再也不要有像今天這種情形。喬，親愛的，我們都有各自的誘惑，有些比你的還嚴重，我們常會用一輩子的時間去克服它們。你以為你的脾氣是全世界最差的，可是從前我的脾氣也像你呢。」

「我會努力去做的，媽媽，我真的會。可是你一定要幫助我、提醒我，使我不要發脾氣。我從前看到爸爸有時候會把手指伸到嘴唇上，用很溫柔卻也很冷靜的神情看你，而你總會把嘴唇緊緊閉上，再不就是走開，他都是在提醒你嗎？」喬輕聲問道。

「是的，是我要他這樣幫助我的，他從來也沒有忘記，而且還用小小的動作和溫柔的神情使我少說了很多尖刻的話。」

喬看到母親的雙眼噙著淚水，說話時雙唇也顫抖著，她害怕自己說太多的話，就焦急地低聲問：「我觀察你而且還告訴你，

這是不是不對呢？我不是故意要不禮貌，可是能把我所想的事全都告訴你，實在是好自在的事，我覺得好安全又快活。」

「我的喬呀，你可以跟媽媽說任何事的，因為我的孩子們肯把心事告訴我，也知道我有多麼愛她們，這是我最大的快慰和驕傲。」

艾美身體動了動，在睡眠中還嘆了口氣。喬像是急著要馬上彌補自己的過失一樣，用一種從未出現過在她臉上的表情抬頭看了看。

「我讓憤怒持續到太陽都下了山。就是因為我不肯原諒她，而今天要不是羅瑞，可能一切都太遲了！我怎麼可以這麼壞心眼？」喬把身體轉向妹妹，微微提高聲音說道，一邊輕撫著散在枕頭上濕漉漉的頭髮。

艾美像是聽到了一樣，她睜開眼睛，伸出雙臂，露出一個深入喬心坎裡的笑容。兩人都沒有說話，但是她們卻隔著毯子緊緊擁抱，在姐妹深情的親吻中一切過錯都得到諒解，也被忘卻了。

第 9 章
上流社會

「金家孩子們這時節剛好得痲疹，眞是全世界最幸運的事了！」四月裡的一天，梅格正在房裡收拾那個「出門皮箱」時說道，周圍是她的妹妹們。

「好在安妮·莫法特也沒有忘記她的諾言，整整兩個星期的玩樂，眞是太好了！」喬回答。她用那雙長長的手臂摺起裙子，看起來眞像座風車。

「而且天氣又這麼好，我眞高興呢。」貝絲加上一句，她正俐落地整理她寶物盒裡的那些領巾和髮帶，這個盒子因為這件大事而借出去了。

「我眞希望是我要出去快活，而可以穿這些漂亮衣服呢。」艾美說，她嘴裡咬滿了針，正用藝術手法為姐姐的衣服填塞襯裡。

「我希望你們全都能去，不過，既然你們不能去，我會記住這次經歷，回來以後說給你們聽。我起碼能做到這一點，你們都對我那麼好，借我東西又幫我準備。」梅格說，她把目光從周遭移到那件在她們眼裡看來幾乎是十全十美的樸素服裝。

「好啦，每樣東西都放進去了，除了我的舞會裝，那要留給媽媽放的。」梅格開懷地說，她的目光從半滿的行李箱轉到幾經

熨燙、修補的白色薄紗裙，她很神氣地稱它作她的「舞會裝」。

第二天天氣晴朗，梅格隆重地出發，準備體驗新奇和快活的兩個星期。瑪區太太其實是不怎麼樂意她去的，因爲她怕梅格回來以後會比去之前更不滿。只是她苦苦哀求，莎麗又保證會好好照顧她，再說做了一個冬天的厭煩工作後，一點小小的娛樂似乎也令人開心。於是做母親的同意了，而做女兒的也就去初嘗時髦生活的滋味了。

莫法特家人的確是很時髦，單純的梅格起初還被那房屋的華美和屋裡人們的優雅嚇了一跳。不過他們雖然過著輕佻嬉鬧的生活，人倒是挺親切，所以很快就使她們的客人輕鬆自在了。也許是梅格感覺到——不知道爲什麼——他們並不是特別有教養或是聰明的人，而他們所有的虛飾仍不太能掩藏他們天生的凡俗資質。過奢華日子、坐豪華馬車、每天穿上最好的衣服，除了讓自己開心外什麼事也不做，這當然是教人快活的事。這種日子正合她意呢，於是她很快模仿起身邊那些人的行爲舉止和言談；略略裝腔作勢，說些法文詞語、把頭髮燙鬈、把衣裙改小，並且盡可能談些時尚的事。她看到安妮·莫法特的漂亮東西越多，就越是羨慕她，也渴望能夠做有錢人。如今她一想到家，就只覺得那兒空盪而且凄涼，工作變得比以前都要辛苦；而她覺得自己雖然有新手套和絲襪，但卻是個貧窮、飽受傷害的女孩。

莫法特先生是個開朗而且胖嘟嘟的老先生，認識她父親；莫法特太太也是個開朗而且胖嘟嘟的老太太，她跟女兒一樣很喜歡梅格。每個人都很疼她，於是「黛西」——她們都這麼稱呼

她──可以說是昏頭轉向了。

「小宴會」要舉行的晚上，她發現那件厚呢裙根本不能穿，因爲其他女孩子都穿著薄裙，顯得非常秀氣；於是她拿出那件薄紗裙，但是在莎麗那件嶄新紗裙旁邊，這件裙子看起來更是老舊、軟趴趴，又寒酸。沒有人對這件裙子說一個字，而莎麗說要幫她梳整頭髮，安妮要幫她綁飾帶，那個訂了婚的姐姐蓓兒，也對她粉白的手臂大加讚揚。但是梅格卻只在她們的好意中看到自己的寒傖，所以當其他人歡笑、交談，像蝴蝶般來來去去之際，她就獨自站在一旁，只覺得心情萬分沉重。她這種難受的感覺正變得更糟時，女僕拿進來一盒花。

「這是送給蓓兒的，當然。喬治每次都會送她花，不過這些可眞是太迷人了。」安妮用力聞了聞花大喊著說。

「那個人說是要送給瑪區小姐的。這裡還有一張紙條。」女僕插嘴說，並且把花交給梅格。

「多有趣呀！花是誰送的？我們還不知道你有情郎了呢！」眾家女孩子在好奇又驚訝的興奮中繞著梅格喊著。

「字條是我媽媽給的，花是羅瑞送的。」梅格簡單說了，但很感激他沒有忘了她。

「噢，可不是嘛！」安妮露出一個滑稽表情說。這時候梅格正把字條塞進口袋，彷彿它是個護身符，可以避開嫉妒、虛榮、浮華，因爲字條上短短幾個字已經發揮了效力，而花朵的美麗也使她開心起來。

這天晚上她開心極了，因爲她舞跳得可盡興了，每個人都好

和善，而她又受到三種讚美：安妮要她唱歌，有個人說她有副好得不得了的嗓子；林肯少校問人說：「那個有一雙美麗眼睛的清純少女是誰？」還有莫法特先生堅持要和她跳舞，因為她「不拖泥帶水，而是充滿活力」——他如此文雅地說。所以，總而言之，她玩得非常愉快，一直到她無意間聽到一段對話，使得她非常困擾。當時她坐在花房裡面，正在等舞伴去為她拿冰水，忽然聽到花牆另一邊有個聲音在問：

「他多大歲數？」

「十六、七歲吧，我想。」另一個聲音回答。

「這對其中一個女孩子會是件好事，不是嗎？莎麗說她們現在很親近，那位老先生很疼她們。」

「我敢說『瑪』太太有她的計畫，而且也會走對棋子的，雖然現在看來還太早。那個女孩子顯然還沒有想到這件事。」莫法特太太說。

「她還扯些什麼她媽媽送的那種謊話，那花送到的時候她臉都紅了，紅得還真可愛呢，可憐的人！如果她能打扮得更像樣就好了。你想如果我們借她一件衣服讓她星期四穿，她會不會生氣？」另一個聲音問。

「她很驕傲的，不過我相信她不會介意，因為她只有那件樣式老舊的薄紗裙。也許今天晚上會不小心把它扯破，那就有理由借她一件像樣裙子穿了。」

「我們再看看好了。我會邀請小羅倫斯來，然後就可以看好戲啦！」

　　這時候梅格的舞伴出現了，發現她看起來面紅耳赤，神情相當激動。她確實是很驕傲的，而她的驕傲這會兒卻非常有用，因為它幫助她藏起對剛才聽到的話感到的屈辱、氣憤和憎惡；雖然她天真無邪，對人不會起疑，但是她卻不可能不明白她朋友們的閒話。

　　可憐的梅格一夜不得安眠，而眼皮沉重、悶悶不樂地起了床，半痛恨她的朋友、半為自己沒有坦誠說出實話，把事情糾正而慚愧。這天早晨大家都在閒晃，過了中午，女孩子們才有氣力做著各自的織毛衣活兒。梅格立刻發現到她朋友們態度有異，她們好像是對她更為尊敬、對她說的話有一種溫柔的興趣，而且毫不隱藏地表露出好奇心的眼神看著她。這些都讓她很驚訝，也挺開心的，只是她起先還不明白，一直到蓓兒小姐從她寫的東西上抬頭看她，並帶著感情地說：

　　「黛西，親愛的，我已經給你的朋友羅倫斯先生送去星期四的請帖了。我們很想要認識他，禮貌上是應該這樣做的。」

　　梅格臉紅了，但是一個想要捉弄這些女孩子們的念頭卻使她故意一本正經地說：

　　「你真好心呢，不過恐怕他不能來。」

　　「為什麼不能呢，親愛的？」蓓兒小姐說。

　　「他太老了。」

　　「我的孩子，你說的是什麼意思？他年齡多大？請告訴我！」克萊拉小姐叫了起來。

　　「差不多七十歲了，我相信。」梅格說，她故意數著針數，

好掩蓋她眼中的促狹笑意。

「你這個淘氣鬼！我們當然是說年輕的那個呀！」蓓兒小姐笑著說。

「他們家沒有年輕男人，羅瑞還只是個小孩子。」梅格也笑了。這些姐妹以為她說到情人而彼此交換的怪異眼神，只讓她感到好笑。

「但是跟你年紀差不多。」南恩說。

「比較接近我妹妹喬的年齡；我到八月就十七歲了。」梅格猛抬頭回了一句。

「那他送你花真是非常好的呢，不是嗎？」安妮說，她看起來像是完全弄不清狀況。

「是呀，他常常這樣對我們所有人，因為他們家種滿了花，而我們都很喜歡花。我媽媽和老羅倫斯先生是朋友，你知道，所以很自然地我們小孩子都在一起玩。」梅格希望她們不要再說了。

「很顯然黛西還沒有入社交界。」克萊拉小姐點點頭對蓓兒說。

「——所以周遭一片純真無邪的狀態。」蓓兒小姐聳聳肩答道。

「我要出去為我們的女娃兒們買點小東西了，各位姑娘，要不要我替你們帶點什麼回來？」穿著一身絲綢和蕾絲的莫法特太太像頭大象般，踩著沉重步子走進來。

「不用，謝謝您，」莎麗說。「我星期四有新的粉紅色絲質

衣裳，什麼也不缺。」

「我也是——」梅格才剛開口就停住了，因為她想到她的確需要幾樣東西，但卻沒能準備好。

「你要穿什麼？」莎麗問。

「還是我那件舊的白色裙子，如果我能把它補得可以見人的話，不幸昨天晚上我卻把它撕破了。」梅格極力要輕鬆自在地說，但卻感到非常不舒服。

「你為什麼不把它送回家，再換一件？」莎麗問，她不是個善於觀察的女孩。

「我沒有別件。」梅格好不容易才說出口，但是莎麗卻不明白，還驚訝嘆道：

「只有那件嗎？多奇怪呀——」她的話沒有說完，因為蓓兒朝她搖頭，又很好心地插嘴說：

「一點也不奇怪，她又沒有入社交界，要那麼多衣服幹什麼？你不必回家拿，黛西，因為我有一件藍色絲綢裙放著沒有用；那件我已經穿不下了，你穿上它讓我開心一下嘛！好嗎，親愛的？」

「你非常好心，但是我不在乎我的舊衣服，只要你不在意就行。對我這樣的小女孩，這件就夠好了。」梅格說。

「你就讓我開心嘛，讓我把你打扮得時髦吧。我好想這麼做呢，而只要這裡妝扮一些，那裡妝扮一些，你會變成個小美人的。」蓓兒用她很有說服力的語氣說。

這麼好心的提議，梅格不能拒絕。想要看看自己在打扮後能

不能成為「小美人」的念頭，使她接受這個提議，而將先前對莫法特家人那些不自在的感覺全忘了。

星期四的黃昏，蓓兒和她的女僕關在房裡，合二人之力把梅格變成了一位窈窕淑女。蓓兒小姐用一個剛剛給洋娃娃打扮好了的小女孩的滿意神情打量她。

「小姐好迷人，好可愛，不是嗎？」荷丹絲叫道，她在感染到的歡樂中把兩手握住。

「過來展示吧。」蓓兒小姐說，一邊帶頭走到眾人正在等著的房間裡。

梅格跟在後頭，拖著長裙窸窸窣窣地走著，耳環發出清脆的聲音，鬈髮也不住晃動、心臟噗通噗通跳著，這時候她才覺得她的「快活」終於真正要開始了！因為鏡子已經很明白地告訴她說，她確實是個「小美人」了。

「我好怕下樓，我覺得好奇怪、好不自然，衣服還沒穿好的樣子。」鈴聲響起，莫法特太太要人來請女孩子們立刻出去時，梅格對莎麗說。

「你一點也不像原來的你了，可是你很好呀。我比起你差得遠呢，因為蓓兒好有品味，而你看起來真有法國味兒呢，我向你保證。」莎麗回答她，極力不讓自己在乎梅格比她漂亮。

梅格牢牢記住這番警告，終於平安地走下樓，翩然走進客廳，莫法特家的人和幾個早到的賓客已經聚在這裡了。她很快就發現，華美的服裝是有某種魅力的，可以吸引某種階級的人，並且獲得他們的尊敬。有幾個之前並沒有注意到她的年輕女孩，突

然之間對她變得十分熱絡；有幾個在上場宴會沒有瞧過她一眼的青年，現在不僅盯著她瞧，還要人為他們介紹，並且對她說盡愚蠢卻很讓人舒服的話；幾個坐在沙發上對著其他人說長道短的老太太們，紛紛流露出有興趣的神情打聽她是何許人。她聽到莫法特太太回答其中一個人說：

「她叫黛西·瑪區，父親是軍中一位上校，原本是我們這裡數一數二的家庭，但後來時運不濟，你知道的；她和羅倫斯家很親近，是個乖孩子，我向你保證；我的耐德對她好迷唷。」

「天啊！」老太太說著，然後再戴上眼鏡仔細端詳梅格，梅格卻做出沒有聽到，也沒有被莫法特太太的話嚇了一跳的樣子。

「奇怪的感覺」並沒有消失，不過她想像自己正在扮演窈窕淑女這個新的角色，所以表現得倒也非常稱職。只是這身緊繃的服裝讓她腰側痛了起來，她又老是踩到長裙的裙襬，又總是害怕耳環會鬆掉，因而弄丟或是摔壞。這會兒她正揮著扇子，對著一個想要顯得風趣機智的年輕男人的無趣笑話笑著，卻突然止住了笑，面露不解之色，因為她看到羅瑞就在她正對面。他正用毫不掩飾的驚訝盯著她，這其中還有不以為然，她想。

「很高興你來了，我起先還怕你不會來呢。」她擺出大人的架勢說。

「喬要我來這裡，然後告訴她你看起來怎麼樣，所以我才來的。」羅瑞回答道，他雖然微微對著她那種媽媽般的語氣笑著，但卻沒把眼光投注她。

「你要告訴她什麼？」梅格問，她心中充滿了好奇心，想要

知道他對她的看法，然而卻又有點感到不安，這還是她頭一次會對他不安呢。

「我不喜歡妳過度招搖的樣子。」

這話出自一個比她小的男孩口中，實在是太過分了，梅格立刻走開，還暴怒地說：

「你是我見過最粗魯無禮的男生！」

盛怒之下，她走到一扇安靜的窗邊站著，讓自己的臉頰涼一涼，這身緊繃的衣服讓她臉色脹得不舒服地亮紅。她站在那裡，林肯少校走過她身邊，一分鐘以後，她聽到他對他母親說：

「她們讓那個姑娘出盡了洋相，我本來想要你看看她的，可是她們把她毀了，今天晚上她只是個玩偶。」

「噢，天啊！」梅格嘆著氣。「真希望我有點頭腦，穿我的舊衣服，那我就不會讓別人那麼討厭我，也不會這麼不自在，又羞辱了自己。」

她把額頭抵著涼涼的窗玻璃，半掩藏地站在窗簾邊，也不在乎她最喜歡的華爾滋舞曲都開始了。一直到有個人碰了碰她，她轉過身，只見羅瑞滿臉懺悔地鞠了個躬，伸出一隻手說：

「請原諒我方才的無禮，和我跳支舞吧。」

「恐怕你會覺得這太可厭了。」梅格說，她想做出生氣的樣子，卻完全失敗了。

「一點也不會，我想得很呢。來嘛，我會乖乖的。我不喜歡你的禮服，不過我真的認為你——實在是豔光四射呢。」他揮著雙手，彷彿言語無法表達他的讚嘆。

梅格露出笑容，心軟了。

「耐德‧莫法特走過來了，他要做什麼呀？」羅瑞說著，皺起了濃眉，看起來似乎不認為這位年輕的主人會給宴會帶來歡愉。

「他講好了要和我跳三支舞，我猜他是要來跟我跳舞了。多無聊呀！」梅格說著，人也變得無精打采了，這倒讓羅瑞樂不可支。

一直到晚餐時間，他才再有機會跟她說話。他看到她和耐德以及耐德的朋友費雪喝著香檳，這兩個人，照羅瑞告訴自己的，舉止簡直「像對傻瓜」一樣。他自覺對瑪區家女孩子有一種兄弟般的權利，要去照顧她們，在需要有人護衛時為她們而戰。

「如果你喝太多這種東西，你明天會頭痛得要命，要是我就不會喝太多，梅格。你媽媽不會高興的，你知道。」耐德轉過身將她酒杯斟滿，費雪也低下身撿起她的扇子時，他彎身到她椅子上方，低聲說道。

「今天晚上我不是梅格，我是個『玩偶』，專門做各種瘋狂的事。明天我就會收拾起這些輕率行為，做個乖寶寶啦！」她故意輕笑著回答。

「那我真希望現在就是明天呢。」羅瑞低聲說著就走開了，對於她的改變很不高興。

梅格像其他女孩子一樣跳舞、賣弄風情、嘰嘰喳喳地說著話，又嗤嗤笑著。晚飯後她開始說起德文，說得結結巴巴、錯誤百出；她那件長裙又幾乎把舞伴給絆倒；她還蹦蹦跳跳地走動，

讓羅瑞非常反感，本想要訓她一頓，但是一直沒有機會。因為梅格總是離他遠遠的，直到他過來道晚安。

隔日的一整天她人都很不舒服，星期六就回家了，兩星期的玩樂讓她筋疲力盡，覺得自己「奢侈富貴」的日子過得已經夠久了。

「能夠安安靜靜，不用時時刻刻拘禮，的確是很快活的事。家是個好地方，即使不富麗堂皇。」星期天晚上，梅格和母親、喬坐著的時候，用一種平靜的表情打量四周說道。

「我真高興聽你這麼說呢，親愛的，我還怕你住過好地方以後，會認為家裡既沉悶又破敗呢。」母親回答道，她在這天當中已經焦慮地看過她好多次了，因為做母親的眼睛很快就能看出孩子臉色的絲毫改變。

「媽，你有像莫法特太太說的那些『計畫』嗎？」梅格不好意思地問。

「有的，我親愛的，我有好多好多計畫呢。所有做母親的都有，不過我想我的計畫和莫法特太太的有些不同。」

喬走過去，坐在椅子的一個扶手上，神情像是要一起去做一件非常肅穆的事情。瑪區太太各握住她們一隻手，充滿期望地望著兩張年輕臉孔，然後用正經卻也開心的神情說：

「我希望我的女兒們個個美麗、有教養、善良，被人仰慕、愛戀、尊敬；有快樂的青春，能聰明地找到好歸宿，過著有益而且快樂的生活，越少的憂煩試煉越好。親愛的女兒們，我對你們是有很大期望的，但是我不願意你們貿貿然就闖進外頭世界——

去嫁給有錢人，只因爲他們有錢或是有華美的房子，然而那只是房子而不是家，因爲房子裡欠缺愛。金錢是不可或缺的珍貴東西──如果使用得當，它也是個高貴的東西──可是我絕不希望你們把它當成最重要或是唯一值得努力追求的東西。如果你們很快樂、受到疼愛、心滿意足，那麼我寧願你們是窮人家的妻子，也不要做個沒有自尊、沒有安寧的皇后。不要煩心，梅格。貧窮很少會嚇退一個眞誠的愛人。我認識幾個最好也最受崇敬的女孩子都是窮人家的女孩，但是她們都很值得人愛，所以不會成爲老小姐。把這些事情交給時間吧，你們要讓這個家快樂，這樣你們有了自己的家以後就會是個宜室宜家的女人；要是沒有自己的家，你們在這裡也可以很滿足。要記住一件事，我的孩子：母親隨時隨地都會傾聽你們的心事，父親永遠是你們的朋友，而我們都相信並且希望我們的女兒們，成爲我們生命中的驕傲和安慰，不管她們有沒有結婚。」

「我們會的，媽媽，我們會的！」母女道晚安時，姐妹倆全心全意地說。

第 10 章

文藝姐妹

　　春天到了，時興的休閒樂事也換了新的一套，白天越來越長，下午也變久了，可以從事各種各樣的工作和遊戲。其中之一是「PC」，這時候正流行祕密社團，她們認為也該有一個，由於這些女孩子全都很崇拜狄更斯，她們就自稱是「匹克威克俱樂部」[1]。除了少數幾次中斷以外，她們這個俱樂部已經成立了一年，每個星期六晚上都在那間大的閣樓裡聚會，聚會的儀式是這樣的：在一張桌子前面擺了一排三張椅子，桌上有盞燈，還有四面白色徽章，每個徽章上都有顏色不同且大大的「P‧C」兩個字；另外還有一份名叫《匹克威克文稿集》的週報，每個人都要投稿，由一向喜歡舞文弄墨的喬擔任編輯。一到七點鐘，四名會員就來到俱樂部，用徽章帶子綁住頭，再煞有介事地在椅子上坐下。梅格因為年齡最大，所以是山謬爾‧匹克威克；喬呢，由於天生喜歡文學，所以是奧古斯塔斯‧史諾格拉斯；貝絲因為身子圓呼呼而且皮膚粉粉嫩嫩，所以是崔西‧塔普曼；艾美這個人總是想要做些自己做不到的事，所以就是納桑尼爾‧溫克爾。會長

1　取自狄更斯（Charles Dickens）的作品《匹克威克外傳》（The Pickwick Papers）。

匹克威克一向負責讀報，報上充滿了新故事、詩、本地新聞、滑稽的廣告，以及心得提示，互相提醒彼此的過錯和缺失。在一次聚會中，匹克威克先生戴上一副沒有鏡片的眼鏡，敲敲桌子並輕咳兩聲，先是狠狠瞪著把身體在椅子上往後仰靠的史諾格拉斯先生，直到他坐正了才開始讀報紙。

主席唸完了報紙，一陣掌聲響起，接著史諾格拉斯先生（喬）起立提議。

「主席和各位先生，」他用慎重而斯文的態度和口氣說了，「我提議讓一位新會員入會，他十分值得這份榮譽，如果能夠入會，他會非常感激；他會給本俱樂部增加許多士氣，也會為本報增加重大的文學價值，他更會非常快樂、非常和善。我提議讓狄奧多‧羅倫斯先生作為本俱樂部的榮譽會員。哎呀，就讓他來吧。」

喬的口氣這麼突然地改變，讓姐妹們都笑了起來，但是史諾格拉斯坐下後，每個人看起來倒是很焦急，誰也沒說話。

「我們付諸表決，」主席說了。「贊成這項提議的會員，請以口頭表示。」

「大家都要記住這是我們的羅瑞，說『贊成』吧！」史諾格拉斯興奮地大喊。

「贊成！贊成！贊成！」立刻有三個聲音回答。

「太好了！上帝保佑你！好啦，既然『擇日不如撞日』。就像溫克爾最會說的——容我介紹我們的新會員出場！」於是，在俱樂部其他成員的驚慌中，喬一把推開了衣櫥門；只見羅瑞坐在

一個裝零星布頭的袋子上，正因為忍住大笑的衝動而脹紅了臉，讓雙頰顯得十分亮紅。

「你這個壞蛋！你這個叛徒！喬！你怎麼可以這樣？」三個女孩都喊著，這時史諾格拉斯領著她的朋友凱旋式地往前走，再拿了一把椅子和一個臂章，不一會兒就讓他入了座。

「你們這兩個惡徒的冷靜真是驚人。」匹克威克先生開口了，他本想皺起眉頭，卻只能露出可掬的笑容。不過這位新會員對這個場合也能應付自如，他站起來，向主席致上感激的行禮，用最最迷人的態度說了：

「主席先生和各位女士──請原諒，是各位先生──容我自我介紹，在下是本俱樂部的卑下僕人山姆‧威勒。」

「妙呀！妙呀！」喬喊道，一邊用暖床器的長柄敲著。

「承蒙他對我的介紹，我忠誠的朋友和高貴的贊助人，」羅瑞把手一揮，繼續說著，「蒙他對我讚譽有加，今晚這個低下的計謀不能怪他，是我計畫的，他只在對我大加揶揄後才同意的。」

「別這樣，不要把責任都攬到你身上，你知道是我提議躲在衣櫥裡的。」史諾格拉斯打斷了他的話，他對這個玩笑挺樂的。

「你別管他說的話。這件事主謀是我，先生，」新會員對匹克威克先生點了個威勒式的點頭。「不過，我用我的名譽擔保，我再也不會這麼做了，而且從此以後我一定會為這個偉大俱樂部的利益全力以赴。」

「好呀！好呀！」喬大叫著，敲起暖床器的蓋子，像是在敲

鈸一樣。

「再說嘛，再說下去呀！」溫克爾和塔普曼也加上一句，主席則是親切地點頭示意。

「我只是想要說，為了略表對各位的感激之意，以及促進兩個鄰國友好關係，我已經在花園角落低處的樹籬中設置了一個郵局；信件、稿件、書籍、包裹都可以放進那裡，而因為我們兩個國家都有鑰匙，所以會非常的方便，我想。容我奉上鑰匙，並且對各位的好意表示無比感激，之後我再回座。」

威勒先生把一把小鑰匙放在桌上，而後退下，這時響起好大的鼓掌聲，暖床器被狂亂的敲擊又揮舞著，好一會兒才恢復了秩序。隨後是一陣長時間的討論，一直到一個小時後會員以三聲尖銳的歡呼聲歡迎新會員入會，這場集會才結束。

「郵局」是個非常好的小小設施，日漸蓬勃發展，因為透過它收送的奇奇怪怪東西就和透過真正郵局的一樣多。悲劇和領巾、詩作和醃黃瓜、花果種子和長信、樂譜和薑餅、膠鞋、請柬、責罵的信件和小狗。老先生很喜歡這件有趣的事，也會送些奇怪的包裹、神祕的短箋、好笑的電報以自娛，他的園丁著迷於漢娜的風采，還真的寫了一封情書由喬轉交呢。這件祕密揭穿的時候他們笑得多開心呀，但是他們做夢也沒有想到，在未來的歲月中，這個小小的郵局會傳送多少的情書呢！

第 11 章

實驗

「六月一號！金家明天就要去海濱，而我就自由了。三個月的假期呢——我可要痛痛快快地享受了！」一個暖和的日子，梅格回到家裡喊道。她看到喬累得不成人形地躺在沙發上，貝絲為她脫下沾滿灰塵的鞋，而艾美正為大家做檸檬汁喝。

「瑪區嬸婆今天走了，噢，真快活啊，」喬說道。「我真怕她會要我跟她一起去呢，如果她要我去，恐怕我就應該陪她去了；可是『梅園』那裡無趣得像座墓園一樣，我可不希望去。在她好端端坐上馬車以前，我可是渾身發抖的，而最後我還是嚇了一大跳。因為當馬車要離開的時候，她還探出頭來說：『喬，你要不要——？』我話沒聽完就卑鄙地掉頭逃走了。我真的是拔腿就跑，一直狂奔到街角，我覺得安全了才停下。」

「可憐的喬！她進屋的時候活像是後頭有大熊在追她呢！」貝絲像個母親一樣地撫摸著姐姐的雙腳。

「瑪區嬸婆真是個不折不扣的海蘆筍呀！」艾美說道。

「她的意思是吸血鬼，不是什麼海草啦。」喬喃喃說道。

「你們這個假期要做什麼呢？」艾美換了個話題。

「我要躺在床上，很晚起床，什麼事也不做。」深陷在搖椅裡的梅格回答。「這整個冬天我都得好早下床，成天為別人工

作，所以現在我可以痛快地休息、尋開心了。」

「不，」喬說，「這種昏昏沉沉的方式不適合我。我已經存了一大堆書了，我要使我的燦爛時光更加燦爛，我要到那棵老蘋果樹上去看書，在我不是像雲——」

「可別說像『雲雀』一樣快活地玩耍！」艾美故意對喬說，藉以回擊「海蘆筍」這一箭之仇。

「那我就說像『夜鶯』一樣好了。」

「別讓我們做功課嘛，貝絲，暫時啦；就讓我們一直玩、一直休息，女孩子本來就是要這樣的。」艾美提議道。

「只要媽媽不在意，我是可以的。我想要學幾首新曲子，而我的孩子們也需要準備夏天的衣服了，它們衣物凌亂，也真的是該有些新衣服了。」貝絲說。

「我們可以嗎，媽媽？」梅格轉頭去問瑪區太太，她正坐在她們稱作「媽媽的角落」裡縫東西。

「你們可以試驗一個禮拜，看看喜不喜歡。我想到了星期六晚上，你們就會發現淨在玩不做事，就跟淨在做事而不玩一樣糟糕。」瑪區太太說。

「噢，才不會呢！那一定會很有意思的。」梅格得意洋洋地說。

「我提議大家喝一杯，就像我的『老友兼夥伴賽利·甘普』所說的，祝大家永遠歡樂，不做苦工！」喬站起來大叫，手裡拿著杯子，這時檸檬汁正在眾人之間傳著。

她們全都高高興興地喝了檸檬汁，然後就開始這個試驗，這

天其餘時間全都懶散了。第二天早晨，梅格過了十點才起床，自個兒吃了早餐，但是似乎沒有什麼味道；屋裡顯得寂寞又凌亂，因為喬沒有把花插到花瓶裡，貝絲沒有打掃，艾美的書四散各處。

現在除了「媽媽的角落」還和平常一樣以外，沒有一個地方是整整齊齊，令人愉快的了。而梅格就坐在那裡「休息和看書」，也就是打著呵欠，想像用她的薪水可以買些什麼漂亮的夏天服裝。喬的上午時光是和羅瑞在小河玩，下午她則是高高坐在蘋果樹上看著《荒野世界》，邊看邊哭。貝絲從住著她一家子的大衣櫃裡翻出每樣東西，但是還整理不到一半就已經厭煩了；於是把娃娃屋凌亂地丟在那裡，去彈她的琴了，一邊為了不用洗碗碟而深自慶幸。

艾美整理了她那部分的園子，穿上漂亮的白色洋裝，把鬈髮整理整齊了，就坐在忍冬樹下畫畫。她希望有人看到，並問這個小小畫家是誰，可是除了一隻好奇的長腳蜘蛛外也沒有人走近；而這蜘蛛又很有興趣地端詳她的畫作，於是她就去散個步，偏偏又遇上一陣雨，最後濕淋淋地回了家。

下午茶時候，她們彼此交換心得，全都同意這是個快活的一天，只不過出奇地漫長。沒有人願意承認自己對這個試驗感到厭倦，不過，到了星期五晚上，每個人都告訴自己，很高興這個禮拜已經快要結束。為了要讓這個教訓更加深印象，幽默感十足的瑪區太太決心用一個適當方式把這個實驗結束，於是她讓漢娜放假，令這些女孩子充分體會到這個遊戲的後果。

星期六早上起床以後，廚房裡沒有爐火，餐廳裡沒有早餐，到處都看不到母親。

「哎呀！出了什麼事啦？」喬大喊，驚惶地四處張望。

梅格跑上樓去，很快又回來了，神情雖然放鬆卻相當昏亂，還有一點點羞愧。

「媽媽沒有生病，只是很累，她說她要在她房裡靜靜休息一天，讓我們自己想辦法。她這麼做非常奇怪，一點也不像她。不過這個禮拜她確實累壞了，所以我們也不可以囉唆，好好照顧自己吧。」

「這容易，而且我喜歡。我好想做點事情──我是說，找些新的樂事呢。」喬很快又加上一句。

其實，有事可做才真是讓她們大大鬆了一口氣呢，她們都樂意去做，不過很快她們就明白漢娜說的「持家可不是開玩笑」這句話的真實了。儲藏室裡食物很多，於是貝絲和艾美擺桌子準備吃飯，梅格和喬就做起早餐了，一邊還納悶僕人們為什麼總會說工作辛苦呢。

「我會端一些上去給媽媽，雖然她要我們不用管她，她可以照顧自己。」當家的梅格說了，她坐在茶壺後方，自覺像個母親一般莊嚴穩重。於是大家還沒有開動前就先準備好一個餐盤，端到樓上去了。燒滾了的茶非常苦，歐姆蛋煎焦了，餅乾上面還沾著點點的小蘇打粉；不過瑪區太太仍然道著謝收下她的早餐，等到喬走了以後才開懷笑了。

「可憐的小東西們，恐怕她們會不好受了，但是這對她們也

有好處。」她說,而後她拿出自己準備的美味佳餚,丟了這一頓不怎麼樣的早餐,免得傷害了她們的自尊心。這是做母親的小小欺瞞伎倆,但是她們會感激她的。

樓下的抱怨連連,大廚對於自己的失敗懊惱得不得了。「沒關係的,我來做午餐,做僕人,你來做女主人。手也別弄髒了,只要招呼客人並發號施令就行了。」喬說,她對烹調的事知道得比梅格還少呢。

梅格欣然接受了這個好心的提議,於是回到了客廳,急忙收拾了一下:把垃圾掃到沙發椅下面,又拉上百葉窗,這就省去撢灰塵的麻煩了。喬對自己的能力深具信心,又想要彌補吵架的事,於是立刻在郵局裡放了一張紙條,邀請羅瑞來吃飯。

「你最好是先看看有什麼東西,再去想到請人來。」梅格知道這個好客卻草率的舉動後如此說道。

「噢,我們有醃牛肉和很多馬鈴薯,我再去買點蘆筍和龍蝦,『好好吃一頓』,就像漢娜說的。我們可以買點生菜做沙拉。我不知道怎麼做,不過書上有教。我要做牛奶凍,我們仍有草莓可以做甜點,還可以有咖啡,如果你們想要優雅一點的話。」喬說。

「不要弄太多麻煩東西,喬,因為你只會做薑餅和糖蜜糖。午餐我是不會幫忙的,因為是你自己要請羅瑞來的,你要招呼他。」

「我也不要你做什麼,你只要客氣對他就行了,並且在我做布丁的時候幫一下。如果我遇到問題的時候你再給我點建議,好

不好？」喬相當委屈地說。

「好啊，可是我除了麵包和一些小事，其他的知道不多，你去買東西以前最好還是問一下媽媽。」梅格謹慎地說。

「我當然會，我又不是傻瓜。」梅格對喬的能力表現出明顯的疑慮，讓喬很生氣地走開了。

「你們想買什麼就買什麼，不要打擾我，我要出去吃午餐，沒辦法擔心家裡的事情。」喬跟母親說了以後，瑪區太太說。「我從來也不喜歡管家事，今天我要放個假，看書、寫信、找朋友，讓自己高興高興。」

忙碌的母親一大早竟然舒舒服服坐在搖椅上看書，這幕少見的景象讓喬感覺像是發生了什麼天災。

「好像每件事都不對勁了呢，」她自言自語著走下樓。「貝絲在哭，保證是這個家裡出了事了。如果是艾美逗她，我可要對付她了。」

喬自己都覺得渾身不對勁了，她匆匆走進客廳裡，卻發現貝絲正對著金絲雀皮寶哭，皮寶在鳥籠裡已經死了，牠那兩隻爪子可憐兮兮的往外伸著，彷彿在乞討牠吃不到而餓死的食物。「都是我的錯——我把牠忘了——籠子裡連一粒鳥食、一滴水都沒有了。噢，皮寶！噢，皮寶！我怎麼能這麼殘忍地對你呢？」貝絲哭著，把這個可憐的鳥兒握在手裡，想要恢復牠的生命。

喬端詳著牠半開的眼睛，摸了摸牠小小的心臟，發現牠已經又冷又硬了，於是搖了搖頭，拿出她的骨牌盒子作棺木。「把牠放進烤箱裡也許牠會變暖和，會活過來。」艾美滿懷希望地說。

「牠是餓死的，不能把牠烤了。我會給牠做件壽衣，把牠埋在花園裡。我再也不要養鳥了，再也不要了，我的皮寶呀！我太壞了，不配養鳥。」貝絲喃喃說著，她坐在地上，兩隻手抱著小鳥。

「葬禮要在今天下午舉行，我們全都要參加。好啦，貝絲，別哭了。這件事很可惜，可是這個禮拜就沒有一件事是順利的，而皮寶是這次實驗裡最倒楣的一個。去做壽衣吧，把牠放在我的骨牌盒子裡。等到午餐派對過後，我們要舉行一場小小的葬禮。」喬說，她已經開始覺得自己做了好多事情了。

她留下其他人去安慰貝絲，自己回到了廚房，廚房裡是一片令人洩氣的混亂。她穿上一件大圍裙就開始工作，等到她把碟子都堆起來準備要洗的時候，才發現火熄了。

「還真是個好兆頭呢！」喬嘀嘀咕咕地說著，邊把火爐門一把拉開，在灰燼裡頭用力撥弄著。

爐火重新燃著以後，她想趁著燒水的時候去市場買菜。走走路使她恢復了精神，她買了一隻幼小的龍蝦、一些很老的蘆筍、兩盒酸草莓，自覺買得真划算之後，她再走回家。等到她清理好，午餐時間也到了，爐火也都燒得火紅了。漢娜留了一盤的麵包要發，梅格很早就把麵包整理過，放在爐床上要發第二遍，後來卻忘了。梅格正在客廳招待莎麗‧葛蒂納，門突然推開，一個沾著麵粉、髒兮兮、脹紅著臉、頭髮蓬亂的人影現了身，尖酸地問：

「嘿，麵包脹出烤盤了，發得夠了吧？」

　　莎麗笑了起來，但是梅格點了點頭，眉毛抬得老高，那個鬼魅似的人形消失了，她立刻毫不遲疑地把那酸麵包放進烤箱了。瑪區太太四處打量了一下，看看情況如何了，她也對貝絲說了些安慰的話，就出門去了。

　　喬在這天早晨所歷經的焦慮、痛苦，是言語也難以形容的，而她做的午餐從此也傳為笑談。由於她不敢再去請教別人，只好一切靠自己，結果她發現要做個好廚子，除了精力和一番好意以外，還需要別的東西才行。

　　「你把鹽當成糖了啦，鮮奶油又是酸的。」梅格比個慘兮兮的手勢回答。

　　喬發出一聲哀嘆，把身體往椅背一靠，這時她想起來她用廚房桌上兩個罐子中的一個匆忙給草莓撒上粉，並且也忘了把牛奶放進冰箱裡了。她的臉脹得通紅，幾乎要哭了出來！這時她和羅瑞的目光相接，他顯然很英勇地極力壓抑，但是目光卻依然是帶著笑；於是這件事的滑稽面突然打動了她，使她哈哈大笑了起來，一直笑到眼淚都流下她的臉頰了。其他人也全都如此，就連女孩子們稱作「嘎嘎叫」的這位老小姐也笑了。於是這頓不幸的午餐就在麵包和奶油、橄欖和歡樂中快快活活地結束了。

　　「我現在完全提不起精神收拾，因此我們就來舉行一場葬禮，讓自己嚴肅些吧。」他們站起來時喬說了。克洛克小姐也準備要走了，她急著要在另一個朋友家的餐桌旁訴說這個新故事。

　　他們為了貝絲也確實嚴肅了：羅瑞在小樹叢的羊齒植物下挖了一個墓，小「皮寶」那個心腸軟的主人哭哭啼啼地把牠放進墓

裡，再用青苔蓋住，一個用紫羅蘭和蘩縷做的花環掛在寫著牠的墓誌銘的石頭上。

儀式結束以後，貝絲因為情緒激動以及肚裡的龍蝦作怪而回到房間，可是房裡沒有地方可以休息，床都沒有鋪好；不過她發現藉著拍打枕頭和整理房間的動作，她的哀傷倒是減緩了許多。梅格幫喬收拾這頓大餐的殘局，花了她們半個下午的時間，把她們累得要命，於是說好了晚餐只要喝茶配土司就行了。羅瑞駕馬車載艾美出去走走，這真是個善行，因為酸奶似乎對她的脾氣有些不好的影響。瑪區太太回到家，看到三個較大的女兒正起勁地在下午做著事，她瞧了櫃櫥一眼，約略知道這個實驗已經成功一部分了。

等到暮色漸濃，四周都寂靜下來時，她們才一個個聚集到門廊，這裡的六月薔薇含苞待放，美麗極了。她們一個個唉聲嘆氣地坐下來，似乎筋疲力盡，又似乎心煩意亂。

「今天是多麼精采的一天！」喬說話了，通常她都是第一個說話的人。

「今天好像比平常短，可是卻多麼地教人不舒服呀。」梅格說。

「一點也不像家。」艾美說。

「沒有媽媽和小皮寶，不可能像是家了。」貝絲嘆了口氣，盯著她腦袋上方空盪盪的鳥籠。

「媽媽來了呢，親愛的，明天你可以再養一隻鳥，如果你想要的話。」

　　瑪區太太邊說邊走過來，在她們中間坐下，看起來像是她的假期也沒有比她們的假日快活多少。

　　「媽媽，你是不是故意走開不管事，好看看我們會怎麼樣？」梅格高喊著，她已經懷疑了一整天。

　　「是的。我希望你們能明白，所有人的舒適是取決於每個人忠誠地做自己分內的事。我和漢娜為你們做事的時候，你們都過得很好，不過我認為你們並不很快樂或是珍惜，所以我就想，我得讓你們看看如果每個人都只顧自己會是什麼樣的情形，算是個小小的教訓吧。你們不覺得能夠彼此幫忙，能夠盡每天的責任，使得休閒更為甜蜜；能夠容忍自制，使家變得舒適可愛，這是要快活得多嗎？」

　　「我們覺得是呢，媽媽！」女孩子們齊聲叫道。

　　「那我要勸你們再扛起你們的小小責任吧，雖然這些責任有時候看起來很沉重，但是它們對我們是有益處的；而且等到我們學會扛起它們以後，它們也會變輕了。工作使我們不至於無聊或是去惹禍，對我們身心有利，而且比金錢或衣飾更能給我們一種力量和獨立感。」

　　「我們會記住的，媽媽！」她們的確是記住了。

第 12 章
羅倫斯營地

　　貝絲是全家人當中最常在家的一個，所以是小小郵局的局長，可以定期前往處理，她又非常喜歡每天打開郵局信箱的小門，分送信件的工作。七月裡有一天，貝絲手裡捧滿物品走進家門，像郵差一樣在各處放下信件和包裹。

　　「媽媽，這是你的花！羅瑞從來都不會忘的。」她說著就把這束新鮮的花插進放在「媽媽的角落」的花瓶裡，花瓶裡的花都是這個重感情的男孩提供的。

　　「梅格・瑪區小姐，你有一封信和一隻手套。」貝絲接著說，並且把物品送給坐在母親旁邊縫袖口的姐姐。

　　「咦，我掉了一副手套，這裡卻只有一隻呢。」梅格說，她盯著這隻灰色的棉質手套。

　　「你有沒有把另外一隻掉到花園裡了？」

　　「沒有，我確定沒有。郵局裡只有一隻。」

　　「我最討厭手套不成雙了！不要緊，另外一隻也許會找到。我的信只是我想要的一首德文歌曲的翻譯，我猜是布魯克先生翻的，因為這不是羅瑞的筆跡。」

　　瑪區太太看了梅格一眼，穿著棉布晨袍的梅格看起來十分美麗，小小的鬈髮在前額飄動；工作小桌上擺放著整齊的白色線

團,她坐在桌邊縫著,看起來像是成年女人。她邊做活兒邊唱著歌,手指飛快來回動著,思緒卻忙碌在如她腰帶上的三色菫一樣無邪而純真的少女幻想上,渾然不知母親的想法。瑪區太太笑了,感到非常滿意。

「喬博士有兩封信、一本書,還有一頂滑稽的舊帽子,這頂帽子塞住了整個信箱,還伸到外頭了。」貝絲哈哈笑著說,一邊走進書房,喬正在書房裡寫東西。

「羅瑞可真是個奸詐鬼!我說我希望流行比較大的帽子,因為大熱天我每天都會晒到臉。他就說:『何必管流行呢?就戴個大帽子,讓自己舒服就行了!』我說如果我有我就戴,他就送過來這頂帽子來試探我。我偏要戴,好玩嘛,讓他知道我才不管時尚流行呢。」說著喬就把這頂古舊的寬邊帽蓋在柏拉圖的胸像上,然後看她的信。

其中一封是母親寫的信,這封信使她臉頰發紅,淚水盈眶,信是這麼寫的:

我親愛的:

我寫這封短信是要告訴你,看到你努力要控制你的脾氣,我有多麼地滿意。你從沒有說起你的磨難、失敗或成功,你以為除了你每天請求協助的在天上的朋友看到之外,沒有人看到──如果我從你那本翻破了封皮的書猜測得沒錯的話。其實我也全都看在眼裡,並且衷心相信你真誠的決心,因為這份決心已經開始要開花結果了。繼續努力吧,親愛的,要有耐心而且勇敢地繼續下

去，也要相信沒有人會比你母親更疼惜你、贊同你。

媽媽

「這真的對我很有幫助呢！這值得上百萬的金錢和千萬的讚美呢。噢，媽媽，我真的是努力了！我會繼續努力下去，不會疲倦的，因為我有你在幫我。」這時候她感覺自己比以往都要堅強，可以迎向她的「惡魔」並且打敗它，所以她把這張紙條用針別在衣服裡面；既作為護身之用，也用來提醒自己，免得自己疏忽了。而後她去拆另一封信，心想不管信裡是好是壞的消息，她都可以面對。羅瑞斗大而活潑的字跡寫道：

親愛的喬：

你好不好？

明天會有一些英國男孩和女孩來看我，我想要開心玩上一陣子。如果天氣好的話，我要在『長草地』紮營，然後大夥兒划船去野餐、打槌球——生火呀、做菜呀，像吉普賽人那樣，玩各種遊戲。他們都很好，也喜歡這種事。布魯克會去，他要管我們男生，凱特．沃恩會指導女生。我希望你們全都來，不管怎麼樣都不能漏了貝絲，不會有人打擾她的。吃的東西不用費心——我會負責的，其他的事也一樣——千萬要來喲，才夠意思！

我可是十萬火急的！

友　　羅瑞

「天大的好消息！」喬喊道。

第二天清晨太陽偷偷往女孩子們的房裡探個臉，要向她們保證這天是個晴天的時候，它看到一幕滑稽的景象。每個人都做了自認為對這場出遊而言是必要而且妥當的準備。梅格額頭上多了一排小小的鬈髮紙捲子，喬在她受罪的臉上塗了過多的冷霜，貝絲讓喬安娜跟自己睡，為即將到來的分別贖罪；而艾美更為這個景象製造了高潮：她把一個曬衣夾夾住鼻子，要補救讓她生氣的塌鼻子。這幕滑稽的景象似乎讓太陽也樂開懷了，因為它突然發出強烈的光和熱，使得喬醒來，看到艾美的裝扮開心地大笑，而吵醒了所有姐妹。

羅瑞跑過去迎接她們，並且非常有禮貌地將她們介紹給他的朋友。草坪成為接待室，當場熱鬧了好幾分鐘。梅格慶幸凱特小姐雖是二十歲的年紀卻穿得非常樸素，這是美國女孩子會樂意模仿的；而耐德先生向她保證自己是特地來看她的，這也教她心花怒放。喬明白羅瑞為什麼在提到凱特時「嘴角一撇」了，因為這位小姐有一種「離我遠點，別碰我」的神情，和其他女孩子輕鬆自在的態度成為強烈的對比。貝絲對新認識的男孩子做了一番觀察，決定行動不方便的那個比較不「可怕」，而且他很溫柔、身體又弱，就為了這一點，她就會對他好的。艾美發現葛蕾絲是個有禮貌又快活的小朋友，她倆定定地互相注視了幾分鐘之後，突然間就變成非常好的朋友。

帳篷、午餐、槌球器材都已經事先運送過去，這群人很快也上了船，兩艘船就一起出發，留下羅倫斯先生在岸邊揮著帽子。

　　羅瑞和喬划一艘船，布魯克先生和耐德划另一艘，而比較調皮搗蛋的雙胞胎之一佛烈得・沃恩自己划著一條單人座小船，拚命想要干擾兩艘船。喬那頂可笑的帽子值得感謝，因為它的用處可真廣：一開始由於它引起眾人的笑聲而打破了彼此間的尷尬；等她划著船，帽子也來回拍動，掀起一陣清涼的微風；而且她還說，如果下起一陣雨來，這頂帽子還可以給大家當傘遮雨呢。凱特對於喬的作風很是驚異，尤其當喬掉了一枝槳而大喊「哎喲喂呀！」以及羅瑞在船上要坐下時絆到喬的腳而說：「我的好傢伙，我有沒有踢到你？」的時候。不過當她戴上眼鏡仔細打量這個奇怪的女孩幾次之後，凱特小姐判定她「雖然古怪，卻挺聰明」，於是老遠就會對著她笑了。

　　另一艘船上的梅格則是姿態優雅地坐著，面對兩個划船者，他們都傾慕眼前這人兒，也因此都以少見的「技術和熟練」划著槳。布魯克先生是個沉默而且嚴肅的年輕人，有一雙秀美的棕色眼睛和悅耳的聲音。梅格喜歡他的沉穩態度，認為他是個裝滿有用知識的活生生的百科全書。他和她說的話不多，但是他卻時常注視她，而她也確信他並不是帶著嫌惡的心理看著她的。耐德是個大學生，自然會擺出新鮮人認為該擺出的態度。他不是很聰明，不過脾氣很好，總體來說是個一起野餐的好玩伴。莎麗・葛蒂納一心只想著不要弄髒她的白色凸花棉布洋裝，並且和那個無處不在的佛烈得嘰喳說著話；佛烈得老是愛惡作劇，讓貝絲無時無刻不提心吊膽。

　　到「長草坪」並不遠，但是他們抵達那裡的時候，帳篷都已

經搭好,而球門也都放下了。這裡是一片悅目的綠色原野,中央有三株橡樹,枝葉茂密,朝四周伸展開來,還有一片平滑的草坪供人打槌球之用。

「歡迎來到羅倫斯營地!」眾人登上岸,看見這裡的景色都歡喜地讚嘆著,這時年輕的主人宣布。

「布魯克是總司令,我是軍需官,其他男生是參謀官,而各位女士呢,你們是客人。帳篷是特別為你們而設的,那棵橡樹是你們的客廳,這棵樹是餐廳,第三棵是營地廚房。現在我們趁天還沒有熱先來比一場槌球,然後再來準備午餐。」

於是法蘭克、貝絲、艾美和葛蕾絲就坐下來,看另外八個人比賽。布魯克先生挑了梅格、凱特和佛烈得組一隊;羅瑞選了莎麗、喬和耐德一隊。英國隊打得不錯,但是美國隊要更勝一籌,兩隊爭奪每一吋的土地,戰況激烈得彷彿一七七六年獨立戰爭的精神激發了他們的鬥志。

「吃午餐囉。」布魯克先生看著手錶說。

「軍需官,麻煩你生個火,拿點水,我和瑪區小姐、莎麗小姐負責鋪桌布好嗎?誰會沖好喝的咖啡?」

「喬會沖。」梅格說,她很高興能推薦自己的妹妹。喬呢,覺得自己近來的烹調技藝會讓她很有面子,於是就去負責看管咖啡壺;小孩子們去撿乾木棍,男生們生了火,還到附近一處山泉裡拿了水回來。凱特小姐畫著素描,法蘭克同貝絲說著話,貝絲一邊用燈芯草編成墊子,當成餐盤。

總司令和他的助手們很快就在桌布上陳列了一批誘人的飲料

和食物，這些東西都用綠葉裝飾得十分美麗。喬宣布咖啡已經煮好，於是每個人都坐下來痛快地享用這一餐，因為年輕人很少會消化不良，而運動更促進健康的胃口。

「鹽在這裡，如果你要用的話。」羅瑞把一碟莓果遞給喬時說。

「謝謝你，我還比較喜歡蜘蛛。」她回答，同時撈起兩隻不小心淹死在奶油湯裡的小蜘蛛；「你好大的膽子，竟敢在你這頓完美的大餐上提醒我那次可怕的午餐盛宴！」喬加上一句，他倆都笑了起來，並且用同一個盤子吃著，因為盤碟不夠。

「我那天很開心，現在都還忘不了呢。這頓飯我是沒有什麼功勞的，你知道；我什麼事也沒有做，是你和梅格、布魯克完成的，我對你有無盡的感謝。我們再也吃不下東西的時候要做什麼呢？」羅瑞問，他覺得午餐結束了，他的王牌也出盡了。

「玩遊戲呀，玩到氣溫涼了。我帶了『作者』遊戲來。我敢說凱特小姐一定知道一些新奇好玩的東西。去問她嘛，她是客人，你應該多陪陪她。」

「你不也是客人嗎？我以為她和布魯克很配，但是他一直在和梅格說話，而凱特就只是隔著她那副可笑的眼鏡盯著他們兩個人。」

凱特小姐的確知道幾種遊戲，而由於女孩子們不想再吃東西，男孩子們再也吃不下東西，他們就都移師到「客廳」，玩起「滑稽接龍」了。

當其他人興高采烈地玩遊戲，此時凱特小姐拿出她的素描

簿,梅格看著她畫,布魯克先生拿本書在草地上,但是他沒有在看。

「那首德文歌曲還可以嗎,瑪區小姐?」布魯克先生打破沉默問道。

「噢,是的,非常好,我很感激為我翻譯的人。」梅格說這話時,她的臉愉快了起來。

「你不會德文嗎?」凱特小姐露出訝異的神情問。

「不太好。我父親教過我,但是他現在不在家,我自己一個人沒法進步很快,因為沒有人可以糾正我的發音。」

「現在來試試看吧。這裡有一本席勒的《瑪麗・史都華》,還有一個很喜歡教人的家教。」說著布魯克先生就露出動人的笑容,把他的書放在她大腿上。

「這很難,我不敢試呢。」梅格說,她很感激,但是當著一個多才多藝的女孩的面,她感到很不好意思。

「我先唸一點,給你打氣。」於是凱特小姐就唸了書中最美的一段詩句,她的發音十分正確,卻也十分沒有感情。

她把書交還給梅格,布魯克先生沒有任何評論,倒是梅格天真地說——

「我還以為這是詩呢。」

「其中一些是。試試看這一段。」

布魯克先生把書翻開到可憐的瑪麗的哀悼詞部分,這時他的嘴角有一抹奇異的笑容。

梅格的新老師拿著用來指著字的長葉片,她乖乖地害羞而緩

慢地唸著，不自覺地用她那銀鈴般的嗓音，溫柔的語調，把堅硬的字句變成了詩。指著字句的綠葉在書頁上移動，梅格很快地在詩人哀傷的場景中忘掉了聽者，彷彿只有自己一個人一般，將詩中不快樂的皇后的言語加上一點悲傷的味道。如果她當時看到那雙棕色眼睛，她會立刻停下，但是她始終沒有往上看，這堂課也就沒有因為她而毀掉。

「非常好！」她停下來以後，布魯克先生說。他忽略她很多錯誤的地方，看起來他像是真的「很喜歡教別人」。

凱特小姐戴上眼鏡，打量了眼前這幕景象，把素描簿合上，用一種紆尊降貴的口氣說：「你的腔很好，過段時間以後會唸得很流暢。我勸你要學會，因為德語是做老師們的一項很寶貴的才藝。我必須去找葛蕾絲了，她跑來跑去的。」說著凱特小姐就漫步走開了，接著又聳聳肩，自言自語地加上一句：「我可不是來這裡陪一個家庭教師的，雖然她的確是年輕又貌美。這些美國佬多麼奇怪呀。我恐怕羅瑞跟他們在一起都會被帶壞了。」

「我忘記英國人挺瞧不起家庭教師的，對待她們也不像我們那樣。」梅格說，她用一種氣惱的神情望著那個遠去的身影。

「據我所知，很不幸的，男性家庭老師在他們那裡也是不好過的。對我們這些工作的人來說，沒有一個地方像美國這樣呢，梅格小姐。」布魯克先生看起來那麼地心滿意足又開心，使得梅格對於哀嘆自己的不幸命運感到慚愧。

「那麼我很高興我生活在這裡。我真不喜歡我的工作，不過畢竟這個工作讓我得到很大的滿足感，所以我不會再抱怨了。我

只希望我能像你一樣喜歡教書的工作。」

「我想如果你有羅瑞這種學生，你就會喜歡了。明年就不能教他了，我會很難過的。」布魯克先生說，他正忙著在草地上戳洞。

「我猜他要去上大學吧？」梅格嘴裡問這個問題，但是她的眼神卻加上一句：「那你要怎麼辦？」

「是的，他該去了，他已經準備好了。而他一走，我也要從軍了。國家需要我。」

「我聽了好高興！」梅格嘆道。「我認為每個青年都會想要從軍，不過，對於待在家裡的母親們和姐妹們卻不好受。」她難過地加上一句。

「我沒有母親也沒有姐妹，朋友更少，沒有人會關心我的死活。」布魯克先生口氣哀怨地說著，這時他正心不在焉地把枯了的玫瑰放進他才剛剛挖的洞裡，再用土把它蓋住，像是一座小墳墓似的。

「羅瑞和他爺爺會很關心，要是你受了什麼傷害，我們也都會為你難過的。」梅格由衷地說。

「謝謝你，這話聽起來很讓我開心……」布魯克先生看起來又開懷了，但是他話還沒有說完，耐德騎著那匹老馬啪嗒啪嗒地過來了，然後在女生面前表演他的騎術，這一天就再也沒有安靜的時候了。

在一場即興表演、一場「狐狸抓鵝」的遊戲，和一場氣氛和諧的槌球賽之後，這個下午就結束了。日落時分，帳篷拆了，食

物籃收拾好了、槌球球門也拔起來、小船上裝好東西，這群人就坐著船向下游漂去，一邊還扯著喉嚨唱歌。

在一小群人先前集合的草坪上，他們互道再見，沃恩家人要去加拿大。四姐妹從花園走回家的時候，凱特看著她們離開，還算客氣地說：「雖然美國女孩子態度很愛炫耀，不過你認識她們以後就會知道她們都很不錯呢。」

「我很同意你的話。」布魯克先生說。

第 13 章
空中樓閣

　　一個暖和的九月天下午，羅瑞舒舒服服地躺在他的吊床上，來回晃著吊床，一邊猜想他的鄰居在做什麼。他抬眼望著上方七葉樹濃濃的綠蔭，做著各種各樣的夢；而當他正想像自己在環繞地球的航行中在海上隨浪起伏時，一陣人聲突然把他打上了岸。他從吊床的網孔看過去，看到瑪區一家人走了出來，好像是要去遠行。

　　「這些女生究竟要做什麼呀？」羅瑞心想，睜開他瞌睡的眼睛好生打量一番，因為他這幾位鄰居外表有些挺奇特的地方。每個人都戴著一頂寬邊帽，一邊肩膀背著一個棕色的棉布包包，還拿著一根長木棍。梅格帶著一個墊子、喬拿著一本書、貝絲提著一個籃子、艾美拿著畫冊。四個人靜靜穿過花園，朝一扇小小的後門走出去，然後開始往房屋和河之間的那座小山爬。

　　「嘿，真絕！」羅瑞自言自語。「她們去野餐竟然沒找我。她們不可能去划船，她們沒有鑰匙。也許她們忘了，我去把鑰匙拿給她們，看看會怎麼樣。」

　　他雖然有六、七頂帽子，但是他卻花了些時間才找到一頂。接著又要找鑰匙，最後鑰匙在他的口袋裡找到了。所以等他翻過圍籬去追她們的時候，她們的身影已經看不見了。他抄了一條最

近的路到了船屋等她們出現，但是沒有人來，於是他到小山上去觀測一番。這座山的一部分被一叢松樹遮蓋，而從這塊綠色的中央傳來一個比松樹的輕嘆或蟋蟀懶洋洋的叫聲，還要清楚的聲音。

「好一幅美麗的景致！」羅瑞從樹叢中往下看，一邊心裡想著，這會兒他非常機警，心情也好多了。

這確實是一幅漂亮的小小圖畫：四姐妹坐在樹蔭幽處，日影在她們身上閃耀，芳香的微風吹起她們的頭髮，吹涼了她們滾燙的雙頰。樹林裡的小動物做著各自的事情，彷彿她們不是陌生人，而是老朋友。梅格坐在墊子上，用她雪白的雙手縫著衣物，那身粉紅色的洋裝在綠樹叢中使她清新、嬌美得像一朵玫瑰。貝絲正為旁邊鐵杉樹下落得厚厚一層的松果分類，因為她會用松果做出美麗的東西。艾美對著一簇羊齒植物素描，而喬一邊大聲唸著書一邊編織。男孩看著她們，臉上閃過一絲陰影，他覺得自己應該走開，因為她們沒有邀請他；可是他又猶豫不定，因為家裡似乎很寂寞，而這場樹林中的小小派對又最能吸引他那浮動不定的心。他動也不動地站著，一隻忙著收穫的松鼠從他近處一棵松樹上跑下去，突然間看到他再跳了回去，吱吱叫罵著，聲音尖銳得使貝絲抬起頭；而瞥見了樺樹後面那張充滿渴望的臉孔，她露出一個令他安心的微笑，算是打招呼。

「我可以過來嗎？還是我會打擾你們？」他一邊慢慢走近一邊問。

梅格揚起眉毛，但是喬不以為然地朝她皺眉頭，立刻說：

「當然可以。我們應該先問過你的,只是我們想你大概不會喜歡像這樣子的女生遊戲。」

「我一向喜歡你們的遊戲,可是如果梅格不想讓我參加,我就走。」羅瑞說。

「如果你也做點事情,我是不會反對的。在這裡沒事做是違反規定的。」梅格嚴肅卻也好心地說。

「那就萬分感激了。只要你們肯讓我待一下,我什麼事情都肯做,因為家裡實在無聊得像是撒哈拉沙漠。我要不要縫衣服、唸書、撿松果、畫畫,或者同時做這些事?把你們的重擔交給我吧,我準備好了。」於是羅瑞就坐下了,他那個逆來順受的表情讓人看了很開心。

「多美麗啊!」羅瑞輕聲說,他能夠迅速地感受到任何種類的美。

「這裡常常都是這樣的,我們都喜歡看,因為它變化萬千,但總是燦爛美麗。」艾美說,她真希望自己能畫下來。

「喬說起我們希望以後能住的鄉下 —— 她說的是真正的鄉下,養豬、養雞、晒乾草。那很好,不過我希望那邊的美麗鄉村是真的,而我們都能去到那裡。」貝絲思索著。

「如果我們每個夢想都變成真的那不是很有趣嗎?」停頓了一會兒後,喬說了。

「我已經有太多的美夢了,要我挑出一個還很困難呢。」羅瑞說。他平躺在地上,朝著那隻洩漏他行蹤的松鼠丟松果。

「你必須挑一個你最喜歡的。是什麼呢?」梅格問。

「如果我說了，你也要說你的喔？」

「好啊，如果其他人也說的話。」

「我們會說的。現在你說吧，羅瑞。」

「等我遊歷過世界上我想要去的地方後，我想要在德國定居，享受我喜歡的音樂。我要成為一個著名的音樂家，所有人都爭著要聽我演奏。我永遠不用為錢或是生意煩惱，只是讓自己快樂，隨我所願地過日子。這是我最喜歡的美夢。你的是什麼，梅格？」

梅格似乎覺得自己的夢有點難以啟齒，她拿著一株羊齒植物在面前揮著，像是要驅散一群想像的蚊蚋，一邊緩緩說道：「我想要有一幢可愛的房子，裡面滿是奢侈豪華的東西——佳餚、華服、漂亮的家具、快活的人，還有大筆的錢。我要做這個房子的女主人，隨我心意掌管這個家，還有很多僕人讓我一點也不用做事。那我會有多高興！因為我不會無聊，又會做好事，而且讓每個人都非常喜歡我。」

「你這場美夢中不用有個男主人嗎？」羅瑞淘氣地問。

「我說了『快活的人』，你知道。」梅格邊說邊仔仔細細綁著鞋帶，不教人看到她的臉。

「你為什麼不說你想要有個很棒很聰明的好丈夫，和幾個天使一樣的小孩？你知道你的夢裡沒有這些就不完美了。」說話直率的喬說，她到目前為止還沒有什麼愛情的幻想，對於浪漫愛情還頗愛嘲弄，除了書裡的以外。

「你的美夢裡只有馬兒、墨水瓶和小說。」梅格突然不耐地

回敬她。

「難道不是嗎？我想要有一個滿是阿拉伯馬的馬廏、堆滿書的房間，我還要用神奇的墨水寫作，讓我的作品和羅瑞的音樂一樣出名。我想在走進我的天國以前做一些了不起的事──英勇或是神奇的事，而在我死後都不會被人忘記。我不知道是什麼事，不過我正在留意，總有一天要讓你們全都嚇一大跳。我想我會寫書，變得有錢又有名，這很適合我，所以這是我最喜歡的美夢。」

「我的美夢是安穩地和爸爸媽媽待在家裡，幫忙照顧家人。」貝絲心滿意足地說。

「你難道不想要別的東西嗎？」羅瑞問。

「從我有了我的小鋼琴以後，我就非常滿足了。我只希望我們全都健康地在一起，沒有別的了。」

「我有好多好多願望，不過我最喜歡的是做個畫家，去羅馬，畫些很好的畫，做全世界最棒的畫家。」這是艾美小小的心願。

「我們可真有野心啊！除了貝絲以外，每個人都想要有錢又有名，在各方面都了不起。我真懷疑我們誰可以達成願望呢。」羅瑞嚼著青草說道，像是一頭沉思的小牛。

「我有完成美夢的鑰匙，但是我能不能打開它的門，就還不知道了。」喬神祕地說道。

「我也有我的美夢的鑰匙，但是我卻不能去試，該死的大學！」羅瑞不耐煩地嘆口氣，低聲發著牢騷。

「我的在這裡！」艾美揮著她的鉛筆。

「我什麼都沒有。」梅格悽慘地說。

一陣微弱的鈴鐺聲提醒他們漢娜已經把茶泡好，正等著泡出茶味兒呢，他們剛好有時間回到家吃晚飯。

「我還可以再來嗎？」羅瑞問。

「可以的，只要你乖，愛讀書，就像初級課本裡教小孩子的那樣。」梅格微笑著說。

「我會試試看的。」

「那你就可以來，而我會教你像蘇格蘭男人一樣打毛線，現在正需要大量的襪子呢。」喬加上一句，他們在大門口分手，她揮了揮她手裡的襪子，像是揮著一面大的藍色毛線旗幟。

第 14 章
祕密

　　喬在屋頂閣樓裡正忙著呢，因為十月天已經開始越來越冷，下午時間也變短了。溫暖的陽光有兩、三個小時照進高高的窗子，喬坐在舊沙發上振筆直書，稿紙散落在她面前一個大箱子上；而家裡的寵物老鼠「史瓜寶」在她頭上的屋梁上漫步，陪著牠的是牠的大兒子，那是隻漂亮的小老鼠，顯然很以牠的鬍子為榮。喬專心在工作上，一直寫到最後一張都寫滿了，她才用花體字簽上名，再把筆摔下，嘆道：

　　「好啦，我已經盡力了！如果這不行，就得等到我能寫出更好東西的時候了。」

　　她靠在沙發上仔細把稿子看過，在這裡那裡劃線又加上很多驚嘆號，再用一條漂亮的紅色緞帶把稿子綁起來，坐在那裡用一種謹慎而渴望的神情看了它一分鐘，這神情明白顯示了她對作品有多麼認真。喬在這裡的書桌是一個靠牆的舊鐵皮櫃櫥。她從這個鐵皮做的藏物處另外拿出一份稿子，把兩份稿子都放進口袋，悄悄走下樓，讓她的朋友們啃她的筆，嚐她的墨水。

　　她盡量無聲無息地戴上帽子、穿上外套，爬出後面窗子，踩在一個低矮門廊的屋頂，縱身跳到路邊草地上，再繞遠路到大馬路上。到了路上，她先讓自己鎮定下來，再攔了一輛正經過的公

129

共馬車，一路搖搖晃晃地進到城裡，看起來很快活也很神祕。

要是有人在觀察她，他會認為她的動作實在是太怪異了，因為她一下馬車就邁著大步走到某條繁忙街道的某個門牌號碼處。她好不容易才找到這個地方，走進門口，抬頭看了看骯髒的樓梯，在那裡動也不動地站了一分鐘以後，突然跑回街上，和來時一樣飛快走開。這番動作她來來回回重複了好幾次，讓對面一幢樓上一個靠窗觀看的黑眼男孩看得非常有趣。第三次走回來了以後，喬甩甩頭，把帽簷拉下蓋到眼睛上頭，接著就走上樓了，那神情像是要拔掉所有的牙齒一樣。

門口許多招牌當中倒是真的有一個牙醫的招牌，年輕男孩盯著一副緩慢開合、用意在吸引人注意的一口假牙一會兒，然後就穿上外套，拿了帽子，走下樓到對面門口站定。他露出微笑，還打了個哆嗦——

「自己一個人來是她的風格，可是如果她受了罪，會需要有人陪她回家。」

十分鐘不到，喬脹著一張通紅的臉跑下樓梯，她的神態是一個剛歷經某種嚴苛考驗的人才有的。她看到這個年輕男孩，毫無開心的表情，只是點點頭就從他身邊走過，但是他卻跟在她後面，用充滿同情的語氣問——

「你會不會很難受？」

「還好。」

「你很快就好了嘛。」

「是呀！謝天謝地！」

「你為什麼要自己來？」

「不想要別人知道。」

「你是我看過最怪的人。你拔了幾顆牙？」

喬看著她的朋友，彷彿聽不懂他的話，然後就哈哈大笑了起來，好像被某件事逗得樂不可支的樣子。

「我希望是兩顆，不過我必須等一個禮拜。」

「你在笑什麼？你在搞什麼鬼啊，喬。」羅瑞說，他看起來很不解。

「你也是呀。你在對面樓上撞球場做什麼？」

「對不起喲，這位女士，那裡不是撞球場而是健身房，我正在學擊劍。」

「那我很高興。」

「為什麼？」

「你可以教我呀，等我們演出《哈姆雷特》的時候，你就可以扮雷爾提了。我們的擊劍場面也可以演得精采了。」

羅瑞開心地放聲大笑，引來幾個行人的微笑。

「不管我們演不演《哈姆雷特》，我都會教你，擊劍很有趣的，而且會讓你思緒非常清晰呢。可是我不相信這是你那麼明確地說『那我很高興』的唯一理由，怎麼樣，是不是？」

「是，我高興的是你沒有去撞球場，因為我希望你永遠也不要去那種地方。你有沒有去呢？」

「不常去。」

「我希望你不要去。」

「沒有什麼壞處的，喬。我家裡也有撞球檯，但是要有一些好手才會好玩，因為我很喜歡打撞球，有時候我會來這裡，跟耐德‧莫法特或是其他人打球。」

「噢，那真糟，因為你會越來越喜歡，然後浪費時間和錢，長大就像那些可怕的男生一樣。」喬搖頭說道。

「你打算一路演說回家嗎？」他很快地問。

「當然不是，為什麼問？」

「因為如果是的話，我就要坐公共馬車；如果不是，我就和你一起走回家，並且告訴你一件很有趣的事。」

「我不會再訓話了。我倒是非常想聽這個消息。」

「那好，走吧。這是個祕密，如果我告訴你，你也要告訴我一個你的祕密。」

「我沒有祕密——」喬才剛說就突然住口，她想到她確實有祕密。

「你有——你是藏不住事情的，所以快承認吧，不然我就不說了。」羅瑞喊道。

「你的祕密是件好事嗎？」

「噢，當然！是關於你認識的人，而且好有趣喔！你應該聽的，我忍了好久，一直想要說呢，好啦，你先。」

「你絕不能在家裡提起喔，好不好？」

「一個字也不說。」

「你也不可以私底下嘲笑我？」

「我從來不會嘲笑人。」

「你才會呢。你可以從別人身上套出你想要的任何事。我不知道你是怎麼做的，可是你天生就會哄人。」

「謝謝你了。說吧。」

「是這樣的，我把兩篇故事交給一個報社的人，他會在下個星期給我回覆。」喬低聲在密友耳邊說。

「美國名女作家瑪區小姐萬歲！」羅瑞大喊，一邊把他的帽子往上拋再接住，這個動作讓兩隻鴨、四隻貓、五隻母雞、六個愛爾蘭小孩子樂不可支。

「噓！這不會有什麼結果的，我敢說。可是我非得試了才能罷休，而我什麼也沒說，因為我不希望別人失望。」

「不會不成的。嘿，你的作品和現在每天刊出的大半垃圾比起來，簡直是莎士比亞的作品呢。看到那些故事登出來，不是很好玩嗎？我們不會以我們的女作家為榮嗎？」

「那你的祕密呢？要公平喔，羅瑞，不然我一輩子都不會相信你了。」她說。

「我說出來可能會惹上麻煩，可是我又沒有答應不說，所以我要說出來。我知道任何一點消息，不告訴你我心裡就不安。我知道梅格那隻手套在哪裡。」

「就這個啊？」喬問，看起來很失望，羅瑞點點頭又眨了眨眼睛，臉上充滿神祕又有智慧的表情。

「目前這樣已經足夠了，等我告訴你它在哪裡以後，你也會同意的。」

「那就說吧。」

　　羅瑞彎腰在喬的耳邊低聲說了三個字，這幾個字造成滑稽的變化。她站定，盯著他好一會兒，既驚訝又不高興，然後她又繼續走，厲聲說：「你怎麼知道的？」

　　「看到的。」

　　「在哪裡？」

　　「口袋裡。」

　　「一直都在嗎？」

　　「是啊。這不是很浪漫嗎？」

　　「才不呢，太可怕了。」

　　「你不高興嗎？」

　　「當然不高興。這太荒唐了，根本不可以的。天啊！梅格會怎麼說？」

　　「你不可以告訴任何人的，拜託。」

　　「我可沒答應。」

　　「可是我們都知道的，而且我信任你。」

　　「呃，反正暫時我不會告訴人。可是我覺得你好討厭，要是你沒跟我講就好了。」

　　「我還以為你會很高興。」

　　「高興有人要把梅格帶走嗎？不會的，多謝了。」

　　「等到有人來把你帶走的時候你就會好受些了。」

　　「我倒想看看有誰敢來試試。」喬惡狠狠地叫著。

　　「我也要看！」羅瑞想到這件事也失聲笑了起來。

　　「我想我這個人不適合聽祕密。你告訴我這個祕密以後，我

的心裡就一直是亂糟糟的。」喬頗不知感激地說。

「我們比賽跑下這座山，你就會好了。」羅瑞提議。

這時候四周不見一個人影，平整的路面在她面前呈誘人的下坡之勢，喬認為這個誘惑實在難以抵擋，於是她拔腿就跑，帽子和梳子立刻飛落身後，髮夾也隨著她的跑步散落地上。羅瑞先跑到終點，對於他這招治療方法十分滿意，只見他這位「亞特蘭大」[2]氣喘吁吁地跑過來，頭髮飛揚、雙眼明亮、臉頰通紅，臉上不見一絲不快。

「真希望我是一匹馬，那麼我就可以在這麼清爽的空氣中跑上好幾哩路都不會喘呢。賽跑是不錯，可是你看看這讓我變成什麼德性了。去啦，把我的東西撿回來，你這個小天使。」喬說著就在一棵楓樹下猛地坐下，落地的紅色楓葉把路邊都鋪滿了。

羅瑞悠哉悠哉地走去撿拾那些掉落的東西，喬就把辮子綁好，希望她把自己弄整齊之前沒有人走過。可是就有人這時候走過，而這人偏巧就是梅格。她穿著一身端莊的服裝，看起來格外有淑女的樣子，因為她去人家家拜訪去了。

「你們在這裡做什麼呀？」她問道，同時用頗有教養的驚訝神情盯著她那個頭髮蓬亂的妹妹。

「撿楓葉。」喬心虛地回答，一邊在她才剛一把抓起的玫瑰色葉子當中挑揀。

「和髮夾。」羅瑞加上一句，把六、七個髮夾丟到喬的裙子

2　Atlanta，希臘神話中一位女獵人，在與追求者賽跑中落敗而下嫁對方。

上。「這條路上長髮夾呢，梅格，也長著髮梳和棕色的草帽。」

「你剛剛去跑步了吧，喬，怎麼可以這樣呢？你要什麼時候才能停止這種蹦蹦跳跳？」梅格語帶責備地說，一邊整理一下她的袖口，撫平才被風吹亂了的頭髮。

「除非等到我老了，身體僵硬，非用枴杖不可。不要逼我長大，梅格。你突然間就改變了，已經讓我夠難過的了，就讓我盡可能做小女生做久一點吧。」

最近她感覺到梅格正快速地變成一個女人，而羅瑞的祕密也使她害怕那勢必到來的分離，如今這分離似乎已經很近了。他看到她臉上的困擾神情，就趕忙開口轉移梅格的注意力：「你去哪裡啦？」

「到葛蒂納家了。莎麗一直告訴我蓓兒‧莫法特的婚禮的事。婚禮非常氣派，他們還去巴黎避寒了。想想看，那有多麼快活呀！」

「你羨慕她嗎，梅格？」羅瑞說。

「恐怕是吧。」

「我很高興！」喬喃喃說道，用力把她的帽子綁上。

「為什麼？」梅格面露驚訝的神情問。

「因為如果你在意財富的話，你就絕不會跑去嫁給一個窮人了。」喬說，她對著羅瑞皺眉頭，因為他正用眼神警告她注意自己說的話。

「我絕不會『跑去嫁』給任何人的。」梅格說，她端莊肅穆地繼續走著，另外兩個人跟在後頭又笑又說著悄悄話，還踢著路

上的石頭，「像小孩子一樣」，梅格自言自語地說。

　　第二個星期六，喬從窗子爬出家裡以後，梅格正坐在她窗前縫東西，卻看到一幕景象而大感駭異：只見羅瑞滿花園追著喬，終於在艾美的涼亭下追到她。那裡出了什麼事，梅格看不到，但是卻能聽到尖銳的笑聲，以及之後的說話聲和好大的報紙翻頁聲。

　　「我們該拿這個女孩子怎麼辦呀？她永遠也不會像個淑女一樣。」梅格嘆口氣，用不以為然的表情看著他們的賽跑。

　　「我希望她不要像淑女，她現在這樣子好好笑又好可愛喔。」貝絲說，但是喬和別人共擁祕密讓她有些傷心這件事，她是絕對不會說的。

　　「這真是很麻煩，可是我們永遠也沒辦法讓她『端端壯壯』。」艾美加上一句，她正在給自己做一些新的荷葉邊，她的鬈髮也綁得很好看，這兩件都是令人快活的事，也讓她覺得優雅而且淑女得不得了。

　　幾分鐘後，喬衝了進來，坐在沙發上假裝在看報。

　　「報上有沒有什麼有趣的事呀？」梅格特意表現親切地問。

　　「只有一篇故事，不過我猜不怎麼樣吧。」喬回答，極力不要讓人看到報紙的名字。

　　「你還是唸出來吧，可以讓我們開心，也可以使你沒機會淘氣。」艾美用她最最大人樣的語氣說。

　　「故事是什麼名字？」貝絲問，她不知道喬為什麼要把報紙擋住她的臉。

「敵對的畫家。」

「聽起來不錯。唸吧。」梅格說。

喬大聲「嗯哼」了一聲，又吸了口大氣，就開始很快地唸起來。姐妹們津津有味地聽著，因為故事很浪漫又有點可憐，結尾時大部分的人物都死了。

「我喜歡關於那幅驚世畫作那部分。」喬停下來之後，艾美發表了她讚許的評論。

「我喜歡講到愛情的部分。」梅格說著揉了揉眼睛，因為那「愛情的部分」很悲慘。

「是誰寫的？」貝絲看到喬的神情，問道。

唸故事的人突然間坐直身體，把報紙丟到一邊，露出脹紅的臉，然後用混合著嚴肅和興奮的口氣，大聲回答：「是你的姐姐。」

「是你！」梅格大叫，丟下手裡的活兒。

「寫得很好。」艾美評論道。

「我就知道！我就知道！噢，我的喬，我真驕傲！」貝絲跑過去摟住她的姐姐，為這個了不起的成就欣喜不已。

「把事情從頭到尾告訴我們吧。」「報紙是什麼時候來的？」「你能拿到多少錢呀？」「爸爸會怎麼說呢？」「羅瑞會不會笑？」全家人齊聲叫喊，全都簇擁著喬。凡家中有任何一點小小的喜事，這些天真而且親愛的人們都會歡樂慶祝。

「別嘰嘰喳喳了，各位，我會告訴你們所有的事。」喬說，

心裡猜想柏尼小姐[3]對於她的作品〈艾芙麗娜〉有沒有她對〈敵對的畫家〉那麼得意。說完了她怎麼處理她的故事後，喬又加上一句：「我去問的時候，那個人說兩篇他都喜歡，但是新人他們是不付稿費的，只會把文章登在他的報上，並且評介一番。這是很好的練習，他說。等到新人有進步了以後，每篇文章都可以有稿費，所以我就把兩篇故事都給他了。而今天這一篇寄來了。羅瑞看到我拿到報紙，堅持要看，我就讓他看。他說故事很好，我要再多寫，下一篇就會有稿費了，我好高興，因為不久以後我也許就可以養活自己和幫助姐妹們了。」

喬直到這時候才吁了口氣。她把頭埋在報紙裡，幾滴眼淚沾濕了她的小小故事。因為她心中最大的願望就是能夠獨立，並且贏得她深愛的人們的稱讚，而這似乎是達到這個目標的第一步。

3　Fanny Burney，一七五二－一八四〇，為英國小說家及日記作家。

第 15 章
電報

「一年裡最討人厭的月份就是十一月。」梅格說，一個無聊的下午，梅格站在窗前望著窗外受到霜害的花園。

「這就是我出生在這個月份的原因。」喬若有所思地說，對於她鼻子上的墨水漬毫無所覺。

「如果現在有一件很快活的事情發生，我們就會認為這是個快活的月份了。」貝絲說，她對每件事都抱持著希望，即使是對十一月。

「或許吧，可是這個家裡從來也沒有發生過快活的事。」梅格正生著悶氣。「我們每天辛苦工作，沒有一點變化，也沒有多少娛樂，跟無止境地原地踏步沒什麼不同。」

梅格嘆口氣，把臉再次轉到受霜害的花園。喬咕噥一聲，把兩隻手肘貼放在桌上，十分消沉的模樣；但是艾美卻朝氣蓬勃地跑開；而坐在另一扇窗前的貝絲微笑著說：「馬上就要有兩件快活的事要發生了：媽媽從街上走來了；羅瑞正穿過花園，好像有好事要說呢。」

他們兩人都走進房裡，瑪區太太問著一向會問的話：「孩子們，有爸爸的信嗎？」

一陣尖銳的鈴聲打斷她的話，一分鐘後，漢娜拿著一封信走

進來。「是嚇人的電報呢，太太。」她說，並且遞給她，好像怕它會爆炸造成損害一樣。

一聽到「電報」兩個字，瑪區太太立刻搶過去，看了上頭的兩行字後就跌坐在椅子上，像是這張小紙朝她心臟發射了一顆子彈一樣。羅瑞衝下樓去拿水，梅格和漢娜扶住她，喬用害怕的聲音大聲唸出來──

「瑪區太太：
令夫病重。盡速前來。
霍爾，華盛頓布蘭克醫院。」

她們屏息靜聽著，房間裡多麼安靜呀！屋外的白日奇怪地黯淡下來，而當她們圍著母親，感覺她們生活中所有的歡樂和支柱都要被奪走的時候，這整個世界改變得多麼突然！瑪區太太很快回復正常，把電報再看了一遍，然後向女兒們伸出雙臂，用她們永遠也忘不了的語氣說：「我要馬上就走，不過可能會來不及了。噢，孩子們，孩子們，幫助我承受這個負擔！」

有幾分鐘的時間，房裡只有輕聲啜泣的聲音，間雜著斷斷續續的安慰話語、溫柔地說一定會幫助的話，以及滿懷希望、說到最後卻因哭泣而說不下去的低語。可憐的漢娜是第一個恢復的，她以不自覺的智慧為其他人做了很好的榜樣，因為對她而言，工作是大半痛苦的萬靈丹。

「上帝會留住好人的！我不會浪費時間去哭，不過快把你的

東西準備好吧，太太。」漢娜誠心誠意地說，一邊拿圍裙擦了擦臉，用她那隻堅硬的手熱情地握住女主人的手，便走開以一抵三地工作去了。

「她的話沒錯，現在沒有時間哭。要鎮靜，孩子們，讓我想一下。」

可憐的人兒，她們試著平靜下來。她們的母親坐直身體，臉色蒼白但神色還算平穩，暫時把悲傷丟到一邊，開始思考情況並且為她們設想計畫。

「羅瑞在哪裡？」她整理好思緒，決定要先做什麼事情後立刻問。

「我在這裡，伯母。噢，讓我做點事吧！」男孩叫著，從隔壁房間趕過來。他先前退到隔壁，是覺得她們的哀傷太神聖了，即使他這雙友善的眼睛也不宜觀看。

「拍電報說我立刻趕去。下一班火車早上很早開。我要坐這班。」

「還有什麼？我的馬已經都準備好了，我可以去任何地方，做任何事。」他說，看他的神情，像是已經準備好飛到天涯海角了。

「留張紙條給瑪區嬸婆。喬，拿那枝筆和紙給我。」

喬把她才新謄寫的一張紙頁上的空白邊緣撕下，把桌子拉到母親身前，心裡明白這趟漫長而且哀傷的旅途所需的錢必須去向人借，不知道可不可以做點事，為父親多籌集哪怕是一小筆錢。

「你去吧，可是不要騎得太快，把自己摔死了。用不著這樣

的。」

顯然瑪區太太的警告被羅瑞拋到腦後了，因爲五分鐘後羅瑞就騎在自己的快馬上，奔馳過窗外，看起來像是在逃命一樣。

「喬，快去告訴金太太我不能去。路上順便買這些東西，我會把它們寫下來，到時候會需要這些的，我也必須準備一些護理用品。」

羅倫斯先生急急忙忙和貝絲一起過來，這位好心的老先生把想得到各種安慰病人的話都說了，還提出最最友善的承諾，要在這個母親離家的這段期間保護她的女兒們，這些話使她大感安慰。他看到她的表情，皺起他的濃眉又搓著兩隻手，突地大步走開，嘴裡說他很快會回來；誰也沒時間想到他，一直到梅格一手拿著一雙膠鞋，另一隻手拿著一杯茶跑過門口，且突然遇上了布魯克先生。

「瑪區小姐，聽到這個消息我很難過。」他說，他的語氣和善而且平靜，安慰了她那煩亂的心思。「我想要陪伴你母親去。羅倫斯先生託我到華盛頓去辦事，能夠在那裡爲她效勞，我會感到非常快活的。」

「你眞是太好心了！我相信我媽媽會接受的。知道有人可以照顧她，我們也放了好大的心了。非常、非常謝謝你！」

等羅瑞帶著一張字條回來以後，每件事情都安排好了，但是喬卻仍然沒有回來。她們開始著急起來，羅瑞就出去找她，因爲從來沒有人知道喬腦子裡想些什麼怪念頭。不過他沒有碰到她，而她走進家門時的神色非常怪異，其中混合了有趣和害怕、滿意

和懊悔，這景象和她放在母親面前的一捲紙鈔同樣讓全家人不解。她微微哽咽地說：「這是我的一些捐款，希望爸爸身體康復，早日回家！」

「天啊，你從哪拿來的錢？二十五塊錢！喬！你可沒做什麼冒失的事吧？」

「沒有。這真的是我的錢。我沒有偷、沒有借、沒有討，是賺來的。而且我想你不會怪我，因為我只賣掉我自己的東西。」

喬邊說邊摘下帽子，這時室內揚起一陣眾人的驚叫聲，她一頭濃密的頭髮剪短了。

「你的頭髮！你那頭漂亮的頭髮！」「噢，喬，你怎麼能這麼做？那是你最迷人的地方呢！」「親愛的孩子，你用不著這樣做的。」「她看起來不像是我的喬，不過我更愛她了！」

每個人都在驚呼，貝絲還去溫柔地抱住這個剪短了頭髮的腦袋，喬雖然做出一副不在乎的神情，但是卻騙不了誰。她把棕色的頭髮撥亂，想要看起來很喜歡這樣。「這又不會影響到我們國家的命運，所以你就別哭了，貝絲。這對於我的虛榮心會有好處的，我對自己的長頭髮已經變得太驕傲了。那頭亂糟糟的頭髮理掉，對我的頭腦也好，我的頭感覺又清爽又涼快；理髮師說我很快就會有一頭鬈鬈的短髮，那樣子會像個男生而且很適合我，又容易整理。我很滿意，所以請收下錢，我們吃晚餐吧。」

十點鐘，瑪區太太收起最後做好的活兒，說：「好啦，孩子們」可是沒有人想要上床睡覺。貝絲還是到鋼琴前彈了父親最喜歡的讚美詩，所有人開始都很勇敢地唱，但卻一個接一個地唱不

下去，最後只剩下貝絲誠心誠意地唱著。對她來說，音樂一向都能給她安慰。

「睡覺去吧，不要在床上聊天，因為我們明天還得早起，需要盡可能充足的睡眠。晚安了，親愛的孩子們。」讚美詩結束時瑪區太太說，這時候也沒有人想要再唱一首了。

她們靜靜地親了她，悄悄地走上床，彷彿生病的父親就躺在隔壁房間裡。雖然家中出了大問題，貝絲和艾美還是很快就睡著了，但是梅格卻還醒著，思索一些她短短的生命中所知最嚴肅的想法。喬一動也不動地躺在那裡，她姐姐以為她睡了，直到一陣壓抑住的啜泣聲讓她摸到一個淚濕的臉頰，她才驚叫起來：

「喬，什麼事啊？你在為爸爸哭嗎？」

「不是，現在不是。」

「那是為什麼？」

「我——我的頭髮！」可憐的喬放聲哭了出來，她想用枕頭搗住她的情緒，但是不成功。

梅格一點也不覺得這句話很滑稽，她最為溫柔地親吻了這位痛苦的女英雄，安撫她。

「不過我不後悔，」喬哽咽著頑強地說，「如果我能夠的話，我明天還會再做。像這樣傻兮兮哭的，是我那個虛榮而又自私的部分。不要告訴別人，現在都沒事了。我以為你們都睡了，才私底下為了我動人的地方小小哀鳴了一下。」

鐘敲十二點，房裡一片闃寂，這時一個人影靜靜地從一張床走到另一張床；撫平這裡的被子，拉一拉那裡的枕頭，然後停下

來溫柔地看著每張沉睡的臉良久，再用她靜靜唸著禱詞的嘴親吻每個人，又熱切地祈禱著只有做母親的人才會祈禱的內容。當她掀開窗簾朝窗外的陰沉夜裡看去時，月亮突然從雲後出現，像是一張明亮而慈祥的臉。它用它的光芒照著她，似乎在寂靜中輕聲對她說：「親愛的人兒啊，安心吧！烏雲後面總是會有光明的！」

第 16 章
書信

在灰暗的寒冷清晨，這些姐妹們點起油燈，用從未感受過的誠懇熱切讀著聖經篇章，如今一個真正的難題陰影逼近了，這些篇章更是充滿了助益和安慰。沒有人多說什麼，但時間越來越近，她們坐在房裡等馬車的時候，瑪區太太對著在身邊忙著的孩子說了：

「孩子們，我把你們託給漢娜照顧，請羅倫斯先生保護你們了。漢娜忠實可靠，而我們的好心鄰居也會把你們當成自己孩子一樣保護。我不會害怕你們的安全，可是我很擔心你們面對這件困難的事做得對不對。我走了以後不要憂傷畏懼，要像平常日子一般繼續你們的工作，因為工作是令人愉快的安慰。要懷抱希望，保持忙碌，不論發生什麼事，要記住你們絕對不會沒有父親的。」

「是的，媽媽。」

「梅格，親愛的，要謹慎，照顧你的妹妹們，有事要向漢娜請教，如果有任何疑惑的地方，去找羅倫斯先生。要有耐心，喬，不要消沉或是草率衝動行事，要時常寫信給我，還要做個勇敢的孩子，隨時隨地幫助大家、給大家打氣。貝絲，用音樂讓自己得到安慰，還要把該做的家事都忠誠地做到；還有你，艾美，

盡量幫助姐姐們，要聽話，要快快樂樂、安全地待在家裡。」

「我們會的，媽媽！我們會的！」

一輛馬車駛近，那啪嗒啪嗒的聲音把她們嚇了一跳，隨後仔細傾聽。這時刻很不好受，不過她們姐妹表現得很好：沒有人放聲哭，沒有人跑開，或是發出哀嘆，雖然她們託母親帶充滿愛意的口信給父親時心情非常沉重，因為她們想到這口信傳過去時或許已經太遲了。她們靜靜地親吻了母親，溫柔地抱住她，在她離開時盡量快活地揮著手。

羅瑞和他爺爺也過來送行，布魯克先生看起來是那麼堅強、體貼又明理，使女孩子們當場就叫他「高貴先生」了。

「再見了，我親愛的孩子們！願上帝保佑我們所有人！」瑪區太太低聲說著，一個接一個地親著心愛的小臉蛋，然後就匆匆進到馬車裡。

她坐馬車離去時，太陽也露臉了，她回頭望去，看到陽光照在門口那群人身上，像是一個好兆頭。他們也看到了，微笑又揮手。馬車轉過街角時她看到的最後一幕就是那四張明亮的臉孔，還有站在她們身後，像是個保鑣的老羅倫斯先生、忠心的漢娜，和盡心盡力的羅瑞。

「每個人對我們都多麼好呀！」她回頭說，這時她又在這個青年臉上那充滿敬意的同情表情上，找到這句話的新證據了。

「我看誰都忍不住要對你們好吧。」布魯克先生回答，一邊笑著，他的笑太具有傳染力了，使得瑪區太太也忍不住笑了起來，於是這趟漫長的旅程一開始就有陽光、微笑、令人開心的言

語這些好兆頭了呢！

「我覺得好像剛經過一場地震。」喬說道。她們的鄰居羅瑞回家吃早餐，留下她們休息，重新打起精神。

「好像半個家都不見了。」梅格可憐兮兮地說。

漢娜很聰明地讓她們發洩了情緒，等到這陣哀戚快要過去的時候，她就帶著咖啡壺來解救她們了。

「好啦，各位親愛的姑娘們，要記住你們母親說的話，不要苦惱。過來喝杯咖啡，然後咱們都開始工作，給這個家增光吧。」

「『要懷抱希望，保持忙碌。』這是我們的座右銘，那就讓我們看看誰牢牢記住這句話。我要去瑪區嬸婆家了，就像平常一樣。噢，只是她又要訓話了！」喬說著，她精神又回來了，喝著咖啡。

「我要去我那金家了，不過我真希望能留在家裡，料理這裡的事情呢。」梅格說，她希望自己沒把眼睛哭得那麼紅就好了。

「用不著。我和貝絲會把家裡照顧好的。」艾美用一種很了不起的神情插嘴說。

「漢娜會告訴我們該做什麼事，等你們回家以後，我們會把家裡每件事都整理好的。」貝絲說，一點也不耽擱就拿出她的拖把和洗碗碟的桶子。

「我認為焦慮是件非常有趣的事。」艾美一邊吃著糖一邊若有所思地說。

其他姐妹們都忍不住笑了起來，心情也好些了。

　　父親那邊的消息讓女孩子們大為放心，因為雖然他病情嚴重，但是最好、最溫柔的護士的在場，已經帶給他好的影響了。布魯克先生每天都會寄來快信，梅格既然身為一家之主，便堅持要唸這些快信，這一週時間過去，快信也變得越來越讓人振奮。起初每個人都急著要寫信，而其中一個以和華盛頓通信為傲的姐妹就會把鼓鼓的信封仔仔細細地塞進信箱裡。

第 17 章
忠誠的小人兒

「梅格，我想你應該去看看胡梅爾家人了。你知道媽媽要我們不要忘了他們。」瑪區太太離開十天後貝絲說。

「我太累了，今天下午不想去。」梅格回答，她一邊縫衣服一邊舒舒服服搖著搖椅。

「你可不可以去呢，喬？」貝絲問。

「我還感冒著，風雨太大了。」

「我還以為你幾乎都好了。」

「我的病好到可以和羅瑞出去，可是還沒有好到可以去胡梅爾家的程度。」喬笑著說，不過她倒是為了自己的矛盾有些羞愧之色。

「你為什麼不自己去？」梅格問。

「我已經都每天去了啊，可是他們家的小娃娃生病了，而我又不知道怎麼辦。胡梅爾太太出門去工作，洛蒂辰在照顧小娃娃，可是他的病越來越重，我想你們或者漢娜應該去一下。」

貝絲懇切地說，梅格答應第二天去。

「向漢娜要些流質食物帶去，貝絲，空氣對你會有好處。」喬說著，帶著歉意又加上一句：「我會去，不過我要先寫完我的東西。」

「我頭疼，我也很累，所以我想你們誰會去。」貝絲說。

「艾美很快就會回來了，她可以替我們去。」梅格提議。

「那我就休息一下，等她回來吧。」

於是貝絲就躺在沙發上，而其他人也回到各自的工作上，胡梅爾一家人就被她們忘記了。一個小時過去了，艾美沒有回家，梅格到她房裡試穿一件新洋裝，喬沉迷在她的故事裡，漢娜在廚房火爐前呼呼大睡。這時候貝絲悄悄戴上兜帽，在籃子裡裝了些要給那些可憐孩子的零星東西，就出門走進冷冽的空氣中；她的頭昏沉沉，那雙有耐心的眼中則是憂傷的神色。她回來時已經很晚了，沒有人看到她靜靜上了樓，把自己關在母親的房裡。半個小時後，喬到「媽媽的衣櫃」裡找什麼東西，看到貝絲坐在醫藥箱上面，神情凝重，眼睛紅紅的，手裡拿著一瓶樟腦。

「哎喲喂呀！出了什麼事啦？」喬大喊一聲，貝絲伸出一隻手，像是警告她不要靠近，然後立刻問。

「你是不是得過猩紅熱？」

「好幾年前，在梅格得的時候得過了。怎麼啦？」

「那我就告訴你吧。噢，喬，那個小娃娃死了！」

「什麼小娃娃？」

「胡梅爾太太的小寶寶，她還沒有回到家，小寶寶就死在我腿上了。」貝絲抽抽搭搭地說著。

「可憐的人兒，那多可怕呀！我應該去的。」喬一臉懊悔的神情坐在母親的大椅子上，把妹妹摟進懷裡。

「那不可怕，喬，只是好悲傷喔！我一下子就看得出他病得

更重了，可是洛蒂辰說她媽媽去找醫生了，所以我就接過小嬰兒，讓洛蒂辰休息一下。小嬰兒好像睡著了，可是他忽然輕輕哭了一聲，全身發抖，然後就不動了。我想讓他的腳暖和一點，洛蒂辰也給他喝了一些牛奶，但是他動也不動，我就知道他死了。」

「別哭，親愛的！那你怎麼辦？」

「我就只是坐在那裡，輕輕抱著他，等到胡梅爾太太帶了醫生回來了。醫生說他死了，然後他看了看亨利區和米娜，他們兩個人都喉嚨痛。『是猩紅熱呢，夫人。你應該早點叫我來的。』他很不高興地說。胡梅爾太太說她沒錢，本來想自己把嬰兒治好的，可是現在已經太遲了，她只能求他幫助其他孩子，並且希望他能好心不收錢。這時候他才笑了笑，也比較溫和了。可是這件事很悲慘，我就在那裡跟他們一起哭，然後他突然轉過身要我回家，吃些顛茄葉[4]，不然我也會得病。」

「不，不會的！」喬大喊一聲，露出驚恐的神情把她抱得更緊。「噢，貝絲，如果你生病了，我永遠不會原諒我自己！我們該怎麼辦？」

「別害怕，我猜我不會很嚴重。我去查了媽媽看的那本書，書上說開始的時候會頭痛、喉嚨痛，還有像我那種奇怪的感覺；所以我吃了一些顛茄，現在我覺得好些了。」貝絲說著把兩隻冰冷的手放在滾燙的額頭上，想要作出若無其事的樣子。

4　一種藥草，用以治療猩紅熱。

「要是媽媽在家就好了！」喬嘆道，她抓起書，心裡感覺華盛頓實在太遠了。她看了一頁的內容，看了看貝絲，摸摸她的額頭又朝她喉部看去，然後正色地說：「你每天去照顧小嬰兒，去了有一個多星期，又跟其他也會發病的人在一起，所以恐怕你也會生病了，貝絲。我要告訴漢娜，生病的事情她都知道。」

「別讓艾美進來，她從沒有得過這個病，我不想把病傳給她。你和梅格會不會再得病呢？」貝絲焦急地問。

「大概不會吧。就算得了也無所謂，我是活該，自私自利，讓你去那裡，自己待在家裡寫些垃圾東西！」喬走出去找漢娜商量，嘴裡一邊喃喃說道。

漢娜這個好人立刻醒來了，馬上就先向喬保證說她不用擔心，每個人都會得猩紅熱，只要正確治療不會有人死的。這些喬全都相信，所以她們上樓去叫梅格的時候，她覺得輕鬆許多了。

「我告訴你們我們要怎麼辦，」漢娜檢查了貝絲，也問了她一些話以後說，「我們去請班斯大夫來給你檢查一下，好確定我們做得沒錯，然後我們把艾美送到瑪區嬸婆家住段時間，讓她不會受到影響，你們兩個人中的一個可以待在家裡一、兩天，給貝絲解解悶。」

「當然是我囉，我最大。」梅格說，她看起來很焦慮，也很自責。

「是我！因為是我害她生病的。我跟媽媽說我會做零星的雜事，結果我沒有做。」喬毅然地說。

「你要誰陪呢，貝絲？只需要一個人就行了。」漢娜說。

「喬。」貝絲說著神色滿足地把頭靠在姐姐身上，解決了這個問題。

「我去告訴艾美。」梅格說，她覺得有一點點不好受，不過大體上倒還放了心，因為她不像喬那麼喜歡看護的工作。

艾美當下就反抗了，她激動地說她情願得猩紅熱也不要去瑪區嬸婆家。梅格跟她講道理、好言相勸，甚至命令，全都沒有用。艾美說她就是不要去，於是梅格絕望地丟下她去問漢娜該怎麼辦。她還沒回來，羅瑞卻走進客廳，發現艾美在啜泣，頭埋在沙發靠墊裡。她把事情原委告訴他，希望羅瑞能安慰她，但是羅瑞卻只是把雙手插在口袋裡在房裡走來走去，一邊輕輕吹口哨，一邊皺著眉頭深思。很快他就在她身邊坐下來，用他最甜蜜的語氣說：「你要懂事，聽她們的話。不，別哭，你聽聽我的快樂計畫嘛。你去瑪區嬸婆家住，我每天都會去帶你出來玩，坐馬車或者是散步，我們可以玩得很開心。那不是比在這裡悶悶不樂要好嗎？」

「我不想被人當成累贅一樣地送走。」艾美用一種自尊心受損的口氣說。

「哎呀，小朋友，這是為了使你身體健康呀。你不希望生病吧？」

「我當然不希望，可是我敢說我一定會生病的，因為我一直都和貝絲一起。」

「就是因為這個原因，你才應該立刻離開，這樣你才能躲過。換換空氣，小心注意，就會使你身體健康的。就算不能完全

避免，至少發燒也比較輕微一些。我勸你最好盡快離開，猩紅熱可不是開玩笑的，小姐。」

「可是瑪區嬸婆家好無聊，她脾氣又壞。」艾美說，看起來很害怕的樣子。

「如果我每天都去找你，告訴你貝絲的情形，還帶你四處閒逛，你就不會無聊啦。老太太喜歡我，我也會盡可能討好她，那不管我們做什麼，她都不會囉唆了。」

「你會帶我坐馬車出去嗎？」

「用我身為紳士的榮譽發誓。」

「而且每天都來？」

「你看我是不是每天都來嘛。」

「而且要等貝絲身體一好起來就帶我回家？」

「一分鐘也不差。」

「還要去看戲喔，真的去喔？」

「如果可以的話，去看十幾場都行。」

「呃，那麼，我就去吧。」艾美慢慢說著。

「這才乖！你叫梅格來，告訴她說你聽話了。」羅瑞說著，讚許地拍了拍她，這個動作比他說的「聽話」更教她不快。

梅格和喬跑下樓來看看這個才剛剛發生的奇蹟；覺得自己很偉大、又肯犧牲自己的艾美說如果醫生說貝絲會生病，她願意去。

「可愛的小妹妹怎麼樣了？」羅瑞問。他最疼貝絲，不覺流露出更多的焦慮。

「她現在躺在媽媽的床上，感覺好多了。小嬰兒的死讓她很難過，不過我相信她只是著了涼。漢娜說她是這麼想，可是她看起來很憂心的樣子，這一點教我不安。」梅格說。

「這是多麼艱苦的人生呀！」喬煩躁地撥弄自己頭髮。「我們才解決了一個問題，就又來了一個問題。媽媽走了以後好像沒有任何東西可以依靠了，我感到很茫然。」

「哎呀，你別把自己弄成個刺蝟的樣子好不好？這樣子很不妥當。把頭髮整一整吧，喬。你說我要不要拍電報給你媽媽，或者做什麼事？」羅瑞問，他一直不能適應朋友那頭漂亮頭髮不見了的這件事。

「我正為這件事傷腦筋呢，」梅格說。「我想如果貝絲真的生病了的話，我們應該告訴她，可是漢娜說不行，因為媽媽不能丟下爸爸，這只會讓他們兩個人心急。貝絲不會病很久，漢娜又知道該怎麼辦。媽媽說過要我們聽她的話，所以我想我們必須聽，可是我覺得這樣好像又不完全對。」

「嗯，我也不知道該說什麼，不然等大夫來過以後你們去問我爺爺好了。」

「好。喬，你馬上去請班斯大夫過來，」梅格發號施令。「要等他來看過以後我們才能決定任何事情。」

「你別動啦，喬。我可是這個家的小跑腿喔。」羅瑞說著拿起帽子。

班斯大夫來了，說貝絲有發燒的症狀，不過可能只是輕微的，不過他聽了胡梅爾家的事以後臉色凝重。他要艾美立刻離開

家，還給她準備一些東西，以保安全。她在喬和羅瑞的護送下離開家，氣派得很呢。

瑪區嬸婆用她一貫的「熱誠」接待他們。

「你們要做什麼啊？」她問，透過眼鏡的目光十分銳利，這時候坐在她椅背上頭的鸚鵡叫著：

「走開！男孩子不准到這裡！」

羅瑞退到窗邊，於是喬就把事情經過說了。

「果然不出我所料，誰教大人准你們跟那些窮人家孩子混在一起！艾美可以住下來，如果她沒有生病，還可以幫點忙，我相信她絕對會生病的——現在看起來就像了。別哭，孩子，聽人吸鼻子就教我擔心呢。」

艾美正要哭出來，但是羅瑞偷偷去扯鸚鵡的尾巴，「波利」受驚地嘎嘎叫著，還喊道：

「哎喲喂呀！」牠叫得好滑稽，讓艾美反而笑了出來。

「你們媽媽信上有沒有說什麼？」老太太聲音沙啞地問。

「我爸爸身體好多了。」喬極力保持冷靜地說。

「哦？是嗎？啊，恐怕也維持不長久吧！瑪區一向體力不行的。」老太太的回答確實讓人不敢恭維。「哈哈！千萬別說死，吸點鼻菸吧，再見，再見！」波利尖聲叫喚著，還跳來跳去，並且用爪子去抓扯牠尾巴的羅瑞戴的帽子。

「閉嘴，你這隻粗俗的老東西！還有，喬，你最好趁早回家去，這麼晚了還跟一個毛躁男孩子閒晃太不成體統了——」

「閉嘴，你這隻粗俗的老東西！」波利大喊，跳下椅子，跑

過去啄這個「毛躁男孩子」，而後者正為了最後一句話笑得全身抖動呢。

　　「我想我大概沒辦法忍受，不過我會試試看。」只剩艾美和瑪區嬸婆在一起時，她想道。

　　「快滾，你這個醜八怪！」波利尖叫起來，聽到這句粗魯的話，艾美終於忍不住啜泣了。

第 18 章
黯淡的日子

貝絲果然是得了猩紅熱,而且比任何人想得都嚴重,只除了漢娜和醫生兩個人。姐姐們對此病一無所知,而羅倫斯先生又不能來看她,所以漢娜就照自己的方式處理一切,忙碌的班斯大夫盡心盡力,而把很多事留給這絕佳的護士去處理。梅格怕傳染給全家人,於是待在家裡管理家事。她寫信給母親時絕口不提貝絲生病的事,自己卻是焦慮又感到一絲愧疚。

喬日日夜夜全心全意照顧貝絲,這件工作並不難,因為貝絲非常有耐心,只要能控制自己,總是不怨天不尤人地忍受著病痛。可是有時候她發著高燒,就會開始用沙啞而且斷斷續續的聲音說話,還會在被單上頭彈琴,並且想要唱歌,但是喉嚨卻腫得唱不出歌來;有時候她會不認得周圍那些熟悉的面孔,反而張冠李戴地亂喊,並且哀求母親過來。這時候喬害怕了,梅格也求漢娜讓她寫信把實情告訴母親,就連漢娜也說她「會想想看這件事,不過眼前是還沒有什麼危險就是了」。華盛頓寄來的一封信更增添了她們的麻煩,因為瑪區先生的病又復發了,有好長一段時間不能有回家的打算。

十二月一日對她們而言的確是個淒冷的一天:刺骨的冷風颼起,大雪簌簌下著,這一年已經準備走向盡頭。這天早晨班斯大

夫來了以後，對著貝絲看了很久，把她火熱的手放在他自己手中
一會兒再輕輕放下，低聲對漢娜說：

「如果瑪區太太能離得開丈夫的話，最好是請她回來吧！」

漢娜不說一語地點點頭，她的嘴唇緊張地抽動著。梅格跌坐
到一張椅子裡，好像一聽到這些話她四肢的力量全都消失了一
樣。喬臉色蒼白地站了一會兒後，立刻跑到客廳抓起電報，匆匆
穿戴好衣帽就衝出屋子，到外頭的風雪中。她很快就回來了，正
無聲無息地脫下斗篷時，羅瑞拿著一封信走進來，信上說瑪區先
生再次康復了。喬很感激地看了信，但是心中的重擔並沒有減
輕，她的臉上充滿了愁苦的神色，羅瑞很快就問：

「怎麼回事？貝絲情況惡化了嗎？」

「我已經請我媽媽趕快回來了。」喬說，她哭喪著臉去扯她
的橡膠鞋。

「很好，喬！是你自己要這麼做的嗎？」羅瑞問，他扶她坐
在門廳的椅子上，還幫她把不聽話的靴子脫掉，因為他看到她兩
隻手抖得厲害。

「不是，是大夫叫我們的。」

「噢，喬，不會這麼糟吧？」羅瑞神情驚愕地叫道。

「是這麼糟了，她不認得我們了；她看起來不是我的貝絲，
而現在又沒有人在旁邊幫助我們面對這種情況：爸爸媽媽都不
在，而上帝又似乎遙不可及，我根本找不到祂！。」

喬的淚水從臉頰上滑落，可憐的她無助地伸出一隻手，像是
在黑暗中摸索一般。羅瑞便握住她的手，喉嚨像哽住了一樣，但

163

他盡可能輕聲細語地說：

「我在這裡，你可以依靠我，喬，親愛的！」

她無法言語，不過她確實「依靠」著他，而這隻友情的手安撫了她哀傷的心。「謝謝你，羅瑞，我現在已經好多了。」

「你要懷著樂觀的希望，這樣可以幫助你，喬。你母親很快就會到家了，那時候一切就都沒事了。」

「我很高興我爸爸好多了，現在她離開他就不會覺得很難過了。」喬嘆了一口氣。

「我昨天就打電報給你母親了，布魯克回電說她會立刻動身，今天晚上就會到家，那時候一切就都沒事了。你高不高興我拍電報了？」

羅瑞話說得飛快，立刻就漲紅了臉，十分興奮；因為他這計畫是偷偷進行的，怕讓這些女孩子失望，也怕會傷害到貝絲。喬的臉色變白，立刻離開椅子，他一停了話，她就用兩手摟住他的脖子並快活地大叫一聲，把他嚇了一大跳：「噢，羅瑞！噢，媽媽！我好高興喔！」她沒有再哭起來，而是歇斯底里地笑著，全身顫抖，緊緊抱著她的朋友，彷彿這突如其來的消息讓她有點慌亂。羅瑞雖然感到很驚異，倒是相當鎮定。他安慰地拍拍她的背，發現她正在回復平靜了，就羞怯地親了她一、兩下，這可教喬立刻回過神來。她抓住欄杆，把他輕輕推開，上氣不接下氣地說：「噢，不要！我不是故意的，我真的是太可怕了。可是你真是個好人，雖然漢娜那麼說你還是拍了電報，所以我忍不住就撲到你身上了。你告訴我全部的情形吧──別再給我酒喝了，喝酒

才害我這樣的。」

「我不在乎呀，」羅瑞一邊整理領帶一邊笑著說。「是這樣的，我很不安心，我爺爺也是。我們認爲你母親應該知道這件事的。萬一貝絲——你知道的，出了什麼事的話，她絕對不會原諒我們的。所以我就跟我爺爺說我們該做點什麼事，於是我昨天就飛快趕去電報局了，你媽媽會回來，我知道，夜班火車要在清晨兩點鐘到，我會去接她。你只要掩藏你的快樂，讓貝絲平靜無事，等那位好心的女士回家就成了。」

「羅瑞，你眞是個天使！我要怎麼感謝你呢？」

「你再撲過來啊，我還挺喜歡的呢。」羅瑞淘氣地說。

「不用了，多謝。等你爺爺來的時候，我請他當你的代理人吧。別鬧了，回家去休息吧，你半夜還得起來呢。上天保佑你，羅瑞，上天保佑你！」

這對姐妹永遠也忘不了那個晚上。因爲她們守護著妹妹時，內心卻有一股任誰在相同情況下都能同理、懼怕的無力感，使她們根本睡不著。

「要是上帝放過貝絲，我永遠都不會再抱怨事情了。」梅格誠誠懇懇地低聲說。

「要是上帝放過貝絲，我會一輩子愛祂、侍奉祂。」喬同樣懇切地說。

「我希望我沒有心臟，我的心好痛。」過了一段時間後，梅格嘆口氣說。

「如果人生經常都要像這般艱苦，我不知道我們要怎麼過完

165

一生。」她妹妹心灰意冷地加上一句。

這時候鐘敲了十二點，她們兩人望著貝絲，把自己的事全忘了，因爲她們彷彿看到貝絲蒼白的臉上有了改變。房裡一片死寂，只有外頭冷風的呼嘯劃破深深的靜寂。已經過了兩點，喬站在窗邊，心想這個世界裏在裹屍布似的白雪當中，看起來是多麼淒涼；這時候她聽到床邊有些動靜，她立刻轉過身，看到梅格在母親的安樂椅前面跪下，臉孔掩住了。一陣駭人的恐懼冰冷地襲上喬的全身，她想：「貝絲死了！梅格不敢告訴我！」

她立刻回到原來的位置，在她激動的目光下，似乎出現了一場重大的改變。那因爲發熱而變得潮紅和痛苦的表情消失了，那張受人疼愛的小臉在完全的安詳中，看起來如此蒼白和平靜，使得喬既不想哭也不感覺傷悲。她低低俯身在這最心愛的妹妹之上，深情地親吻她濕濕的額頭，並且柔聲低語：「再見了，我的貝絲，永別了！」

漢娜像是被這番騷動喚醒了一樣，突地從睡夢中醒來，急忙趕到床邊；她看了看貝絲，又去摸了她兩隻手，接著湊到她嘴邊去聽，然後把圍裙從頭上一把脫了，坐在搖椅裡來回搖著。她低聲嘆道：「燒已經退了，她睡著了。現在她的皮膚很濕，呼吸也順暢了。讚美上天！噢，天啊！」

這對姐妹還不敢相信這快樂的實情呢，大夫就過來證實了。「是的，我親愛的孩子們，我相信這個小姑娘這次可以熬過了。不要吵到她，讓她睡覺，等她醒來以後，就給她──」

她們該給她什麼，誰也沒聽到，因爲她倆悄悄走進暗黑的門

廳，坐在樓階上彼此緊緊相擁，開心得說不出話來。當梅格和喬
這次漫長而哀傷的守夜結束，兩人朝屋外的清晨景象看出去時，
兩雙沉重的眼睛看到的，是從沒見過的美麗日出，是從沒有見過
的可愛世界。

　　「看起來像是童話世界呢。」梅格站在窗簾後看著耀眼的景
象說著，兀自微笑。

　　「你聽！」喬大喊一聲，立刻跳起來。

　　沒錯，樓下門口響起了鈴聲，接著是漢娜的叫聲，然後是羅
瑞的說話聲，他輕聲欣喜地說：「各位姑娘，你們的媽媽回家
了！回家了！」

第 19 章
艾美的遺囑

　　家中發生這些事情的時候，艾美在瑪區嬸婆家的日子才難過呢。她深切地感受到自己流放在外，而生平頭一次明白在家裡是多麼被人疼、受人寵。瑪區嬸婆從來也不會寵任何人，她對這種事是很不以為然的，不過她倒存心要表現和善，因為這個行為乖巧的小姑娘很討她的喜歡。但是瑪區嬸婆那些規矩和命令、她那些一本正經的行事風格及那些冗長乏味的話，全教艾美煩得不得了。這位老太太發現這孩子比她的姐姐們都聽話、脾氣好之後，覺得自己有責任盡可能要消滅家庭裡自由和放任給孩子的惡劣影響。於是她盯住艾美，像自己在六十年前被教導的那樣教導她，這可讓艾美膽戰心驚，覺得自己像隻蒼蠅，落入一隻嚴格的蜘蛛所織的網中。

　　要不是有羅瑞和女僕艾絲特，她覺得自己永遠也熬不過這段可怕的時間。艾絲特是法國人，她和她的主人——她稱作「夫人」——一起生活好多年，她對這位老太太有一定的操縱權，因為後者不能沒有她。她的真名是艾絲特兒，可是瑪區嬸婆要她把名字改了，她也照做，不過說有個條件，就是不能要她改變宗教。她很喜歡這位「小姐」，在艾美陪她為夫人的衣服縫蕾絲花邊的時候，會說些在法國生活時候的稀奇故事，讓艾美開心。她

也准她在這幢大宅裡四處閒逛，細看收藏在大衣櫥和舊箱子裡的奇怪而且漂亮的東西，瑪區嬸婆很愛收集東西。艾美最喜歡的是一個印度櫃子，櫃子全是奇特的一格格抽屜和祕密空間，裡面放著各種各樣的擺飾品。細細觀賞並且擺放這些東西，帶給艾美很大的滿足，尤其是那個珠寶盒。

「小姐可以選的話，會想要哪一樣？」艾絲特問，她總是坐在旁邊看著，事後再把這些值錢的東西鎖上。

「我最喜歡鑽石，可是這裡沒有鍊子，我喜歡項鍊，項鍊很適合我呢。如果可以的話，我會選這個。」艾美回答，她用著羨慕的眼神望著一串黃金和黑檀木珠串，這個珠串下還吊著一個同樣材質的沉甸甸的十字架。

「我真希望知道瑪區嬸婆死了以後這些漂亮東西要怎麼辦。」她說，她慢慢放回這串閃亮的念珠，然後把首飾寶盒一個個關上。

「要給您和您的姐姐們，我知道的。夫人告訴我了。我是她遺囑的見證人，她的遺願是這樣的。」艾絲特微笑著輕聲說。

「那多好呀！可是我希望她現在就給我們。拖——延——可不是件快樂的事呢。」艾美說著，並朝鑽石看了最後一眼。

「年輕姑娘佩戴這些東西嫌早了些。珍珠是給最先訂婚的人——夫人說了的。我覺得您走的時候夫人會送您那個小小的土耳其玉戒指，因為夫人很稱讚您的乖巧禮貌。」

「你也這樣想嗎？唉，要是我能得到那個可愛的戒指，多乖我都會願意呢！」艾美說著，並開心地試戴了這枚藍色戒指，她

有堅強的決心要得到它。

從這天起,她簡直乖得可以,老太太爲自己訓練的成果感到十分滿意。艾美決定立下遺囑,就像瑪區嬸婆一樣,那麼萬一她眞的生病死掉,她的財產可以公平而且大方地分給別人。光是想到要把在她眼中和嬸婆的首飾同樣珍貴的小小財富給別人,她都會感到一陣心痛呢。

她在一次遊戲時間裡靠著艾絲特在某些法律名詞方面的幫忙,盡可能地寫好了這份重要文件,讓這位好脾氣的法國女人簽了名。艾美鬆了一口氣,就把它放在一邊,準備給羅瑞看,她想要羅瑞做第二個見證人。這天是個下雨的日子,於是她就帶著「波利」到樓上一間大房間去玩。這間房間裡有一個衣櫃,裡面全是老式的服裝,艾絲特准她去玩這些衣服;她最喜歡的消遣就是穿上那些褪了色的織錦衣裙,在長鏡子前面神氣地走來走去,行莊嚴的彎腰屈膝禮,並且讓裙襬在地面掃過,發出她很喜歡聽的窸窣聲。這一天她正忙著這些,根本沒聽到羅瑞按鈴的聲音,也沒有看到他探頭進來看著她 —— 這時候她正神情肅穆地大步來回,一邊搧動扇子一邊神氣地把頭揚起,她的頭上包著一條粉紅色的包頭巾,和她的藍色織錦裙、黃色鋪錦襯裙形成奇怪的對比。

羅瑞好不容易克制了嬉鬧的念頭,免得惹火了這位女王陛下,他敲了敲門,蒙這位女王接見。

「拜託你唸一下這個,然後告訴我合不合法、對不對。我覺得我應該寫下這些,因爲生命無常,我不希望我死了以後還讓人很不高興。」

羅瑞咬著嘴唇，稍稍把臉轉開，不去看這個哀傷的說話者，然後用一種值得讚頌的正經態度，一字一字仔細唸出：

我的遺囑

本人，艾美·柯蒂斯·瑪區，係在心智健全情況下將我的世間財產遺贈如下：

我父親：可以得到我最好的圖畫、素描、地圖以及藝術品，包括畫框。還有一百元整，他可以自由處置。

我母親：我所有的衣服——除了藍色有口袋的圍兜之外；還有我的相片和獎牌，附上我許多的愛。

我親愛的姐姐梅格：我要給她我的土耳其玉戒指（如果我能得到它的話），還有我那個上頭有鴿子圖樣的綠盒子，以及我那個真正的蕾絲花邊，送給她當頸飾；另外我再送她我為她畫的素描，算是紀念物，讓她記著她的「小丫頭」。

喬：我要送給她我的胸針，就是用火蠟補過的那個，還要送她銅的墨水瓶架——瓶蓋被她弄丟了——和我最寶貴的石膏兔子，因為我把她的小說燒了我很難過。

貝絲（如果她活得比我久的話）：我要給她我的娃娃和小櫃子、我的扇子、我的亞麻領圈；如果她病好了，人也變瘦了，穿得下鞋子的話，我的便鞋也要送她。在此我也要為我開過老喬安娜的玩笑表達我的懊悔。

我的鄰居朋友狄奧多·羅倫斯：我要留給他我的紙板畫冊、我的一匹馬的陶土模型，不過他說過這匹馬連個頸子也沒有。同

時為了報答在困苦時刻他的善心，他可以任意在我的美術作品中間選一件，〈巴黎聖母院〉是最好的。

可敬的贊助人羅倫斯先生：我送給他我那個盒蓋上有一面鏡子的紫色盒子讓他裝他的筆，並且使他回想起那個過世的女孩，她謝謝他對她家人的恩情，尤其是對貝絲。

我希望我的好玩伴吉蒂‧布萊恩能夠收下那件藍色絲圍兜和我的金色珠珠的戒指，附上我的吻。

漢娜：我要送給她她想要的硬紙盒，和我所有的拼布作品，希望她能夠看到它們就想到我。

處置了所有貴重財產後，我希望人人都能滿意，不要責怪死者。我原諒每個人，也相信當號角吹起時我們都能再次相聚，阿門。

本人立此遺囑，簽名並封緘於西元後 1861 年 11 月 20 日。

艾美‧柯蒂斯‧瑪區

見證人：艾絲特‧佛爾納

狄奧多‧羅倫斯

最後一個名字是用鉛筆寫的，艾美解釋說他要再用墨水寫一遍，再把信封起。

「你怎麼會有這種想法？有人告訴你說貝絲把東西分送的事嗎？」羅瑞正色地問，艾美在他面前放了一小截紅色帶子，和封蠟、蠟燭、墨水台。

她解釋這件事的原因，然後焦急地問：「貝絲怎麼樣啦？」

「我不應該說的，不過既然都說了，我就告訴你吧。有一天她覺得自己病情很糟，所以她告訴喬說她要把她的琴留給梅格，把她的貓給你，那個可憐的舊娃娃給喬，喬會因為她而愛它的。她很難過自己沒有什麼東西可以送人，所以她要把她的頭髮送給我們其他人，還要給爺爺她最大最多的愛。她從來沒有想到要立遺囑。」

羅瑞一邊說一邊簽名、上封蠟，頭也沒有抬，直到一顆好大的淚珠滴到紙上。艾美的臉上滿是不解的神情，但是她只說：「是不是有時候也可以在遺囑上加上後記？」

「是的，這叫作『遺囑追加條款』。」

「那在我的遺囑裡加上一條追加條款吧──說我希望在我死後把我全部的鬃髮剪下來，分送給我的朋友。起先我忘了，不過我希望這樣做，雖然這樣子會破壞我的外觀。」

羅瑞把這一條加上去，為艾美這最後也是最大的犧牲露出微笑。然後他跟她玩了一個小時，對她所有的磨難也深感興趣。但是他要走的時候，艾美卻拉住他，顫抖著嘴唇低聲問：「貝絲是不是真的有危險？」

「恐怕是的，不過我們必須樂觀，所以不要哭喲，乖。」說著羅瑞像個哥哥一樣用一隻手臂摟住她，這個動作很讓她心安。

他走了以後，她走到她的小小教堂，在暮色中坐在那裡為貝絲祈禱；她的眼淚簌簌流下，胸口好痛，只覺得就算是一百萬個土耳其玉戒指，也不能撫慰她失去這個溫柔小姐姐的損失。

第 20 章

情愫

　　我想我找不出任何文字訴說這家人母女相會的情形。這種時刻美麗溫馨，是讓人去經歷的，但是要描述卻是非常地困難，所以我就把這個情景留給我的讀者們去想像，而只說這個家裡充滿了真正的快樂。梅格的溫柔心願終於實現了，因為當貝絲從那漫長而有療效的睡眠中醒來以後，她眼睛看到的第一樣東西就是那朵小小的玫瑰花和母親的臉。她身體虛弱得連驚嘆的力氣都沒有，只能微笑，挨近那雙環著她的手臂，感到自己的渴望終於滿足了。

　　這一天，這座城裡裡外外也許有很多快活的小女生，但是我個人認為，當艾美坐在母親懷裡訴說她的磨難，得到母親讚許的微笑和充滿疼愛的撫摸，她是那些人當中最快樂的了。她們還到了小禮拜堂裡，艾美告訴母親這個地方的目的，母親倒沒有反對。

　　「相反的，我很喜歡呢，乖孩子。」她把目光從布滿灰塵的念珠移到破舊的小本聖經，以及掛著綠葉花圈的聖像上。「當我們為事情煩惱和憂傷的時候，能有地方讓我們沉靜一下，這是非常好的想法呢。我們生活中常會有不如意，不過只要我們用正確的方法尋求援助，我們總是能熬過去的。我想我的小女兒也明白

這件事囉？」

「是的，媽媽。等我回家以後，我想要在大櫃子裡騰出一個
角落，放我的書和一幅同樣的這個聖像。我照著畫了這幅像，聖
母的臉畫得不好——她太漂亮了，我畫不出來。不過聖嬰畫得比
較好，我很喜歡。我喜歡把祂想成從前也是一個嬰兒，那樣我就
不會覺得距離很遙遠，而這樣子的想法可以幫助我。」

艾美指著坐在聖母膝頭的聖嬰時，瑪區太太看到她舉起的手
上有樣東西，不禁微微一笑。她沒有說什麼，不過艾美明白，停
頓了一會兒後嚴肅地說了：

「我本來要告訴你的，不過我忘了。這個戒指是嬸婆今天給
我的。她把我叫到她面前，然後親親我，就把戒指戴在我手指
上，說她很以我為榮，她希望我能一直待在這裡。她還給我這個
古怪的戒指釦，免得土耳其玉戒指戴不牢，因為它太大了。媽
媽，我想戴著，可不可以呢？」

「這戒指很漂亮，不過我想你戴這種飾物還太小了，艾
美。」瑪區太太說。

「我會盡量不要虛榮，」艾美說。「我想我不是因為它很漂
亮才喜歡它，而是像那個故事裡戴手鍊的女孩一樣，是為了提醒
我自己才戴的。」

「你是說要想到瑪區嬸婆？」她母親笑著問。

「不是的，是要提醒我不要自私自利。」艾美一臉的誠懇，
使她母親停住了笑，尊重地聽起她的小小計畫。

「最近我對自己一大堆不乖的事情想了很多，而自私就是其

中最不乖的事，所以我想要努力盡我所能去改掉。我很容易忘掉我的決心，不過如果我有個東西一直在身邊提醒，我猜我會表現得比較好。我可以試試這種方法嗎？」

「可以的，不過我對大櫃子的角落更有信心。親愛的，戴著你的戒指吧，盡你的力量去做，我想你是會成功的；因為有心向善，你就已經贏了半場戰爭了。我現在要回去看貝絲了。打起精神喲，小女兒，我們很快就可以把你接回來了。」

這天晚上，梅格正寫信給父親，要向他報告母親已安抵家門之時，喬一溜煙上了樓，進到貝絲的房間。她看到母親坐在平常的位置上，站了一會兒後，把手指頭在頭髮裡轉呀轉，舉止是憂慮的，而神情猶豫不定。

「有什麼事呀，親愛的？」瑪區太太問，她伸出一隻手，臉上是讓人信賴的神情。

「我要告訴你一件事，媽媽。」

「是梅格的事嗎？」

「您怎麼這麼快就猜到了？是呀，是她的事，雖然是件小事，可是卻讓我不安呢。」

「貝絲睡了，你小聲點說，把事情全告訴我。那個莫法特可沒有來家裡吧，我希望？」瑪區太太小聲地問。

「沒有，如果他來我絕對當他的面把門關上。」喬說著就在母親的腳邊坐下。「去年夏天梅格丟了一雙手套在羅倫斯家，結果只找回一隻。我們本來都忘記這件事了，後來是羅瑞告訴我說另外一隻被布魯克先生拿去了。他把手套放在背心口袋，有一次

手套掉出來，羅瑞就和他開玩笑，布魯克先生承認他喜歡梅格，但是不敢講，因為梅格太年輕而他又太窮。你看，這是不是很糟糕的情況呢？」

「你想梅格喜不喜歡他？」瑪區太太神色焦急地問。

「拜託！我對愛情和這種無稽之談一無所知！」喬大叫，口氣裡可笑地混雜著興趣和鄙視。「小說裡的女孩子表現戀愛的方式是驚慌失措和面紅耳赤、昏倒、日益消瘦、做出種種愚蠢的行為。而梅格可沒有這些事，她能吃能睡，理智得很；我提到那個男人的時候她也直直盯著我，只有在羅瑞開情侶玩笑的時候才會有一點臉紅。我不准羅瑞開她玩笑，可是他根本不管我。」

「那麼你認為梅格對約翰沒有意思了？」

「誰？」喬瞪大眼睛問。

「布魯克先生啊。我現在都叫他約翰。我們是在醫院裡的時候就開始了，他很喜歡我這樣叫他呢。」

「噢，天啊！我知道你會站在他那邊了：他之前對爸爸很好，如果梅格願意嫁他，你不會把他趕走，而會答應的。好卑劣的傢伙！討好爸爸，幫你的忙，就為了哄你們好喜歡他！」喬憤怒地又扯了扯頭髮。

「親愛的，別生氣，我告訴你事情是怎麼發生的。約翰應羅倫斯先生之請陪我去醫院，他對可憐的爸爸盡心盡力，我們不由得越來越喜歡他。他對梅格是坦蕩蕩的，因為他告訴我們他愛她，但是他希望能先有個舒適的家，再向她求婚。他只希望我們准許他愛她，為她而努力，以及盡量讓她能愛他。他真的是個非

常優秀的青年，我們不能不聽他的話，不過我不贊成梅格這麼年輕就訂婚。」

「你不會希望她嫁個有錢人嗎？」喬問道，她母親的話在最後有一些遲疑。

「金錢是好東西，是有用的東西，喬。而我希望我的女兒們永遠不會急需要錢，也不會受太多錢的誘惑。我希望約翰能在某個正經事業裡做穩了，讓他有相當豐厚的收入，不要欠債，還能給梅格舒服的生活。我不會貪圖女兒們有多麼了不得的財富、多麼神氣的地位，或是豪門鉅富的婆家。如果地位和金錢是隨著愛情和美德一起而來，我會很感激地接受，並且為你們的好運感到高興；但是我從經驗裡得知，在一間樸素的小屋子裡，辛勤賺得每天的開銷、某些匱乏使得少許的快樂更加甜美，在這樣的家庭中會有何其多的真正快樂。梅格從簡陋的生活開始，我很滿足，因為如果我沒有看錯的話，她擁有一個好男人的真心，這方面就是富足的，而這要比大筆的財富更好。」

「我了解的，媽媽，也很同意你的看法，只是我對梅格很失望，因為我本來計畫要讓她嫁給羅瑞，一生一世過著豪華的生活。那樣不是很好嗎？」喬的神色開朗許多，她抬頭往上看。

「他比她年輕呢，你知道。」瑪區太太才剛開始說，就被喬打斷了──

「只小一點點。他比較老成，又高，只要他願意，他可以很像大人的。而且他有錢又大方，心地又好，也愛我們所有人。很可惜，我的計畫吹了。」

「恐怕羅瑞對梅格來說根本不像大人，而且目前也太心思不定，沒法讓人依靠。這種事情我們不能干預，而且最好不要滿腦子『浪漫的胡亂心思』，像你所說的，免得它破壞我們的友情。」

「哎呀，我不會的，可是我不喜歡看到事情弄得糾纏不清，亂成一團；我希望能在我們頭上戴熨斗讓我們不要長大，可是花蕾會長成玫瑰，小貓會長成大貓──越來越糟！」

「熨斗和貓是怎麼回事呀？」梅格問，她悄悄走進房裡，手裡拿著寫好的信。

「只是我的一段胡言亂語。我要去睡了，走吧。」喬說著，一邊伸直身體。

「很對，而且寫得很好。請再加上一句，說代向約翰送上我的關愛。」瑪區太太把信瀏覽了一下，遞了回去。

「你叫他『約翰』嗎？」梅格笑著問，那雙純真的眼睛低頭望著母親的眼睛。

「是呀，他就像我們的兒子一樣，我們都喜歡他呢。」瑪區太太回答，並且用一個銳利的目光回了女兒一眼。

「我很高興，他很寂寞呢。晚安媽媽。有你在家裡真是有說不出的安心呢。」梅格平靜地回答。

她母親給她的親吻十分溫柔，她走開後，瑪區太太用一種兼具滿意和遺憾的口氣說：「她現在還不愛約翰，但是她很快就會愛他了。」

第 21 章

坦途

　　之後幾週平靜的日子就像是暴風雨後的陽光一樣。家中的病患進步神速，瑪區先生也開始提到會在新年時早點回家。貝絲不久後也能躺在書房沙發上一整天，找事情給自己解悶了：她先是跟她喜歡的貓兒玩，不久後她就開始縫起娃娃的衣物了，因為這些活兒的進度都已經落後了。她從前那麼靈巧的手腳，如今僵硬又虛弱，所以喬每天都會用她強壯的手臂抱著她在屋子附近透透氣。梅格高高興興地為「小乖乖」做美味的食物，而把她白皙的雙手都弄得黑忽忽，還燙傷了；而忠於那枚戒指的艾美，為了慶祝自己終能回家，也拚命把自己的寶貝分送給姐姐們。

　　好幾天暖和的氣候果然帶來了一個晴朗的聖誕節。漢娜說「骨頭裡就能感覺到」當天會是少見的好天氣，事後證明她的預言可真準，因為每個人和每件事似乎都一定會順利。先是瑪區先生寫信來，說他很快就會回到她們身邊，然後是貝絲當天早上感覺身體格外地好，穿上了母親送的禮物——一件柔軟的深紅色美利諾羊毛長袍——之後就被很神氣地抬到窗前，觀賞喬和羅瑞獻上的禮物。這對打不倒的寶貝盡心盡力使自己不負盛名，因為他們像是傳說中的小精靈，在夜裡做活，變出一個滑稽的驚喜出來。只見花園裡站著一個好大的白雪堆起來的女孩子，頭上戴著

冬青的葉冠，一隻手提著一個裡頭有水果和鮮花的籃子，另一隻手上拿著一大本樂譜，一條彩虹色的毛毯披在她那冰雪的肩膀上，從她嘴裡伸出一條粉紅色的紙帶子，上頭是一首聖誕歌曲。

貝絲看到這張紙條笑得樂不可支，羅瑞來來回回跑著，把禮物一一送進來，而喬送禮物時說的那些話又是多麼滑稽呀！

「我快活極了，要是爸爸也在這裡的話，我恐怕就會高興得承受不了了。」貝絲心滿意足地嘆著氣說，讓喬抱她到書房裡休息一下，並且吃點喬送給她的香甜葡萄。喬加上一句「我也是」，還拍了拍她的口袋，她口袋裡是那本她想了好久的《渦堤孩》。

「我很確定我也是。」艾美也回應著說，一邊對著聖母聖子的雕刻沉思，這是她母親送給她的，放在一個很漂亮的畫框中。

「我當然也是！」梅格也叫道，她正在撫平她生平第一件絲質洋裝上銀光閃閃的衣褶。羅倫斯先生堅持要送她這件衣服。

「我怎麼可能不是？」瑪區太太心懷感激地說，她的目光從丈夫的信移到貝絲那張綻放笑容的臉。

在這個平凡的世界上，偶爾事情也會像故事書上那樣發生、讓人開心，而這是多大的安慰呀！在每個人都說她們已經快活得再也承受不了任何快樂事的半小時之後，這最後一件快樂的事也來了。羅瑞打開客廳門，靜靜地探頭進來，他的臉上滿是壓抑住的興奮表情，他的聲音有像是藏了什麼祕密似地快活，所以雖然他只是用一種奇怪的平淡語氣說：「這是送給瑪區家的另一份聖誕禮物。」但是每個人卻都跳了起來。

　　他的話還沒有完全說完，人就像是被拉開了一樣，在他位置上的是一個高大的男人，圍巾圍住了口鼻，正靠在另一個高個子男人的手臂上，這個人想要說話卻說不出來。當然屋裡所有人都迎過去，有幾分鐘的時間每個人似乎都不知道該怎麼辦，因為這麼一件最最奇怪的事發生了，卻沒有一個人說一個字。瑪區先生淹沒在四雙深情手臂的擁抱下，喬很丟臉地幾乎要昏過去，還得由羅瑞為她在放瓷器的櫃子裡找東西救治一番；布魯克先生斷斷續續解釋著，不小心親吻了梅格；而一向端莊的艾美也被一張凳子絆倒，索性連站也不站起來，逕自摟住父親的靴子，令人動容地大哭了起來。瑪區太太是第一個恢復正常的人，她舉起一隻手警告說：「噓！別忘了貝絲也在！」

　　不過已經來不及了，書房打開了，小小的紅色袍子出現在門口，喜悅將氣力注入貝絲虛弱的四肢中，她直奔過來，撲進父親懷中。這以後發生的事，我們就別管了吧，因為這些滿足的心滿溢出快樂，沖走過去的愁苦，只留下此刻的甜美。

　　瑪區先生說他很想要給她們一個驚喜，等到好天氣來臨以後大夫准他利用這個時機，他又說布魯克有多麼盡心盡力、他是個多麼值得尊敬又正直的年輕人。話說到這裡，瑪區先生停頓了一下，朝著正用力撥著柴火的梅格看了一眼，再詢問式地對妻子抬了眉毛，為什麼這麼做，留待讀者自己去想像；而瑪區太太輕輕點點頭，頗突兀地問他要不要吃點東西，這是什麼原因呢，也留待讀者去猜測了。喬看到這一切，也明白這目光是怎麼回事，就悶悶不樂地邁著大步走去拿酒和牛肉汁。她用力把門摔上時還喃

喃自語：「我最討厭棕色眼睛有涵養的年輕人！」

　　從來沒有一頓聖誕大餐有他們這頓那麼精采。光是看漢娜端上來的肥美火雞就很可觀了，火雞肚裡塞滿了餡料，烤得黃澄澄，裝飾得漂漂亮亮；棗子布丁也是同樣地美觀可口，幾乎是入口即化。入口即化的還有果凍，艾美像是一隻追到蜂蜜罐裡的蒼蠅，開懷大吃。每件事都很順利，這真是拜天之賜，漢娜說：「因為我腦子亂成一團。我沒把布丁放進烤箱，把葡萄乾塞進火雞肚裡，這還真是奇蹟呢。」

　　羅倫斯先生和他的孫子也和他們共餐，還有布魯克先生——喬偷偷對著他露出不悅之色，讓羅瑞樂不可支。餐桌首位並排放著兩張安樂椅，貝絲和父親各據一位，少量地吃著火雞肉和一點水果。他們舉杯互祝健康、說故事、唱歌，像老人家說的那樣「緬懷往日」，過了非常快活的一段時光。本來計畫了要坐雪車出遊，但是女孩子們不肯離開父親，所以客人們也早早離開，這快樂的一家人圍著爐火坐著。

　　「才一年以前，我們還在為了我們要過個悽慘的聖誕節哀嘆，你們還記得嗎？」閒聊許多事情的漫長談話過後，喬打破了短暫的靜默開口。

　　「大體上說來，這一年還挺愉快的！」梅格說，她對著爐火露出微笑，為了自己保持端莊地對待了布魯克先生而慶幸。

　　「我覺得這一年很辛苦呢。」艾美用若有所思的眼神望著照亮在她戒指上的火光說道。

　　「我很高興這一年已經結束了，因為爸爸回到我們身邊。」

坐在父親膝頭上的貝絲輕聲說。

「這是一條很艱難的路呢,我的小朝聖者們,尤其在這條路的後半。不過我們很勇敢地往前走了,我想你們的重擔可以說很快就要卸下了。」瑪區先生用做父親的滿意神情看著圍在他旁邊的四張年輕臉孔。

「你怎麼知道?是媽媽告訴你的嗎?」喬問。

「媽媽說的不多,從小草就可以看得出風向。而且我今天也有些發現呢。」

「噢,你告訴我們是什麼樣的發現嘛!」坐在父親旁邊的梅格喊著。

「這就是其中一樣,」父親說著拿起搭在他椅子扶手上那隻手,指了指粗糙的手指、手背上一處燙傷的地方,和手心兩、三處起硬皮的地方。「我還記得從前這隻手是白皙而且光滑的,而你一心一意,就是要保持它的美麗。從前這隻手很漂亮,但是對我來說,現在它更漂亮,因為在這些看似瑕疵的地方,我能看出它的過往情形。這處燙傷是拋開虛榮才換得的,而這隻粗硬的手心換來的是比水泡要好的東西,而我相信這些被針刺到的手指縫出來的東西會維持得更久,因為在它的一針一線中,縫進了太多的善良。梅格,我親愛的女兒,比起一雙細白的手或是時尚方面的本事,我更珍視女孩子的持家本領。我對於能夠握住這麼一隻善良、勤勞的手感到很自豪,我希望不要很快就有人來提親,把這雙手的主人給帶走了。」

如果梅格希望得到耐心工作好幾個小時的報酬,那麼她父親大手用力地握緊和他投給她的讚許笑容，就是這個報酬了。

「那喬怎麼樣呢？請爸爸說些好話吧，因為她很努力，而且對我好好喲。」貝絲對著父親耳朵說。

他笑了，注視著坐在對面、棕色臉上有少見的溫柔表情的高個子女孩。

「雖然鬢髮剪短了，但是我卻看不到我一年前離開時那個『喬兒子』了。」瑪區先生說。「我看到的是一個衣領夾得挺直、鞋帶綁得整齊的年輕淑女，她既不吹口哨、說粗話，也不像以前那樣躺在地毯上。現在她的臉因為看顧病人和焦慮而瘦了，也蒼白了，但是我喜歡看著這張臉，因為它變得柔和了，她的聲音也放低了。她不再橫衝直撞，走起路來是靜悄悄的；她還像個母親一樣照顧一個小朋友，這讓我很欣慰。我挺懷念從前那個野丫頭，但是如果取而代之的是一個堅強、助人的溫柔女郎，我也會非常滿意了。」

聽到父親的稱讚，喬那雙銳利的眼睛黯淡了一分鐘，瘦削的臉孔在爐火照射下淡成粉紅色，她覺得自己倒的確有些受之無愧。

「輪到貝絲了。」艾美說，她很希望輪到自己，不過她願意等一等。

「她能說的不多，我怕說太多她就會溜走了，不過她已經不像從前那麼地害羞了。」父親高興地說，但是想起他差一點就要失去這個女兒，便把她摟得更緊，並且用臉頰貼著她的臉，溫柔地說，「你總算平安無事了，貝絲，求主保佑，我要盡力讓你平

安。」

　　過了一陣子的安靜之後，他低頭看看坐在他腳邊小凳子上的艾美，揉了揉她那頭閃亮的頭髮：

　　「我注意到艾美在吃晚餐時幫忙拿火雞腿，整個下午幫媽媽跑腿，晚上還把位置讓給梅格，對每個人又有耐心脾氣又好。我也注意到她不常煩躁或是看鏡子，甚至對她戴的漂亮戒指也沒有提起；所以我的結論是，她已經學會多替別人設想，少顧到自己，而且她也決定要像她用黏土塑小人兒那樣，小心謹慎地塑造她的性情了。我很高興，雖然我應該為她那優雅的風度感到驕傲，但是我更為擁有一個能使自己和別人生活更美好的可愛女兒而驕傲。」

　　「你在想什麼呀，貝絲？」艾美謝過父親，並且說了戒指的事情之後，喬問道。

　　「我今天在看《天路歷程》，裡面說到基督徒和『希望』在經歷許多困難後來到一片怡人的綠色草地。那裡的百合花終年開放，而他們在走到旅程終點之前，都會在那裡快樂地休息，就像我們現在一樣。」貝絲回答，然後她從父親懷裡溜下來，慢慢走到鋼琴旁，又加上一句：「現在是歌唱時間，我想要坐到我的老位置上。我要唱那些朝聖者聽到的牧童唱的歌。我為爸爸作了曲，因為爸爸喜歡那個歌詞。」

　　於是貝絲坐在她心愛的小鋼琴前，輕輕彈著琴鍵，用他們以為再也聽不見的甜美嗓音配著她自己的伴奏唱了出來，這是首古怪的讚美詩，但是對她而言卻是再適合不過的了。

第 22 章
無心的撮合

第二天，做母親的和做女兒們的全都像是簇擁著女王蜂的蜜蜂一樣，前前後後跟著瑪區先生，只顧著看這個新回家的病人、侍候他、聽他說話，而忘記別的一切。這個新的病人只差沒被這番好意給害死。當他被支撐著坐在貝絲沙發旁邊的一張大椅子上，另外三個人就在不遠處，漢娜偶爾還會探頭進來，「瞧瞧這個可愛的人」的時候，他們的幸福似乎已經完備，再也不需要什麼了。但是事實上確實還少了某樣東西，年紀大的人都能感覺得到，只是沒有人承認。瑪區夫婦兩人視線緊跟著梅格，彼此用焦急的表情望著。喬會突然間一陣子陰沉下來，有人還看她對著布魯克先生忘在門廳裡的那把傘揮著拳頭。梅格變得心不在焉，容易害羞，沉默不語，門鈴一響就嚇一大跳，別人提到約翰的名字她就臉紅。艾美說：「每個人好像都在等一件事，心神不定的樣子，這可真怪呀，因為爸爸已經好端端地在家裡了。」貝絲還純真地納悶起來，不知道她們的鄰居為什麼不像平常那樣子過來了呢。

羅瑞下午過來了，看到梅格站在窗前，突然間似乎想要要寶；他單膝跪在雪地上，搥胸扯髮，又雙手合十做懇求狀，像是在祈求什麼恩賜。梅格叫他正經些，快走開，他又假裝從手帕裡

擰出眼淚，又垂頭喪氣地繞過屋角，好似灰心絕望了一般。

「那個傻瓜在做什麼？」梅格笑著說，並且努力做出不知情的樣子。

「他在表演你的約翰以後會做的動作。真感人呀，不是嗎？」喬語帶嘲諷地說。

「別說『我的約翰』，既不妥當也不正確。」但是梅格的聲音卻似乎在這幾個字上徘徊，好像這些字聽起來很悅耳。「拜託別煩我好不好，喬？我說過我沒有很喜歡他，而且我們之間也沒有什麼事好說的，我們全都是朋友，以後也像從前一樣。」

「可是我們不行，因為有人說了什麼話，而羅瑞的惡作劇已經害到你了。我看得出來，媽媽也看得出來，你一點也不像從前了，而且你現在距離我如此遙遠。我不是存心要煩你，而且我也會像個男子漢一樣地承受這件事，可是我真的希望這一切都快快定下來。我討厭等你，所以如果你有心要這麼做，你就動作快一點，快快把事情弄好。」喬急躁地說。

「他沒開口，我不能說什麼也不能做什麼，而他又不會開口，因為爸爸說我還太小。」梅格說著，她低頭在手裡的活兒上，臉上掛著奇異的微笑，這笑容讓人覺得她對父親的看法頗不同意。

「就算他真的開口，你也不知道該說什麼，而只會哭或者面紅耳赤，抑或是讓他稱心如意，而不會堅決地回絕他。」

「我才沒有你以為的那麼傻，那麼沒有用呢。我知道我該說什麼，因為我已經都計畫好了，以免突如其來時不知道該怎麼

辦。我不知道會發生什麼事，但是我希望自己有所準備。」

「你願不願意告訴我你會怎麼說？」喬用一種比較尊敬的語氣問。

「噢，我只會平靜而且堅決地說：『謝謝你，布魯克先生，你很好心，可是我和家父的看法一致：就是我年紀還小，目前不會和任何人訂終生。所以請不要再說什麼了，就讓我們繼續做朋友吧。』」

「嗯！這話夠冷漠無情了，不過我不相信你會說出來，而且就算你說出來，我知道他也不會滿意的。如果他像書裡那些被拒絕了的情人一樣繼續鍥而不捨，你就會軟了心腸，不肯傷他的心了。」

「我不會的。我會告訴他說我已經打定主意，然後充滿尊嚴地走出房間。」

梅格邊說邊站了起來，正要表演如何充滿尊嚴退出房間的動作，突然門廳裡傳來一陣腳步聲，把她嚇得連忙坐回位置，開始縫起衣物，好像她的性命全繫在要在某個時間裡縫完這道接縫一樣。喬忍住了笑。當有人客氣地敲了敲門時，她神色嚴肅地開了門，這張臉毫無慇懃待客之意。

「午安，我是來拿回我的傘的——我是說，我來看看你父親今天怎麼樣了。」布魯克先生說，他的目光從一張有心事的臉轉到另一張有心事的臉上，使他也面帶困惑。

「傘很好，我父親在架子上，我去拿我父親，並且告訴傘你來了。」喬的回答把父親和傘都弄混了，說完她立刻溜出房間，

要給梅格一個發表她那番話、展現尊嚴的機會。但是她才一走，梅格就側著身子朝門過去，一邊喃喃說道：

「我媽媽會想要見你。請坐，我去叫她。」

「別走。你怕我嗎，瑪格麗特？」布魯克先生流露出十分受傷的表情，使得梅格認為自己一定是做了非常不客氣的事。她的臉立刻脹紅到了額頭鬢髮的地方，因為他從來沒有叫她瑪格麗特過，而她很驚訝地發現，他說起來竟是那麼地自然、甜蜜。她急著想要表現得既友善又自在的樣子，所以狀似親熱地伸出一隻手，很感激地說：

「你對我爸爸那麼好，我怎麼可能會怕你？我只希望我能夠感謝你的照顧呢。」

「你可以告訴我，你要怎麼感謝我嗎？」布魯克先生問道，同時兩隻手也緊緊握住她那隻小手，低頭用充滿愛戀的棕色眼睛望著她，眼中的深情使她的心噗通噗通跳，她又想逃走又想留下來聽他說。

「噢，不要，請不要——我想還是別說好。」她說，她想要抽出她的手，梅格雖然說不怕，但是她神情卻顯得很害怕。

「我不會打擾你，我只想知道你會不會有一點喜歡我，梅格。我非常愛你，親愛的。」布魯克又溫柔地加上一句。

「我年紀太小了。」梅格猶豫地說，不知道自己為什麼會這麼心慌，卻又挺喜歡這種感覺。

「我可以等，而在這同時，你也可以學著喜歡我。這會是一門很困難的功課嗎，親愛的？」

「如果我選擇去學習的話就不會，但是——」

「求你選擇去學習吧，梅格。我喜歡教人家，而這要比德文還好學呢。」約翰打斷她的話，同時把她另一隻手也握住了，如此一來她就沒辦法掩住臉了，他低頭注視著她。

他的語氣是懇求的，但是梅格含羞偷偷看了他一眼時，卻看到他的眼神既溫柔卻也很快活，而且他臉上還露出那種很有把握自己會成功的滿意笑容。她只覺得很激動而且很怪異，由於不知道該怎麼辦，就任性地發作出來。她抽出兩隻手，暴躁地說：「我是不會去選擇的。請你走開，別惹我！」

可憐的布魯克先生，他的臉色看起來像是空中樓閣坍塌在他身邊了一樣，他從沒有看過梅格發這樣子的脾氣，使他很困惑。

「你說的話是真的嗎？」他焦急地問，邊追著走開的她。

「是的，是真的。我不想要煩這種事。我爸爸說我還用不著。這事情來得太快了，我還是不要理會得好。」

「我可不可以希望你會慢慢改變心意呢？我願意等，而且在你有更多時間去想以前，什麼話都不要說。不要捉弄我，梅格。我想你不是這種人。」

「你根本連想都不用想我。我希望你不要。」梅格說，對於考驗情人的耐心以及試試自己的力量，有一種調皮的滿足。

此刻他神色嚴肅，臉色蒼白，只是站在那裡，用那麼充滿渴望、那麼溫柔的眼神看著她，使她發覺自己早已心軟了。而要不是瑪區嬸婆在這個有趣的時刻蹣跚走進來，接著會發生什麼事我都不知道呢。

　　這位老太太忍不住想要去看看她的姪子。她出門散步的時候遇到羅瑞，聽說瑪區先生回來了，就立刻坐著馬車來探望了。全家人都在屋子後半部忙，她又悄悄走進房裡，本來要給他們一個驚喜的。不過她倒是讓這一對男女嚇了一跳，梅格一驚，像是見了鬼一樣，布魯克先生則隱入書房。

　　「哎呀，這是怎麼回事啊？」老太太大聲問，她用柺杖在地上敲了敲，目光從那個面色蒼白的男生移到滿臉脹紅的少女。

　　「那是爸爸的朋友。我沒料到您來了！」梅格結結巴巴地說，心想她少不了要聽到一些話了。

　　「看得出來。」瑪區嬸婆回了她一句，坐了下來。「可是這個爸爸的朋友跟你說了什麼，讓你看起來氣成這個樣子？這中間一定有什麼把戲，我一定要知道這是怎麼回事。」她又敲了敲柺杖。

　　「我們只是在說話呢。布魯克先生是來拿他的傘的。」梅格說，她心裡真希望布魯克先生和那把傘都已經安然出了房門。

　　「布魯克？那個男孩子的家庭老師？啊！我明白了。我全明白了。喬有一次不小心看到你爸爸的信裡寫的東西，我就要她告訴我了。你還沒有接受他吧，孩子？」瑪區嬸婆露出駭異的表情嚷道。

　　「噓！他會聽見。我去找媽媽來好嗎？」梅格說，她的心都慌亂了。

　　「還不要。我有事情要跟你說，我必須一吐為快。你告訴我，你真的要嫁給這個布魯克嗎？如果你要嫁他，我一毛錢也不

會給你。你記住這件事，腦筋清楚一點。」老太太凜然地說。

瑪區嬸婆有獨到的本事，能把最最溫和的人的反抗心激發出來，而她也樂此不疲。

「我願意嫁給誰就嫁給誰，瑪區嬸婆，而你也可以愛把錢留給誰就留給誰。」她說，並且毅然決然地點點頭。

瑪區嬸婆不理會，繼續訓她的話。「這個布魯克沒有錢，也沒有什麼有錢親戚吧？」

「是沒有，不過他有很多好朋友。」

「你不能靠朋友過活，試試看，你就會知道朋友會變得多麼冷漠。他也沒有做什麼生意吧？」

「還沒有。羅倫斯先生會幫他。」

「孩子，他知道你有有錢的親戚，這才是他喜歡你的原因呢，我猜。」

「瑪區嬸婆，你怎麼這樣說話？約翰才不會這麼卑鄙呢，如果你再這樣子說話，我連一分鐘都不要聽。」梅格氣急敗壞地喊著，除了老太太的疑心以外，什麼都忘了。「我的約翰才不會為了錢結婚，就像我也不會為錢結婚一樣！我們願意工作，我們也願意等。我不怕窮，因為我到目前為止都很快樂，而且我知道我會和他在一起，因為他愛我，而我——」。

說到這裡，梅格住口了，因為她突然想起她還沒有打定主意呀，她起先是要「她的約翰」走開，而且他或許聽到了她那番並不連貫的話了呢。

瑪區嬸婆大為震怒，她老早打定主意要把她這個漂亮的孫姪

女配戶好人家，但這個女孩快樂的年輕臉龐上有某種東西，令這個孤寂的老女人感到既哀傷又不是滋味。

「好，這整件事我都不管了！你是個任性的孩子，而你這件錯事會讓你失去的比你想像得要多。不，我不待在這兒了。我對你真是失望，現在也沒心情見你爸爸了。別指望你結婚我會送你任何東西。你那位布先生的朋友得照顧你們了，我永遠也不管你了。」

說罷瑪區嬸婆當著梅格的面砰然一聲摔上門，氣呼呼地坐著馬車走了。她似乎也把這個女孩子的勇氣全都帶走了，因為當房裡只剩下梅格一個人，她站了一會兒，不知道自己是該哭還是該笑。她還沒有決定，就被布魯克先生一把抱住，他一口氣說了：「我忍不住聽了你們的話，梅格。謝謝你替我說話，也謝謝瑪區嬸婆證明了你的確是有一點喜歡我的。」

「我也不知道自己有多喜歡你，一直到她侮辱你以後。」梅格說。

「而我用不著走開，可以留下來，做個快樂的人嗎？我可以嗎，親愛的？」

此刻又是一次發表那決定性的演說，並且莊嚴退場的好機會，只是梅格一樣也沒有想到，反而做了一件在喬眼裡丟臉丟一輩子的事——她嬌弱地輕聲說：「可以，約翰。」並且把臉貼著布魯克先生的背心。

瑪區嬸婆走後十五分鐘，喬輕步走下樓。本來是要前去為一個落敗的敵人歡慶，為了讚揚意志堅決的姐姐逐走了一個討人厭

的情人；不料卻看到前面提到的這個敵人竟平靜地坐在沙發上，而那個意志堅決的姐姐端坐在他膝頭，臉上是最最卑屈的服從表情，這當然是莫大的震驚啦！

喬倒抽了一口氣，像是突然被澆了一頭冷水——這種從未料到的情勢大逆轉真的讓她喘不過氣來了。這對情侶聽到不尋常的聲音便轉過頭來看著她。梅格一躍而起，神情是既得意又害羞的，而「那個人」——喬這麼稱呼他——還笑了起來，一邊親吻這個驚駭的新來者，一邊冷靜地說：「喬妹妹，你要恭喜我們喔！」

這是傷心之外再加上侮辱了。喬激動地雙手比劃了一番後，一句話也沒說就走了。她衝上樓，進到房間裡，悽慘的叫聲把兩個病人都驚動了：「噢！誰快下去吧！約翰‧布魯克的行為太可怕了，梅格還很喜歡呢！」

瑪區夫婦迅速離開房間。喬重重地在床上坐下，又哭又罵地把這個糟糕的消息告訴貝絲和艾美。這兩個小一點的妹妹都覺得這件事很好玩、很有趣，喬從她們那裡得不到什麼安慰，於是就到她在閣樓的避難所，把她的困擾告訴小老鼠們。

沒有人知道這天下午在客廳裡發生了什麼事，不過他們說了很多的事，而一向不多話的布魯克先生倒是讓他的朋友們大為驚異了，因為他言辭流利，興致高昂地提出他的示愛請求、說出他的計畫，並且說動他們照他的希望安排每件事。

他還沒有說出他打算為梅格打造的天堂生活，喝茶鈴已經響起，於是他驕傲地帶著梅格一起去吃晚餐，而他倆看起來都是那

197

麼地快活，使得喬不忍心嫉妒或是不悅。艾美對於約翰的癡情和梅格的莊重深為感動，貝絲隔著一段距離朝他倆微笑，而瑪區夫婦則以充滿溫柔的滿意之情打量這對年輕人。這頓飯誰都吃得不多，可是每個人看起來都好快樂，這間老舊的房間在家中第一樁浪漫愛情就此展開之後，神奇地明亮燦爛多了。

「你現在可不能說從來沒有一件快樂的事情發生了吧，梅格？」艾美說，她正在決定要怎麼樣把這對情侶安排在她打算畫的素描中。

「是的，我絕對不能這麼說了。自從我說了那句話以後發生了多少事呀！那好像是一年前的事了。」梅格回答。她此刻正置身在一場幸福的美夢中，高高飄浮在日常瑣事之上。

前門砰的一聲關上，這時喬鬆了一口氣，對自己說：「羅瑞來了，現在我們總可以有段合乎理智的談話了。」

不料喬錯了，因為羅瑞蹦蹦跳跳地進來，手捧著好大一束像是新娘捧花的花束，說要送給「約翰·布魯克太太」。

「我就知道布魯克一定會達成心願，他一向是這樣。當他打定主意要做到一件事，事情就能做成，即使天塌下來也要做成。」羅瑞獻上他的花和他的道賀之後說道。

「多謝你的稱讚，我把它看成未來的一個好兆頭。我現在就邀請你參加我的婚禮。」布魯克先生說，此刻他心平氣和地看待世人，即使是他這個頑皮的學生。

「即使我在天涯海角，我也會來參加的。因為光是在那個場合的喬的表情就值得我長途跋涉了。這位女士，你看起來並不怎

麼歡樂，是怎麼回事啊？」羅瑞一邊問一邊跟著她走到客廳的角
落，其他人則都走過去迎接羅倫斯先生。

「我不贊成這門婚事，可是我已經打定主意要接受。」喬莊
嚴地說。「你不會知道要我放開梅格有多難。」她繼續說，聲音
都有點不穩了。

「你並不是放開她，而只是跟別人共同擁有她而已。」羅瑞
安慰地說。

「那再也不一樣了。我已經失去我最親的朋友了。」喬嘆口
氣說。

「好啦，別難過了，他是個好人。不要緊的，你知道。梅格
很快樂，布魯克會很快安定下來，爺爺會照顧他的，我們也會很
高興看到梅格有自己的小小家園。她離開以後我們也會過快活的
時光，因為我不久就會讀完大學，到時候我們可以出國，去旅行
或是什麼的。這樣子能不能讓你安慰一些？」

「我希望可以，可是我們不能知道三年裡會發生什麼事。」
喬邊思索邊說。

「這倒是真的。你難道不想往前看，知道我們到時候會在哪
裡嗎？我可願意。」羅瑞回答。

「我不想，因為我也許會看到一些悲傷的事，而此刻每個人
看起來都是這麼地快樂。」喬的眼睛慢慢環顧著房裡，房裡的景
象十分歡樂，使她的目光也隨之一亮。

爸爸媽媽坐在一起，他們正靜靜回味大約二十年前他們的浪
漫情懷開始的第一章。艾美正在畫這對戀人，這對戀人坐離眾人

一小段距離，正沉浸在兩人的美麗世界中，那個世界的光芒照在他倆臉上，其中有種優雅是這位小畫家無法摹畫的。貝絲躺在沙發上，正開心地和她的「老」朋友說著話，而這位老朋友握著她的一隻小手，彷彿感受到這隻手擁有牽引他走在她所走的平靜路途的力量。喬懶洋洋地坐在她最喜歡的矮椅子上，那種嚴肅而沉靜的神情是最適合她的。而羅瑞則靠在她的椅背上，他的下巴正好在她那頭鬈髮之上。他露出最友善的笑容，在長玻璃窗的倒影中，他朝她點了點頭。

在梅格、喬、貝絲和艾美前方，簾幕落下了。幕還會不會升起，要看各位讀者對於這齣名叫《小婦人》的戲中第一幕的喜好了。

01

PLAYING PILGRIMS

"Christmas won't be Christmas without any presents," grumbled Jo, lying on the rug.

"It's so dreadful to be poor!" sighed Meg, looking down at her old dress.

"I don't think it's fair for some girls to have plenty of pretty things, and other girls nothing at all," added little Amy, with an injured sniff.

"We've got Father and Mother, and each other," said Beth contentedly from her corner.

The four young faces on which the firelight shone brightened at the cheerful words, but darkened again as Jo said sadly, "We haven't got Father, and shall not have him for a long time." They all think of Father far away, where the fighting was.

Nobody spoke for a minute; then Meg said in an altered tone, "You know the reason Mother proposed not having any presents this Christmas was because it is going to be a hard winter for everyone; and she thinks we ought not to spend money for pleasure, when our men are suffering so in the army. We can't do much, but we can make our little sacrifices, and ought to do it gladly. But I am afraid I don't," and Meg shook her head, as she thought regretfully of all the pretty things she wanted.

"But I don't think the little we should spend would do any good. We've each got a dollar, and the army wouldn't be much helped by our giving that. I agree not to expect anything from Mother or you,

but I do want to buy *Undine and Sintram* for myself. I've wanted it so long," said Jo, who was a bookworm.

"I planned to spend mine in new music," said Beth, with a little sigh, which no one heard but the hearth brush and kettle-holder.

"I shall get a nice box of Faber's drawing pencils; I really need them," said Amy decidedly.

"Mother didn't say anything about our money, and she won't wish us to give up everything. Let's each buy what we want, and have a little fun; I'm sure we work hard enough to earn it," cried Jo, examining the heels of her shoes in a gentlemanly manner.

"I know I do—teaching those tiresome children nearly all day, when I'm longing to enjoy myself at home," began Meg, in the complaining tone again.

"You don't have half such a hard time as I do," said Jo. "How would you like to be shut up for hours with a nervous, fussy old lady, who keeps you trotting, is never satisfied, and worries you till you're ready to fly out of the window or cry?"

"It's naughty to fret, but I do think washing dishes and keeping things tidy is the worst work in the world. It makes me cross, and my hands get so stiff, I can't practice well at all." And Beth looked at her rough hands with a sigh that any one could hear that time.

"I don't believe any of you suffer as I do," cried Amy, "for you don't have to go to school with impertinent girls, who plague you if you don't know your lessons, and laugh at your dresses, and label your father if he isn't rich, and insult you when your nose isn't nice."

"If you mean libel, I'd say so, and not talk about labels, as if Papa was a pickle bottle," advised Jo, laughing.

"I know what I mean, and you needn't be statirical about it. It's proper to use good words, and improve your vocabilary," returned Amy, with dignity.

"Don't peck at one another, children. Don't you wish we had the money Papa lost when we were little, Jo? Dear me! How happy and good we'd be, if we had no worries!" said Meg, who could remember better times.

"You said the other day you thought we were a deal happier than the King children, for they were fighting and fretting all the time, in spite of their money."

"So I did, Beth. Well, I think we are. For though we do have to work, we make fun for ourselves, and are a pretty jolly set, as Jo would say."

"Jo does use such slang words!" observed Amy, with a reproving look at the long figure stretched on the rug.

Jo immediately sat up, put her hands in her pockets, and began to whistle.

"Don't, Jo. It's so boyish!"

"That's why I do it."

"I detest rude, unladylike girls!"

"I hate affected, niminy-piminy chits!"

"Birds in their little nests agree," sang Beth, the peacemaker, with such a funny face that both sharp voices softened to a laugh, and the "pecking" ended for that time.

"Really, girls, you are both to be blamed," said Meg, beginning to lecture in her elder-sisterly fashion. "You are old enough to leave off boyish tricks, and to behave better, Josephine. It didn't matter so much when you were a little girl, but now you are so tall, and turn up your hair, you should remember that you are a young lady."

"I'm not! And if turning up my hair makes me one, I'll wear it in two tails till I'm twenty," cried Jo, pulling off her net, and shaking down a chestnut mane. "I hate to think I've got to grow up, and be Miss March, and wear long gowns, and look as prim as a China Aster!

It's bad enough to be a girl, anyway, when I like boys' games and work and manners! I can't get over my disappointment in not being a boy. And it's worse than ever now, for I'm dying to go and fight with Papa. And I can only stay at home and knit, like a poky old woman!"

And Jo shook the blue army sock till the needles rattled like castanets, and her ball bounded across the room.

"Poor Jo! It's too bad, but it can't be helped. So you must try to be contented with making your name boyish, and playing brother to us girls," said Beth, stroking the rough head with a hand that all the dish washing and dusting in the world could not make ungentle in its touch.

"As for you, Amy," continued Meg, "you are altogether too particular and prim. Your airs are funny now, but you'll grow up an affected little goose, if you don't take care. I like your nice manners and refined ways of speaking, when you don't try to be elegant. But your absurd words are as bad as Jo's slang."

"If Jo is a tomboy and Amy a goose, what am I, please?" asked Beth, ready to share the lecture.

"You're a dear, and nothing else," answered Meg warmly, and no one contradicted her, for the 'Mouse' was the pet of the family.

As young readers like to know 'how people look', we will take this moment to give them a little sketch of the four sisters, who sat knitting away in the twilight, while the December snow fell quietly without, and the fire crackled cheerfully within. It was a comfortable room, though the carpet was faded and the furniture very plain, for a good picture or two hung on the walls, books filled the recesses, chrysanthemums and Christmas roses bloomed in the windows, and a pleasant atmosphere of home peace pervaded it.

Margaret, the eldest of the four, was sixteen, and very pretty, being plump and fair, with large eyes, plenty of soft brown hair, a

sweet mouth, and white hands, of which she was rather vain. Fifteen-year-old Jo was very tall, thin, and brown, and reminded one of a colt, for she never seemed to know what to do with her long limbs, which were very much in her way. She had a decided mouth, a comical nose, and sharp, gray eyes, which appeared to see everything, and were by turns fierce, funny, or thoughtful. Her long, thick hair was her one beauty, but it was usually bundled into a net, to be out of her way. Round shoulders had Jo, big hands and feet, a flyaway look to her clothes, and the uncomfortable appearance of a girl who was rapidly shooting up into a woman and didn't like it. Elizabeth, or Beth, as everyone called her, was a rosy, smooth-haired, bright-eyed girl of thirteen, with a shy manner, a timid voice, and a peaceful expression which was seldom disturbed. Her father called her 'Little Miss Tranquility', and the name suited her excellently, for she seemed to live in a happy world of her own, only venturing out to meet the few whom she trusted and loved. Amy, though the youngest, was a most important person, in her own opinion at least. A regular snow maiden, with blue eyes, and yellow hair curling on her shoulders, pale and slender, and always carrying herself like a young lady mindful of her manners. What the characters of the four sisters were we will leave to be found out.

The clock struck six and, having swept up the hearth, Beth put a pair of slippers down to warm. Somehow the sight of the old shoes had a good effect upon the girls, for Mother was coming, and everyone brightened to welcome her. Meg stopped lecturing, and lighted the lamp, Amy got out of the easy chair without being asked, and Jo forgot how tired she was as she sat up to hold the slippers nearer to the blaze.

"They are quite worn out. Marmee must have a new pair."

"I thought I'd get her some with my dollar," said Beth.

"No, I shall!" cried Amy.

"I'm the oldest," began Meg, but Jo cut in with a decided, "I'm the man of the family now Papa is away, and I shall provide the slippers, for he told me to take special care of Mother while he was gone."

"I'll tell you what we'll do," said Beth, "let's each get her something for Christmas, and not get anything for ourselves."

"That's like you, dear! What will we get?" exclaimed Jo.

Everyone thought soberly for a minute, then Meg announced, as if the idea was suggested by the sight of her own pretty hands, "I shall give her a nice pair of gloves."

"Army shoes, best to be had," cried Jo.

"Some handkerchiefs, all hemmed," said Beth.

"I'll get a little bottle of cologne. She likes it, and it won't cost much, so I'll have some left to buy my pencils," added Amy.

"How will we give the things?" asked Meg.

"Put them on the table, and bring her in and see her open the bundles. Don't you remember how we used to do on our birthdays? Let Marmee think we are getting things for ourselves, and then surprise her. We must go shopping tomorrow afternoon, Meg." said Jo.

From the door came a cheery voice , and actors and audience turned to welcome a tall, motherly lady with a 'can I help you' look about her which was truly delightful. She was not elegantly dressed, but a noble-looking woman, and the girls thought the gray cloak and unfashionable bonnet covered the most splendid mother in the world.

"Well, dearies, how have you got on today? There was so much to do, getting the boxes ready to go tomorrow, that I didn't come home to dinner. Has anyone called, Beth? How is your cold, Meg? Jo, you look tired to death. Come and kiss me, baby."

While making these maternal inquiries Mrs. March got her wet things off, her warm slippers on, and sitting down in the easy chair, drew Amy to her lap, preparing to enjoy the happiest hour of her busy day. The girls flew about, trying to make things comfortable, each in her own way. As they gathered about the table, Mrs. March said, with a particularly happy face, "I've got a treat for you after supper."

A quick, bright smile went round like a streak of sunshine. Beth clapped her hands, regardless of the biscuit she held, and Jo tossed up her napkin, crying, "A letter! A letter! Three cheers for Father!"

"Yes, a nice long letter. He is well, and thinks he shall get through the cold season better than we feared. He sends all sorts of loving wishes for Christmas, and an especial message to you girls," said Mrs. March, patting her pocket as if she had got a treasure there.

They all drew to the fire, Mother in the big chair with Beth at her feet, Meg and Amy perched on either arm of the chair, and Jo leaning on the back, where no one would see any sign of emotion if the letter should happen to be touching. Very few letters were written in those hard times that were not touching, especially those which fathers sent home. In this one little was said of the hardships endured, the dangers faced, or the homesickness conquered. It was a cheerful, hopeful letter, full of lively descriptions of camp life, marches, and military news, and only at the end did the writer's heart over-flow with fatherly love and longing for the little girls at home.

"Give them all of my dear love and a kiss. Tell them I think of them by day, pray for them by night, and find my best comfort in their affection at all times. A year seems very long to wait before I see them, but remind them that while we wait we may all work, so that these hard days need not be wasted. I know they will remember all I said to them, that they will be loving children to you, will do their duty faithfully, fight their bosom enemies bravely, and conquer themselves

so beautifully that when I come back to them I may be fonder and prouder than ever of my little women." Everybody sniffed when they came to that part.

"We all will," cried Meg. "I think too much of my looks and hate to work, but won't any more, if I can help it."

"I'll try and be what he loves to call me, 'a little woman' and not be rough and wild, but do my duty here instead of wanting to be somewhere else," said Jo, thinking that keeping her temper at home was a much harder task than facing a rebel or two down South.

Beth said nothing, but wiped away her tears with the blue army sock and began to knit with all her might, losing no time in doing the duty that lay nearest her, while she resolved in her quiet little soul to be all that Father hoped to find her when the year brought round the happy coming home.

Mrs. March broke the silence that followed Jo's words, by saying in her cheery voice, "Do you remember how you used to play Pilgrim's Progress when you were little things?"

"What fun it was, especially going by the lions, fighting Apollyon, and passing through the valley where the hob-goblins were," said Jo.

"I liked the place where the bundles fell off and tumbled downstairs," said Meg.

"My favorite part was when we came out on the flat roof where our flowers and arbors and pretty things were, and all stood and sung for joy up there in the sunshine," said Beth, smiling, as if that pleasant moment had come back to her.

"I don't remember much about it, except that I was afraid of the cellar and the dark entry, and always liked the cake and milk we had up at the top. If I wasn't too old for such things, I'd rather like to play it over again," said Amy, who began to talk of renouncing

childish things at the mature age of twelve.

"We never are too old for this, my dear, because it is a play we are playing all the time in one way or another. Our burdens are here, our road is before us, and the longing for goodness and happiness is the guide that leads us through many troubles and mistakes to the peace which is a true Celestial City. Now, my little pilgrims, suppose you begin again, not in play, but in earnest, and see how far on you can get before Father comes home."

"Really, Mother? Where are our bundles?" asked Amy, who was a very literal young lady.

"Each of you told what your burden was just now, except Beth. I rather think she hasn't got any," said her mother.

"Yes, I have. Mine is dishes and dusters, and envying girls with nice pianos, and being afraid of people."

Beth's bundle was such a funny one that everybody wanted to laugh, but nobody did, for it would have hurt her feelings very much.

"Let us do it," said Meg thoughtfully. "It is only another name for trying to be good, and the story may help us, for though we do want to be good, it's hard work and we forget, and don't do our best."

"We were in the Slough of Despond tonight, and Mother came and pulled us out as Help did in the book. We ought to have our roll of directions, like Christian. What shall we do about that?" asked Jo, delighted with the fancy which lent a little romance to the very dull task of doing her duty.

"Look under your pillows Christmas morning, and you will find your guidebook," replied Mrs. March.

They talked over the new plan while old Hannah cleared the table, then out came the four little work baskets, and the needles flew as the girls made sheets for Aunt March. It was uninteresting sewing,

but tonight no one grumbled.

At nine they stopped work, and sang, as usual, before they went to bed. No one but Beth could get much music out of the old piano, but she had a way of softly touching the yellow keys and making a pleasant accompaniment to the simple songs they sang. Meg had a voice like a flute, and she and her mother led the little choir. Amy chirped like a cricket, and Jo wandered through the airs at her own sweet will, always coming out at the wrong place with a croak or a quaver that spoiled the most pensive tune. They had always done this from the time they could lisp...

Crinkle, crinkle, 'ittle 'tar,

and it had become a household custom, for the mother was a born singer. The first sound in the morning was her voice as she went about the house singing like a lark, and the last sound at night was the same cheery sound, for the girls never grew too old for that familiar lullaby.

02

A MERRY CHRISTMAS

Jo was the first to wake in the gray dawn of Christmas morning. No stockings hung at the fireplace, and for a moment she felt as much disappointed as she did long ago, when her little sock fell down because it was crammed so full of goodies. Then she remembered her mother's promise and, slipping her hand under her pillow, drew out a little crimson-covered book. She knew it very well, for it was that beautiful old story of the best life ever lived, and Jo felt that it was a true guidebook for any pilgrim going on a long journey. She woke Meg with a "Merry Christmas," and bade her see what was under her pillow. A green-covered book appeared, with the same picture inside, and a few words written by their mother, which made their one present very precious in their eyes. Presently Beth and Amy woke to rummage and find their little books also, one dove-colored, the other blue, and all sat looking at and talking about them, while the east grew rosy with the coming day.

"Where is Mother?" asked Meg, as she and Jo ran down to thank her for their gifts, half an hour later.

"Goodness only knows. Some poor creeter came a-beggin', and your ma went straight off to see what was needed. There never was such a woman for givin' away vittles and drink, clothes and firin'," replied Hannah, who had lived with the family since Meg was born, and was considered by them all more as a friend than a servant.

"She will be back soon, I think, so fry your cakes, and have everything ready," said Meg, looking over the presents which were

212

collected in a basket and kept under the sofa, ready to be produced at the proper time. "Why, where is Amy's bottle of cologne?" she added, as the little flask did not appear.

"She took it out a minute ago, and went off with it to put a ribbon on it, or some such notion," replied Jo, dancing about the room to take the first stiffness off the new army slippers.

"How nice my handkerchiefs look, don't they? Hannah washed and ironed them for me, and I marked them all myself," said Beth, looking proudly at the somewhat uneven letters which had cost her such labor.

"Bless the child! She's gone and put 'Mother' on them!" cried Jo, taking one up.

"Isn't that right? I thought it was better to do it so. 'I don't want anyone to use these but Marmee," said Beth, looking troubled.

"Dear, it's a very pretty idea. It will please her very much, I know," said Meg, with a frown for Jo and a smile for Beth.

"There's Mother. Hide the basket, quick!" cried Jo, as a door slammed and steps sounded in the hall.

"Merry Christmas, Marmee! Many of them! Thank you for our books. We read some, and mean to every day," they all cried in chorus.

"Merry Christmas, little daughters! I'm glad you began at once, and hope you will keep on. But I want to say one word before we sit down. Not far away from here lies a poor woman with a little newborn baby. Six children are huddled into one bed to keep from freezing, for they have no fire. There is nothing to eat over there, and the oldest boy came to tell me they were suffering hunger and cold. My girls, will you give them your breakfast as a Christmas present?"

They were all unusually hungry, having waited nearly an hour, and for a minute no one spoke, only a minute, for Jo exclaimed impetuously, "I'm so glad you came before we began!"

"May I go and help carry the things to the poor little children?" asked Beth eagerly.

"I shall take the cream and the muffins," added Amy, heroically giving up the article she most liked.

Meg was already covering the buckwheats, and piling the bread into one big plate.

"I thought you'd do it," said Mrs. March, smiling as if satisfied. "You shall all go and help me, and when we come back we will have bread and milk for breakfast, and make it up at dinnertime."

They were soon ready, and the procession set out.

A poor, bare, miserable room it was, with broken windows, no fire, ragged bedclothes, a sick mother, wailing baby, and a group of pale, hungry children cuddled under one old quilt, trying to keep warm.

"Ach, mein Gott! It is good angels come to us!" said the poor woman, crying for joy.

"Funny angels in hoods and mittens," said Jo, and set them to laughing.

"Das ist gut!" "Die Engel-kinder!" cried the poor things as they ate and warmed their purple hands at the comfortable blaze. The girls had never been called angel children before, and thought it very agreeable, especially Jo, who had been considered a 'Sancho' ever since she was born. That was a very happy breakfast, though they didn't get any of it. And when they went away, leaving comfort behind, I think there were not in all the city four merrier people than the hungry little girls who gave away their breakfasts and contented themselves with bread and milk on Christmas morning.

"That's loving our neighbor better than ourselves, and I like it," said Meg, as they set out their presents while their mother was upstairs collecting clothes for the poor Hummels.

Not a very splendid show, but there was a great deal of love done up in the few little bundles, and the tall vase of red roses, white chrysanthemums, and trailing vines, which stood in the middle, gave quite an elegant air to the table.

"She's coming! Strike up, Beth! Open the door, Amy! Three cheers for Marmee!" cried Jo, prancing about while Meg went to conduct Mother to the seat of honor.

Beth played her gayest march, Amy threw open the door, and Meg enacted escort with great dignity. Mrs. March was both surprised and touched, and smiled with her eyes full as she examined her presents and read the little notes which accompanied them. The slippers went on at once, a new handkerchief was slipped into her pocket, well scented with Amy's cologne, the rose was fastened in her bosom, and the nice gloves were pronounced a perfect fit.

There was a good deal of laughing and kissing and explaining, in the simple, loving fashion which makes these home festivals so pleasant at the time, so sweet to remember long afterward, and then all fell to work.

The morning charities and ceremonies took so much time that the rest of the day was devoted to preparations for the evening festivities. Being still too young to go often to the theater, and not rich enough to afford any great outlay for private performances, the girls put their wits to work, and necessity being the mother of invention, made whatever they needed. The smallness of the company made it necessary for the two principal actors to take several parts apiece, and they certainly deserved some credit for the hard work they did in learning three or four different parts, whisking in and out of various costumes, and managing the stage besides. It was excellent drill for their memories, a harmless amusement, and employed many hours which otherwise would have been idle, lonely, or spent in less profitable society.

On Christmas night, a dozen girls piled onto the bed which was the dress circle, and sat before the blue and yellow chintz curtains in a most flattering state of expectancy. There was a good deal of rustling and whispering behind the curtain, a trifle of lamp smoke, and an occasional giggle from Amy, who was apt to get hysterical in the excitement of the moment. Presently a bell sounded, the curtains flew apart, and the operatic tragedy began.

After curtain has fallen, Hannah appeared, with "Mrs. March's compliments, and would the ladies walk down to supper."

This was a surprise even to the actors, and when they saw the table, they looked at one another in rapturous amazement. It was like Marmee to get up a little treat for them, but anything so fine as this was unheard of since the departed days of plenty. There was ice cream, actually two dishes of it, pink and white, and cake and fruit and distracting French bonbons and, in the middle of the table, four great bouquets of hot house flowers.

It quite took their breath away, and they stared first at the table and then at their mother, who looked as if she enjoyed it immensely.

"Is it fairies?" asked Amy.

"Santa Claus," said Beth.

"Mother did it." And Meg smiled her sweetest, in spite of her gray beard and white eyebrows.

"Aunt March had a good fit and sent the supper," cried Jo, with a sudden inspiration.

"All wrong. Old Mr. Laurence sent it," replied Mrs. March.

"The Laurence boy's grandfather! What in the world put such a thing into his head? We don't know him!" exclaimed Meg.

"Hannah told one of his servants about your breakfast party. He is an odd old gentleman, but that pleased him. He knew my father years ago, and he sent me a polite note this afternoon, saying he hoped

I would allow him to express his friendly feeling toward my children by sending them a few trifles in honor of the day. I could not refuse, and so you have a little feast at night to make up for the bread-and-milk breakfast."

"That boy put it into his head, I know he did! He's a capital fellow, and I wish we could get acquainted. He looks as if he'd like to know us but he's bashful, and Meg is so prim she won't let me speak to him when we pass," said Jo.

"You mean the people who live in the big house next door, don't you?" asked one of the girls. "My mother knows old Mr. Laurence, but says he's very proud and doesn't like to mix with his neighbors. He keeps his grandson shut up, when he isn't riding or walking with his tutor, and makes him study very hard. We invited him to our party, but he didn't come. Mother says he's very nice, though he never speaks to us girls."

"Our cat ran away once, and he brought her back, and we talked over the fence, and were getting on capitally, all about cricket, and so on, when he saw Meg coming, and walked off. I mean to know him some day, for he needs fun, I'm sure he does," said Jo decidedly.

"I like his manners, and he looks like a little gentleman."

"It's a mercy you didn't, Mother!" laughed Jo, looking at her boots. "But we'll have another play sometime that he can see. Perhaps he'll help act. Wouldn't that be jolly?"

"I never had such a fine bouquet before! How pretty it is!" And Meg examined her flowers with great interest.

"They are lovely. But Beth's roses are sweeter to me," said Mrs. March, smelling the half-dead posy in her belt.

Beth nestled up to her, and whispered softly, "I wish I could send my bunch to Father. I'm afraid he isn't having such a merry Christmas as we are."

03

THE LAURENCE BOY

"Jo! Jo! Where are you?" cried Meg at the foot of the garret stairs.

"Here!" answered a husky voice from above, and, running up, Meg found her sister eating apples and crying over the Heir of Redclyffe, wrapped up in a comforter on an old three-legged sofa by the sunny window. This was Jo's favorite refuge, and here she loved to retire with half a dozen russets and a nice book, to enjoy the quiet and the society of a pet rat who lived near by and didn't mind her a particle. As Meg appeared, Scrabble whisked into his hole. Jo shook the tears off her cheeks and waited to hear the news.

"Such fun! Only see! A regular note of invitation from Mrs. Gardiner for tomorrow night!" cried Meg, waving the precious paper.

" 'Mrs. Gardiner would be happy to see Miss March and Miss Josephine at a little dance on New Year's Eve.' Marmee is willing we should go, now what shall we wear?"

"What's the use of asking that, when you know we shall wear our poplins, because we haven't got anything else?" answered Jo with her mouth full.

"If I only had a silk!" sighed Meg. "Mother says I may when I'm eighteen perhaps, but two years is an everlasting time to wait."

"I'm sure our pops look like silk, and they are nice enough for us. Yours is as good as new, but I forgot the burn and the tear in mine. Whatever shall I do? The burn shows badly, and I can't take any

out."

"You must sit still all you can and keep your back out of sight. The front is all right. I shall have a new ribbon for my hair, and Marmee will lend me her little pearl pin, and my new slippers are lovely, and my gloves will do, though they aren't as nice as I'd like."

"Mine are spoiled with lemonade, and I can't get any new ones, so I shall have to go without," said Jo, who never troubled herself much about dress.

"You must have gloves, or I won't go," cried Meg decidedly. "Gloves are more important than anything else. You can't dance without them, and if you don't I should be so mortified."

"I can hold them crumpled up in my hand, so no one will know how stained they are. That's all I can do. No! I'll tell you how we can manage, each wear one good one and carry a bad one. Don't you see?"

"Your hands are bigger than mine, and you will stretch my glove dreadfully," began Meg, whose gloves were a tender point with her.

"Then I'll go without. I don't care what people say!" cried Jo, taking up her book.

"You may have it, you may! Only don't stain it, and do behave nicely. Don't put your hands behind you, or stare, or say 'Christopher Columbus!' will you?"

"Don't worry about me. I'll be as prim as I can and not get into any scrapes, if I can help it. Now go and answer your note, and let me finish this splendid story."

So Meg went away to 'accept with thanks', look over her dress, and sing blithely as she did up her one real lace frill, while Jo finished her story, her four apples, and had a game of romps with Scrabble.

On New Year's Eve the parlor was deserted, for the two younger

girls played dressing maids and the two elder were absorbed in the all-important business of 'getting ready for the party'.

Meg was finished at last, and by the united exertions of the entire family Jo's hair was got up and her dress on. They looked very well in their simple suits, Meg's in silvery drab, with a blue velvet snood, lace frills, and the pearl pin. Jo in maroon, with a stiff, gentlemanly linen collar, and a white chrysanthemum or two for her only ornament. Each put on one nice light glove, and carried one soiled one, and all pronounced the effect "quite easy and fine". Meg's high-heeled slippers were very tight and hurt her, though she would not own it, and Jo's nineteen hairpins all seemed stuck straight into her head, which was not exactly comfortable, but, dear me, let us be elegant or die.

"Have a good time, dearies!" said Mrs. March, as the sisters went daintily down the walk. "Don't eat much supper, and come away at eleven when I send Hannah for you." As the gate clashed behind them, a voice cried from a window...

"Girls, girls! Have you both got nice pocket handkerchiefs?"

"Yes, yes, spandy nice, and Meg has cologne on hers," cried Jo, adding with a laugh as they went on, "I do believe Marmee would ask that if we were all running away from an earthquake."

"It is one of her aristocratic tastes, and quite proper, for a real lady is always known by neat boots, gloves, and handkerchief," replied Meg, who had a good many little 'aristocratic tastes' of her own.

"Now don't forget to keep the bad breadth out of sight, Jo. Is my sash right? And does my hair look very bad?" said Meg, as she turned from the glass in Mrs. Gardiner's dressing room after a prolonged prink.

"I know I shall forget. If you see me doing anything wrong, just

remind me by a wink, will you?" returned Jo, giving her collar a twitch and her head a hasty brush.

"No, winking isn't ladylike. I'll lift my eyebrows if any thing is wrong, and nod if you are all right. Now hold your shoulder straight, and take short steps, and don't shake hands if you are introduced to anyone. It isn't the thing."

"How do you learn all the proper ways? I never can. Isn't that music gay?"

Down they went, feeling a trifle timid, for they seldom went to parties, and informal as this little gathering was, it was an event to them. Mrs. Gardiner, a stately old lady, greeted them kindly and handed them over to the eldest of her six daughters. Meg knew Sallie and was at her ease very soon, but Jo, who didn't care much for girls or girlish gossip, stood about, with her back carefully against the wall, and felt as much out of place as a colt in a flower garden. She could not roam about and amuse herself, for the burned breadth would show, so she stared at people rather forlornly till the dancing began. Meg was asked at once, and the tight slippers tripped about so briskly that none would have guessed the pain their wearer suffered smilingly. Jo saw a big red headed youth approaching her corner, and fearing he meant to engage her, she slipped into a curtained recess, intending to peep and enjoy herself in peace. Unfortunately, another bashful person had chosen the same refuge, for, as the curtain fell behind her, she found herself face to face with the 'Laurence boy'.

"Dear me, I didn't know anyone was here!" stammered Jo, preparing to back out as speedily as she had bounced in.

But the boy laughed and said pleasantly, though he looked a little startled, "Don't mind me, stay if you like."

"Shan't I disturb you?"

"Not a bit. I only came here because I don't know many people

and felt rather strange at first, you know."

"So did I. Don't go away, please, unless you'd rather."

The boy sat down again and looked at his pumps, till Jo said, trying to be polite and easy, "I think I've had the pleasure of seeing you before. You live near us, don't you?"

"Next door." And he looked up and laughed outright, for Jo's prim manner was rather funny when he remembered how they had chatted about cricket when he brought the cat home.

That put Jo at her ease and she laughed too, as she said, in her heartiest way, "We did have such a good time over your nice Christmas present."

"Grandpa sent it."

"But you put it into his head, didn't you, now?"

"How is your cat, Miss March?" asked the boy, trying to look sober while his black eyes shone with fun.

"Nicely, thank you, Mr. Laurence. But I am not Miss March, I'm only Jo," returned the young lady.

"I'm not Mr. Laurence, I'm only Laurie."

"Laurie Laurence, what an odd name."

"Don't you like to dance, Miss Jo?" asked Laurie, looking as if he thought the name suited her.

"I like it well enough if there is plenty of room, and everyone is lively. In a place like this I'm sure to upset something, tread on people's toes, or do something dreadful, so I keep out of mischief and let Meg sail about. Don't you dance?"

"Sometimes. You see I've been abroad a good many years, and haven't been into company enough yet to know how you do things here."

"Abroad!" cried Jo. "Oh, tell me about it! I love dearly to hear people describe their travels."

Laurie didn't seem to know where to begin, but Jo's eager questions soon set him going.

Laurie's bashfulness soon wore off, for Jo's gentlemanly demeanor amused and set him at his ease, and Jo was her merry self again, because her dress was forgotten and nobody lifted their eyebrows at her. She liked the 'Laurence boy' better than ever and took several good looks at him, so that she might describe him to the girls, for they had no brothers, very few male cousins, and boys were almost unknown creatures to them.

"Curly black hair, brown skin, big black eyes, handsome nose, fine teeth, small hands and feet, taller than I am, very polite, for a boy, and altogether jolly. Wonder how old he is?"

It was on the tip of Jo's tongue to ask, but she checked herself in time and, with unusual tact, tried to find out in a round-about way.

"I suppose you are going to college soon? I see you pegging away at your books, no, I mean studying hard." And Jo blushed at the dreadful 'pegging' which had escaped her.

Laurie smiled but didn't seem shocked, and answered with a shrug. "Not for a year or two. I won't go before seventeen, anyway."

"Aren't you but fifteen?" asked Jo, looking at the tall lad, whom she had imagined seventeen already.

"Sixteen, next month."

"How I wish I was going to college! You don't look as if you liked it."

"I hate it!"

"What do you like?"

"To live in Italy, and to enjoy myself in my own way."

Jo wanted very much to ask what his own way was, but his black brows looked rather threatening as he knit them, so she changed the

subject by saying, as her foot kept time, "That's a splendid polka! Why don't you go and try it?"

"If you will come too," he answered, with a gallant little bow.

"I can't, for I told Meg I wouldn't, because..." There Jo stopped, and looked undecided whether to tell or to laugh.

"Because, what?"

"You won't tell?"

"Never!"

"Well, I scorched my frock, and though it's nicely mended, it shows, and Meg told me to keep still so no one would see it. You may laugh, if you want to. It is funny, I know."

But Laurie didn't laugh. He only looked down a minute, and the expression of his face puzzled Jo when he said very gently, "Never mind that. I'll tell you how we can manage. There's a long hall out there, and we can dance grandly, and no one will see us. Please come."

Jo thanked him and gladly went, wishing she had two neat gloves when she saw the nice, pearl-colored ones her partner wore. The hall was empty, and they had a grand polka, for Laurie danced well, and taught her the German step, which delighted Jo. When the music stopped, they sat down on the stairs to get their breath, and Laurie was in the midst of an account of a students' festival at Heidelberg when Meg appeared in search of her sister. She beckoned, and Jo reluctantly followed her into a side room, where she found her on a sofa, holding her foot, and looking pale.

"I've sprained my ankle. That stupid high heel turned and gave me a sad wrench. It aches so, I can hardly stand, and I don't know how I'm ever going to get home," she said, rocking to and fro in pain.

"I knew you'd hurt your feet with those silly shoes. I'm sorry.

But I don't see what you can do, except get a carriage, or stay here all night," answered Jo, softly rubbing the poor ankle as she spoke.

"I can't have a carriage without its costing ever so much. I dare say I can't get one at all, for most people come in their own, and it's a long way to the stable, and no one to send."

"I'll go."

"No, indeed! It's past nine, and dark as Egypt. I'll rest till Hannah comes, and then do the best I can."

"I'll ask Laurie. He will go," said Jo, looking relieved as the idea occurred to her.

"Mercy, no! Don't ask or tell anyone. Get me my rubbers, and put these slippers with our things. I can't dance anymore, but as soon as supper is over, watch for Hannah and tell me the minute she comes."

They had a merry time over the bonbons and mottoes, and were in the midst of a quiet game of Buzz, with two or three other young people who had strayed in, when Hannah appeared. Meg forgot her foot and rose so quickly that she was forced to catch hold of Jo, with an exclamation of pain.

"Hush! Don't say anything," she whispered, adding aloud, "It's nothing. I turned my foot a little, that's all," and limped upstairs to put her things on.

Hannah scolded, Meg cried, and Jo was at her wits' end, till she decided to take things into her own hands. Slipping out, she ran down and, finding a servant, asked if he could get her a carriage. It happened to be a hired waiter who knew nothing about the neighborhood and Jo was looking round for help when Laurie, who had heard what she said, came up and offered his grandfather's carriage, which had just come for him, he said.

"It's so early! You can't mean to go yet?" began Jo, looking

relieved but hesitating to accept the offer.

"I always go early, I do, truly! Please let me take you home. It's all on my way, you know, and it rains, they say."

That settled it, and telling him of Meg's mishap, Jo gratefully accepted and rushed up to bring down the rest of the party. Hannah hated rain as much as a cat does so she made no trouble, and they rolled away in the luxurious close carriage, feeling very festive and elegant. Laurie went on the box so Meg could keep her foot up, and the girls talked over their party in freedom.

"I had a capital time. Did you?" asked Jo, rumpling up her hair, and making herself comfortable.

"Yes, till I hurt myself. Sallie's friend, Annie Moffat, took a fancy to me, and asked me to come and spend a week with her when Sallie does. She is going in the spring when the opera comes, and it will be perfectly splendid, if Mother only lets me go," answered Meg, cheering up at the thought.

Jo told her adventures, and by the time she had finished they were at home. With many thanks, they said good night and crept in, hoping to disturb no one, but the instant their door creaked, two little nightcaps bobbed up, and two sleepy but eager voices cried out...

"Tell about the party! Tell about the party!"

With what Meg called 'a great want of manners' Jo had saved some bonbons for the little girls, and they soon subsided, after hearing the most thrilling events of the evening.

04

BURDENS

"Oh, dear, how hard it does seem to take up our packs and go on," sighed Meg the morning after the party, for now the holidays were over, the week of merrymaking did not fit her for going on easily with the task she never liked.

"I wish it was Christmas or New Year's all the time. Wouldn't it be fun?" answered Jo, yawning dismally.

"We shouldn't enjoy ourselves half so much as we do now. But it does seem so nice to have little suppers and bouquets, and go to parties, and drive home, and read and rest, and not work. It's like other people, you know, and I always envy girls who do such things, I'm so fond of luxury," said Meg, trying to decide which of two shabby gowns was the least shabby.

"Well, we can't have it, so don't let us grumble but shoulder our bundles and trudge along as cheerfully as Marmee does."

But Meg didn't brighten, for her burden, consisting of four spoiled children, seemed heavier than ever. She had not heart enough even to make herself pretty as usual by putting on a blue neck ribbon and dressing her hair in the most becoming way.

"Where's the use of looking nice, when no one sees me but those cross midgets, and no one cares whether I'm pretty or not?" she muttered, shutting her drawer with a jerk. "I shall have to toil and moil all my days, with only little bits of fun now and then, and get old and ugly and sour, because I'm poor and can't enjoy my life as other girls do. It's a shame!"

So Meg went down, wearing an injured look, and wasn't at all agreeable at breakfast time. Everyone seemed rather out of sorts and inclined to croak.

"There never was such a cross family!" cried Jo.

"Girls, girls, do be quiet one minute! I must get this off by the early mail, and you drive me distracted with your worry," cried Mrs. March, crossing out the third spoiled sentence in her letter.

There was a momentary lull, broken by Hannah, who stalked in, laid two hot turnovers on the table, and stalked out again. Hannah never forgot to make them, no matter how busy or grumpy she might be, for the walk was long and bleak. The poor things got no other lunch and were seldom home before two.

"Goodbye, Marmee. We are a set of rascals this morning, but we'll come home regular angels. Now then, Meg!" And Jo tramped away, feeling that the pilgrims were not setting out as they ought to do.

They always looked back before turning the corner, for their mother was always at the window to nod and smile, and wave her hand to them. Somehow it seemed as if they couldn't have got through the day without that, for whatever their mood might be, the last glimpse of that motherly face was sure to affect them like sunshine.

Jo gave her sister an encouraging pat on the shoulder as they parted for the day, each going a different way, each hugging her little warm turnover, and each trying to be cheerful in spite of wintry weather, hard work, and the unsatisfied desires of pleasure-loving youth.

When Mr. March lost his property in trying to help an unfortunate friend, the two oldest girls begged to be allowed to do something toward their own support, at least. Believing that they could not begin too early to cultivate energy, industry, and independence, their parents consented, and both fell to work with the hearty good will which in spite of all obstacles is sure to succeed at last.

Margaret found a place as nursery governess and felt rich with her small salary. As she said, she was 'fond of luxury', and her chief trouble was poverty. She found it harder to bear than the others because she could remember a time when home was beautiful, life full of ease and pleasure, and want of any kind unknown. She tried not to be envious or discontented, but it was very natural that the young girl should long for pretty things, gay friends, accomplishments, and a happy life. At the Kings' she daily saw all she wanted, for the children's older sisters were just out, and Meg caught frequent glimpses of dainty ball dresses and bouquets, heard lively gossip about theaters, concerts, sleighing parties, and merrymakings of all kinds, and saw money lavished on trifles which would have been so precious to her. Poor Meg seldom complained, but a sense of injustice made her feel bitter toward everyone sometimes, for she had not yet learned to know how rich she was in the blessings which alone can make life happy.

Jo happened to suit Aunt March, who was lame and needed an active person to wait upon her. The childless old lady had offered to adopt one of the girls when the troubles came, and was much offended because her offer was declined. Other friends told the Marches that they had lost all chance of being remembered in the rich old lady's will, but the unworldly Marches only said...

"We can't give up our girls for a dozen fortunes. Rich or poor, we will keep together and be happy in one another."

The old lady wouldn't speak to them for a time, but happening to meet Jo at a friend's, something in her comical face and blunt manners struck the old lady's fancy, and she proposed to take her for a companion. This did not suit Jo at all, but she accepted the place since nothing better appeared and, to every one's surprise, got on remarkably well with her irascible relative. There was an occasional tempest, and once Jo had marched home, declaring she couldn't bear it any longer, but Aunt March always cleared up quickly, and sent for her to come back again with such urgency that she could not refuse, for in her heart she rather liked the peppery old lady.

I suspect that the real attraction was a large library of fine books, which was left to dust and spiders since Uncle March died. The dim, dusty room, with the busts staring down from the tall bookcases, the cozy chairs, the globes, and best of all, the wilderness of books in which she could wander where she liked, made the library a region of bliss to her.

The moment Aunt March took her nap, or was busy with company, Jo hurried to this quiet place, and curling herself up in the easy chair, devoured poetry, romance, history, travels, and pictures like a regular bookworm. But, like all happiness, it did not last long, for as sure as she had just reached the heart of the story, the sweetest verse of a song, or the most perilous adventure of her traveler, a shrill voice called, "Josy-phine! Josy-phine!" and she had to leave her paradise to wind yarn, wash the poodle, or read Belsham's Essays by the hour together.

Jo's ambition was to do something very splendid. What it was, she had no idea as yet, but left it for time to tell her, and meanwhile, found her greatest affliction in the fact that she couldn't read, run, and ride as much as she liked. A quick temper, sharp tongue, and restless spirit were always getting her into scrapes, and her life was a series of ups and downs, which were both comic and pathetic. But the training she received at Aunt March's was just what she needed, and the thought that she was doing something to support herself made her happy in spite of the perpetual "Josy-phine!"

Beth was too bashful to go to school. It had been tried, but she suffered so much that it was given up, and she did her lessons at home with her father. Even when he went away, and her mother was called to devote her skill and energy to Soldiers' Aid Societies, Beth went faithfully on by herself and did the best she could. She was a housewifely little creature, and helped Hannah keep home neat and comfortable for the workers, never thinking of any reward but to be loved. Long, quiet days she spent, not lonely nor idle, for her little world was peopled with imaginary friends, and she was by nature a busy bee. There were six dolls to be taken up and dressed every morning, for Beth was a child still and loved her pets as well as ever. Not one whole or handsome one among them, all were outcasts till Beth took them in, for when her sisters outgrew these idols, they passed to her because Amy would have nothing old or ugly. Beth cherished them all the more tenderly for that very reason, and set up a hospital for infirm dolls.

Beth had her troubles as well as the others, and not being an angel but a very human little girl, she often 'wept a little weep' as Jo said, because she couldn't take music lessons and have a fine piano. She loved music so dearly, tried so hard to learn, and practiced away so patiently at the jingling old instrument, that it did seem as if someone ought to help her. Nobody did, however, and nobody saw Beth wipe the tears off the yellow keys, that wouldn't keep in tune, when she was all alone. She sang like a little lark about her work, never was too tired to play for Marmee and the girls, and day after day said hopefully to herself, "I know I'll get my music some time, if I'm good."

If anybody had asked Amy what the greatest trial of her life was, she would have answered at once, "My nose." When she was a baby, Jo had accidently dropped her into the coal hod, and Amy

insisted that the fall had ruined her nose forever. It was not big nor red, like poor 'Petrea's', it was only rather flat, and all the pinching in the world could not give it an aristocratic point. No one minded it but herself, and it was doing its best to grow, but Amy felt deeply the want of a Grecian nose, and drew whole sheets of handsome ones to console herself.

"Little Raphael," as her sisters called her, had a decided talent for drawing, and was never so happy as when copying flowers, designing fairies, or illustrating stories with queer specimens of art. She was a great favorite with her mates, being good-tempered and possessing the happy art of pleasing without effort.

Amy was in a fair way to be spoiled, for everyone petted her, and her small vanities and selfishnesses were growing nicely. One thing, however, rather quenched the vanities. She had to wear her cousin's clothes. Florence's mama hadn't a particle of taste. Everything was good, well made, and little worn, but Amy's artistic eyes were much afflicted, especially this winter, when her school dress was a dull purple with yellow dots and no trimming.

Meg was Amy's confidant and monitor, and by some strange attraction of opposites Jo was gentle Beth's. To Jo alone did the shy child tell her thoughts, and over her big harum-scarum sister Beth unconsciously exercised more influence than anyone in the family. The two older girls were a great deal to one another, but each took one of the younger sisters into her keeping and watched over her in her own way, 'playing mother' they called it, and put their sisters in the places of discarded dolls with the maternal instinct of little women.

"Has anybody got anything to tell? It's been such a dismal day I'm really dying for some amusement," said Meg, as they sat sewing together that evening.

Beth told a story. Then they asked their mother for one, and after a moments thought, she said soberly, "Once upon a time, there were four girls, who had enough to eat and drink and wear, a good many comforts and pleasures, kind friends and parents who loved them dearly, and yet they were not contented." (Here the listeners stole sly looks at one another, and began to sew diligently.) "These girls were anxious to be good and made many excellent resolutions, but they did not keep them very well, and were constantly saying, 'If only we had this,' or 'If we could only do that,' quite forgetting how much they already had, and how many things they actually could do. So they asked an old woman what spell they could use to make them happy, and she said, 'When you feel discontented, think over your blessings, and be grateful.'" (Here Jo looked up quickly, as if about to speak, but changed her mind, seeing that the story was not done yet.)

"Being sensible girls, they decided to try her advice, and soon were surprised to see how well off they were. One discovered that money couldn't keep shame and sorrow out of rich people's houses, another that, though she was poor, she was a great deal happier, with her youth, health, and good spirits, than a certain fretful, feeble old lady who couldn't enjoy her comforts, a third that, disagreeable as it was to help get dinner, it was harder still to go begging for it and the fourth, that even carnelian rings were not so valuable as good behavior. So they agreed to stop complaining, to enjoy the blessings already possessed, and try to deserve them, lest they should be taken away entirely, instead of increased, and I believe they were never disappointed or sorry that they took the old woman's advice."

"Now, Marmee, that is very cunning of you to turn our own stories against us, and give us a sermon instead of a romance!" cried Meg.

"I like that kind of sermon. It's the sort Father used to tell us," said Beth thoughtfully, putting the needles straight on Jo's

cushion.

"I don't complain near as much as the others do, and I shall be more careful than ever now, for I've had warning from Susie's downfall," said Amy morally.

"We needed that lesson, and we won't forget it. If we do so, you just say to us, as old Chloe did in Uncle Tom, 'Tink ob yer marcies, chillen!' 'Tink ob yer marcies!'" added Jo, who could not, for the life of her, help getting a morsel of fun out of the little sermon, though she took it to heart as much as any of them.

05

BEING NEIGHBORLY

"What in the world are you going to do now, Jo?" asked Meg one snowy afternoon, as her sister came tramping through the hall, in rubber boots, old sack, and hood, with a broom in one hand and a shovel in the other.

"Going out for exercise," answered Jo with a mischievous twinkle in her eyes.

Meg went back to toast her feet and read Ivanhoe, and Jo began to dig paths with great energy. The snow was light, and with her broom she soon swept a path all round the garden, for Beth to walk in when the sun came out and the invalid dolls needed air. Now, the garden separated the Marches' house from that of Mr. Laurence. Both stood in a suburb of the city, which was still country-like, with groves and lawns, large gardens, and quiet streets. A low hedge parted the two estates. On one side was an old, brown house, looking rather bare and shabby, robbed of the vines that in summer covered its walls and the flowers, which then surrounded it. On the other side was a stately stone mansion, plainly betokening every sort of comfort and luxury, from the big coach house and well-kept grounds to the conservatory and the glimpses of lovely things one caught between the rich curtains.

Yet it seemed a lonely, lifeless sort of house, for no children frolicked on the lawn, no motherly face ever smiled at the windows, and few people went in and out, except the old gentleman and his grandson.

To Jo's lively fancy, this fine house seemed a kind of enchanted palace, full of splendors and delights which no one enjoyed. She had long wanted to behold these hidden glories, and to know the Laurence boy, who looked as if he would like to be known, if he only knew how to begin. Since the party, she had been more eager than ever, and had planned many ways of making friends with him, but he had not been seen lately, and Jo began to think he had gone away, when she one day spied a brown face at an upper window, looking wistfully down into their garden, where Beth and Amy were snow-balling one another.

"That boy is suffering for society and fun," she said to herself. "His grandpa does not know what's good for him, and keeps him shut up all alone. He needs a party of jolly boys to play with, or somebody young and lively. I've a great mind to go over and tell the old gentleman so!"

The idea amused Jo, who liked to do daring things and was always scandalizing Meg by her queer performances. The plan of 'going over' was not forgotten. And when the snowy afternoon came, Jo resolved to try what could be done. She saw Mr. Laurence drive off, and then sallied out to dig her way down to the hedge, where she paused and took a survey. All quiet, curtains down at the lower windows, servants out of sight, and nothing human visible but a curly black head leaning on a thin hand at the upper window.

"There he is," thought Jo, "Poor boy! All alone and sick this dismal day. It's a shame! I'll toss up a snowball and make him look out, and then say a kind word to him."

Up went a handful of soft snow, and the head turned at once, showing a face which lost its listless look in a minute, as the big eyes brightened and the mouth began to smile. Jo nodded and laughed, and flourished her broom as she called out...

"How do you do? Are you sick?"

Laurie opened the window, and croaked out as hoarsely as a raven...

"Better, thank you. I've had a bad cold, and been shut up a week."

"I'm sorry. What do you amuse yourself with?"

"Nothing. It's dull as tombs up here."

"Don't you read?"

"Not much. They won't let me."

"Can't somebody read to you?"

"Grandpa does sometimes, but my books don't interest him, and I hate to ask Brooke all the time."

"Have someone come and see you then."

"There isn't anyone I'd like to see. Boys make such a row, and my head is weak."

"Isn't there some nice girl who'd read and amuse you? Girls are quiet and like to play nurse."

"Don't know any."

"You know us," began Jo, then laughed and stopped.

"So I do! Will you come, please?" cried Laurie.

"I'm not quiet and nice, but I'll come, if Mother will let me. I'll go ask her. Shut the window, like a good boy, and wait till I come."

With that, Jo shouldered her broom and marched into the house, wondering what they would all say to her. Laurie was in a flutter of excitement at the idea of having company, and flew about to get ready, for as Mrs. March said, he was 'a little gentleman', and did honor to the coming guest by brushing his curly pate, putting on a fresh color, and trying to tidy up the room, which in spite of half a dozen servants, was anything but neat. Presently there came a loud ring, then a decided voice, asking for 'Mr. Laurie', and a surprised-looking servant came running up to announce a young lady.

"All right, show her up, it's Miss Jo," said Laurie, going to the door of his little parlor to meet Jo, who appeared, looking rosy and quite at her ease, with a covered dish in one hand and Beth's three kittens in the other.

"Here I am, bag and baggage," she said briskly. "Mother sent her love, and was glad if I could do anything for you. Meg wanted me to bring some of her blanc mange, she makes it very nicely, and Beth thought her cats would be comforting. I knew you'd laugh at them, but I couldn't refuse, she was so anxious to do something."

It so happened that Beth's funny loan was just the thing, for in laughing over the kits, Laurie forgot his bashfulness, and grew sociable at once.

"That looks too pretty to eat," he said, smiling with pleasure, as Jo uncovered the dish, and showed the blanc mange, surrounded by a garland of green leaves, and the scarlet flowers of Amy's pet geranium.

"It isn't anything, only they all felt kindly and wanted to show it. Tell the girl to put it away for your tea. It's so simple you can eat it, and being soft, it will slip down without hurting your sore throat. What a cozy room this is!"

"It might be if it was kept nice, but the maids are lazy, and I don't know how to make them mind. It worries me though."

"I'll right it up in two minutes, for it only needs to have the hearth brushed, so—and the things made straight on the mantelpiece, so—and the books put here, and the bottles there, and your sofa turned from the light, and the pillows plumped up a bit. Now then, you're fixed."

And so he was, for, as she laughed and talked, Jo had whisked things into place and given quite a different air to the room. Laurie watched her in respectful silence, and when she beckoned him to his

sofa, he sat down with a sigh of satisfaction, saying gratefully...

"How kind you are! Yes, that's what it wanted. Now please take the big chair and let me do something to amuse my company."

"No, I came to amuse you. Shall I read aloud?" and Jo looked affectionately toward some inviting books near by.

"Thank you! I've read all those, and if you don't mind, I'd rather talk," answered Laurie.

"Not a bit. I'll talk all day if you'll only set me going. Beth says I never know when to stop."

"Is Beth the rosy one, who stays at home good deal and sometimes goes out with a little basket?" asked Laurie with interest.

"Yes, that's Beth. She's my girl, and a regular good one she is, too."

"The pretty one is Meg, and the curly-haired one is Amy, I believe?"

"How did you find that out?"

Laurie colored up, but answered frankly, "Why, you see I often hear you calling to one another, and when I'm alone up here, I can't help looking over at your house, you always seem to be having such good times. I beg your pardon for being so rude, but sometimes you forget to put down the curtain at the window where the flowers are. And when the lamps are lighted, it's like looking at a picture to see the fire, and you all around the table with your mother. Her face is right opposite, and it looks so sweet behind the flowers, I can't help watching it. I haven't got any mother, you know." And Laurie poked the fire to hide a little twitching of the lips that he could not control.

Laurie was sick and lonely, and feeling how rich she was in home and happiness, she gladly tried to share it with him. Her face was very friendly and her sharp voice unusually gentle as she said...

"We'll never draw that curtain any more, and I give you leave to

look as much as you like. I just wish, though, instead of peeping, you'd come over and see us. Mother is so splendid, she'd do you heaps of good, and Beth would sing to you if I begged her to, and Amy would dance. Meg and I would make you laugh over our funny stage properties, and we'd have jolly times. Wouldn't your grandpa let you?"

"I think he would, if your mother asked him. He's very kind, though he does not look so, and he lets me do what I like, pretty much, only he's afraid I might be a bother to strangers," began Laurie, brightening more and more.

"We are not strangers, we are neighbors, and you needn't think you'd be a bother. We want to know you, and I've been trying to do it this ever so long. We haven't been here a great while, you know, but we have got acquainted with all our neighbors but you."

"You see, Grandpa lives among his books, and doesn't mind much what happens outside. Mr. Brooke, my tutor, doesn't stay here, you know, and I have no one to go about with me, so I just stop at home and get on as I can."

"That's bad. You ought to make an effort and go visiting everywhere you are asked, then you'll have plenty of friends, and pleasant places to go to. Never mind being bashful. It won't last long if you keep going."

Laurie turned red again, but wasn't offended at being accused of bashfulness, for there was so much good will in Jo it was impossible not to take her blunt speeches as kindly as they were meant.

"Do you like your school?" asked the boy, changing the subject, after a little pause, during which he stared at the fire and Jo looked about her, well pleased.

"Don't go to school, I'm a businessman—girl, I mean. I go to wait on my great-aunt, and a dear, cross old soul she is, too,"

answered Jo.

Laurie opened his mouth to ask another question, but remembering just in time that it wasn't manners to make too many inquiries into people's affairs, he shut it again, and looked uncomfortable.

Jo liked his good breeding, and didn't mind having a laugh at Aunt March, so she gave him a lively description of the fidgety old lady, her fat poodle, the parrot that talked Spanish, and the library where she reveled.

Then they got to talking about books, and to Jo's delight, she found that Laurie loved them as well as she did, and had read even more than herself.

"If you like them so much, come down and see ours. Grandfather is out, so you needn't be afraid," said Laurie, getting up.

"I'm not afraid of anything," returned Jo, with a toss of the head.

"I don't believe you are!" exclaimed the boy, looking at her with much admiration, though he privately thought she would have good reason to be a trifle afraid of the old gentleman, if she met him in some of his moods.

The atmosphere of the whole house being summerlike, Laurie led the way from room to room. And so, at last they came to the library, where she clapped her hands and pranced, as she always did when especially delighted. It was lined with books, and there were pictures and statues, and distracting little cabinets full of coins and curiosities, and Sleepy Hollow chairs, and queer tables, and bronzes, and best of all, a great open fireplace with quaint tiles all round it.

"What richness!" sighed Jo, sinking into the depth of a velour chair and gazing about her with an air of intense satisfaction.

"Theodore Laurence, you ought to be the happiest boy in the

world," she added impressively.

"A fellow can't live on books," said Laurie, shaking his head as he perched on a table opposite.

Before he could say more, a bell rang, and Jo flew up, exclaiming with alarm, "Mercy me! It's your grandpa!"

"Well, what if it is? You are not afraid of anything, you know," returned the boy, looking wicked.

"I think I am a little bit afraid of him, but I don't know why I should be. Marmee said I might come, and I don't think you're any the worse for it," said Jo, composing herself, though she kept her eyes on the door.

"I'm a great deal better for it, and ever so much obliged. I'm only afraid you are very tired of talking to me. It was so pleasant, I couldn't bear to stop," said Laurie gratefully.

"The doctor to see you, sir," and the maid beckoned as she spoke.

"Would you mind if I left you for a minute? I suppose I must see him," said Laurie.

"Don't mind me. I'm happy as a cricket here," answered Jo.

Laurie went away, and his guest amused herself in her own way. She was standing before a fine portrait of the old gentleman when the door opened again, and without turning, she said decidedly, "I'm sure now that I shouldn't be afraid of him, for he's got kind eyes, though his mouth is grim, and he looks as if he had a tremendous will of his own. He isn't as handsome as my grandfather, but I like him."

"Thank you, ma'am," said a gruff voice behind her, and there, to her great dismay, stood old Mr. Laurence.

Poor Jo blushed till she couldn't blush any redder, and her heart began to beat uncomfortably fast as she thought what she had said. For a minute a wild desire to run away possessed her, but that was

cowardly, and the girls would laugh at her, so she resolved to stay and get out of the scrape as she could. A second look showed her that the living eyes, under the bushy eyebrows, were kinder even than the painted ones, and there was a sly twinkle in them, which lessened her fear a good deal. The gruff voice was gruffer than ever, as the old gentleman said abruptly, after the dreadful pause, "So you're not afraid of me, hey?"

"Not much, sir."

"And you don't think me as handsome as your grandfather?"

"Not quite, sir."

"And I've got a tremendous will, have I?"

"I only said I thought so."

"But you like me in spite of it?"

"Yes, I do, sir."

That answer pleased the old gentleman. He gave a short laugh, shook hands with her, and, putting his finger under her chin, turned up her face, examined it gravely, and let it go, saying with a nod,

"You've got your grandfather's spirit, if you haven't his face. He was a fine man, my dear, but what is better, he was a brave and an honest one, and I was proud to be his friend."

"Thank you, sir," And Jo was quite comfortable after that, for it suited her exactly.

"What have you been doing to this boy of mine, hey?" was the next question, sharply put.

"Only trying to be neighborly, sir." And Jo told how her visit came about.

"You think he needs cheering up a bit, do you?"

"Yes, sir, he seems a little lonely, and young folks would do him good perhaps. We are only girls, but we should be glad to help if we could, for we don't forget the splendid Christmas present you sent

us," said Jo eagerly.

"Tut, tut, tut! That was the boy's affair. How is the poor woman?"

"Doing nicely, sir." And off went Jo, talking very fast, as she told all about the Hummels, in whom her mother had interested richer friends than they were.

"Just her father's way of doing good. I shall come and see your mother some fine day. Tell her so. There's the tea bell, we have it early on the boy's account. Come down and go on being neighborly."

"If you'd like to have me, sir."

"Shouldn't ask you, if I didn't." And Mr. Laurence offered her his arm with old-fashioned courtesy.

"What would Meg say to this?" thought Jo, as she was marched away, while her eyes danced with fun as she imagined herself telling the story at home.

Laurie came running downstairs and brought up with a start of surprise at the astounding sight of Jo arm in arm with his redoubtable grandfather.

"I didn't know you'd come, sir," he began, as Jo gave him a triumphant little glance.

"That's evident, by the way you racket downstairs. Come to your tea, sir, and behave like a gentleman." And having pulled the boy's hair by way of a caress, Mr. Laurence walked on, while Laurie went through a series of comic evolutions behind their backs, which nearly produced an explosion of laughter from Jo.

The old gentleman did not say much as he drank his four cups of tea, but he watched the young people, who soon chatted away like old friends, and the change in his grandson did not escape him. There was color, light, and life in the boy's face now, vivacity in his manner, and genuine merriment in his laugh.

"She's right, the lad is lonely. I'll see what these little girls can do for him," thought Mr. Laurence, as he looked and listened. He liked Jo, for her odd, blunt ways suited him, and she seemed to understand the boy almost as well as if she had been one herself.

If the Laurences had been what Jo called 'prim and poky', she would not have got on at all, for such people always made her shy and awkward. But finding them free and easy, she was so herself, and made a good impression. When they rose she proposed to go, but Laurie said he had something more to show her, and took her away to the conservatory, which had been lighted for her benefit. It seemed quite fairylike to Jo, as she went up and down the walks, enjoying the blooming walls on either side, the soft light, the damp sweet air, and the wonderful vines and trees that hung about her, while her new friend cut the finest flowers till his hands were full. Then he tied them up, saying, with the happy look Jo liked to see, "Please give these to your mother, and tell her I like the medicine she sent me very much."

They found Mr. Laurence standing before the fire in the great drawing room, but Jo's attention was entirely absorbed by a grand piano, which stood open.

"Do you play?" she asked, turning to Laurie with a respectful expression.

"Sometimes," he answered modestly.

"Please do now. I want to hear it, so I can tell Beth."

"Won't you first?"

"Don't know how. Too stupid to learn, but I love music dearly."

So Laurie played and Jo listened, with her nose luxuriously buried in heliotrope and tea roses. Her respect and regard for the 'Laurence' boy increased very much, for he played remarkably well and didn't put on any airs. She wished Beth could hear him, but she

did not say so, only praised him till he was quite abashed, and his grandfather came to his rescue.

"That will do, that will do, young lady. Too many sugarplums are not good for him. His music isn't bad, but I hope he will do as well in more important things. Going? well, I'm much obliged to you, and I hope you'll come again. My respects to your mother. Good night, Doctor Jo."

He shook hands kindly, but looked as if something did not please him. When they got into the hall, Jo asked Laurie if she had said anything amiss. He shook his head.

"No, it was me. He doesn't like to hear me play."

"Why not?"

"I'll tell you some day. John is going home with you, as I can't."

"No need of that. I am not a young lady, and it's only a step. Take care of yourself, won't you?"

"Yes, but you will come again, I hope?"

"If you promise to come and see us after you are well."

"I will."

"Good night, Laurie!"

"Good night, Jo, good night!"

When all the afternoon's adventures had been told, the family felt inclined to go visiting in a body, for each found something very attractive in the big house on the other side of the hedge. Mrs. March wanted to talk of her father with the old man who had not forgotten him, Meg longed to walk in the conservatory, Beth sighed for the grand piano, and Amy was eager to see the fine pictures and statues.

"Mother, why didn't Mr. Laurence like to have Laurie play?" asked Jo, who was of an inquiring disposition.

"I am not sure, but I think it was because his son, Laurie's

father, married an Italian lady, a musician, which displeased the old man, who is very proud. The lady was good and lovely and accomplished, but he did not like her, and never saw his son after he married. They both died when Laurie was a little child, and then his grandfather took him home. I fancy the boy, who was born in Italy, is not very strong, and the old man is afraid of losing him, which makes him so careful. Laurie comes naturally by his love of music, for he is like his mother, and I dare say his grandfather fears that he may want to be a musician. At any rate, his skill reminds him of the woman he did not like, and so he 'glowered' as Jo said."

"Dear me, how romantic!" exclaimed Meg.

"How silly!" said Jo. "Let him be a musician if he wants to, and not plague his life out sending him to college, when he hates to go."

"That's why he has such handsome black eyes and pretty manners, I suppose. Italians are always nice," said Meg, who was a little sentimental.

"What do you know about his eyes and his manners? You never spoke to him, hardly," cried Jo, who was not sentimental.

"I saw him at the party, and what you tell shows that he knows how to behave. That was a nice little speech about the medicine Mother sent him."

"He meant the blanc mange, I suppose."

"How stupid you are, child! He meant you, of course."

"Did he?" And Jo opened her eyes as if it had never occurred to her before.

"I never saw such a girl! You don't know a compliment when you get it," said Meg, with the air of a young lady who knew all about the matter.

"I think they are great nonsense, and I'll thank you not to be

silly and spoil my fun. Laurie's a nice boy and I like him, and I won't have any sentimental stuff about compliments and such rubbish. We'll all be good to him because he hasn't got any mother, and he may come over and see us, mayn't he, Marmee?"

"Yes, Jo, your little friend is very welcome, and I hope Meg will remember that children should be children as long as they can."

"I don't call myself a child, and I'm not in my teens yet," observed Amy. "What do you say, Beth?"

"I was thinking about our 'Pilgrim's Progress'," answered Beth, who had not heard a word. "How we got out of the Slough and through the Wicket Gate by resolving to be good, and up the steep hill by trying, and that maybe the house over there, full of splendid things, is going to be our Palace Beautiful."

"We have got to get by the lions first," said Jo, as if she rather liked the prospect.

06

BETH FINDS THE PALACE BEAUTIFUL

The big house did prove a Palace Beautiful. All sorts of pleasant things happened about that time, for the new friendship flourished like grass in spring. Every one liked Laurie, and he privately informed his tutor that "the Marches were regularly splendid girls." Never having known mother or sisters, he was quick to feel the influences they brought about him, and their busy, lively ways made him ashamed of the indolent life he led. He was tired of books, and found people so interesting now that Mr. Brooke was obliged to make very unsatisfactory reports, for Laurie was always playing truant and running over to the Marches'.

"Never mind, let him take a holiday, and make it up afterward," said the old gentleman. "The good lady next door says he is studying too hard and needs young society, amusement, and exercise. I suspect she is right, and that I've been coddling the fellow as if I'd been his grandmother. Let him do what he likes, as long as he is happy. He can't get into mischief in that little nunnery over there, and Mrs. March is doing more for him than we can."

What good times they had, to be sure. Such plays and tableaux, such sleigh rides and skating frolics, such pleasant evenings in the old parlor, and now and then such gay little parties at the great house. Meg could walk in the conservatory whenever she liked and revel in bouquets, Jo browsed over the new library voraciously, and convulsed

the old gentleman with her criticisms, Amy copied pictures and enjoyed beauty to her heart's content, and Laurie played 'lord of the manor' in the most delightful style.

But Beth, though yearning for the grand piano, could not pluck up courage to go to the 'Mansion of Bliss', as Meg called it. She went once with Jo, but the old gentleman, not being aware of her infirmity, stared at her so hard from under his heavy eyebrows, and said "Hey!" so loud, that he frightened her so much her 'feet chattered on the floor', she never told her mother, and she ran away, declaring she would never go there any more, not even for the dear piano. No persuasions or enticements could overcome her fear, till, the fact coming to Mr. Laurence's ear in some mysterious way, he set about mending matters. During one of the brief calls he made, he artfully led the conversation to music, and talked away about great singers whom he had seen, fine organs he had heard, and told such charming anecdotes that Beth found it impossible to stay in her distant corner, but crept nearer and nearer, as if fascinated. At the back of his chair she stopped and stood listening, with her great eyes wide open and her cheeks red with excitement of this unusual performance. Taking no more notice of her than if she had been a fly, Mr. Laurence talked on about Laurie's lessons and teachers. And presently, as if the idea had just occurred to him, he said to Mrs. March...

"The boy neglects his music now, and I'm glad of it, for he was getting too fond of it. But the piano suffers for want of use. Wouldn't some of your girls like to run over, and practice on it now and then, just to keep it in tune, you know, ma'am?"

Before Mrs. March could reply, Mr. Laurence went on with an odd little nod and smile...

"They needn't see or speak to anyone, but run in at any time.

For I'm shut up in my study at the other end of the house, Laurie is out a great deal, and the servants are never near the drawing room after nine o'clock."

Here he rose, as if going, and Beth made up her mind to speak, for that last arrangement left nothing to be desired. "Please, tell the young ladies what I say, and if they don't care to come, why, never mind." Here a little hand slipped into his, and Beth looked up at him with a face full of gratitude, as she said, in her earnest yet timid way...

"Oh sir, they do care, very very much!"

"Are you the musical girl?" he asked, without any startling "Hey!" as he looked down at her very kindly.

"I'm Beth. I love it dearly, and I'll come, if you are quite sure nobody will hear me, and be disturbed," she added, fearing to be rude, and trembling at her own boldness as she spoke.

"Not a soul, my dear. The house is empty half the day, so come and drum away as much as you like, and I shall be obliged to you."

"How kind you are, sir!"

Beth blushed like a rose under the friendly look he wore, but she was not frightened now, and gave the hand a grateful squeeze because she had no words to thank him for the precious gift he had given her. The old gentleman softly stroked the hair off her forehead, and, stooping down, he kissed her, saying, in a tone few people ever heard...

"I had a little girl once, with eyes like these. God bless you, my dear! Good day, madam." And away he went, in a great hurry.

Beth had a rapture with her mother. How blithely she sang that evening, and how they all laughed at her because she woke Amy in the night by playing the piano on her face in her sleep. Next day, having seen both the old and young gentleman out of the house, Beth, after two or three retreats, fairly got in at the side door, and made her way

as noiselessly as any mouse to the drawing room where her idol stood. Quite by accident, of course, some pretty, easy music lay on the piano, and with trembling fingers and frequent stops to listen and look about, Beth at last touched the great instrument, and straightway forgot her fear, herself, and everything else but the unspeakable delight which the music gave her, for it was like the voice of a beloved friend.

She stayed till Hannah came to take her home to dinner, but she had no appetite, and could only sit and smile upon everyone in a general state of beatitude.

After that, the little brown hood slipped through the hedge nearly every day, and the great drawing room was haunted by a tuneful spirit that came and went unseen. She never knew that Mr. Laurence often opened his study door to hear the old-fashioned airs he liked. She never saw Laurie mount guard in the hall to warn the servants away. She never suspected that the exercise books and new songs which she found in the rack were put there for her especial benefit, and when he talked to her about music at home, she only thought how kind he was to tell things that helped her so much. So she enjoyed herself heartily, and found, what isn't always the case, that her granted wish was all she had hoped.

"Mother, I'm going to work Mr. Laurence a pair of slippers. He is so kind to me, I must thank him, and I don't know any other way. Can I do it?" asked Beth, a few weeks after that eventful call of his.

"Yes, dear. It will please him very much, and be a nice way of thanking him." replied Mrs. March, who took peculiar pleasure in granting Beth's requests because she so seldom asked anything for herself.

She was a nimble little needlewoman, and they were finished before anyone got tired of them. Then she wrote a short, simple note,

and with Laurie's help, got them smuggled onto the study table one morning before the old gentleman was up.

When this excitement was over, Beth waited to see what would happen. All day passed and a part of the next before any acknowledgement arrived, and she was beginning to fear she had offended her crotchety friend. On the afternoon of the second day, she went out to do an errand, and give poor Joanna, the invalid doll, her daily exercise. As she came up the street, on her return, she saw three, yes, four heads popping in and out of the parlor windows, and the moment they saw her, several hands were waved, and several joyful voices screamed...

"Here's a letter from the old gentleman! Come quick, and read it!"

"Oh, Beth, he's sent you..." began Amy, gesticulating with unseemly energy, but she got no further, for Jo quenched her by slamming down the window.

Beth hurried on in a flutter of suspense. At the door her sisters seized and bore her to the parlor in a triumphal procession, all pointing and all saying at once, "Look there! Look there!" Beth did look, and turned pale with delight and surprise, for there stood a little cabinet piano, with a letter lying on the glossy lid, directed like a sign board to "Miss Elizabeth March."

"For me?" gasped Beth, holding onto Jo and feeling as if she should tumble down, it was such an overwhelming thing altogether.

"Yes, all for you, my precious! Isn't it splendid of him? Don't you think he's the dearest old man in the world? Here's the key in the letter. We didn't open it, but we are dying to know what he says," cried Jo, hugging her sister and offering the note.

"You read it! I can't, I feel so queer! Oh, it is too lovely!" and Beth hid her face in Jo's apron, quite upset by her present.

Jo opened the paper and began to laugh, for the first words she saw were...

"Miss March: "Dear Madam—"

"How nice it sounds! I wish someone would write to me so!" said Amy, who thought the old-fashioned address very elegant.

" 'I have had many pairs of slippers in my life, but I never had any that suited me so well as yours,' " continued Jo. " 'Heart's-ease is my favorite flower, and these will always remind me of the gentle giver. I like to pay my debts, so I know you will allow 'the old gentleman' to send you something which once belonged to the little grand daughter he lost. With hearty thanks and best wishes, I remain " 'Your grateful friend and humble servant, 'JAMES LAURENCE' .'"

"There, Beth, that's an honor to be proud of, I'm sure! Laurie told me how fond Mr. Laurence used to be of the child who died, and how he kept all her little things carefully. Just think, he's given you her piano. That comes of having big blue eyes and loving music," said Jo, trying to soothe Beth, who trembled and looked more excited than she had ever been before.

"Try it, honey. Let's hear the sound of the baby pianny," said Hannah, who always took a share in the family joys and sorrows.

So Beth tried it, and everyone pronounced it the most remarkable piano ever heard. "You'll have to go and thank him," said Jo, by way of a joke, for the idea of the child's really going never entered her head.

"Yes, I mean to. I guess I'll go now, before I get frightened thinking about it." And, to the utter amazement of the assembled family, Beth walked deliberately down the garden, through the hedge, and in at the Laurences' door.

They would have been still more amazed if they had seen what

Beth did afterward. If you will believe me, she went and knocked at the study door before she gave herself time to think, and when a gruff voice called out, "Come in!" she did go in, right up to Mr. Laurence, who looked quite taken aback, and held out her hand, saying, with only a small quaver in her voice, "I came to thank you, sir, for..." But she didn't finish, for he looked so friendly that she forgot her speech and, only remembering that he had lost the little girl he loved, she put both arms round his neck and kissed him.

If the roof of the house had suddenly flown off, the old gentleman wouldn't have been more astonished. But he liked it. Oh, dear, yes, he liked it amazingly! And was so touched and pleased by that confiding little kiss that all his crustiness vanished, and he just set her on his knee, and laid his wrinkled cheek against her rosy one, feeling as if he had got his own little granddaughter back again. Beth ceased to fear him from that moment, and sat there talking to him as cozily as if she had known him all her life, for love casts out fear, and gratitude can conquer pride. When she went home, he walked with her to her own gate, shook hands cordially, and touched his hat as he marched back again, looking very stately and erect, like a handsome, soldierly old gentleman, as he was.

When the girls saw that performance, Jo began to dance a jig, by way of expressing her satisfaction, Amy nearly fell out of the window in her surprise, and Meg exclaimed, with up-lifted hands, "Well, I do believe the world is coming to an end."

07

AMY's VALLEY OF HUMILIATION

"I need money so much. I'm dreadfully in debt, and it won't be my turn to have the rag money for a month." said Amy.

"In debt, Amy? What do you mean?" And Meg looked sober.

"Why, I owe at least a dozen pickled limes, and I can't pay them, you know, till I have money, for Marmee forbade my having anything charged at the shop."

"Tell me all about it. Are limes the fashion now? It used to be pricking bits of rubber to make balls." And Meg tried to keep her countenance, Amy looked so grave and important.

"Why, you see, the girls are always buying them, and unless you want to be thought mean, you must do it too. It's nothing but limes now, for everyone is sucking them in their desks in schooltime, and trading them off for pencils, bead rings, paper dolls, or something else, at recess. If one girl likes another, she gives her a lime. If she's mad with her, she eats one before her face, and doesn't offer even a suck. They treat by turns, and I've had ever so many but haven't returned them, and I ought for they are debts of honor, you know."

"How much will pay them off and restore your credit?" asked Meg, taking out her purse.

"A quarter would more than do it, and leave a few cents over for a treat for you."

"Here's the money. Make it last as long as you can, for it isn't

very plenty, you know."

"Oh, thank you! It must be so nice to have pocket money!"

Next day Amy was rather late at school, but could not resist the temptation of displaying, with pardonable pride, a moist brown-paper parcel, before she consigned it to the inmost recesses of her desk. During the next few minutes the rumor that Amy March had got twenty-four delicious limes (she ate one on the way) and was going to treat circulated through her 'set', and the attentions of her friends became quite overwhelming. Katy Brown invited her to her next party on the spot. Mary Kingsley insisted on lending her her watch till recess, and Jenny Snow, a satirical young lady, who had basely twitted Amy upon her limeless state, promptly buried the hatchet and offered to furnish answers to certain appalling sums. But Amy had not forgotten Miss Snow's cutting remarks.

A distinguished personage happened to visit the school that morning, and Amy's beautifully drawn maps received praise, which honor to her foe rankled in the soul of Miss Snow, and caused Miss March to assume the airs of a studious young peacock. But, alas, alas! Pride goes before a fall, and the revengeful Snow turned the tables with disastrous success. No sooner had the guest paid the usual stale compliments and bowed himself out, than Jenny, under pretense of asking an important question, informed Mr. Davis, the teacher, that Amy March had pickled limes in her desk.

Now Mr. Davis had declared limes a contraband article, and solemnly vowed to publicly ferrule the first person who was found breaking the law.

"Miss March, come to the desk."

Amy rose to comply with outward composure, but a secret fear oppressed her, for the limes weighed upon her conscience.

"Bring with you the limes you have in your desk," was the

unexpected command which arrested her before she got out of her seat.

With a despairing glance at her set, she obeyed.

"Now take these disgusting things two by two, and throw them out of the window."

Scarlet with shame and anger, Amy went to and fro six dreadful times. As Amy returned from her last trip, Mr. Davis gave a portentous "Hem!" and said, in his most impressive manner...

"Young ladies, you remember what I said to you a week ago. I am sorry this has happened, but I never allow my rules to be infringed, and I never break my word. Miss March, hold out your hand."

Amy started, and put both hands behind her, turning on him an imploring look which pleaded for her better than the words she could not utter.

"Your hand, Miss March!" was the only answer her mute appeal received, and too proud to cry or beseech, Amy set her teeth, threw back her head defiantly, and bore without flinching several tingling blows on her little palm. For the first time in her life she had been struck, and the disgrace, in her eyes, was as deep as if he had knocked her down.

"You will now stand on the platform till recess," said Mr. Davis, resolved to do the thing thoroughly, since he had begun.

During the fifteen minutes that followed, the proud and sensitive little girl suffered a shame and pain which she never forgot. To others it might seem a ludicrous or trivial affair, but to her it was a hard experience, for during the twelve years of her life she had been governed by love alone, and a blow of that sort had never touched her before. The smart of her hand and the ache of her heart were forgotten in the sting of the thought, "I shall have to tell at home,

and they will be so disappointed in me!"

The fifteen minutes seemed an hour, but they came to an end at last, and the word 'Recess!' had never seemed so welcome to her before.

"You can go, Miss March," said Mr. Davis, looking, as he felt, uncomfortable.

He did not soon forget the reproachful glance Amy gave him, as she went, without a word to anyone, straight into the anteroom, snatched her things, and left the place "forever," as she passionately declared to herself. She was in a sad state when she got home, and when the older girls arrived, some time later, an indignation meeting was held at once. Mrs. March did not say much but looked disturbed, and comforted her afflicted little daughter in her tenderest manner. Meg bathed the insulted hand with glycerine and tears, Beth felt that even her beloved kittens would fail as a balm for griefs like this, Jo wrathfully proposed that Mr. Davis be arrested without delay, and Hannah shook her fist at the 'villain' and pounded potatoes for dinner as if she had him under her pestle.

"Yes, you can have a vacation from school, but I want you to study a little every day with Beth," said Mrs. March that evening. "I don't approve of corporal punishment, especially for girls. I dislike Mr. Davis's manner of teaching and don't think the girls you associate with are doing you any good, so I shall ask your father's advice before I send you anywhere else."

"That's good! I wish all the girls would leave, and spoil his old school. It's perfectly maddening to think of those lovely limes," sighed Amy, with the air of a martyr.

"I am not sorry you lost them, for you broke the rules, and deserved some punishment for disobedience," was the severe reply, which rather disappointed the young lady, who expected nothing but sympathy.

"Do you mean you are glad I was disgraced before the whole school?" cried Amy.

"I should not have chosen that way of mending a fault," replied her mother, "but I'm not sure that it won't do you more good than a bolder method. You are getting to be rather conceited, my dear, and it is quite time you set about correcting it. You have a good many little gifts and virtues, but there is no need of parading them, for conceit spoils the finest genius. There is not much danger that real talent or goodness will be overlooked long, even if it is, the consciousness of possessing and using it well should satisfy one, and the great charm of all power is modesty."

"So it is!" cried Laurie, who was playing chess in a corner with Jo. "I knew a girl once, who had a really remarkable talent for music, and she didn't know it, never guessed what sweet little things she composed when she was alone, and wouldn't have believed it if anyone had told her."

Beth suddenly turned very red, and hid her face in the sofa cushion, quite overcome by such an unexpected discovery. So the lecture ended in a laugh.

08

JO MEETS APOLLYON

"Girls, where are you going?" asked Amy, coming into their room one Saturday afternoon, and finding them getting ready to go out with an air of secrecy which excited her curiosity.

"Never mind. Little girls shouldn't ask questions," returned Jo sharply.

"You are going somewhere with Laurie, I know you are. You were whispering and laughing together on the sofa last night, and you stopped when I came in. Aren't you going with him?"

"Yes, we are. Now do be still, and stop bothering."

Amy held her tongue, but used her eyes, and saw Meg slip a fan into her pocket.

"I know! I know! You're going to the theater to see the Seven Castles!" she cried, adding resolutely, "and I shall go, for Mother said I might see it, and I've got my rag money, and it was mean not to tell me in time."

"You can't sit with us, for our seats are reserved, and you mustn't sit alone, so Laurie will give you his place, and that will spoil our pleasure. Or he'll get another seat for you, and that isn't proper when you weren't asked. You shan't stir a step, so you may just stay where you are," scolded Jo, crosser than ever, having just pricked her finger in her hurry.

Sitting on the floor with one boot on, Amy began to cry and Meg to reason with her, when Laurie called from below, and the two girls hurried down, leaving their sister wailing. Just as the party was setting

out, Amy called over the banisters in a threatening tone, "You'll be sorry for this, Jo March, see if you ain't."

"Fiddlesticks!" returned Jo, slamming the door.

They had a charming time, for The Seven Castles of the Diamond Lake was as brilliant and wonderful as heart could wish. But in spite of the comical red imps, sparkling elves, and the gorgeous princes and princesses, Jo's pleasure had a drop of bitterness in it. The fairy queen's yellow curls reminded her of Amy, and between the acts she amused herself with wondering what her sister would do to make her 'sorry for it'.

When they got home, they found Amy reading in the parlor. She assumed an injured air as they came in, never lifted her eyes from her book, or asked a single question. Perhaps curiosity might have conquered resentment, if Beth had not been there to inquire and receive a glowing description of the play. On going up to put away her best hat, Jo's first look was toward the bureau, for in their last quarrel Amy had soothed her feelings by turning Jo's top drawer upside down on the floor. Everything was in its place, however, and after a hasty glance into her various closets, bags, and boxes, Jo decided that Amy had forgiven and forgotten her wrongs.

There Jo was mistaken, for next day she made a discovery which produced a tempest. Meg, Beth, and Amy were sitting together, late in the afternoon, when Jo burst into the room, looking excited and demanding breathlessly, "Has anyone taken my book?"

Meg and Beth said, "No." at once, and looked surprised. Amy poked the fire and said nothing. Jo saw her color rise and was down upon her in a minute.

"Amy, you've got it!"

"I burned it up."

"What! My little book I was so fond of, and worked over, and

meant to finish before Father got home? Have you really burned it?"
said Jo, turning very pale, while her eyes kindled and her hands
clutched Amy nervously.

"Yes, I did! I told you I'd make you pay for being so cross
yesterday, and I have, so..."

Amy got no farther, for Jo's hot temper mastered her, and she
shook Amy till her teeth chattered in her head, crying in a passion of
grief and anger...

"You wicked, wicked girl! I never can write it again, and I'll
never forgive you as long as I live."

Meg flew to rescue Amy, and Beth to pacify Jo, but Jo was quite
beside herself, and with a parting box on her sister's ear, she rushed
out of the room up to the old sofa in the garret, and finished her fight
alone.

The storm cleared up below, for Mrs. March came home, and,
having heard the story, soon brought Amy to a sense of the wrong she
had done her sister. Jo's book was the pride of her heart, and was
regarded by her family as a literary sprout of great promise. It was
only half a dozen little fairy tales, but Jo had worked over them
patiently, putting her whole heart into her work, hoping to make
something good enough to print. She had just copied them with great
care, and had destroyed the old manuscript, so that Amy's bonfire had
consumed the loving work of several years. It seemed a small loss to
others, but to Jo it was a dreadful calamity, and she felt that it never
could be made up to her. Beth mourned as for a departed kitten, and
Meg refused to defend her pet. Mrs. March looked grave and grieved,
and Amy felt that no one would love her till she had asked pardon for
the act which she now regretted more than any of them.

When the tea bell rang, Jo appeared, looking so grim and
unapproachable that it took all Amy's courage to say meekly...

"Please forgive me, Jo. I'm very, very sorry."

"I never shall forgive you," was Jo's stern answer, and from that moment she ignored Amy entirely.

As Jo received her good-night kiss, Mrs. March whispered gently, "My dear, don't let the sun go down upon your anger. Forgive each other, help each other, and begin again tomorrow."

Jo wanted to lay her head down on that motherly bosom, and cry her grief and anger all away, but tears were an unmanly weakness, and she felt so deeply injured that she really couldn't quite forgive yet. So she winked hard, shook her head, and said gruffly because Amy was listening, "It was an abominable thing, and she doesn't deserve to be forgiven."

With that she marched off to bed, and there was no merry or confidential gossip that night.

Amy was much offended that her overtures of peace had been repulsed, and began to wish she had not humbled herself, to feel more injured than ever, and to plume herself on her superior virtue in a way which was particularly exasperating. Jo still looked like a thunder cloud, and nothing went well all day. It was bitter cold in the morning, she dropped her precious turnover in the gutter, Aunt March had an attack of the fidgets, Meg was sensitive, Beth would look grieved and wistful when she got home, and Amy kept making remarks about people who were always talking about being good and yet wouldn't even try when other people set them a virtuous example.

"Everybody is so hateful, I'll ask Laurie to go skating. He is always kind and jolly, and will put me to rights, I know," said Jo to herself, and off she went.

Amy heard the clash of skates, and looked out with an impatient exclamation.

"There! She promised I should go next time, for this is the last

ice we shall have. But it's no use to ask such a crosspatch to take me."

"Don't say that. You were very naughty, and it is hard to forgive the loss of her precious little book, but I think she might do it now," said Meg. "Go after them. Don't say anything till Jo has got good-natured with Laurie, than take a quiet minute and just kiss her, or do some kind thing, and I'm sure she'll be friends again with all her heart."

"I'll try," said Amy, for the advice suited her, and after a flurry to get ready, she ran after the friends, who were just disappearing over the hill.

Jo heard Amy panting after her run, stamping her feet and blowing on her fingers as she tried to put her skates on, but Jo never turned and went slowly zigzagging down the river, taking a bitter, unhappy sort of satisfaction in her sister's troubles. As Laurie turned the bend, he shouted back...

"Keep near the shore. It isn't safe in the middle." Jo heard, but Amy was struggling to her feet and did not catch a word. Jo glanced over her shoulder, and the little demon she was harboring said in her ear...

"No matter whether she heard or not, let her take care of herself."

Laurie had vanished round the bend, Jo was just at the turn, and Amy, far behind, striking out toward the smoother ice in the middle of the river. For a minute Jo stood still with a strange feeling in her heart, then she resolved to go on, but something held and turned her round, just in time to see Amy throw up her hands and go down, with a sudden crash of rotten ice, the splash of water, and a cry that made Jo's heart stand still with fear. She tried to call Laurie, but her voice was gone. She tried to rush forward, but her feet seemed to have no

strength in them, and for a second, she could only stand motionless, staring with a terror-stricken face at the little blue hood above the black water. Something rushed swiftly by her, and Laurie's voice cried out...

"Bring a rail. Quick, quick!"

How she did it, she never knew, but for the next few minutes she worked as if possessed, blindly obeying Laurie, who was quite self-possessed, and lying flat, held Amy up by his arm and hockey stick till Jo dragged a rail from the fence, and together they got the child out, more frightened than hurt.

Shivering, dripping, and crying, they got Amy home, and after an exciting time of it, she fell asleep, rolled in blankets before a hot fire.

"Are you sure she is safe?" whispered Jo, looking remorsefully at the golden head, which might have been swept away from her sight forever under the treacherous ice.

"Quite safe, dear. She is not hurt, and won't even take cold, I think, you were so sensible in covering and getting her home quickly," replied her mother cheerfully.

"Laurie did it all. I only let her go. Mother, if she should die, it would be my fault." And Jo dropped down beside the bed in a passion of penitent tears, telling all that had happened, bitterly condemning her hardness of heart, and sobbing out her gratitude for being spared the heavy punishment which might have come upon her.

"It seems as if I could do anything when I'm in a passion. I get so savage, I could hurt anyone and enjoy it. I'm afraid I shall do something dreadful some day, and spoil my life, and make everybody hate me. Oh, Mother, help me, do help me!"

"I will, my child, I will. Don't cry so bitterly, but remember this day, and resolve with all your soul that you will never know another like it. Jo, dear, we all have our temptations, some far greater than yours, and it often takes us all our lives to conquer them. You think

your temper is the worst in the world, but mine used to be just like it."

"I will try, Mother, I truly will. But you must help me, remind me, and keep me from flying out. I used to see Father sometimes put his finger on his lips, and look at you with a very kind but sober face, and you always folded your lips tight and went away. Was he reminding you then?" asked Jo softly.

"Yes. I asked him to help me so, and he never forgot it, but saved me from many a sharp word by that little gesture and kind look."

Jo saw that her mother's eyes filled and her lips trembled as she spoke, and fearing that she had said too much, she whispered anxiously, "Was it wrong to watch you and to speak of it? I didn't mean to be rude, but it's so comfortable to say all I think to you, and feel so safe and happy here."

"My Jo, you may say anything to your mother, for it is my greatest happiness and pride to feel that my girls confide in me and know how much I love them."

"I thought I'd grieved you."

Amy stirred and sighed in her sleep, and as if eager to begin at once to mend her fault, Jo looked up with an expression on her face which it had never worn before.

"I let the sun go down on my anger. I wouldn't forgive her, and today, if it hadn't been for Laurie, it might have been too late! How could I be so wicked?" said Jo, half aloud, as she leaned over her sister softly stroking the wet hair scattered on the pillow.

As if she heard, Amy opened her eyes, and held out her arms, with a smile that went straight to Jo's heart. Neither said a word, but they hugged one another close, in spite of the blankets, and everything was forgiven and forgotten in one hearty kiss.

09

MEG GOES TO VANITY FAIR

"I do think it was the most fortunate thing in the world that those children should have the measles just now," said Meg, one April day, as she stood packing the 'go abroady' trunk in her room, surrounded by her sisters.

"And so nice of Annie Moffat not to forget her promise. A whole fortnight of fun will be regularly splendid," replied Jo, looking like a windmill as she folded skirts with her long arms.

"And such lovely weather, I'm so glad of that," added Beth, tidily sorting neck and hair ribbons in her best box, lent for the great occasion.

"I wish I was going to have a fine time and wear all these nice things," said Amy with her mouth full of pins, as she artistically replenished her sister's cushion.

"I wish you were all going, but as you can't, I shall keep my adventures to tell you when I come back. I'm sure it's the least I can do when you have been so kind, lending me things and helping me get ready," said Meg, glancing round the room at the very simple outfit, which seemed nearly perfect in their eyes.

"There now, the trays are ready, and everything in but my ball dress, which I shall leave for Mother to pack," said Meg, cheering up, as she glanced from the half-filled trunk to the many times pressed and mended white tarlatan, which she called her 'ball dress' with an important air.

The next day was fine, and Meg departed in style for a fortnight

of novelty and pleasure. Mrs. March had consented to the visit rather reluctantly, fearing that Margaret would come back more discontented than she went. But she begged so hard, and Sallie had promised to take good care of her, and a little pleasure seemed so delightful after a winter of irksome work that the mother yielded, and the daughter went to take her first taste of fashionable life.

The Moffats were very fashionable, and simple Meg was rather daunted, at first, by the splendor of the house and the elegance of its occupants. But they were kindly people, in spite of the frivolous life they led, and soon put their guest at her ease. Perhaps Meg felt, without understanding why, that they were not particularly cultivated or intelligent people, and that all their gilding could not quite conceal the ordinary material of which they were made. It certainly was agreeable to fare sumptuously, drive in a fine carriage, wear her best frock every day, and do nothing but enjoy herself. It suited her exactly, and soon she began to imitate the manners and conversation of those about her, to put on little airs and graces, use French phrases, crimp her hair, take in her dresses, and talk about the fashions as well as she could. The more she saw of Annie Moffat's pretty things, the more she envied her and sighed to be rich. Home now looked bare and dismal as she thought of it, work grew harder than ever, and she felt that she was a very destitute and much-injured girl, in spite of the new gloves and silk stockings.

Mr. Moffat was a fat, jolly old gentleman, who knew her father, and Mrs. Moffat, a fat, jolly old lady, who took as great a fancy to Meg as her daughter had done. Everyone petted her, and 'Daisy', as they called her, was in a fair way to have her head turned.

When the evening for the small party came, she found that the poplin wouldn't do at all, for the other girls were putting on thin dresses and making themselves very fine indeed. So out came the

tarlatan, looking older, limper, and shabbier than ever beside Sallie's crisp new one. No one said a word about it, but Sallie offered to dress her hair, and Annie to tie her sash, and Belle, the engaged sister, praised her white arms. But in their kindness Meg saw only pity for her poverty, and her heart felt very heavy as she stood by herself, while the others laughed, chattered, and flew about like gauzy butterflies. The hard, bitter feeling was getting pretty bad, when the maid brought in a box of flowers.

"It's for Belle, of course, George always sends her some, but these are altogether ravishing," cried Annie, with a great sniff.

"They are for Miss March, the man said. And here's a note," put in the maid, holding it to Meg.

"What fun! Who are they from? Didn't know you had a lover," cried the girls, fluttering about Meg in a high state of curiosity and surprise.

"The note is from Mother, and the flowers from Laurie," said Meg simply, yet much gratified that he had not forgotten her.

"Oh, indeed!" said Annie with a funny look, as Meg slipped the note into her pocket as a sort of talisman against envy, vanity, and false pride, for the few loving words had done her good, and the flowers cheered her up by their beauty.

She enjoyed herself very much that evening, for she danced to her heart's content. Everyone was very kind, and she had three compliments. Annie made her sing, and some one said she had a remarkably fine voice. Major Lincoln asked who 'the fresh little girl with the beautiful eyes' was, and Mr. Moffat insisted on dancing with her because she 'didn't dawdle, but had some spring in her', as he gracefully expressed it. So altogether she had a very nice time, till she overheard a bit of conversation, which disturbed her extremely. She was sitting just inside the conservatory, waiting for her partner to

bring her an ice, when she heard a voice ask on the other side of the flowery wall...

"How old is he?"

"Sixteen or seventeen, I should say," replied another voice.

"It would be a grand thing for one of those girls, wouldn't it? Sallie says they are very intimate now, and the old man quite dotes on them."

"Mrs. M. has made her plans, I dare say, and will play her cards well, early as it is. The girl evidently doesn't think of it yet," said Mrs. Moffat.

"She told that fib about her momma, as if she did know, and colored up when the flowers came quite prettily. Poor thing! She'd be so nice if she was only got up in style. Do you think she'd be offended if we offered to lend her a dress for Thursday?" asked another voice.

"She's proud, but I don't believe she'd mind, for that dowdy tarlatan is all she has got. She may tear it tonight, and that will be a good excuse for offering a decent one."

"We'll see. I shall ask young Laurence, as a compliment to her, and we'll have fun about it afterward."

Here Meg's partner appeared, to find her looking much flushed and rather agitated. She was proud, and her pride was useful just then, for it helped her hide her mortification, anger, and disgust at what she had just heard. For, innocent and unsuspicious as she was, she could not help understanding the gossip of her friends.

Poor Meg had a restless night, and got up heavy-eyed, unhappy, half resentful toward her friends, and half ashamed of herself for not speaking out frankly and setting everything right. Everybody dawdled that morning, and it was noon before the girls found energy enough even to take up their worsted work. Something in the manner of her friends struck Meg at once. They treated her with more respect, she

thought, took quite a tender interest in what she said, and looked at her with eyes that plainly betrayed curiosity. All this surprised and flattered her, though she did not understand it till Miss Belle looked up from her writing, and said, with a sentimental air...

"Daisy, dear, I've sent an invitation to your friend, Mr. Laurence, for Thursday. We should like to know him, and it's only a proper compliment to you."

Meg colored, but a mischievous fancy to tease the girls made her reply demurely, "You are very kind, but I'm afraid he won't come."

"Why not, Cherie?" asked Miss Belle.

"He's too old."

"My child, what do you mean? What is his age, I beg to know!" cried Miss Clara.

"Nearly seventy, I believe," answered Meg, counting stitches to hide the merriment in her eyes.

"You sly creature! Of course we meant the young man," exclaimed Miss Belle, laughing.

"There isn't any, Laurie is only a little boy." And Meg laughed also at the queer look which the sisters exchanged as she thus described her supposed lover.

"About your age," Nan said.

"Nearer my sister Jo's; I am seventeen in August," returned Meg, tossing her head.

"It's very nice of him to send you flowers, isn't it?" said Annie, looking wise about nothing.

"Yes, he often does, to all of us, for their house is full, and we are so fond of them. My mother and old Mr. Laurence are friends, you know, so it is quite natural that we children should play together," and Meg hoped they would say no more.

"It's evident Daisy isn't out yet," said Miss Clara to Belle with

a nod.

"Quite a pastoral state of innocence all round," returned Miss Belle with a shrug.

"I'm going out to get some little matters for my girls. Can I do anything for you, young ladies?" asked Mrs. Moffat, lumbering in like an elephant in silk and lace.

"No, thank you, ma'am," replied Sallie. "I've got my new pink silk for Thursday and don't want a thing."

"Nor I..." began Meg, but stopped because it occurred to her that she did want several things and could not have them.

"What shall you wear?" asked Sallie.

"My old white one again, if I can mend it fit to be seen, it got sadly torn last night," said Meg, trying to speak quite easily, but feeling very uncomfortable.

"Why don't you send home for another?" said Sallie, who was not an observing young lady.

"I haven't got any other." It cost Meg an effort to say that, but Sallie did not see it and exclaimed in amiable surprise, "Only that? How funny..." She did not finish her speech, for Belle shook her head at her and broke in, saying kindly...

"Not at all. Where is the use of having a lot of dresses when she isn't out yet? There's no need of sending home, Daisy, even if you had a dozen, for I've got a sweet blue silk laid away, which I've outgrown, and you shall wear it to please me, won't you, dear?"

"You are very kind, but I don't mind my old dress if you don't, it does well enough for a little girl like me," said Meg.

"Now do let me please myself by dressing you up in style. I admire to do it, and you'd be a regular little beauty with a touch here and there. I shan't let anyone see you till you are done, and then we'll burst upon them like Cinderella and her godmother going to the

ball," said Belle in her persuasive tone.

Meg couldn't refuse the offer so kindly made, for a desire to see if she would be 'a little beauty' after touching up caused her to accept and forget all her former uncomfortable feelings toward the Moffats.

On the Thursday evening, Belle shut herself up with her maid, and between them they turned Meg into a fine lady. Miss Belle surveyed her with the satisfaction of a little girl with a newly dressed doll.

"Mademoiselle is charmante, tres jolie, is she not?" cried Hortense, clasping her hands in an affected rapture.

"Come and show yourself," said Miss Belle, leading the way to the room where the others were waiting.

As Meg went rustling after, with her long skirts trailing, her earrings tinkling, her curls waving, and her heart beating, she felt as if her fun had really begun at last, for the mirror had plainly told her that she was 'a little beauty' .

"I'm afraid to go down, I feel so queer and stiff and half-dressed," said Meg to Sallie, as the bell rang, and Mrs. Moffat sent to ask the young ladies to appear at once.

"You don't look a bit like yourself, but you are very nice. I'm nowhere beside you, for Belle has heaps of taste, and you're quite French, I assure you. Let your flowers hang, don't be so careful of them, and be sure you don't trip," returned Sallie, trying not to care that Meg was prettier than herself.

Keeping that warning carefully in mind, Margaret got safely down stairs and sailed into the drawing rooms where the Moffats and a few early guests were assembled. She very soon discovered that there is a charm about fine clothes which attracts a certain class of people and secures their respect. Several young ladies, who had taken no

notice of her before, were very affectionate all of a sudden. Several young gentlemen, who had only stared at her at the other party, now not only stared, but asked to be introduced, and said all manner of foolish but agreeable things to her, and several old ladies, who sat on the sofas, and criticized the rest of the party, inquired who she was with an air of interest. She heard Mrs. Moffat reply to one of them...

"Daisy March—father a colonel in the army—one of our first families, but reverses of fortune, you know; intimate friends of the Laurences; sweet creature, I assure you; my Ned is quite wild about her."

"Dear me!" said the old lady, putting up her glass for another observation of Meg, who tried to look as if she had not heard and been rather shocked at Mrs. Moffat's fibs. The 'queer feeling' did not pass away, but she imagined herself acting the new part of fine lady and so got on pretty well, though the tight dress gave her a side-ache, the train kept getting under her feet, and she was in constant fear lest her earrings should fly off and get lost or broken. She was flirting her fan and laughing at the feeble jokes of a young gentleman who tried to be witty, when she suddenly stopped laughing and looked confused, for just opposite, she saw Laurie. He was staring at her with undisguised surprise, and disapproval also, she thought.

"I'm glad you came, I was afraid you wouldn't." she said, with her most grown-up air.

"Jo wanted me to come, and tell her how you looked, so I did," answered Laurie, without turning his eyes upon her, though he half smiled at her maternal tone.

"What shall you tell her?" asked Meg, full of curiosity to know his opinion of her, yet feeling ill at ease with him for the first time.

"I don't like fuss and feathers."

That was altogether too much from a lad younger than herself,

and Meg walked away, saying petulantly, "You are the rudest boy I ever saw."

Feeling very much ruffled, she went and stood at a quiet window to cool her cheeks, for the tight dress gave her an uncomfortably brilliant color. As she stood there, Major Lincoln passed by, and a minute after she heard him saying to his mother...

"They are making a fool of that little girl. I wanted you to see her, but they have spoiled her entirely. She's nothing but a doll tonight."

"Oh, dear!" sighed Meg. "I wish I'd been sensible and worn my own things, then I should not have disgusted other people, or felt so uncomfortable and ashamed of myself."

She leaned her forehead on the cool pane, and stood half hidden by the curtains, never minding that her favorite waltz had begun, till some one touched her, and turning, she saw Laurie, looking penitent, as he said, with his very best bow and his hand out...

"Please forgive my rudeness, and come and dance with me."

"I'm afraid it will be too disagreeable to you," said Meg, trying to look offended and failing entirely.

"Not a bit of it, I'm dying to do it. Come, I'll be good. I don't like your gown, but I do think you are just splendid." And he waved his hands, as if words failed to express his admiration.

Meg smiled and relented.

"Here comes Ned Moffat. What does he want?" said Laurie, knitting his black brows as if he did not regard his young host in the light of a pleasant addition to the party.

"He put his name down for three dances, and I suppose he's coming for them. What a bore!" said Meg, assuming a languid air which amused Laurie immensely.

He did not speak to her again till suppertime, when he saw her

drinking champagne with Ned and his friend Fisher, who were behaving 'like a pair of fools', as Laurie said to himself, for he felt a brotherly sort of right to watch over the Marches and fight their battles whenever a defender was needed.

"You'll have a splitting headache tomorrow, if you drink much of that. I wouldn't, Meg, your mother doesn't like it, you know," he whispered, leaning over her chair, as Ned turned to refill her glass and Fisher stooped to pick up her fan.

"I'm not Meg tonight, I'm 'a doll' who does all sorts of crazy things. Tomorrow I shall put away my 'fuss and feathers' and be desperately good again," she answered with an affected little laugh.

"Wish tomorrow was here, then," muttered Laurie, walking off, ill-pleased at the change he saw in her.

Meg danced and flirted, chattered and giggled, as the other girls did. After supper she undertook the German, and blundered through it, nearly upsetting her partner with her long skirt, and romping in a way that scandalized Laurie, who looked on and meditated a lecture. But he got no chance to deliver it, for Meg kept away from him till he came to say good night.

She was sick all the next day, and on Saturday went home, quite used up with her fortnight's fun and feeling that she had 'sat in the lap of luxury' long enough.

"It does seem pleasant to be quiet, and not have company manners on all the time. Home is a nice place, though it isn't splendid," said Meg, looking about her with a restful expression, as she sat with her mother and Jo on the Sunday evening.

"I'm glad to hear you say so, dear, for I was afraid home would seem dull and poor to you after your fine quarters," replied her mother, who had given her many anxious looks that day. For motherly eyes are quick to see any change in children's faces.

"Mother, do you have 'plans', as Mrs. Moffat said?" asked Meg bashfully.

"Yes, my dear, I have a great many, all mothers do, but mine differ somewhat from Mrs. Moffat's, I suspect."

Jo went and sat on one arm of the chair, looking as if she thought they were about to join in some very solemn affair. Holding a hand of each, and watching the two young faces wistfully, Mrs. March said, in her serious yet cheery way...

"I want my daughters to be beautiful, accomplished, and good. To be admired, loved, and respected. To have a happy youth, to be well and wisely married, and to lead useful, pleasant lives, with as little care and sorrow to try them as God sees fit to send. My dear girls, I am ambitious for you, but not to have you make a dash in the world, marry rich men merely because they are rich, or have splendid houses, which are not homes because love is wanting. Money is a needful and precious thing, and when well used, a noble thing, but I never want you to think it is the first or only prize to strive for. I'd rather see you poor men's wives, if you were happy, beloved, contented, than queens on thrones, without self-respect and peace. Don't be troubled, Meg, poverty seldom daunts a sincere lover. Some of the best and most honored women I know were poor girls, but so love-worthy that they were not allowed to be old maids. Leave these things to time. Make this home happy, so that you may be fit for homes of your own, if they are offered you, and contented here if they are not. One thing remember, my girls. Mother is always ready to be your confidant, Father to be your friend, and both of us hope and trust that our daughters, whether married or single, will be the pride and comfort of our lives."

"We will, Marmee, we will!" cried both, with all their hearts, as she bade them good night.

10

THE P.C. AND P.O.

As spring came on, a new set of amusements became the fashion, and the lengthening days gave long afternoons for work and play of all sorts. One of these was the 'P.C.', for as secret societies were the fashion, it was thought proper to have one, and as all of the girls admired Dickens, they called themselves the Pickwick Club. With a few interruptions, they had kept this up for a year, and met every Saturday evening in the big garret, on which occasions the ceremonies were as follows: Three chairs were arranged in a row before a table on which was a lamp, also four white badges, with a big 'P.C.' in different colors on each, and the weekly newspaper called, The Pickwick Portfolio, to which all contributed something, while Jo, who reveled in pens and ink, was the editor. At seven o'clock, the four members ascended to the clubroom, tied their badges round their heads, and took their seats with great solemnity. Meg, as the eldest, was Samuel Pickwick, Jo, being of a literary turn, Augustus Snodgrass, Beth, because she was round and rosy, Tracy Tupman, and Amy, who was always trying to do what she couldn't, was Nathaniel Winkle. Pickwick, the president, read the paper, which was filled with original tales, poetry, local news, funny advertisements, and hints, in which they good-naturedly reminded each other of their faults and short comings. On one occasion, Mr. Pickwick put on a pair of spectacles without any glass, rapped upon the table, hemmed, and having stared hard at Mr. Snodgrass, who was tilting back in his chair, till he arranged himself properly, began to read.

As the President finished reading the paper, a round of applause followed, and then Mr. Snodgrass rose to make a proposition.

"Mr. President and gentlemen," he began, assuming a parliamentary attitude and tone, "I wish to propose the admission of a new member—one who highly deserves the honor, would be deeply grateful for it, and would add immensely to the spirit of the club, the literary value of the paper, and be no end jolly and nice. I propose Mr. Theodore Laurence as an honorary member of the P. C. Come now, do have him."

Jo's sudden change of tone made the girls laugh, but all looked rather anxious, and no one said a word as Snodgrass took his seat.

"We'll put it to a vote," said the President. "All in favor of this motion please to manifest it by saying, 'Aye'."

"Everybody remember it's our Laurie, and say, 'Aye!'" cried Snodgrass excitedly.

"Aye! Aye! Aye!" replied three voices at once.

"Good! Bless you! Now, as there's nothing like 'taking time by the fetlock', as Winkle characteristically observes, allow me to present the new member." And, to the dismay of the rest of the club, Jo threw open the door of the closet, and displayed Laurie sitting on a rag bag, flushed and twinkling with suppressed laughter.

"You rogue! You traitor! Jo, how could you?" cried the three girls, as Snodgrass led her friend triumphantly forth, and producing both a chair and a badge, installed him in a jiffy.

"The coolness of you two rascals is amazing," began Mr. Pickwick, trying to get up an awful frown and only succeeding in producing an amiable smile. But the new member was equal to the occasion, and rising, with a grateful salutation to the Chair, said in the most engaging manner, "Mr. President and ladies—I beg pardon, gentlemen—allow me to introduce myself as Sam Weller, the very

humble servant of the club."

"Good! Good!" cried Jo, pounding with the handle of the old warming pan on which she leaned.

"My faithful friend and noble patron," continued Laurie with a wave of the hand, "who has so flatteringly presented me, is not to be blamed for the base stratagem of tonight. I planned it, and she only gave in after lots of teasing."

"Come now, don't lay it all on yourself. You know I proposed the cupboard," broke in Snodgrass, who was enjoying the joke amazingly.

"Never mind what she says. I'm the wretch that did it, sir," said the new member, with a Welleresque nod to Mr. Pickwick. "But on my honor, I never will do so again, and henceforth devote myself to the interest of this immortal club."

"Hear! Hear!" cried Jo, clashing the lid of the warming pan like a cymbal.

"Go on, go on!" added Winkle and Tupman, while the President bowed benignly.

"I merely wish to say, that as a slight token of my gratitude for the honor done me, and as a means of promoting friendly relations between adjoining nations, I have set up a post office in the hedge in the lower corner of the garden. Letters, manuscripts, books, and bundles can be passed in there, and as each nation has a key, it will be uncommonly nice, I fancy. Allow me to present the club key, and with many thanks for your favor, take my seat."

Great applause as Mr. Weller deposited a little key on the table and subsided, the warming pan clashed and waved wildly, and it was some time before order could be restored. A long discussion followed, and did not adjourn till a late hour, when it broke up with three shrill cheers for the new member.

The P. O. was a capital little institution, and flourished wonderfully, for nearly as many queer things passed through it as through the real post office. Tragedies and cravats, poetry and pickles, garden seeds and long letters, music and gingerbread, rubbers, invitations, scoldings, and puppies. The old gentleman liked the fun, and amused himself by sending odd bundles, mysterious messages, and funny telegrams, and his gardener, who was smitten with Hannah's charms, actually sent a love letter to Jo's care. How they laughed when the secret came out, never dreaming how many love letters that little post office would hold in the years to come.

11
EXPERIMENTS

"The first of June! The Kings are off to the seashore tomorrow, and I'm free. Three months' vacation—how I shall enjoy it!" exclaimed Meg, coming home one warm day to find Jo laid upon the sofa in an unusual state of exhaustion, while Beth took off her dusty boots, and Amy made lemonade for the refreshment of the whole party.

"Aunt March went today, for which, oh, be joyful!" said Jo. "I was mortally afraid she'd ask me to go with her. If she had, I should have felt as if I ought to do it, but Plumfield is about as gay as a churchyard, you know, and I'd rather be excused. I quaked till she was fairly in the carriage, and had a final fright, for as it drove of, she popped out her head, saying, 'Josyphine, won't you—?' I didn't hear any more, for I basely turned and fled. I did actually run, and whisked round the corner where I felt safe."

"Poor old Jo! She came in looking as if bears were after her," said Beth, as she cuddled her sister's feet with a motherly air.

"Aunt March is a regular samphire, is she not?" observed Amy, tasting her mixture critically.

"She means vampire, not seaweed, but it doesn't matter. It's too warm to be particular about one's parts of speech," murmured Jo.

"What shall you do all your vacation?" asked Amy, changing the subject.

"I shall lie abed late, and do nothing," replied Meg, from the depths of the rocking chair. "I've been routed up early all winter and

had to spend my days working for other people, so now I'm going to rest and revel to my heart's content."

"No," said Jo, "that dozy way wouldn't suit me. I've laid in a heap of books, and I'm going to improve my shining hours reading on my perch in the old apple tree, when I'm not having l——"

"Don't say 'larks!'" implored Amy, as a return snub for the 'samphire' correction.

"I'll say 'nightingales' then, with Laurie. That's proper and appropriate, since he's a warbler."

"Don't let us do any lessons, Beth, for a while, but play all the time and rest, as the girls mean to," proposed Amy.

"Well, I will, if Mother doesn't mind. I want to learn some new songs, and my children need fitting up for the summer. They are dreadfully out of order and really suffering for clothes."

"May we, Mother?" asked Meg, turning to Mrs. March, who sat sewing in what they called 'Marmee's corner'.

"You may try your experiment for a week and see how you like it. I think by Saturday night you will find that all play and no work is as bad as all work and no play."

"Oh, dear, no! It will be delicious, I'm sure," said Meg complacently.

"I now propose a toast, as my 'friend and pardner, Sairy Gamp', says. Fun forever, and no grubbing!" cried Jo, rising, glass in hand, as the lemonade went round.

They all drank it merrily, and began the experiment by lounging for the rest of the day. Next morning, Meg did not appear till ten o'clock. Her solitary breakfast did not taste good, and the room seemed lonely and untidy, for Jo had not filled the vases, Beth had not dusted, and Amy's books lay scattered about. Nothing was neat and pleasant but 'Marmee's corner', which looked as usual. And there

Meg sat, to 'rest and read', which meant to yawn and imagine what pretty summer dresses she would get with her salary. Jo spent the morning on the river with Laurie and the afternoon reading and crying over The Wide, Wide World, up in the apple tree. Beth began by rummaging everything out of the big closet where her family resided, but getting tired before half done, she left her establishment topsy-turvy and went to her music, rejoicing that she had no dishes to wash. Amy arranged her bower, put on her best white frock, smoothed her curls, and sat down to draw under the honeysuckles, hoping someone would see and inquire who the young artist was. As no one appeared but an inquisitive daddy-longlegs, who examined her work with interest, she went to walk, got caught in a shower, and came home dripping.

At teatime they compared notes, and all agreed that it had been a delightful, though unusually long day. No one would own that they were tired of the experiment, but by Friday night each acknowledged to herself that she was glad the week was nearly done. Hoping to impress the lesson more deeply, Mrs. March, who had a good deal of humor, resolved to finish off the trial in an appropriate manner, so she gave Hannah a holiday and let the girls enjoy the full effect of the play system.

When they got up on Saturday morning, there was no fire in the kitchen, no breakfast in the dining room, and no mother anywhere to be seen.

"Mercy on us! What has happened?" cried Jo, staring about her in dismay.

Meg ran upstairs and soon came back again, looking relieved but rather bewildered, and a little ashamed.

"Mother isn't sick, only very tired, and she says she is going to stay quietly in her room all day and let us do the best we can. It's a

very queer thing for her to do, she doesn't act a bit like herself. But she says it has been a hard week for her, so we mustn't grumble but take care of ourselves."

"That's easy enough, and I like the idea, I'm aching for something to do, that is, some new amusement, you know," added Jo quickly.

In fact it was an immense relief to them all to have a little work, and they took hold with a will, but soon realized the truth of Hannah's saying, "Housekeeping ain't no joke." There was plenty of food in the larder, and while Beth and Amy set the table, Meg and Jo got breakfast, wondering as they did why servants ever talked about hard work.

"I shall take some up to Mother, though she said we were not to think of her, for she'd take care of herself," said Meg, who presided and felt quite matronly behind the teapot.

So a tray was fitted out before anyone began, and taken up with the cook's compliments. The boiled tea was very bitter, the omelet scorched, and the biscuits speckled with saleratus, but Mrs. March received her repast with thanks and laughed heartily over it after Jo was gone.

"Poor little souls, they will have a hard time, I'm afraid, but they won't suffer, and it will do them good," she said, producing the more palatable viands with which she had provided herself, and disposing of the bad breakfast, so that their feelings might not be hurt, a motherly little deception for which they were grateful.

Many were the complaints below, and great the chagrin of the head cook at her failures. "Never mind, I'll get the dinner and be servant, you be mistress, keep your hands nice, see company, and give orders," said Jo, who knew still less than Meg about culinary affairs.

This obliging offer was gladly accepted, and Margaret retired to the parlor, which she hastily put in order by whisking the litter under the sofa and shutting the blinds to save the trouble of dusting. Jo, with perfect faith in her own powers and a friendly desire to make up the quarrel, immediately put a note in the office, inviting Laurie to dinner.

"You'd better see what you have got before you think of having company," said Meg, when informed of the hospitable but rash act.

"Oh, there's corned beef and plenty of potatoes, and I shall get some asparagus and a lobster, 'for a relish', as Hannah says. We'll have lettuce and make a salad. I don't know how, but the book tells. I'll have blanc mange and strawberries for dessert, and coffee too, if you want to be elegant."

"Don't try too many messes, Jo, for you can't make anything but gingerbread and molasses candy fit to eat. I wash my hands of the dinner party, and since you have asked Laurie on your own responsibility, you may just take care of him."

"I don't want you to do anything but be civil to him and help to the pudding. You'll give me your advice if I get in a muddle, won't you?" asked Jo, rather hurt.

"Yes, but I don't know much, except about bread and a few trifles. You had better ask Mother's leave before you order anything," returned Meg prudently.

"Of course I shall. I'm not a fool." And Jo went off in a huff at the doubts expressed of her powers.

"Get what you like, and don't disturb me. I'm going out to dinner and can't worry about things at home," said Mrs. March, when Jo spoke to her. "I never enjoyed housekeeping, and I'm going to take a vacation today, and read, write, go visiting, and amuse myself."

The unusual spectacle of her busy mother rocking comfortably and reading early in the morning made Jo feel as if some unnatural

phenomenon had occurred.

"Everything is out of sorts, somehow," she said to herself, going downstairs. "There's Beth crying, that's a sure sign that something is wrong with this family. If Amy is bothering, I'll shake her."

Feeling very much out of sorts herself, Jo hurried into the parlor to find Beth sobbing over Pip, the canary, who lay dead in the cage with his little claws pathetically extended, as if imploring the food for want of which he had died.

"It's all my fault, I forgot him, there isn't a seed or a drop left. Oh, Pip! Oh, Pip! How could I be so cruel to you?" cried Beth, taking the poor thing in her hands and trying to restore him.

Jo peeped into his half-open eye, felt his little heart, and finding him stiff and cold, shook her head, and offered her domino box for a coffin.

"Put him in the oven, and maybe he will get warm and revive," said Amy hopefully.

"He's been starved, and he shan't be baked now he's dead. I'll make him a shroud, and he shall be buried in the garden, and I'll never have another bird, never, my Pip! for I am too bad to own one," murmured Beth, sitting on the floor with her pet folded in her hands.

"The funeral shall be this afternoon, and we will all go. Now, don't cry, Bethy. It's a pity, but nothing goes right this week, and Pip has had the worst of the experiment. Make the shroud, and lay him in my box, and after the dinner party, we'll have a nice little funeral," said Jo, beginning to feel as if she had undertaken a good deal.

Leaving the others to console Beth, she departed to the kitchen, which was in a most discouraging state of confusion. Putting on a big apron, she fell to work and got the dishes piled up ready for washing, when she discovered that the fire was out.

"Here's a sweet prospect!" muttered Jo, slamming the stove door open, and poking vigorously among the cinders.

Having rekindled the fire, she thought she would go to market while the water heated. The walk revived her spirits, and flattering herself that she had made good bargains, she trudged home again, after buying a very young lobster, some very old asparagus, and two boxes of acid strawberries. By the time she got cleared up, the dinner arrived and the stove was red-hot. Hannah had left a pan of bread to rise, Meg had worked it up early, set it on the hearth for a second rising, and forgotten it. Meg was entertaining Sallie Gardiner in the parlor, when the door flew open and a floury, crocky, flushed, and disheveled figure appeared, demanding tartly...

"I say, isn't bread 'riz' enough when it runs over the pans?"

Sallie began to laugh, but Meg nodded and lifted her eyebrows as high as they would go, which caused the apparition to vanish and put the sour bread into the oven without further delay. Mrs. March went out, after peeping here and there to see how matters went, also saying a word of comfort to Beth.

Language cannot describe the anxieties, experiences, and exertions which Jo underwent that morning, and the dinner she served up became a standing joke. Fearing to ask any more advice, she did her best alone, and discovered that something more than energy and good will is necessary to make a cook.

"Salt instead of sugar, and the cream is sour," Meg said with a tragic gesture.

Jo uttered a groan and fell back in her chair, remembering that she had given a last hasty powdering to the berries out of one of the two boxes on the kitchen table, and had neglected to put the milk in the refrigerator. She turned scarlet and was on the verge of crying,

when she met Laurie's eyes, which would look merry in spite of his heroic efforts. The comical side of the affair suddenly struck her, and she laughed till the tears ran down her cheeks. So did everyone else, even 'Croaker' as the girls called the old lady, and the unfortunate dinner ended gaily, with bread and butter, olives and fun.

"I haven't strength of mind enough to clear up now, so we will sober ourselves with a funeral," said Jo, as they rose, and Miss Crocker made ready to go, being eager to tell the new story at another friend's dinner table.

They did sober themselves for Beth's sake. Laurie dug a grave under the ferns in the grove, little Pip was laid in, with many tears by his tender-hearted mistress, and covered with moss, while a wreath of violets and chickweed was hung on the stone.

At the conclusion of the ceremonies, Beth retired to her room, overcome with emotion and lobster, but there was no place of repose, for the beds were not made, and she found her grief much assuaged by beating up the pillows and putting things in order. Meg helped Jo clear away the remains of the feast, which took half the afternoon and left them so tired that they agreed to be contented with tea and toast for supper.

Laurie took Amy to drive, which was a deed of charity, for the sour cream seemed to have had a bad effect upon her temper. Mrs. March came home to find the three older girls hard at work in the middle of the afternoon, and a glance at the closet gave her an idea of the success of one part of the experiment.

As twilight fell, dewy and still, one by one they gathered on the porch where the June roses were budding beautifully, and each groaned or sighed as she sat down, as if tired or troubled.

"What a dreadful day this has been!" began Jo, usually the first to speak.

"It has seemed shorter than usual, but so uncomfortable," said Meg.

"Not a bit like home," added Amy.

"It can't seem so without Marmee and little Pip," sighed Beth, glancing with full eyes at the empty cage above her head.

"Here's Mother, dear, and you shall have another bird tomorrow, if you want it."

As she spoke, Mrs. March came and took her place among them, looking as if her holiday had not been much pleasanter than theirs.

"Mother, did you go away and let everything be, just to see how we'd get on?" cried Meg, who had had suspicions all day.

"Yes, I wanted you to see how the comfort of all depends on each doing her share faithfully. While Hannah and I did your work, you got on pretty well, though I don't think you were very happy or amiable. So I thought, as a little lesson, I would show you what happens when everyone thinks only of herself. Don't you feel that it is pleasanter to help one another, to have daily duties which make leisure sweet when it comes, and to bear and forbear, that home may be comfortable and lovely to us all?"

"We do, Mother, we do!" cried the girls.

"Then let me advise you to take up your little burdens again, for though they seem heavy sometimes, they are good for us, and lighten as we learn to carry them. keeps us from ennui and mischief, is good for health and spirits, and gives us a sense of power and independence better than money or fashion."

"We'll remember, Mother!" and they did.

12

CAMP LAURENCE

Beth was postmistress, for, being most at home, she could attend to it regularly, and dearly liked the daily task of unlocking the little door and distributing the mail. One July day she came in with her hands full, and went about the house leaving letters and parcels like the penny post.

"Here's your posy, Mother! Laurie never forgets that," she said, putting the fresh nosegay in the vase that stood in 'Marmee's corner', and was kept supplied by the affectionate boy.

"Miss Meg March, one letter and a glove," continued Beth, delivering the articles to her sister, who sat near her mother, stitching wristbands.

"Why, I left a pair over there, and here is only one," said Meg, looking at the gray cotton glove. "Didn't you drop the other in the garden?"

"No, I'm sure I didn't, for there was only one in the office."

"I hate to have odd gloves! Never mind, the other may be found. My letter is only a translation of the German song I wanted. I think Mr. Brooke did it, for this isn't Laurie's writing."

Mrs. March glanced at Meg, who was looking very pretty in her gingham morning gown, with the little curls blowing about her forehead, and very womanly, as she sat sewing at her little worktable, full of tidy white rolls, so unconscious of the thought in her mother's mind as she sewed and sang, while her fingers flew and her thoughts were busied with girlish fancies as innocent and fresh as the pansies in her belt, that Mrs. March smiled and was satisfied.

"Two letters for Doctor Jo, a book, and a funny old hat, which covered the whole post office and stuck outside," said Beth, laughing as she went into the study where Jo sat writing.

"What a sly fellow Laurie is! I said I wished bigger hats were the fashion, because I burn my face every hot day. He said, 'Why mind the fashion? Wear a big hat, and be comfortable!' I said I would if I had one, and he has sent me this, to try me. I'll wear it for fun, and show him I don't care for the fashion." And hanging the antique broad-brim on a bust of Plato, Jo read her letters.

One from her mother made her cheeks glow and her eyes fill, for it said to her...

My Dear:

I write a little word to tell you with how much satisfaction I watch your efforts to control your temper. You say nothing about your trials, failures, or successes, and think, perhaps, that no one sees them but the Friend whose help you daily ask, if I may trust the well-worn cover of your guidebook. I, too, have seen them all, and heartily believe in the sincerity of your resolution, since it begins to bear fruit. Go on, dear, patiently and bravely, and always believe that no one sympathizes more tenderly with you than your loving...

Mother

"That does me good! That's worth millions of money and pecks of praise. Oh, Marmee, I do try! I will keep on trying, and not get tired, since I have you to help me."

Feeling stronger than ever to meet and subdue her Apollyon, she pinned the note inside her frock, as a shield and a reminder, lest she be taken unaware, and proceeded to open her other letter, quite ready for either good or bad news. In a big, dashing hand, Laurie wrote...

Dear Jo, What ho!

Some English girls and boys are coming to see me tomorrow and I want to have a jolly time. If it's fine, I'm going to pitch my tent in Longmeadow, and row up the whole crew to lunch and croquet—have a fire, make messes, gypsy fashion, and all sorts of larks. They are nice people, and like such things. Brooke will go to keep us boys steady, and Kate Vaughn will play propriety for the girls. I want you all to come, can't let Beth off at any price, and nobody shall worry her. Don't bother about rations, I'll see to that and everything else, only do come, there's a good fellow!

In a tearing hurry, Yours ever, Laurie.

"Here's richness!" cried Jo.

When the sun peeped into the girls' room early next morning to promise them a fine day, he saw a comical sight. Each had made such preparation for the fete as seemed necessary and proper. Meg had an extra row of little curlpapers across her forehead, Jo had copiously anointed her afflicted face with cold cream, Beth had taken Joanna to bed with her to atone for the approaching separation, and Amy had capped the climax by putting a clothespin on her nose to uplift the offending feature. This funny spectacle appeared to amuse the sun, for he burst out with such radiance that Jo woke up and roused her sisters by a hearty laugh at Amy's ornament.

Laurie ran to meet and present them to his friends in the most cordial manner. The lawn was the reception room, and for several minutes a lively scene was enacted there. Meg was grateful to see that Miss Kate, though twenty, was dressed with a simplicity which American girls would do well to imitate, and who was much flattered by Mr. Ned's assurances that he came especially to see her. Jo understood why Laurie 'primmed up his mouth' when speaking of Kate, for that young lady had a standoff-don't-touch-me air, which contrasted strongly with the free and easy demeanor of the other girls. Beth took an observation of the new boys and decided that the lame one was not 'dreadful', but gentle and feeble, and she would be kind to him on that account. Amy found Grace a well-mannered, merry, little person, and after staring dumbly at one another for a few minutes, they suddenly became very good friends.

Tents, lunch, and croquet utensils having been sent on beforehand, the party was soon embarked, and the two boats pushed off together, leaving Mr. Laurence waving his hat on the shore. Laurie and Jo rowed one boat, Mr. Brooke and Ned the other, while Fred Vaughn, the riotous twin, did his best to upset both by paddling about in a wherry like a disturbed water bug. Jo's funny hat deserved a vote of thanks, for it was of general utility. It broke the ice in the beginning by producing a laugh, it created quite a refreshing breeze, flapping to and fro as she rowed, and would make an excellent umbrella for the whole party, if a shower came up, she said. Miss Kate decided that she was 'odd', but rather clever, and smiled upon her from afar.

Meg, in the other boat, was delightfully situated, face to face with the rowers, who both admired the prospect and feathered their oars with uncommon 'skill and dexterity'. Mr. Brooke was a grave, silent young man, with handsome brown eyes and a pleasant voice. Meg liked his quiet manners and considered him a walking encyclopedia of useful knowledge. He never talked to her much, but he looked at her a good deal, and she felt sure that he did not regard her with aversion. Ned, being in college, of course put on all the airs which freshmen think it their bounden duty to assume. He was not very wise, but very good-natured, and altogether an excellent person

to carry on a picnic. Sallie Gardiner was absorbed in keeping her white pique dress clean and chattering with the ubiquitous Fred, who kept Beth in constant terror by his pranks.

It was not far to Longmeadow, but the tent was pitched and the wickets down by the time they arrived. A pleasant green field, with three wide-spreading oaks in the middle and a smooth strip of turf for croquet.

"Welcome to Camp Laurence!" said the young host, as they landed with exclamations of delight.

"Brooke is commander in chief, I am commissary general, the other fellows are staff officers, and you, ladies, are company. The tent is for your especial benefit and that oak is your drawing room, this is the messroom and the third is the camp kitchen. Now, let's have a game before it gets hot, and then we'll see about dinner."

Frank, Beth, Amy, and Grace sat down to watch the croquet game played by the other eight. Mr. Brooke chose Meg, Kate, and Fred. Laurie took Sallie, Jo, and Ned. The English played well, but the Americans played better, and contested every inch of the ground as strongly as if the spirit of '76 inspired them.

"Time for lunch," said Mr. Brooke, looking at his watch.

"Commissary general, will you make the fire and get water, while Miss March, Miss Sallie, and I spread the table? Who can make good coffee?"

"Jo can," said Meg, glad to recommend her sister. So Jo, feeling that her late lessons in cookery were to do her honor, went to preside over the coffeepot, while the children collected dry sticks, and the boys made a fire and got water from a spring near by. Miss Kate sketched and Frank talked to Beth, who was making little mats of braided rushes to serve as plates.

The commander in chief and his aides soon spread the tablecloth

with an inviting array of eatables and drinkables, prettily decorated with green leaves. Jo announced that the coffee was ready, and everyone settled themselves to a hearty meal, for youth is seldom dyspeptic, and exercise develops wholesome appetites.

"There's salt here," said Laurie, as he handed Jo a saucer of berries.

"Thank you, I prefer spiders," she replied, fishing up two unwary little ones who had gone to a creamy death. "How dare you remind me of that horrid dinner party, when yours is so nice in every way?" added Jo, as they both laughed and ate out of one plate, the china having run short.

"I had an uncommonly good time that day, and haven't got over it yet. This is no credit to me, you know, I don't do anything. It's you and Meg and Brooke who make it all go, and I'm no end obliged to you. What shall we do when we can't eat anymore?" asked Laurie, feeling that his trump card had been played when lunch was over.

"Have games till it's cooler. I brought Authors, and I dare say Miss Kate knows something new and nice. Go and ask her. She's company, and you ought to stay with her more."

"Aren't you company too? I thought she'd suit Brooke, but he keeps talking to Meg, and Kate just stares at them through that ridiculous glass of hers."

Miss Kate did know several new games, and as the girls would not, and the boys could not, eat any more, they all adjourned to the drawing room to play Rig-marole.

"While it went on, Miss Kate took out her sketch, and Margaret watched her, while Mr. Brooke lay on the grass with a book, which he did not read."

"Did the German song suit, Miss March?" inquired Mr. Brooke, breaking the silence.

"Oh, yes! It was very sweet, and I'm much obliged to whoever translated it for me." And Meg's face brightened as she spoke.

"Don't you read German?" asked Miss Kate with a look of surprise.

"Not very well. My father, who taught me, is away, and I don't get on very fast alone, for I've no one to correct my pronunciation."

"Try a little now. Here is Schiller's Mary Stuart and a tutor who loves to teach." And Mr. Brooke laid his book on her lap with an inviting smile.

"It's so hard I'm afraid to try," said Meg, grateful, but bashful in the presence of the accomplished young lady beside her.

"I'll read a bit to encourage you." And Miss Kate read one of the most beautiful passages in a perfectly correct but perfectly expressionless manner.

Mr. Brooke made no comment as she returned the book to Meg, who said innocently, "I thought it was poetry."

"Some of it is. Try this passage."

There was a queer smile about Mr. Brooke's mouth as he opened at poor Mary's lament.

Meg obediently following the long grass-blade which her new tutor used to point with, read slowly and timidly, unconsciously making poetry of the hard words by the soft intonation of her musical voice. Down the page went the green guide, and presently, forgetting her listener in the beauty of the sad scene, Meg read as if alone, giving a little touch of tragedy to the words of the unhappy queen. If she had seen the brown eyes then, she would have stopped short, but she never looked up, and the lesson was not spoiled for her.

"Very well indeed!" said Mr. Brooke, as she paused, quite ignoring her many mistakes, and looking as if he did indeed love to teach.

Miss Kate put up her glass, and, having taken a survey of the little tableau before her, shut her sketch book, saying with condescension, "You've a nice accent and in time will be a clever reader. I advise you to learn, for German is a valuable accomplishment to teachers. I must look after Grace, she is romping." And Miss Kate strolled away, adding to herself with a shrug, "I didn't come to chaperone a governess, though she is young and pretty. What odd people these Yankees are. I'm afraid Laurie will be quite spoiled among them."

"I forgot that English people rather turn up their noses at governesses and don't treat them as we do," said Meg, looking after the retreating figure with an annoyed expression.

"Tutors also have rather a hard time of it there, as I know to my sorrow. There's no place like America for us workers, Miss Margaret." And Mr. Brooke looked so contented and cheerful that Meg was ashamed to lament her hard lot.

"I'm glad I live in it then. I don't like my work, but I get a good deal of satisfaction out of it after all, so I won't complain. I only wished I liked teaching as you do."

"I think you would if you had Laurie for a pupil. I shall be very sorry to lose him next year," said Mr. Brooke, busily punching holes in the turf.

"Going to college, I suppose?" Meg's lips asked the question, but her eyes added, "And what becomes of you?"

"Yes, it's high time he went, for he is ready, and as soon as he is off, I shall turn soldier. I am needed."

"I am glad of that!" exclaimed Meg. "I should think every young man would want to go, though it is hard for the mothers and sisters who stay at home," she added sorrowfully.

"I have neither, and very few friends to care whether I live or

die," said Mr. Brooke rather bitterly as he absently put the dead rose in the hole he had made and covered it up, like a little grave.

"Laurie and his grandfather would care a great deal, and we should all be very sorry to have any harm happen to you," said Meg heartily.

"Thank you, that sounds pleasant," began Mr. Brooke, looking cheerful again, but before he could finish his speech, Ned, mounted on the old horse, came lumbering up to display his equestrian skill before the young ladies, and there was no more quiet that day.

An impromptu circus, fox and geese, and an amicable game of croquet finished the afternoon. At sunset the tent was struck, hampers packed, wickets pulled up, boats loaded, and the whole party floated down the river, singing at the tops of their voices.

On the lawn where it had gathered, the little party separated with cordial good nights and good-byes, for the Vaughns were going to Canada. As the four sisters went home through the garden, Miss Kate looked after them, saying, without the patronizing tone in her voice,

"In spite of their demonstrative manners, American girls are very nice when one knows them."

"I quite agree with you," said Mr. Brooke.

13

CASTLES IN THE AIR

Laurie lay luxuriously swinging to and fro in his hammock one warm September afternoon, wondering what his neighbors were about. Staring up into the green gloom of the horse-chestnut trees above him, he dreamed dreams of all sorts, and was just imagining himself tossing on the ocean in a voyage round the world, when the sound of voices brought him ashore in a flash. Peeping through the meshes of the hammock, he saw the Marches coming out, as if bound on some expedition.

"What in the world are those girls about now?" thought Laurie, opening his sleepy eyes to take a good look, for there was something rather peculiar in the appearance of his neighbors. Each wore a large, flapping hat, a brown linen pouch slung over one shoulder, and carried a long staff. Meg had a cushion, Jo a book, Beth a basket, and Amy a portfolio. All walked quietly through the garden, out at the little back gate, and began to climb the hill that lay between the house and river.

"Well, that's cool," said Laurie to himself, "to have a picnic and never ask me! They can't be going in the boat, for they haven't got the key. Perhaps they forgot it. I'll take it to them, and see what's going on."

Though possessed of half a dozen hats, it took him some time to find one, then there was a hunt for the key, which was at last discovered in his pocket, so that the girls were quite out of sight when he leaped the fence and ran after them. Taking the shortest way to the

boathouse, he waited for them to appear, but no one came, and he went up the hill to take an observation. A grove of pines covered one part of it, and from the heart of this green spot came a clearer sound than the soft sigh of the pines or the drowsy chirp of the crickets.

"Here's a landscape!" thought Laurie, peeping through the bushes, and looking wide-awake and good-natured already.

It was a rather pretty little picture, for the sisters sat together in the shady nook, with sun and shadow flickering over them, the aromatic wind lifting their hair and cooling their hot cheeks, and all the little wood people going on with their affairs as if these were no strangers but old friends. Meg sat upon her cushion, sewing daintily with her white hands, and looking as fresh and sweet as a rose in her pink dress among the green. Beth was sorting the cones that lay thick under the hemlock near by, for she made pretty things with them. Amy was sketching a group of ferns, and Jo was knitting as she read aloud. A shadow passed over the boy's face as he watched them, feeling that he ought to go away because uninvited; yet lingering because home seemed very lonely and this quiet party in the woods most attractive to his restless spirit. He stood so still that a squirrel, busy with its harvesting, ran down a pine close beside him, saw him suddenly and skipped back, scolding so shrilly that Beth looked up, espied the wistful face behind the birches, and beckoned with a reassuring smile.

"May I come in, please? Or shall I be a bother?" he asked, advancing slowly.

Meg lifted her eyebrows, but Jo scowled at her defiantly and said at once, "Of course you may. We should have asked you before, only we thought you wouldn't care for such a girl's game as this."

"I always like your games, but if Meg doesn't want me, I'll go away."

302

"I've no objection, if you do something. It's against the rules to be idle here," replied Meg gravely but graciously.

"Much obliged. I'll do anything if you'll let me stop a bit, for it's as dull as the Desert of Sahara down there. Shall I sew, read, cone, draw, or do all at once? Bring on your bears. I'm ready." And Laurie sat down with a submissive expression delightful to behold.

"How beautiful that is!" said Laurie softly, for he was quick to see and feel beauty of any kind.

"It's often so, and we like to watch it, for it is never the same, but always splendid," replied Amy, wishing she could paint it.

"Jo talks about the country where we hope to live sometime—the real country, she means, with pigs and chickens and haymaking. It would be nice, but I wish the beautiful country up there was real, and we could ever go to it," said Beth musingly.

"Wouldn't it be fun if all the castles in the air which we make could come true, and we could live in them?" said Jo, after a little pause.

"I've made such quantities it would be hard to choose which I'd have," said Laurie, lying flat and throwing cones at the squirrel who had betrayed him.

"You'd have to take your favorite one. What is it?" asked Meg.

"If I tell mine, will you tell yours?"

"Yes, if the girls will too."

"We will. Now, Laurie."

"After I'd seen as much of the world as I want to, I'd like to settle in Germany and have just as much music as I choose. I'm to be a famous musician myself, and all creation is to rush to hear me. And I'm never to be bothered about money or business, but just enjoy myself and live for what I like. That's my favorite castle. What's yours, Meg?"

Margaret seemed to find it a little hard to tell hers, and waved a brake before her face, as if to disperse imaginary gnats, while she said slowly, "I should like a lovely house, full of all sorts of luxurious things—nice food, pretty clothes, handsome furniture, pleasant people, and heaps of money. I am to be mistress of it, and manage it as I like, with plenty of servants, so I never need work a bit. How I should enjoy it! For I wouldn't be idle, but do good, and make everyone love me dearly."

"Wouldn't you have a master for your castle in the air?" asked Laurie slyly.

"I said 'pleasant people', you know," and Meg carefully tied up her shoe as she spoke, so that no one saw her face.

"Why don't you say you'd have a splendid, wise, good husband and some angelic little children? You know your castle wouldn't be perfect without," said blunt Jo, who had no tender fancies yet, and rather scorned romance, except in books.

"You'd have nothing but horses, inkstands, and novels in yours," answered Meg petulantly.

"Wouldn't I though? I'd have a stable full of Arabian steeds, rooms piled high with books, and I'd write out of a magic inkstand, so that my works should be as famous as Laurie's music. I want to do something splendid before I go into my castle, something heroic or wonderful that won't be forgotten after I'm dead. I don't know what, but I'm on the watch for it, and mean to astonish you all some day. I think I shall write books, and get rich and famous, that would suit me, so that is my favorite dream."

"Mine is to stay at home safe with Father and Mother, and help take care of the family," said Beth contentedly.

"Don't you wish for anything else?" asked Laurie.

"Since I had my little piano, I am perfectly satisfied. I only wish

we may all keep well and be together, nothing else."

"I have ever so many wishes, but the pet one is to be an artist, and go to Rome, and do fine pictures, and be the best artist in the whole world," was Amy's modest desire.

"We're an ambitious set, aren't we? Every one of us, but Beth, wants to be rich and famous, and gorgeous in every respect. I do wonder if any of us will ever get our wishes," said Laurie, chewing grass like a meditative calf.

"I've got the key to my castle in the air, but whether I can unlock the door remains to be seen," observed Jo mysteriously.

"I've got the key to mine, but I'm not allowed to try it. Hang college!" muttered Laurie with an impatient sigh.

"Here's mine!" and Amy waved her pencil.

"I haven't got any," said Meg forlornly.

The faint sound of a bell warned them that Hannah had put the tea 'to draw', and they would just have time to get home to supper.

"May I come again?" asked Laurie.

"Yes, if you are good, and love your book, as the boys in the primer are told to do," said Meg, smiling.

"I'll try."

"Then you may come, and I'll teach you to knit as the Scotchmen do. There's a demand for socks just now," added Jo, waving hers like a big blue worsted banner as they parted at the gate.

14

SECRETS

Jo was very busy in the garret, for the October days began to grow chilly, and the afternoons were short. For two or three hours the sun lay warmly in the high window, showing Jo seated on the old sofa, writing busily, with her papers spread out upon a trunk before her, while Scrabble, the pet rat, promenaded the beams overhead, accompanied by his oldest son, a fine young fellow, who was evidently very proud of his whiskers. Quite absorbed in her work, Jo scribbled away till the last page was filled, when she signed her name with a flourish and threw down her pen, exclaiming...

"There, I've done my best! If this won't suit I shall have to wait till I can do better."

Lying back on the sofa, she read the manuscript carefully through, making dashes here and there, and putting in many exclamation points. Then she tied it up with a smart red ribbon, and sat a minute looking at it with a sober, wistful expression, which plainly showed how earnest her work had been. Jo's desk up here was an old tin kitchen which hung against the wall. From this tin receptacle Jo produced another manuscript, and putting both in her pocket, crept quietly downstairs, leaving her friends to nibble her pens and taste her ink.

She put on her hat and jacket as noiselessly as possible, and going to the back entry window, got out upon the roof of a low porch, swung herself down to the grassy bank, and took a roundabout way to the road. Once there, she composed herself, hailed a passing omnibus,

SECRETS

and rolled away to town, looking very merry and mysterious.

If anyone had been watching her, he would have thought her movements decidedly peculiar, for on alighting, she went off at a great pace till she reached a certain number in a certain busy street. Having found the place with some difficulty, she went into the doorway, looked up the dirty stairs, and after standing stock still a minute, suddenly dived into the street and walked away as rapidly as she came. This maneuver she repeated several times, to the great amusement of a black-eyed young gentleman lounging in the window of a building opposite. On returning for the third time, Jo gave herself a shake, pulled her hat over her eyes, and walked up the stairs, looking as if she were going to have all her teeth out.

There was a dentist's sign, among others, which adorned the entrance, and after staring a moment at the pair of artificial jaws which slowly opened and shut to draw attention to a fine set of teeth, the young gentleman put on his coat, took his hat, and went down to post himself in the opposite doorway, saying with a smile and a shiver,

"It's like her to come alone, but if she has a bad time she'll need someone to help her home."

In ten minutes Jo came running downstairs with a very red face and the general appearance of a person who had just passed through a trying ordeal of some sort. When she saw the young gentleman she looked anything but pleased, and passed him with a nod. But he followed, asking with an air of sympathy, "Did you have a bad time?"

"Not very."

"You got through quickly."

"Yes, thank goodness!"

"Why did you go alone?"

"Didn't want anyone to know."

307

"You're the oddest fellow I ever saw. How many did you have out?"

Jo looked at her friend as if she did not understand him, then began to laugh as if mightily amused at something.

"There are two which I want to have come out, but I must wait a week."

"What are you laughing at? You are up to some mischief, Jo," said Laurie, looking mystified.

"So are you. What were you doing, sir, up in that billiard saloon?"

"Begging your pardon, ma'am, it wasn't a billiard saloon, but a gymnasium, and I was taking a lesson in fencing."

"I'm glad of that."

"Why?"

"You can teach me, and then when we play Hamlet, you can be Laertes, and we'll make a fine thing of the fencing scene."

Laurie burst out with a hearty boy's laugh, which made several passers-by smile in spite of themselves.

"I'll teach you whether we play Hamlet or not. It's grand fun and will straighten you up capitally. But I don't believe that was your only reason for saying 'I'm glad' in that decided way, was it now?"

"No, I was glad that you were not in the saloon, because I hope you never go to such places. Do you?"

"Not often."

"I wish you wouldn't."

"It's no harm, Jo. I have billiards at home, but it's no fun unless you have good players, so, as I'm fond of it, I come sometimes and have a game with Ned Moffat or some of the other fellows."

"Oh, dear, I'm so sorry, for you'll get to liking it better and

SECRETS

better, and will waste time and money, and grow like those dreadful boys." said Jo, shaking her head.

"Are you going to deliver lectures all the way home?" he asked presently.

"Of course not. Why?"

"Because if you are, I'll take a bus. If you're not, I'd like to walk with you and tell you something very interesting."

"I won't preach any more, and I'd like to hear the news immensely."

"Very well, then, come on. It's a secret, and if I tell you, you must tell me yours."

"I haven't got any," began Jo, but stopped suddenly, remembering that she had.

"You know you have—you can't hide anything, so up and 'fess, or I won't tell," cried Laurie.

"Is your secret a nice one?"

"Oh, isn't it! All about people you know, and such fun! You ought to hear it, and I've been aching to tell it this long time. Come, you begin."

"You'll not say anything about it at home, will you?"

"Not a word."

"And you won't tease me in private?"

"I never tease."

"Yes, you do. You get everything you want out of people. I don't know how you do it, but you are a born wheedler."

"Thank you. Fire away."

"Well, I've left two stories with a newspaperman, and he's to give his answer next week," whispered Jo, in her confidant's ear.

"Hurrah for Miss March, the celebrated American authoress!" cried Laurie, throwing up his hat and catching it again, to the great

309

delight of two ducks, four cats, five hens, and half a dozen Irish children.

"Hush! It won't come to anything, I dare say, but I couldn't rest till I had tried, and I said nothing about it because I didn't want anyone else to be disappointed."

"It won't fail. Why, Jo, your stories are works of Shakespeare compared to half the rubbish that is published every day. Won't it be fun to see them in print, and shan't we feel proud of our authoress?"

"Where's your secret? Play fair, Teddy, or I'll never believe you again," she said.

"I may get into a scrape for telling, but I didn't promise not to, so I will, for I never feel easy in my mind till I've told you any plummy bit of news I get. I know where Meg's glove is."

"Is that all?" said Jo, looking disappointed, as Laurie nodded and twinkled with a face full of mysterious intelligence.

"It's quite enough for the present, as you'll agree when I tell you where it is."

"Tell, then."

Laurie bent, and whispered three words in Jo's ear, which produced a comical change. She stood and stared at him for a minute, looking both surprised and displeased, then walked on, saying sharply, "How do you know?"

"Saw it."

"Where?"

"Pocket."

"All this time?"

"Yes, isn't that romantic?"

"No, it's horrid."

"Don't you like it?"

"Of course I don't. It's ridiculous, it won't be allowed. My patience! What would Meg say?"

"You are not to tell anyone. Mind that."

"I didn't promise."

"That was understood, and I trusted you."

"Well, I won't for the present, anyway, but I'm disgusted, and wish you hadn't told me."

"I thought you'd be pleased."

"At the idea of anybody coming to take Meg away? No, thank you."

"You'll feel better about it when somebody comes to take you away."

"I'd like to see anyone try it," cried Jo fiercely.

"So should I!" and Laurie chuckled at the idea.

"I don't think secrets agree with me, I feel rumpled up in my mind since you told me that," said Jo rather ungratefully.

"Race down this hill with me, and you'll be all right," suggested Laurie.

No one was in sight, the smooth road sloped invitingly before her, and finding the temptation irresistible, Jo darted away, soon leaving hat and comb behind her and scattering hairpins as she ran. Laurie reached the goal first and was quite satisfied with the success of his treatment, for his Atlanta came panting up with flying hair, bright eyes, ruddy cheeks, and no signs of dissatisfaction in her face.

"I wish I was a horse, then I could run for miles in this splendid air, and not lose my breath. It was capital, but see what a guy it's made me. Go, pick up my things, like a cherub, as you are," said Jo, dropping down under a maple tree, which was carpeting the bank with crimson leaves.

Laurie leisurely departed to recover the lost property, and Jo bundled up her braids, hoping no one would pass by till she was tidy

again. But someone did pass, and who should it be but Meg, looking particularly ladylike in her state and festival suit, for she had been making calls.

"What in the world are you doing here?" she asked, regarding her disheveled sister with well-bred surprise.

"Getting leaves," meekly answered Jo, sorting the rosy handful she had just swept up.

"And hairpins," added Laurie, throwing half a dozen into Jo's lap. "They grow on this road, Meg, so do combs and brown straw hats."

"You have been running, Jo. How could you? When will you stop such romping ways?" said Meg reprovingly, as she settled her cuffs and smoothed her hair, with which the wind had taken liberties.

"Never till I'm stiff and old and have to use a crutch. Don't try to make me grow up before my time, Meg. It's hard enough to have you change all of a sudden. Let me be a little girl as long as I can."

Lately, she had felt that Margaret was fast getting to be a woman, and Laurie's secret made her dread the separation which must surely come some time and now seemed very near. He saw the trouble in her face and drew Meg's attention from it by asking quickly, "Where have you been calling, all so fine?"

"At the Gardiners', and Sallie has been telling me all about Belle Moffat's wedding. It was very splendid, and they have gone to spend the winter in Paris. Just think how delightful that must be!"

"Do you envy her, Meg?" said Laurie.

"I'm afraid I do."

"I'm glad of it!" muttered Jo, tying on her hat with a jerk.

"Why?" asked Meg, looking surprised.

"Because if you care much about riches, you will never go and marry a poor man," said Jo, frowning at Laurie, who was mutely warning her to mind what she said.

"I shall never 'go and marry' anyone," observed Meg, walking on with great dignity while the others followed, laughing, whispering, skipping stones, and 'behaving like children', as Meg said to herself.

On the second Saturday after Jo got out of the window, Meg, as she sat sewing at her window, was scandalized by the sight of Laurie chasing Jo all over the garden and finally capturing her in Amy's bower. What went on there, Meg could not see, but shrieks of laughter were heard, followed by the murmur of voices and a great flapping of newspapers.

"What shall we do with that girl? She never will behave like a young lady," sighed Meg, as she watched the race with a disapproving face.

"I hope she won't. She is so funny and dear as she is," said Beth, who had never betrayed that she was a little hurt at Jo's having secrets with anyone but her.

"It's very trying, but we never can make her commy la fo," added Amy, who sat making some new frills for herself, with her curls tied up in a very becoming way, two agreeable things that made her feel unusually elegant and ladylike.

In a few minutes Jo bounced in, laid herself on the sofa, and affected to read.

"Have you anything interesting there?" asked Meg, with condescension.

"Nothing but a story, won't amount to much, I guess," returned Jo, carefully keeping the name of the paper out of sight.

"You'd better read it aloud. That will amuse us and keep you out of mischief," said Amy in her most grown-up tone.

"What's the name?" asked Beth, wondering why Jo kept her

face behind the sheet.

"The Rival Painters."

"That sounds well. Read it," said Meg.

With a loud "Hem!" and a long breath, Jo began to read very fast. The girls listened with interest, for the tale was romantic, and somewhat pathetic, as most of the characters died in the end. "I like that about the splendid picture," was Amy's approving remark, as Jo paused.

"I prefer the lovering part." said Meg, wiping her eyes, for the lovering part was tragical.

"Who wrote it?" asked Beth, who had caught a glimpse of Jo's face.

The reader suddenly sat up, cast away the paper, displaying a flushed countenance, and with a funny mixture of solemnity and excitement replied in a loud voice, "Your sister."

"You?" cried Meg, dropping her work.

"It's very good," said Amy critically.

"I knew it! I knew it! Oh, my Jo, I am so proud!" and Beth ran to hug her sister and exult over this splendid success.

"Tell us about it." "When did it come?" "How much did you get for it?" "What will Father say?" "Won't Laurie laugh?" cried the family, all in one breath as they clustered about Jo, for these foolish, affectionate people made a jubilee of every little household joy.

"Stop jabbering, girls, and I'll tell you everything," said Jo, wondering if Miss Burney felt any grander over her Evelina than she did over her 'Rival Painters'. Having told how she disposed of her tales, Jo added, "And when I went to get my answer, the man said he liked them both, but didn't pay beginners, only let them print in his paper, and noticed the stories. It was good practice, he said, and when

the beginners improved, anyone would pay. So I let him have the two stories, and today this was sent to me, and Laurie caught me with it and insisted on seeing it, so I let him. And he said it was good, and I shall write more, and he's going to get the next paid for, and I am so happy, for in time I may be able to support myself and help the girls."

Jo's breath gave out here, and wrapping her head in the paper, she bedewed her little story with a few natural tears, for to be independent and earn the praise of those she loved were the dearest wishes of her heart, and this seemed to be the first step toward that happy end.

15

A TELEGRAM

"November is the most disagreeable month in the whole year," said Margaret, standing at the window one dull afternoon, looking out at the frostbitten garden.

"That's the reason I was born in it," observed Jo pensively, quite unconscious of the blot on her nose.

"If something very pleasant should happen now, we should think it a delightful month," said Beth, who took a hopeful view of everything, even November.

"I dare say, but nothing pleasant ever does happen in this family," said Meg, who was out of sorts. "We go grubbing along day after day, without a bit of change, and very little fun. We might as well be in a treadmill."

Meg sighed, and turned to the frostbitten garden again. Jo groaned and leaned both elbows on the table in a despondent attitude, but Amy spatted away energetically, and Beth, who sat at the other window, said, smiling, "Two pleasant things are going to happen right away. Marmee is coming down the street, and Laurie is tramping through the garden as if he had something nice to tell."

In they both came, Mrs. March with her usual question, "Any letter from Father, girls?"

A sharp ring interrupted her, and a minute after Hannah came in with a letter.

"It's one of them horrid telegraph things, mum," she said, handling it as if she was afraid it would explode and do some damage.

At the word 'telegraph', Mrs. March snatched it, read the two lines it contained, and dropped back into her chair as white as if the little paper had sent a bullet to her heart. Laurie dashed downstairs for water, while Meg and Hannah supported her, and Jo read aloud, in a frightened voice...

Mrs. March:
Your husband is very ill. Come at once.
S. HALE
Blank Hospital, Washington.

How still the room was as they listened breathlessly, how strangely the day darkened outside, and how suddenly the whole world seemed to change, as the girls gathered about their mother, feeling as if all the happiness and support of their lives was about to be taken from them.

Mrs. March was herself again directly, read the message over, and stretched out her arms to her daughters, saying, in a tone they never forgot, "I shall go at once, but it may be too late. Oh, children, children, help me to bear it!"

For several minutes there was nothing but the sound of sobbing in the room, mingled with broken words of comfort, tender assurances of help, and hopeful whispers that died away in tears. Poor Hannah was the first to recover, and with unconscious wisdom she set all the rest a good example, for with her, work was panacea for most afflictions.

"The Lord keep the dear man! I won't waste no time a-cryin', but git your things ready right away, mum," she said heartily, as she wiped her face on her apron, gave her mistress a warm shake of the hand with her own hard one, and went away to work like three women

in one.

"She's right, there's no time for tears now. Be calm, girls, and let me think."

They tried to be calm, poor things, as their mother sat up, looking pale but steady, and put away her grief to think and plan for them.

"Where's Laurie?" she asked presently, when she had collected her thoughts and decided on the first duties to be done.

"Here, ma'am. Oh, let me do something!" cried the boy, hurrying from the next room whither he had withdrawn, feeling that their first sorrow was too sacred for even his friendly eyes to see.

"Send a telegram saying I will come at once. The next train goes early in the morning. I'll take that."

"What else? The horses are ready. I can go anywhere, do anything," he said, looking ready to fly to the ends of the earth.

"Leave a note at Aunt March's. Jo, give me that pen and paper."

Tearing off the blank side of one of her newly copied pages, Jo drew the table before her mother, well knowing that money for the long, sad journey must be borrowed, and feeling as if she could do anything to add a little to the sum for her father.

"Now go, dear, but don't kill yourself driving at a desperate pace. There is no need of that."

Mrs. March's warning was evidently thrown away, for five minutes later Laurie tore by the window on his own fleet horse, riding as if for his life.

"Jo, run to the rooms, and tell Mrs. King that I can't come. On the way get these things. I'll put them down, they'll be needed and I must go prepared for nursing.

Mr. Laurence came hurrying back with Beth, bringing every comfort the kind old gentleman could think of for the invalid, and friendliest promises of protection for the girls during the mother's absence, which comforted her very much. He saw the look, knit his heavy eyebrows, rubbed his hands, and marched abruptly away, saying he'd be back directly. No one had time to think of him again till, as Meg ran through the entry, with a pair of rubbers in one hand and a cup of tea in the other, she came suddenly upon Mr. Brooke.

"I'm very sorry to hear of this, Miss March," he said, in the kind, quiet tone which sounded very pleasantly to her perturbed spirit. "I came to offer myself as escort to your mother. Mr. Laurence has commissions for me in Washington, and it will give me real satisfaction to be of service to her there."

"How kind you all are! Mother will accept, I'm sure, and it will be such a relief to know that she has someone to take care of her. Thank you very, very much!"

Everything was arranged by the time Laurie returned, but still Jo did not come. They began to get anxious, and Laurie went off to find her, for no one knew what freak Jo might take into her head. He missed her, however, and she came walking in with a very queer expression of countenance, for there was a mixture of fun and fear, satisfaction and regret in it, which puzzled the family as much as did the roll of bills she laid before her mother, saying with a little choke in her voice, "That's my contribution toward making Father comfortable and bringing him home!"

"My dear, where did you get it? Twenty-five dollars! Jo, I hope you haven't done anything rash?"

"No, it's mine honestly. I didn't beg, borrow, or steal it. I earned it, and I don't think you'll blame me, for I only sold what was my own."

As she spoke, Jo took off her bonnet, and a general outcry arose, for all her abundant hair was cut short.

"Your hair! Your beautiful hair!" "Oh, Jo, how could you? Your one beauty." "My dear girl, there was no need of this." "She doesn't look like my Jo any more, but I love her dearly for it!"

As everyone exclaimed, and Beth hugged the cropped head tenderly, Jo assumed an indifferent air, which did not deceive anyone a particle, and said, rumpling up the brown bush and trying to look as if she liked it, "It doesn't affect the fate of the nation, so don't wail, Beth. It will be good for my vanity, I was getting too proud of my wig. It will do my brains good to have that mop taken off. My head feels deliciously light and cool, and the barber said I could soon have a curly crop, which will be boyish, becoming, and easy to keep in order. I'm satisfied, so please take the money and let's have supper."

No one wanted to go to bed when at ten o'clock Mrs. March put by the last finished job, and said, "Come girls." Beth went to the piano and played the father's favorite hymn. All began bravely, but broke down one by one till Beth was left alone, singing with all her heart, for to her music was always a sweet consoler.

"Go to bed and don't talk, for we must be up early and shall need all the sleep we can get. Good night, my darlings," said Mrs. March, as the hymn ended, for no one cared to try another.

They kissed her quietly, and went to bed as silently as if the dear invalid lay in the next room. Beth and Amy soon fell asleep in spite of the great trouble, but Meg lay awake, thinking the most serious thoughts she had ever known in her short life. Jo lay motionless, and her sister fancied that she was asleep, till a stifled sob made her exclaim, as she touched a wet cheek...

"Jo, dear, what is it? Are you crying about father?"

"No, not now."

"What then?"

"My... My hair!" burst out poor Jo, trying vainly to smother

her emotion in the pillow.

It did not seem at all comical to Meg, who kissed and caressed the afflicted heroine in the tenderest manner.

"I'm not sorry," protested Jo, with a choke. "I'd do it again tomorrow, if I could. It's only the vain part of me that goes and cries in this silly way. Don't tell anyone, it's all over now. I thought you were asleep, so I just made a little private moan for my one beauty."

The clocks were striking midnight and the rooms were very still as a figure glided quietly from bed to bed, smoothing a coverlet here, settling a pillow there, and pausing to look long and tenderly at each unconscious face, to kiss each with lips that mutely blessed, and to pray the fervent prayers which only mothers utter. As she lifted the curtain to look out into the dreary night, the moon broke suddenly from behind the clouds and shone upon her like a bright, benignant face, which seemed to whisper in the silence, "Be comforted, dear soul! There is always light behind the clouds."

16

LETTERS

In the cold gray dawn the sisters lit their lamp and read their chapter with an earnestness never felt before. For now the shadow of a real trouble had come, the little books were full of help and comfort.

Nobody talked much, but as the time drew very near and they sat waiting for the carriage, Mrs. March said to the girls.

"Children, I leave you to Hannah's care and Mr. Laurence's protection. Hannah is faithfulness itself, and our good neighbor will guard you as if you were his own. I have no fears for you, yet I am anxious that you should take this trouble rightly. Don't grieve and fret when I am gone. Go on with your work as usual, for work is a blessed solace. Hope and keep busy, and whatever happens, remember that you never can be fatherless."

"Yes, Mother."

"Meg, dear, be prudent, watch over your sisters, consult Hannah, and in any perplexity, go to Mr. Laurence. Be patient, Jo, don't get despondent or do rash things, write to me often, and be my brave girl, ready to help and cheer all. Beth, comfort yourself with your music, and be faithful to the little home duties, and you, Amy, help all you can, be obedient, and keep happy safe at home."

"We will, Mother! We will!"

The rattle of an approaching carriage made them all start and listen. That was the hard minute, but the girls stood it well. No one cried, no one ran away or uttered a lamentation, though their hearts were very heavy as they sent loving messages to Father, remembering, as they spoke that it might be too late to deliver them. They kissed their mother quietly, clung about her tenderly, and tried to wave their hands cheerfully when she drove away.

Laurie and his grandfather came over to see her off, and Mr. Brooke looked so strong and sensible and kind that the girls christened him 'Mr. Greatheart' on the spot.

"Good-by, my darlings! God bless and keep us all!" whispered Mrs. March, as she kissed one dear little face after the other, and hurried into the carriage.

As she rolled away, the sun came out, and looking back, she saw it shining on the group at the gate like a good omen. They saw it also, and smiled and waved their hands, and the last thing she beheld as she turned the corner was the four bright faces, and behind them like a bodyguard, old Mr. Laurence, faithful Hannah, and devoted Laurie.

"How kind everyone is to us!" she said, turning to find fresh proof of it in the respectful sympathy of the young man's face.

"I don't see how they can help it," returned Mr. Brooke, laughing so infectiously that Mrs. March could not help smiling. And so the journey began with the good omens of sunshine, smiles, and cheerful words.

"I feel as if there had been an earthquake," said Jo, as their neighbors went home to breakfast, leaving them to rest and refresh themselves.

"It seems as if half the house was gone," added Meg forlornly.

Hannah wisely allowed them to relieve their feelings, and when the shower showed signs of clearing up, she came to the rescue, armed with a coffeepot.

"Now, my dear young ladies, remember what your ma said, and don't fret. Come and have a cup of coffee all round, and then let's fall to work and be a credit to the family."

Chapter 16

" 'Hope and keep busy', that's the motto for us, so let's see who will remember it best. I shall go to Aunt March, as usual. Oh, won't she lecture though!" said Jo, as she sipped with returning spirit.

"I shall go to my Kings, though I'd much rather stay at home and attend to things here," said Meg, wishing she hadn't made her eyes so red.

"No need of that. Beth and I can keep house perfectly well," put in Amy, with an important air.

"Hannah will tell us what to do, and we'll have everything nice when you come home," added Beth, getting out her mop and dish tub without delay.

"I think anxiety is very interesting," observed Amy, eating sugar pensively.

The girls couldn't help laughing, and felt better for it.

News from their father comforted the girls very much, for though dangerously ill, the presence of the best and tenderest of nurses had already done him good. Mr. Brooke sent a bulletin every day, and as the head of the family, Meg insisted on reading the dispatches, which grew more cheerful as the week passed. At first, everyone was eager to write, and plump envelopes were carefully poked into the letter box by one or other of the sisters, who felt rather important with their Washington correspondence.

17

LITTLE FAITHFUL

"Meg, I wish you'd go and see the Hummels. You know Mother told us not to forget them." said Beth, ten days after Mrs. March's departure.

"I'm too tired to go this afternoon," replied Meg, rocking comfortably as she sewed.

"Can't you, Jo?" asked Beth.

"Too stormy for me with my cold."

"I thought it was almost well."

"It's well enough for me to go out with Laurie, but not well enough to go to the Hummels'," said Jo, laughing, but looking a little ashamed of her inconsistency.

"Why don't you go yourself?" asked Meg.

"I have been every day, but the baby is sick, and I don't know what to do for it. Mrs. Hummel goes away to work, and Lottchen takes care of it. But it gets sicker and sicker, and I think you or Hannah ought to go."

Beth spoke earnestly, and Meg promised she would go tomorrow.

"Ask Hannah for some nice little mess, and take it round, Beth, the air will do you good," said Jo, adding apologetically, "I'd go but I want to finish my writing."

"My head aches and I'm tired, so I thought maybe some of you would go," said Beth.

"Amy will be in presently, and she will run down for us," suggested Meg.

So Beth lay down on the sofa, the others returned to their work, and the Hummels were forgotten. An hour passed. Amy did not come, Meg went to her room to try on a new dress, Jo was absorbed in her story, and Hannah was sound asleep before the kitchen fire, when Beth quietly put on her hood, filled her basket with odds and ends for the poor children, and went out into the chilly air with a heavy head and a grieved look in her patient eyes. It was late when she came back, and no one saw her creep upstairs and shut herself into her mother's room. Half an hour after, Jo went to 'Mother's closet' for something, and there found little Beth sitting on the medicine chest, looking very grave, with red eyes and a camphor bottle in her hand.

"Christopher Columbus! What's the matter?" cried Jo, as Beth put out her hand as if to warn her off, and asked quickly. . .

"You've had the scarlet fever, haven't you?"

"Years ago, when Meg did. Why?"

"Then I'll tell you. Oh, Jo, the baby's dead!"

"What baby?"

"Mrs. Hummel's. It died in my lap before she got home," cried Beth with a sob.

"My poor dear, how dreadful for you! I ought to have gone," said Jo, taking her sister in her arms as she sat down in her mother's big chair, with a remorseful face.

"It wasn't dreadful, Jo, only so sad! I saw in a minute it was sicker, but Lottchen said her mother had gone for a doctor, so I took Baby and let Lotty rest. It seemed asleep, but all of a sudden if gave a little cry and trembled, and then lay very still. I tried to warm its feet, and Lotty gave it some milk, but it didn't stir, and I knew it was dead."

"Don't cry, dear! What did you do?"

"I just sat and held it softly till Mrs. Hummel came with the doctor. He said it was dead, and looked at Heinrich and Minna, who have sore throats. 'Scarlet fever, ma'am. Ought to have called me before,' he said crossly. Mrs. Hummel told him she was poor, and had tried to cure baby herself, but now it was too late, and she could only ask him to help the others and trust to charity for his pay. He smiled then, and was kinder, but it was very sad, and I cried with them till he turned round all of a sudden, and told me to go home and take belladonna right away, or I'd have the fever."

"No, you won't!" cried Jo, hugging her close, with a frightened look. "Oh, Beth, if you should be sick I never could forgive myself! What shall we do?"

"Don't be frightened, I guess I shan't have it badly. I looked in Mother's book, and saw that it begins with headache, sore throat, and queer feelings like mine, so I did take some belladonna, and I feel better," said Beth, laying her cold hands on her hot forehead and trying to look well.

"If Mother was only at home!" exclaimed Jo, seizing the book, and feeling that Washington was an immense way off. She read a page, looked at Beth, felt her head, peeped into her throat, and then said gravely, "You've been over the baby every day for more than a week, and among the others who are going to have it, so I'm afraid you are going to have it, Beth. I'll call Hannah, she knows all about sickness."

"Don't let Amy come. She never had it, and I should hate to give it to her. Can't you and Meg have it over again?" asked Beth, anxiously.

"I guess not. Don't care if I do. Serve me right, selfish pig, to let you go, and stay writing rubbish myself!" muttered Jo, as she went to consult Hannah.

The good soul was wide awake in a minute, and took the lead at

once, assuring Jo that there was no need to worry; every one had
scarlet fever, and if rightly treated, nobody died, all of which Jo
believed, and felt much relieved as they went up to call Meg.

"Now I'll tell you what we'll do," said Hannah, when she had
examined and questioned Beth, "we will have Dr. Bangs, just to take
a look at you, dear, and see that we start right. Then we'll send Amy
off to Aunt March's for a spell, to keep her out of harm's way, and
one of you girls can stay at home and amuse Beth for a day or two."

"I shall stay, of course, I'm oldest," began Meg, looking
anxious and self-reproachful.

"I shall, because it's my fault she is sick. I told Mother I'd do
the errands, and I haven't," said Jo decidedly.

"Which will you have, Beth? There ain't no need of but one,"
said Hannah.

"Jo, please." And Beth leaned her head against her sister with
a contented look, which effectually settled that point.

"I'll go and tell Amy," said Meg, feeling a little hurt, yet rather
relieved on the whole, for she did not like nursing, and Jo did.

Amy rebelled outright, and passionately declared that she had
rather have the fever than go to Aunt March. Meg reasoned, pleaded,
and commanded, all in vain. Amy protested that she would not go,
and Meg left her in despair to ask Hannah what should be done.
Before she came back, Laurie walked into the parlor to find Amy
sobbing, with her head in the sofa cushions. She told her story,
expecting to be consoled, but Laurie only put his hands in his pockets
and walked about the room, whistling softly, as he knit his brows in
deep thought. Presently he sat down beside her, and said, in his most
wheedlesome tone, "Now be a sensible little woman, and do as they
say. No, don't cry, but hear what a jolly plan I've got. You go to Aunt
March's, and I'll come and take you out every day, driving or walking,

and we'll have capital times. Won't that be better than moping here?"

"I don't wish to be sent off as if I was in the way," began Amy, in an injured voice.

"Bless your heart, child, it's to keep you well. You don't want to be sick, do you?"

"No, I'm sure I don't, but I dare say I shall be, for I've been with Beth all the time."

"That's the very reason you ought to go away at once, so that you may escape it. Change of air and care will keep you well, I dare say, or if it does not entirely, you will have the fever more lightly. I advise you to be off as soon as you can, for scarlet fever is no joke, miss."

"But it's dull at Aunt March's, and she is so cross," said Amy, looking rather frightened.

"It won't be dull with me popping in every day to tell you how Beth is, and take you out gallivanting. The old lady likes me, and I'll be as sweet as possible to her, so she won't peck at us, whatever we do."

"Will you take me out in the trotting wagon with Puck?"

"On my honor as a gentleman."

"And come every single day?"

"See if I don't!"

"And bring me back the minute Beth is well?"

"The identical minute."

"And go to the theater, truly?"

"A dozen theaters, if we may."

"Well—I guess I will," said Amy slowly.

"Good girl! Call Meg, and tell her you'll give in," said Laurie, with an approving pat, which annoyed Amy more than the 'giving in'.

Meg and Jo came running down to behold the miracle which had

been wrought, and Amy, feeling very precious and self-sacrificing, promised to go, if the doctor said Beth was going to be ill.

"How is the little dear?" asked Laurie, for Beth was his especial pet, and he felt more anxious about her than he liked to show.

"She is lying down on Mother's bed, and feels better. The baby's death troubled her, but I dare say she has only got cold. Hannah says she thinks so, but she looks worried, and that makes me fidgety," answered Meg.

"What a trying world it is!" said Jo, rumpling up her hair in a fretful way. "No sooner do we get out of one trouble than down comes another. There doesn't seem to be anything to hold on to when Mother's gone, so I'm all at sea."

"Well, don't make a porcupine of yourself, it isn't becoming. Settle your wig, Jo, and tell me if I shall telegraph to your mother, or do anything?" asked Laurie, who never had been reconciled to the loss of his friend's one beauty.

"That is what troubles me," said Meg. "I think we ought to tell her if Beth is really ill, but Hannah says we mustn't, for Mother can't leave Father, and it will only make them anxious. Beth won't be sick long, and Hannah knows just what to do, and Mother said we were to mind her, so I suppose we must, but it doesn't seem quite right to me."

"Hum, well, I can't say. Suppose you ask Grandfather after the doctor has been."

"We will. Jo, go and get Dr. Bangs at once," commanded Meg. "We can't decide anything till he has been."

"Stay where you are, Jo. I'm errand boy to this establishment," said Laurie, taking up his cap.

Dr. Bangs came, said Beth had symptoms of the fever, but he thought she would have it lightly, though he looked sober over the

Hummel story. Amy was ordered off at once, and provided with something to ward off danger, she departed in great state, with Jo and Laurie as escort.

Aunt March received them with her usual hospitality.

"What do you want now?" she asked, looking sharply over her spectacles, while the parrot, sitting on the back of her chair, called out...

"Go away. No boys allowed here."

Laurie retired to the window, and Jo told her story.

"No more than I expected, if you are allowed to go poking about among poor folks. Amy can stay and make herself useful if she isn't sick, which I've no doubt she will be, looks like it now. Don't cry, child, it worries me to hear people sniff."

Amy was on the point of crying, but Laurie slyly pulled the parrot's tail, which caused Polly to utter an astonished croak and call out, "Bless my boots!" in such a funny way, that she laughed instead.

"What do you hear from your mother?" asked the old lady gruffly.

"Father is much better," replied Jo, trying to keep sober.

"Oh, is he? Well, that won't last long, I fancy. March never had any stamina," was the cheerful reply.

"Ha, ha! Never say die, take a pinch of snuff, goodbye, goodbye!" squalled Polly, dancing on her perch, and clawing at the old lady's cap as Laurie tweaked him in the rear.

"Hold your tongue, you disrespectful old bird! And, Jo, you'd better go at once. It isn't proper to be gadding about so late with a rattlepated boy like..."

"Hold your tongue, you disrespectful old bird!" cried Polly, tumbling off the chair with a bounce, and running to peck the

'rattlepated' boy, who was shaking with laughter at the last speech.

"I don't think I can bear it, but I'll try," thought Amy, as she was left alone with Aunt March.

"Get along, you fright!" screamed Polly, and at that rude speech Amy could not restrain a sniff.

18

DARK DAYS

Beth did have the fever, and was much sicker than anyone but Hannah and the doctor suspected. The girls knew nothing about illness, and Mr. Laurence was not allowed to see her, so Hannah had everything her own way, and busy Dr. Bangs did his best, but left a good deal to the excellent nurse. Meg stayed at home, lest she should infect the Kings, and kept house, feeling very anxious and a little guilty when she wrote letters in which no mention was made of Beth's illness.

Jo devoted herself to Beth day and night, not a hard task, for Beth was very patient, and bore her pain uncomplainingly as long as she could control herself. But there came a time when during the fever fits she began to talk in a hoarse, broken voice, to play on the coverlet as if on her beloved little piano, and try to sing with a throat so swollen that there was no music left, a time when she did not know the familiar faces around her, but addressed them by wrong names, and called imploringly for her mother. Then Jo grew frightened, Meg begged to be allowed to write the truth, and even Hannah said she 'would think of it, though there was no danger yet'. A letter from Washington added to their trouble, for Mr. March had had a relapse, and could not think of coming home for a long while.

The first of December was a wintry day indeed to them, for a bitter wind blew, snow fell fast, and the year seemed getting ready for its death. When Dr. Bangs came that morning, he looked long at Beth, held the hot hand in both his own for a minute, and laid it gently

down, saying, in a low voice to Hannah, "If Mrs. March can leave her husband she'd better be sent for."

Hannah nodded without speaking, for her lips twitched nervously, Meg dropped down into a chair as the strength seemed to go out of her limbs at the sound of those words, and Jo, standing with a pale face for a minute, ran to the parlor, snatched up the telegram, and throwing on her things, rushed out into the storm. She was soon back, and while noiselessly taking off her cloak, Laurie came in with a letter, saying that Mr. March was mending again. Jo read it thankfully, but the heavy weight did not seem lifted off her heart, and her face was so full of misery that Laurie asked quickly, "What is it? Is Beth worse?"

"I've sent for Mother," said Jo, tugging at her rubber boots with a tragic expression.

"Good for you, Jo! Did you do it on your own responsibility?" asked Laurie, as he seated her in the hall chair and took off the rebellious boots, seeing how her hands shook.

"No. The doctor told us to."

"Oh, Jo, it's not so bad as that?" cried Laurie, with a startled face.

"Yes, it is. She doesn't know us. She doesn't look like my Beth, and there's nobody to help us bear it. Mother and father both gone, and God seems so far away I can't find Him."

As the tears streamed fast down poor Jo's cheeks, she stretched out her hand in a helpless sort of way, as if groping in the dark, and Laurie took it in his, whispering as well as he could with a lump in his throat, "I'm here. Hold on to me, Jo, dear!"

She could not speak, but she did 'hold on', and the warm grasp of the friendly human hand comforted her sore heart, and seemed to lead her nearer to the Divine arm which alone could uphold her in her trouble.

"Thank you, Teddy, I'm better now. I don't feel so forlorn, and will try to bear it if it comes."

"Keep hoping for the best, that will help you, Jo. Soon your mother will be here, and then everything will be all right."

"I'm so glad Father is better. Now she won't feel so bad about leaving him." sighed Jo.

"I telegraphed to your mother yesterday, and Brooke answered she'd come at once, and she'll be here tonight, and everything will be all right. Aren't you glad I did it?"

Laurie spoke very fast, and turned red and excited all in a minute, for he had kept his plot a secret, for fear of disappointing the girls or harming Beth. Jo grew quite white, flew out of her chair, and the moment he stopped speaking she electrified him by throwing her arms round his neck, and crying out, with a joyful cry, "Oh, Laurie! Oh, Mother! I am so glad!" She did not weep again, but laughed hysterically, and trembled and clung to her friend as if she was a little bewildered by the sudden news.

Laurie, though decidedly amazed, behaved with great presence of mind. He patted her back soothingly, and finding that she was recovering, followed it up by a bashful kiss or two, which brought Jo round at once. Holding on to the banisters, she put him gently away, saying breathlessly, "Oh, don't! I didn't mean to, it was dreadful of me, but you were such a dear to go and do it in spite of Hannah that I couldn't help flying at you. Tell me all about it, and don't give me wine again, it makes me act so."

"I don't mind," laughed Laurie, as he settled his tie. "Why, you see I got fidgety, and so did Grandpa. We thought your mother ought to know. She'd never forgive us if Beth... Well, if anything happened, you know. So I got grandpa to say it was high time we did

something, and off I pelted to the office yesterday. Your mother will come, I know, and the late train is in at two A.M. I shall go for her, and you've only got to bottle up your rapture, and keep Beth quiet till that blessed lady gets here."

"Laurie, you're an angel! How shall I ever thank you?"

"Fly at me again. I rather liked it," said Laurie, looking mischievous, a thing he had not done for a fortnight.

"No, thank you. I'll do it by proxy, when your grandpa comes. Don't tease, but go home and rest, for you'll be up half the night. Bless you, Teddy, bless you!"

The girls never forgot that night, for no sleep came to them as they kept their watch, with that dreadful sense of powerlessness which comes to us in hours like those.

"If God spares Beth, I never will complain again," whispered Meg earnestly.

"If God spares Beth, I'll try to love and serve Him all my life," answered Jo, with equal fervor.

"I wish I had no heart, it aches so," sighed Meg, after a pause.

"If life is often as hard as this, I don't see how we ever shall get through it," added her sister despondently.

Here the clock struck twelve, and both forgot themselves in watching Beth, for they fancied a change passed over her wan face. The house was still as death, and nothing but the wailing of the wind broke the deep hush.

It was past two, when Jo, who stood at the window thinking how dreary the world looked in its winding sheet of snow, heard a movement by the bed, and turning quickly, saw Meg kneeling before their mother's easy chair with her face hidden. A dreadful fear passed coldly over Jo, as she thought, "Beth is dead, and Meg is afraid to tell me."

She was back at her post in an instant, and to her excited eyes a great change seemed to have taken place. The fever flush and the look of pain were gone, and the beloved little face looked so pale and peaceful in its utter repose that Jo felt no desire to weep or to lament. Leaning low over this dearest of her sisters, she kissed the damp forehead with her heart on her lips, and softly whispered, "Good-by, my Beth. Good-by!"

As if awaked by the stir, Hannah started out of her sleep, hurried to the bed, looked at Beth, felt her hands, listened at her lips, and then, throwing her apron over her head, sat down to rock to and fro, exclaiming, under her breath, "The fever's turned, she's sleepin' nat'ral, her skin's damp, and she breathes easy. Praise be given! Oh, my goodness me!"

Before the girls could believe the happy truth, the doctor came to confirm it. "Yes, my dears, I think the little girl will pull through this time. Keep the house quiet, let her sleep, and when she wakes, give her..."

What they were to give, neither heard, for both crept into the dark hall, and, sitting on the stairs, held each other close, rejoicing with hearts too full for words.

Never had the sun risen so beautifully, and never had the world seemed so lovely as it did to the heavy eyes of Meg and Jo, as they looked out in the early morning, when their long, sad vigil was done.

"It looks like a fairy world," said Meg, smiling to herself, as she stood behind the curtain, watching the dazzling sight.

"Hark!" cried Jo, starting to her feet.

Yes, there was a sound of bells at the door below, a cry from Hannah, and then Laurie's voice saying in a joyful whisper, "Girls, she's come! She's come!"

19

AMY's WILL

While these things were happening at home, Amy was having hard times at Aunt March's. She felt her exile deeply, and for the first time in her life, realized how much she was beloved and petted at home. Aunt March never petted any one; she did not approve of it, but she meant to be kind, for the well-behaved little girl pleased her very much. But she worried Amy very much with her rules and orders, her prim ways, and long, prosy talks. Finding the child more docile and amiable than her sister, the old lady felt it her duty to try and counteract, as far as possible, the bad effects of home freedom and indulgence. So she took Amy by the hand, and taught her as she herself had been taught sixty years ago, a process which carried dismay to Amy's soul, and made her feel like a fly in the web of a very strict spider.

If it had not been for Laurie, and old Esther, the maid, she felt that she never could have got through that dreadful time. Esther was a Frenchwoman, who had lived with 'Madame', as she called her mistress, for many years, and who rather tyrannized over the old lady, who could not get along without her. Her real name was Estelle, but Aunt March ordered her to change it, and she obeyed, on condition that she was never asked to change her religion. She took a fancy to Mademoiselle, and amused her very much with odd stories of her life in France, when Amy sat with her while she got up Madame's laces. She also allowed her to roam about the great house, and examine the curious and pretty things stored away in the big wardrobes and the ancient chests, for Aunt March hoarded like a magpie. Amy's chief delight was an Indian cabinet, full of queer drawers, little pigeonholes, and secret places, in which were kept all sorts of ornaments, some precious, some merely curious, all more or less antique. To examine and arrange these things gave Amy great satisfaction, especially the jewel cases.

"Which would Mademoiselle choose if she had her will?" asked Esther, who always sat near to watch over and lock up the valuables.

"I like the diamonds best, but there is no necklace among them, and I'm fond of necklaces, they are so becoming. I should choose this if I might," replied Amy, looking with great admiration at a string of gold and ebony beads from which hung a heavy cross of the same.

"I wish I knew where all these pretty things would go when Aunt March dies," she said, as she slowly replaced the shining rosary and shut the jewel cases one by one.

"To you and your sisters. I know it, Madame confides in me. I witnessed her will, and it is to be so," whispered Esther smiling.

"How nice! But I wish she'd let us have them now. Procrastination is not agreeable," observed Amy, taking a last look at the diamonds.

"It is too soon yet for the young ladies to wear these things. The first one who is affianced will have the pearls, Madame has said it, and I have a fancy that the little turquoise ring will be given to you when you go, for Madame approves your good behavior and charming manners."

"Do you think so? Oh, I'll be a lamb, if I can only have that lovely ring!" And Amy tried on the blue ring with a delighted face and a firm resolve to earn it.

From that day she was a model of obedience, and the old lady complacently admired the success of her training. She decided to

make her will, as Aunt March had done, so that if she did fall ill and die, her possessions might be justly and generously divided. It cost her a pang even to think of giving up the little treasures which in her eyes were as precious as the old lady's jewels.

During one of her play hours she wrote out the important document as well as she could, with some help from Esther as to certain legal terms, and when the good-natured Frenchwoman had signed her name, Amy felt relieved and laid it by to show Laurie, whom she wanted as a second witness. As it was a rainy day, she went upstairs to amuse herself in one of the large chambers, and took Polly with her for company. In this room there was a wardrobe full of old-fashioned costumes with which Esther allowed her to play, and it was her favorite amusement to array herself in the faded brocades, and parade up and down before the long mirror, making stately curtsies, and sweeping her train about with a rustle which delighted her ears. So busy was she on this day that she did not hear Laurie's ring nor see his face peeping in at her as she gravely promenaded to and fro, flirting her fan and tossing her head, on which she wore a great pink turban, contrasting oddly with her blue brocade dress and yellow quilted petticoat.

Having with difficulty restrained an explosion of merriment, lest it should offend her majesty, Laurie tapped and was graciously received.

"I want you to read that, please, and tell me if it is legal and right. I felt I ought to do it, for life is uncertain and I don't want any ill feeling over my tomb."

Laurie bit his lips, and turning a little from the pensive speaker, read the following document, with praiseworthy gravity, considering the spelling:

MY LAST WILL AND TESTIMENT

I, Amy Curtis March, being in my sane mind, go give and bequeethe all my earthly property—viz. to wit:—namely

To my father, my best pictures, sketches, maps, and works of art, including frames. Also my $100, to do what he likes with.

To my mother, all my clothes, except the blue apron with pockets—also my likeness, and my medal, with much love.

To my dear sister Margaret, I give my turkquoise ring (if I get it), also my green box with the doves on it, also my piece of real lace for her neck, and my sketch of her as a memorial of her 'little girl'.

To Jo I leave my breastpin, the one mended with sealing wax, also my bronze inkstand—she lost the cover—and my most precious plaster rabbit, because I am sorry I burned up her story.

To Beth (if she lives after me) I give my dolls and the little bureau, my fan, my linen collars and my new slippers if she can wear them being thin when she gets well. And I herewith also leave her my regret that I ever made fun of old Joanna.

To my friend and neighbor Theodore Laurence I bequeethe my paper mashay portfolio, my clay model of a horse though he did say it hadn't any neck. Also in return for his great kindness in the hour of affliction any one of my artistic works he likes, Noter Dame is the best.

To our venerable benefactor Mr. Laurence I leave my purple box with a looking glass in the cover which will be nice for his pens and remind him of the departed girl who thanks him for his favors to her family, especially Beth.

I wish my favorite playmate Kitty Bryant to have the blue silk apron and my gold-bead ring with a kiss.

To Hannah I give the bandbox she wanted and all the patchwork I leave hoping she 'will remember me, when it you see'.

And now having disposed of my most valuable property I hope all will be satisfied and not blame the dead. I forgive everyone, and trust we may all meet when the trump shall sound. Amen.

To this will and testament I set my hand and seal on this 20th day of Nov. Anni Domino 1861.

Amy Curtis March
Witnesses:
Estelle Valnor, Theodore Laurence.

The last name was written in pencil, and Amy explained that he was to rewrite it in ink and seal it up for her properly.

"What put it into your head? Did anyone tell you about Beth's giving away her things?" asked Laurie soberly, as Amy laid a bit of red tape, with sealing wax, a taper, and a standish before him.

She explained and then asked anxiously, "What about Beth?"

"I'm sorry I spoke, but as I did, I'll tell you. She felt so ill one day that she told Jo she wanted to give her piano to Meg, her cats to you, and the poor old doll to Jo, who would love it for her sake. She was sorry she had so little to give, and left locks of hair to the rest of us, and her best love to Grandpa. She never thought of a will."

Laurie was signing and sealing as he spoke, and did not look up till a great tear dropped on the paper. Amy's face was full of trouble, but she only said, "Don't people put sort of postscripts to their wills, sometimes?"

"Yes, 'codicils', they call them."

"Put one in mine then, that I wish all my curls cut off, and given round to my friends. I forgot it, but I want it done though it will spoil my looks."

Laurie added it, smiling at Amy's last and greatest sacrifice. Then he amused her for an hour, and was much interested in all her trials.

But when he came to go, Amy held him back to whisper with trembling lips, "Is there really any danger about Beth?"

"I'm afraid there is, but we must hope for the best, so don't cry, dear." And Laurie put his arm about her with a brotherly gesture which was very comforting.

When he had gone, she went to her little chapel, and sitting in the twilight, prayed for Beth, with streaming tears and an aching heart, feeling that a million turquoise rings would not console her for the loss of her gentle little sister.

20

CONFIDENTIAL

I don't think I have any words in which to tell the meeting of the mother and daughters. Such hours are beautiful to live, but very hard to describe, so I will leave it to the imagination of my readers, merely saying that the house was full of genuine happiness, and that Meg's tender hope was realized, for when Beth woke from that long, healing sleep, the first objects on which her eyes fell were the little rose and Mother's face. Too weak to wonder at anything, she only smiled and nestled close in the loving arms about her, feeling that the hungry longing was satisfied at last.

There probably were a good many happy little girls in and about the city that day, but it is my private opinion that Amy was the happiest of all, when she sat in her mother's lap and told her trials, receiving consolation and compensation in the shape of approving smiles and fond caresses. They were alone together in the chapel, to which her mother did not object when its purpose was explained to her.

"On the contrary, I like it very much, dear," looking from the dusty rosary to the well-worn little book, and the lovely picture with its garland of evergreen. "It is an excellent plan to have some place where we can go to be quiet, when things vex or grieve us. There are a good many hard times in this life of ours, but we can always bear them if we ask help in the right way. I think my little girl is learning this."

"Yes, Mother, and when I go home I mean to have a corner in the big closet to put my books and the copy of that picture which I've tried to make. The woman's face is not good, it's too beautiful for me to draw, but the baby is done better, and I love it very much. I like to think He was a little child once, for then I don't seem so far away, and that helps me."

As Amy pointed to the smiling Christ child on his Mother's knee, Mrs. March saw something on the lifted hand that made her smile. She said nothing, but Amy understood the look, and after a minute's pause, she added gravely, "I wanted to speak to you about this, but I forgot it. Aunt gave me the ring today. She called me to her and kissed me, and put it on my finger, and said I was a credit to her, and she'd like to keep me always. She gave that funny guard to keep the turquoise on, as it's too big. I'd like to wear them Mother, can I?"

"They are very pretty, but I think you're rather too young for such ornaments, Amy," said Mrs. March.

"I'll try not to be vain," said Amy. "I don't think I like it only because it's so pretty, but I want to wear it as the girl in the story wore her bracelet, to remind me of something."

"Do you mean Aunt March?" asked her mother, laughing.

"No, to remind me not to be selfish." Amy looked so earnest and sincere about it that her mother stopped laughing, and listened respectfully to the little plan.

"I've thought a great deal lately about my 'bundle of naughties', and being selfish is the largest one in it, so I'm going to try hard to cure it, if I can. I'm apt to forget my resolutions, but if I had something always about me to remind me, I guess I should do better. May we try this way?"

"Yes, but I have more faith in the corner of the big closet. Wear your ring, dear, and do your best. I think you will prosper, for the sincere wish to be good is half the battle. Now I must go back to Beth. Keep up your heart, little daughter, and we will soon have you

home again."

That evening while Meg was writing to her father to report the traveler's safe arrival, Jo slipped upstairs into Beth's room, and finding her mother in her usual place, stood a minute twisting her fingers in her hair, with a worried gesture and an undecided look.

"What is it, deary?" asked Mrs. March, holding out her hand, with a face which invited confidence.

"I want to tell you something, Mother."

"About Meg?"

"How quickly you guessed! Yes, it's about her, and though it's a little thing, it fidgets me."

"Beth is asleep. Speak low, and tell me all about it. That Moffat hasn't been here, I hope?" asked Mrs. March rather sharply.

"No. I should have shut the door in his face if he had," said Jo, settling herself on the floor at her mother's feet. "Last summer Meg left a pair of gloves over at the Laurences' and only one was returned. We forgot about it, till Teddy told me that Mr. Brooke owned that he liked Meg but didn't dare say so, she was so young and he so poor. Now, isn't it a dreadful state of things?"

"Do you think Meg cares for him?" asked Mrs. March, with an anxious look.

"Mercy me! I don't know anything about love and such nonsense!" cried Jo, with a funny mixture of interest and contempt. "In novels, the girls show it by starting and blushing, fainting away, growing thin, and acting like fools. Now Meg does not do anything of the sort. She eats and drinks and sleeps like a sensible creature, she looks straight in my face when I talk about that man, and only blushes a little bit when Teddy jokes about lovers. I forbid him to do it, but he doesn't mind me as he ought."

"Then you fancy that Meg is not interested in John?"

"Who?" cried Jo, staring.

"Mr. Brooke. I call him 'John' now. We fell into the way of doing so at the hospital, and he likes it."

"Oh, dear! I know you'll take his part. He's been good to Father, and you won't send him away, but let Meg marry him, if she wants to. Mean thing! To go petting Papa and helping you, just to wheedle you into liking him." And Jo pulled her hair again with a wrathful tweak.

"My dear, don't get angry about it, and I will tell you how it happened. John went with me at Mr. Laurence's request, and was so devoted to poor Father that we couldn't help getting fond of him. He was perfectly open and honorable about Meg, for he told us he loved her, but would earn a comfortable home before he asked her to marry him. He only wanted our leave to love her and work for her, and the right to make her love him if he could. He is a truly excellent young man, and we could not refuse to listen to him, but I will not consent to Meg's engaging herself so young."

"Hadn't you rather have her marry a rich man?" asked Jo, as her mother's voice faltered a little over the last words.

"Money is a good and useful thing, Jo, and I hope my girls will never feel the need of it too bitterly, nor be tempted by too much. I should like to know that John was firmly established in some good business, which gave him an income large enough to keep free from debt and make Meg comfortable. I'm not ambitious for a splendid fortune, a fashionable position, or a great name for my girls. If rank and money come with love and virtue, also, I should accept them gratefully, and enjoy your good fortune, but I know, by experience, how much genuine happiness can be had in a plain little house, where the daily bread is earned, and some privations give sweetness to the few pleasures. I am content to see Meg begin humbly, for if I am not mistaken, she will be rich in the possession of a good man's heart, and

that is better than a fortune."

"I understand, Mother, and quite agree, but I'm disappointed about Meg, for I'd planned to have her marry Teddy by-and-by and sit in the lap of luxury all her days. Wouldn't it be nice?" asked Jo, looking up with a brighter face.

"He is younger than she, you know," began Mrs. March, but Jo broke in...

"Only a little, he's old for his age, and tall, and can be quite grown-up in his manners if he likes. Then he's rich and generous and good, and loves us all, and I say it's a pity my plan is spoiled."

"I'm afraid Laurie is hardly grown-up enough for Meg, and altogether too much of a weathercock just now for anyone to depend on. Don't make plans, Jo, but let time and their own hearts mate your friends. We can't meddle safely in such matters, and had better not get 'romantic rubbish' as you call it, into our heads, lest it spoil our friendship."

"Well, I won't, but I hate to see things going all crisscross and getting snarled up. I wish wearing flatirons on our heads would keep us from growing up. But buds will be roses, and kittens cats, more's the pity!"

"What's that about flatirons and cats?" asked Meg, as she crept into the room with the finished letter in her hand.

"Only one of my stupid speeches. I'm going to bed. Come, Peggy," said Jo, unfolding herself like an animated puzzle.

"Quite right, and beautifully written. Please add that I send my love to John," said Mrs. March, as she glanced over the letter and gave it back.

"Do you call him 'John'?" asked Meg, smiling, with her innocent eyes looking down into her mother's.

"Yes, he has been like a son to us, and we are very fond of

him," replied Mrs. March, returning the look with a keen one.

"I'm glad of that, he is so lonely. Good night, Mother, dear. It is so inexpressibly comfortable to have you here," was Meg's answer.

The kiss her mother gave her was a very tender one, and as she went away, Mrs. March said, with a mixture of satisfaction and regret, "She does not love John yet, but will soon learn to."

21

PLEASANT MEADOWS

Like sunshine after a storm were the peaceful weeks which followed. The invalids improved rapidly, and Mr. March began to talk of returning early in the new year. Beth was soon able to lie on the study sofa all day, amusing herself with the well-beloved cats at first, and in time with doll's sewing, which had fallen sadly behind-hand. Her once active limbs were so stiff and feeble that Jo took her for a daily airing about the house in her strong arms. Meg cheerfully blackened and burned her white hands cooking delicate messes for 'the dear', while Amy, a loyal slave of the ring, celebrated her return by giving away as many of her treasures as she could prevail on her sisters to accept.

Several days of unusually mild weather fitly ushered in a splendid Christmas Day. Hannah 'felt in her bones' that it was going to be an unusually fine day, and she proved herself a true prophetess, for everybody and everything seemed bound to produce a grand success. To begin with, Mr. March wrote that he should soon be with them, then Beth felt uncommonly well that morning, and, being dressed in her mother's gift, a soft crimson merino wrapper, was borne in high triumph to the window to behold the offering of Jo and Laurie. The Unquenchables had done their best to be worthy of the name, for like elves they had worked by night and conjured up a comical surprise. Out in the garden stood a stately snow maiden, crowned with holly, bearing a basket of fruit and flowers in one hand, a great roll of music in the other, a perfect rainbow of an Afghan round her chilly

shoulders, and a Christmas carol issuing from her lips on a pink paper streamer.

How Beth laughed when she saw it, how Laurie ran up and down to bring in the gifts, and what ridiculous speeches Jo made as she presented them.

"I'm so full of happiness, that if Father was only here, I couldn't hold one drop more," said Beth, quite sighing with contentment as Jo carried her off to the study to rest after the excitement, and to refresh herself with some of the delicious grapes that Jo had sent her.

"So am I," added Jo, slapping the pocket wherein reposed the long-desired *Undine and Sintram.*

"I'm sure I am," echoed Amy, poring over the engraved copy of the Madonna and Child, which her mother had given her in a pretty frame.

"Of course I am!" cried Meg, smoothing the silvery folds of her first silk dress, for Mr. Laurence had insisted on giving it. "How can I be otherwise?" said Mrs. March gratefully, as her eyes went from her husband's letter to Beth's smiling face.

Now and then, in this workaday world, things do happen in the delightful storybook fashion, and what a comfort it is. Half an hour after everyone had said they were so happy they could only hold one drop more, the drop came. Laurie opened the parlor door and popped his head in very quietly. He might just as well have turned a somersault and uttered an Indian war whoop, for his face was so full of suppressed excitement and his voice so treacherously joyful that everyone jumped up, though he only said, in a queer, breathless voice,

"Here's another Christmas present for the March family."

Before the words were well out of his mouth, he was whisked away somehow, and in his place appeared a tall man, muffled up to the

eyes, leaning on the arm of another tall man, who tried to say something and couldn't. Of course there was a general stampede, and for several minutes everybody seemed to lose their wits, for the strangest things were done, and no one said a word.

Mr. March became invisible in the embrace of four pairs of loving arms. Jo disgraced herself by nearly fainting away, and had to be doctored by Laurie in the china closet. Mr. Brooke kissed Meg entirely by mistake, as he somewhat incoherently explained. And Amy, the dignified, tumbled over a stool, and never stopping to get up, hugged and cried over her father's boots in the most touching manner. Mrs. March was the first to recover herself, and held up her hand with a warning, "Hush! Remember Beth."

But it was too late. The study door flew open, the little red wrapper appeared on the threshold, joy put strength into the feeble limbs, and Beth ran straight into her father's arms. Never mind what happened just after that, for the full hearts overflowed, washing away the bitterness of the past and leaving only the sweetness of the present.

Mr. March told how he had longed to surprise them, and how, when the fine weather came, he had been allowed by his doctor to take advantage of it, how devoted Brooke had been, and how he was altogether a most estimable and upright young man. Why Mr. March paused a minute just there, and after a glance at Meg, who was violently poking the fire, looked at his wife with an inquiring lift of the eyebrows, I leave you to imagine. Also why Mrs. March gently nodded her head and asked, rather abruptly, if he wouldn't like to have something to eat. Jo saw and understood the look, and she stalked grimly away to get wine and beef tea, muttering to herself as she slammed the door, "I hate estimable young men with brown eyes!"

There never was such a Christmas dinner as they had that day.

The fat turkey was a sight to behold, when Hannah sent him up, stuffed, browned, and decorated. So was the plum pudding, which melted in one's mouth, likewise the jellies, in which Amy reveled like a fly in a honeypot. Everything turned out well, which was a mercy, Hannah said, "For my mind was that flustered, Mum, that it's a merrycle I didn't roast the pudding, and stuff the turkey with raisins, let alone bilin' of it in a cloth."

Mr. Laurence and his grandson dined with them, also Mr. Brooke, at whom Jo glowered darkly, to Laurie's infinite amusement. Two easy chairs stood side by side at the head of the table, in which sat Beth and her father, feasting modestly on chicken and a little fruit. They drank healths, told stories, sang songs, 'reminisced', as the old folks say, and had a thoroughly good time. A sleigh ride had been planned, but the girls would not leave their father, so the guests departed early, and as twilight gathered, the happy family sat together round the fire.

"Just a year ago we were groaning over the dismal Christmas we expected to have. Do you remember?" asked Jo, breaking a short pause which had followed a long conversation about many things.

"Rather a pleasant year on the whole!" said Meg, smiling at the fire, and congratulating herself on having treated Mr. Brooke with dignity.

"I think it's been a pretty hard one," observed Amy, watching the light shine on her ring with thoughtful eyes.

"I'm glad it's over, because we've got you back," whispered Beth, who sat on her father's knee.

"Rather a rough road for you to travel, my little pilgrims, especially the latter part of it. But you have got on bravely, and I think the burdens are in a fair way to tumble off very soon," said Mr. March, looking with fatherly satisfaction at the four young faces

gathered round him.

"How do you know? Did Mother tell you?" asked Jo.

"Not much. Straws show which way the wind blows, and I've made several discoveries today."

"Oh, tell us what they are!" cried Meg, who sat beside him.

"Here is one." And taking up the hand which lay on the arm of his chair, he pointed to the roughened forefinger, a burn on the back, and two or three little hard spots on the palm. "I remember a time when this hand was white and smooth, and your first care was to keep it so. It was very pretty then, but to me it is much prettier now, for in this seeming blemishes I read a little history. A burnt offering has been made of vanity, this hardened palm has earned something better than blisters, and I'm sure the sewing done by these pricked fingers will last a long time, so much good will went into the stitches. Meg, my dear, I value the womanly skill which keeps home happy more than white hands or fashionable accomplishments. I'm proud to shake this good, industrious little hand, and hope I shall not soon be asked to give it away."

If Meg had wanted a reward for hours of patient labor, she received it in the hearty pressure of her father's hand and the approving smile he gave her.

"What about Jo? Please say something nice, for she has tried so hard and been so very, very good to me," said Beth in her father's ear.

He laughed and looked across at the tall girl who sat opposite, with an unusually mild expression in her face.

"In spite of the curly crop, I don't see the 'son Jo' whom I left a year ago," said Mr. March. "I see a young lady who pins her collar straight, laces her boots neatly, and neither whistles, talks slang, nor lies on the rug as she used to do. Her face is rather thin and pale

just now, with watching and anxiety, but I like to look at it, for it has grown gentler, and her voice is lower. She doesn't bounce, but moves quietly, and takes care of a certain little person in a motherly way which delights me. I rather miss my wild girl, but if I get a strong, helpful, tenderhearted woman in her place, I shall feel quite satisfied."

Jo's keen eyes were rather dim for a minute, and her thin face grew rosy in the firelight as she received her father's praise, feeling that she did deserve a portion of it.

"Now, Beth," said Amy, longing for her turn, but ready to wait.

"There's so little of her, I'm afraid to say much, for fear she will slip away altogether, though she is not so shy as she used to be," began their father cheerfully. But recollecting how nearly he had lost her, he held her close, saying tenderly, with her cheek against his own,

"I've got you safe, my Beth, and I'll keep you so, please God."

After a minute's silence, he looked down at Amy, who sat on the cricket at his feet, and said, with a caress of the shining hair...

"I observed that Amy took drumsticks at dinner, ran errands for her mother all the afternoon, gave Meg her place tonight, and has waited on every one with patience and good humor. I also observe that she does not fret much nor look in the glass, and has not even mentioned a very pretty ring which she wears, so I conclude that she has learned to think of other people more and of herself less, and has decided to try and mold her character as carefully as she molds her little clay figures. I am glad of this, for though I should be very proud of a graceful statue made by her, I shall be infinitely prouder of a lovable daughter with a talent for making life beautiful to herself and others."

"What are you thinking of, Beth?" asked Jo, when Amy had

thanked her father and told about her ring.

"I read in Pilgrim's Progress today how, after many troubles, Christian and Hopeful came to a pleasant green meadow where lilies bloomed all year round, and there they rested happily, as we do now, before they went on to their journey's end," answered Beth, adding, as she slipped out of her father's arms and went to the instrument,

"It's singing time now, and I want to be in my old place. I'll try to sing the song of the shepherd boy which the Pilgrims heard. I made the music for Father, because he likes the verses."

So, sitting at the dear little piano, Beth softly touched the keys, and in the sweet voice they had never thought to hear again, sang to her own accompaniment the quaint hymn, which was a singularly fitting song for her.

22

AUNT MARCH SETTLES THE QUESTION

Like bees swarming after their queen, mother and daughters hovered about Mr. March the next day, neglecting everything to look at, wait upon, and listen to the new invalid, who was in a fair way to be killed by kindness. As he sat propped up in a big chair by Beth's sofa, with the other three close by, and Hannah popping in her head now and then 'to peek at the dear man', nothing seemed needed to complete their happiness. But something was needed, and the elder ones felt it, though none confessed the fact. Mr. and Mrs. March looked at one another with an anxious expression, as their eyes followed Meg. Jo had sudden fits of sobriety, and was seen to shake her fist at Mr. Brooke's umbrella, which had been left in the hall. Meg was absent-minded, shy, and silent, started when the bell rang, and colored when John's name was mentioned. Amy said, "Everyone seemed waiting for something, and couldn't settle down, which was queer, since Father was safe at home," and Beth innocently wondered why their neighbors didn't run over as usual.

Laurie went by in the afternoon, and seeing Meg at the window, seemed suddenly possessed with a melodramatic fit, for he fell down on one knee in the snow, beat his breast, tore his hair, and clasped his hands imploringly, as if begging some boon. And when Meg told him to behave himself and go away, he wrung imaginary tears out of his handkerchief, and staggered round the corner as if in utter despair.

"What does the goose mean?" said Meg, laughing and trying to look unconscious.

"He's showing you how your John will go on by-and-by. Touching, isn't it?" answered Jo scornfully.

"Don't say my John, it isn't proper or true," but Meg's voice lingered over the words as if they sounded pleasant to her. "Please don't plague me, Jo, I've told you I don't care much about him, and there isn't to be anything said, but we are all to be friendly, and go on as before."

"We can't, for something has been said, and Laurie's mischief has spoiled you for me. I see it, and so does Mother. You are not like your old self a bit, and seem ever so far away from me. I don't mean to plague you and will bear it like a man, but I do wish it was all settled. I hate to wait, so if you mean ever to do it, make haste and have it over quickly," said Jo pettishly.

"I can't say anything till he speaks, and he won't, because Father said I was too young," began Meg, bending over her work with a queer little smile, which suggested that she did not quite agree with her father on that point.

"If he did speak, you wouldn't know what to say, but would cry or blush, or let him have his own way, instead of giving a good, decided no."

"I'm not so silly and weak as you think. I know just what I should say, for I've planned it all, so I needn't be taken unawares. There's no knowing what may happen, and I wished to be prepared."

"Would you mind telling me what you'd say?" asked Jo more respectfully.

"Oh, I should merely say, quite calmly and decidedly, 'Thank you, Mr. Brooke, you are very kind, but I agree with Father that I am too young to enter into any engagement at present, so please say no

358

more, but let us be friends as we were.' "

"Hum, that's stiff and cool enough! I don't believe you'll ever say it, and I know he won't be satisfied if you do. If he goes on like the rejected lovers in books, you'll give in, rather than hurt his feelings."

"No, I won't. I shall tell him I've made up my mind, and shall walk out of the room with dignity."

Meg rose as she spoke, and was just going to rehearse the dignified exit, when a step in the hall made her fly into her seat and begin to sew as fast as if her life depended on finishing that particular seam in a given time. Jo smothered a laugh at the sudden change, and when someone gave a modest tap, opened the door with a grim aspect which was anything but hospitable.

"Good afternoon. I came to get my umbrella, that is, to see how your father finds himself today," said Mr. Brooke, getting a trifle confused as his eyes went from one telltale face to the other.

"It's very well, he's in the rack. I'll get him, and tell it you are here." And having jumbled her father and the umbrella well together in her reply, Jo slipped out of the room to give Meg a chance to make her speech and air her dignity. But the instant she vanished, Meg began to sidle toward the door, murmuring...

"Mother will like to see you. Pray sit down, I'll call her."

"Don't go. Are you afraid of me, Margaret?" and Mr. Brooke looked so hurt that Meg thought she must have done something very rude. She blushed up to the little curls on her forehead, for he had never called her Margaret before, and she was surprised to find how natural and sweet it seemed to hear him say it. Anxious to appear friendly and at her ease, she put out her hand with a confiding gesture, and said gratefully...

"How can I be afraid when you have been so kind to Father? I

only wish I could thank you for it."

"Shall I tell you how?" asked Mr. Brooke, holding the small hand fast in both his own, and looking down at Meg with so much love in the brown eyes that her heart began to flutter, and she both longed to run away and to stop and listen.

"Oh no, please don't, I'd rather not," she said, trying to withdraw her hand, and looking frightened in spite of her denial.

"I won't trouble you. I only want to know if you care for me a little, Meg. I love you so much, dear," added Mr. Brooke tenderly.

"I'm too young," faltered Meg, wondering why she was so fluttered, yet rather enjoying it.

"I'll wait, and in the meantime, you could be learning to like me. Would it be a very hard lesson, dear?"

"Not if I chose to learn it, but. . ."

"Please choose to learn, Meg. I love to teach, and this is easier than German," broke in John, getting possession of the other hand, so that she had no way of hiding her face as he bent to look into it.

His tone was properly beseeching, but stealing a shy look at him, Meg saw that his eyes were merry as well as tender, and that he wore the satisfied smile of one who had no doubt of his success. She felt excited and strange, and not knowing what else to do, followed a capricious impulse, and, withdrawing her hands, said petulantly, "I don't choose. Please go away and let me be!"

Poor Mr. Brooke looked as if his lovely castle in the air was tumbling about his ears, for he had never seen Meg in such a mood before, and it rather bewildered him.

"Do you really mean that?" he asked anxiously, following her as she walked away.

"Yes, I do. I don't want to be worried about such things. Father says I needn't, it's too soon and I'd rather not."

"Mayn't I hope you'll change your mind by-and-by? I'll wait and say nothing till you have had more time. Don't play with me, Meg. I didn't think that of you."

"Don't think of me at all. I'd rather you wouldn't," said Meg, taking a naughty satisfaction in trying her lover's patience and her own power.

He was grave and pale now. He just stood looking at her so wistfully, so tenderly, that she found her heart relenting in spite of herself. What would have happened next I cannot say, if Aunt March had not come hobbling in at this interesting minute.

The old lady couldn't resist her longing to see her nephew, for she had met Laurie as she took her airing, and hearing of Mr. March's arrival, drove straight out to see him. The family were all busy in the back part of the house, and she had made her way quietly in, hoping to surprise them. She did surprise two of them so much that Meg started as if she had seen a ghost, and Mr. Brooke vanished into the study.

"Bless me, what's all this?" cried the old lady with a rap of her cane as she glanced from the pale young gentleman to the scarlet young lady.

"It's Father's friend. I'm so surprised to see you!" stammered Meg, feeling that she was in for a lecture now.

"That's evident," returned Aunt March, sitting down. "But what is Father's friend saying to make you look like a peony? There's mischief going on, and I insist upon knowing what it is," with another rap.

"We were only talking. Mr. Brooke came for his umbrella," began Meg, wishing that Mr. Brooke and the umbrella were safely out of the house.

"Brooke? That boy's tutor? Ah! I understand now. I know all

about it. Jo blundered into a wrong message in one of your Father's letters, and I made her tell me. You haven't gone and accepted him, child?" cried Aunt March, looking scandalized.

"Hush! He'll hear. Shan't I call Mother?" said Meg, much troubled.

"Not yet. I've something to say to you, and I must free my mind at once. Tell me, do you mean to marry this Cook? If you do, not one penny of my money ever goes to you. Remember that, and be a sensible girl," said the old lady impressively.

Now Aunt March possessed in perfection the art of rousing the spirit of opposition in the gentlest people, and enjoyed doing it.

"I shall marry whom I please, Aunt March, and you can leave your money to anyone you like," she said, nodding her head with a resolute air.

Aunt March took no notice, but went on with her lecture. "This Rook is poor and hasn't got any rich relations, has he?"

"No, but he has many warm friends."

"You can't live on friends, try it and see how cool they'll grow. He hasn't any business, has he?"

"Not yet. Mr. Laurence is going to help him."

"He knows you have got rich relations, child. That's the secret of his liking, I suspect."

"Aunt March, how dare you say such a thing? John is above such meanness, and I won't listen to you a minute if you talk so," cried Meg indignantly, forgetting everything but the injustice of the old lady's suspicions. "My John wouldn't marry for money, any more than I would. We are willing to work and we mean to wait. I'm not afraid of being poor, for I've been happy so far, and I know I shall be with him because he loves me, and I..."

Meg stopped there, remembering all of a sudden that she hadn't

made up her mind, that she had told 'her John' to go away, and that he might be overhearing her inconsistent remarks.

Aunt March was very angry, for she had set her heart on having her pretty niece make a fine match, and something in the girl's happy young face made the lonely old woman feel both sad and sour.

"Well, I wash my hands of the whole affair! You are a willful child, and you've lost more than you know by this piece of folly. No, I won't stop. I'm disappointed in you, and haven't spirits to see your father now. Don't expect anything from me when you are married. Your Mr. Brooke's friends must take care of you. I'm done with you forever."

And slamming the door in Meg's face, Aunt March drove off in high dudgeon. She seemed to take all the girl's courage with her, for when left alone, Meg stood for a moment, undecided whether to laugh or cry. Before she could make up her mind, she was taken possession of by Mr. Brooke, who said all in one breath, "I couldn't help hearing, Meg. Thank you for defending me, and Aunt March for proving that you do care for me a little bit."

"I didn't know how much till she abused you," began Meg.

"And I needn't go away, but may stay and be happy, may I, dear?"

Here was another fine chance to make the crushing speech and the stately exit, but Meg never thought of doing either, and disgraced herself forever in Jo's eyes by meekly whispering, "Yes, John," and hiding her face on Mr. Brooke's waistcoat.

Fifteen minutes after Aunt March's departure, Jo came softly downstairs. Going in to exult over a fallen enemy and to praise a strong-minded sister for the banishment of an objectionable lover, it certainly was a shock to behold the aforesaid enemy serenely sitting on the sofa, with the strongminded sister enthroned upon his knee and wearing an expression of the most abject submission. Jo gave a sort of gasp, as if a cold shower bath had suddenly fallen upon her, for such an unexpected turning of the tables actually took her breath away. At the odd sound the lovers turned and saw her. Meg jumped up, looking both proud and shy, but 'that man', as Jo called him, actually laughed and said coolly, as he kissed the astonished newcomer,

"Sister Jo, congratulate us!"

That was adding insult to injury, and making some wild demonstration with her hands, Jo vanished without a word. Rushing upstairs, she startled the invalids by exclaiming tragically as she burst into the room, "Oh, do somebody go down quick! John Brooke is acting dreadfully, and Meg likes it!"

Mr. and Mrs. March left the room with speed, and casting herself upon the bed, Jo cried and scolded tempestuously as she told the awful news to Beth and Amy. The little girls, however, considered it a most agreeable and interesting event, and Jo got little comfort from them, so she went up to her refuge in the garret, and confided her troubles to the rats.

Nobody ever knew what went on in the parlor that afternoon, but a great deal of talking was done, and quiet Mr. Brooke astonished his friends by the eloquence and spirit with which he pleaded his suit, told his plans, and persuaded them to arrange everything just as he wanted it.

The tea bell rang before he had finished describing the paradise which he meant to earn for Meg, and he proudly took her in to supper, both looking so happy that Jo hadn't the heart to be jealous or dismal. Amy was very much impressed by John's devotion and Meg's dignity, Beth beamed at them from a distance, while Mr. and Mrs. March surveyed the young couple with such tender satisfaction. No one ate much, but everyone looked very happy, and the old room

seemed to brighten up amazingly when the first romance of the family began there.

"You can't say nothing pleasant ever happens now, can you, Meg?" said Amy, trying to decide how she would group the lovers in a sketch she was planning to make.

"No, I'm sure I can't. How much has happened since I said that! It seems a year ago," answered Meg, who was in a blissful dream lifted far above such common things as bread and butter.

Jo shake her head, and then say to herself with an air of relief as the front door banged, "Here comes Laurie. Now we shall have some sensible conversation."

But Jo was mistaken, for Laurie came prancing in, overflowing with good spirits, bearing a great bridal-looking bouquet for 'Mrs. John Brooke'.

"I knew Brooke would have it all his own way, he always does, for when he makes up his mind to accomplish anything, it's done though the sky falls," said Laurie, when he had presented his offering and his congratulations.

"Much obliged for that recommendation. I take it as a good omen for the future and invite you to my wedding on the spot," answered Mr. Brooke, who felt at peace with all mankind, even his mischievous pupil.

"I'll come if I'm at the ends of the earth, for the sight of Jo's face alone on that occasion would be worth a long journey. You don't look festive, ma'am, what's the matter?" asked Laurie, following her into a corner of the parlor, whither all had adjourned to greet Mr. Laurence.

"I don't approve of the match, but I've made up my mind to bear it, and shall not say a word against it," said Jo solemnly. "You can't know how hard it is for me to give up Meg," she continued

with a little quiver in her voice.

"You don't give her up. You only go halves," said Laurie consolingly.

"It can never be the same again. I've lost my dearest friend," sighed Jo.

"Well, now, don't be dismal, there's a good fellow. It's all right you see. Meg is happy, Brooke will fly round and get settled immediately, Grandpa will attend to him, and it will be very jolly to see Meg in her own little house. We'll have capital times after she is gone, for I shall be through college before long, and then we'll go abroad on some nice trip or other. Wouldn't that console you?"

"I rather think it would, but there's no knowing what may happen in three years," said Jo thoughtfully.

"That's true. Don't you wish you could take a look forward and see where we shall all be then? I do," returned Laurie.

"I think not, for I might see something sad, and everyone looks so happy now, I don't believe they could be much improved." And Jo's eyes went slowly round the room, brightening as they looked, for the prospect was a pleasant one.

Father and Mother sat together, quietly reliving the first chapter of the romance which for them began some twenty years ago. Amy was drawing the lovers, who sat apart in a beautiful world of their own, the light of which touched their faces with a grace the little artist could not copy. Beth lay on her sofa, talking cheerily with her old friend, who held her little hand as if he felt that it possessed the power to lead him along the peaceful way she walked. Jo lounged in her favorite low seat, with the grave quiet look which best became her, and Laurie, leaning on the back of her chair, his chin on a level with her curly head, smiled with his friendliest aspect, and nodded at her in the long glass which reflected them both.

So the curtain falls upon Meg, Jo, Beth, and Amy. Whether it ever rises again, depends upon the reception given the first act of the domestic drama called Little Women.

L. M. Alcott.

國家圖書館出版品預行編目資料

小婦人（中英雙語典藏版）/ 露意莎・梅・艾考特（Louisa May
Alcott）著；那培玄、法蘭克・T・麥瑞爾（Frank T. Merrill）、
鐘文君繪；張琰譯. -- 二版. -- 臺中市：晨星，2022.12
　　面；　公分. --（愛藏本；110）
中英雙語典藏版
譯自：Little Women
ISBN 978-626-320-276-4（精裝）

874.59　　　　　　　　　　　　　　　　　　　111015950

愛藏本：110

小婦人（中英雙語典藏版）
Little Women

填寫線上回函，立刻享有
晨星網路書店50元購書金

作　　　者｜露意莎・梅・艾考特（Louisa May Alcott）
封面繪者｜鐘文君
內頁繪者｜那培玄、法蘭克・T・麥瑞爾（Frank T. Merrill）
譯　　　者｜張琰

責任編輯｜呂曉婕、江品如
文字編輯｜陳涵紀
封面設計｜鐘文君
美術編輯｜黃偵瑜
文字校潤｜陳涵紀、江品如

創 辦 人｜陳銘民
發 行 所｜晨星出版有限公司
　　　　　台中市 407 工業 30 路 1 號
　　　　　TEL：04-23595820　　FAX：04-23550581
　　　　　http://star.morningstar.com.tw
　　　　　行政院新聞局版台業字第 2500 號
法律顧問｜陳思成律師

讀者專線｜TEL：02-23672044 / 04-2359-5819#212
傳真專線｜FAX：02-23635741 / 04-23595493
讀者信箱｜service@morningstar.com.tw
網路書店｜http://www.morningstar.com.tw
郵政劃撥｜15060393　知己圖書股份有限公司

初版日期｜2007 年 08 月 30 日
二版日期｜2022 年 12 月 01 日
　ISBN｜978-626-320-276-4
　定價｜新台幣 330 元

印　　　刷｜上好印刷股份有限公司